ALSO BY DAVID ROLLINS

A Knife Edge
The Death Trust

HARD RAIN

HARD RAIN

A THRILLER

DAVID ROLLINS

BANTAM BOOKS

Hard Rain is a work of fiction. Names, characters, places, and incidents either are the product of the author's imagination or are used fictitiously. Any resemblance to actual persons, living or dead, events, or locales is entirely coincidental.

Published in the United States by Bantam Books, an imprint of The Random House Publishing Group, a division of Random House, Inc., New York.

BANTAM BOOKS and the rooster colophon are registered trademarks of Random House, Inc.

Originally published in hardcover in Australia by Pan MacMillan Australia Pty Limited, Sydney, in 2008.

Library of Congress Cataloging-in-Publication Data
Rollins, David
Hard rain : a thriller / David Rollins. — 1st ed.
p. cm.
ISBN 978-0-553-80536-9
eBook ISBN 978-0-553-90730-8
1. Military attachés—Crimes against—Turkey—Fiction. 2. Government investigators—United States—Fiction. 3. Americans—Turkey—Fiction.
I. Title.
PR9619.4.R66H37 2010
823'.92—dc22 2009039761

Printed in the United States of America on acid-free paper

www.bantamdell.com

2 4 6 8 9 7 5 3 1

First Edition

Text design by Diane Hobbing

Stolen waters are sweet, and bread eaten in secret is pleasant.

—Proverbs 9:17

ACKNOWLEDGMENTS

Thanks to Sarge, Trish, Mike, Jennifer, and Sam for reading earlier drafts.

Thanks to Woody for comments and direction.

Thanks to Lieutenant Colonel Michael "Panda" Pandolfo for helping me rewrite the prologue, for reading and proofing the manuscript, and for the hours of patient schooling (of me).

Thanks to the men and women at Eglin AFB, Langley AFB, Offutt AFB, Kirtland AFB, and Vandenberg AFB for showing me around.

Thanks to Dana Drury for sorting out my website.

Thanks to my lawyer, Eric Feig, and my literary agent, Kathleen Anderson, for making this my day job.

Thanks to Joe Marich, my publicist, and his account manager, Kyle Hensley, for all the great ideas.

Thanks to my publisher at Random House, Vice President Kate Miciak, for all the support and patience.

And thanks to you, Sam, for continuing to put up with me.

HARD RAIN

PROLOGUE

February 26, 1991
Southern Iraq, Highway 80

Amjad, Raaghib, and Daleel watched the Mercedes speed by in the last rays of the afternoon sun. A refrigerator was strapped to its roof, the power cord whipping around in the dusty slipstream like an angry viper.

"I like those cars," said Daleel from the backseat. At age twenty, he was the oldest of the soldiers. "They're fast and comfortable. With a car like that, you could drive all the way from Kuwait City to Baghdad in a single day and not feel like you'd driven at all."

"We could have had one of those—there were many for the taking." Amjad swerved around a rock on the road, just as the vehicle ahead of them had done, before resuming his search of the airwaves, hunting for rock music. "Kuwait was a Mercedes-Benz parking lot. But this Range Rover was a more sensible choice. We wanted space, remember?"

"Amjad's right about the car," said Raaghib, trying on one of the pairs of looted sunglasses from the rack nestled between his knees. "Just look at all the treasures we've managed to squeeze into it. With all this jewelry and perfume, our mothers and sisters will think they're in heaven. We can set up a shop—make money, get rich and fat like the Kuwaitis. Yes, this car was a good choice. And if the traffic slows down and we have to leave the road, it'll eat up the desert sand like an American tank."

Amjad shivered at the mention of American armor. From the shelter of a slit trench, slack-jawed and terrified, he'd watched as a few Abrams M1A1s had annihilated twenty-eight Iraqi T-72 main battle tanks in a matter of minutes.

A sign flashed by in the wash from their headlights, indicating the turnoff to Basra a kilometer ahead.

"I think Saddam was a fool to taunt the Americans," he blurted.

"I'd keep that to yourself, Amjad," Raaghib taunted. "There's still plenty of room in Abu Ghraib."

"He's not the only person to say it," Daleel commented. "But look at all the cars behind and in front of us—all the way to the horizon in both directions. Every one is full of spoils. The army is coming home rich. Iraq cannot fail to prosper from this."

Raaghib felt a change of subject was in order. "I found pictures of Madonna. She has incredible pointed breasts. You should see them."

"That woman is a whore," Amjad commented, forcing aside the memories of battle. "Not worthy of Iraqi semen. Though I'd still like to see those pictures."

"So you can hide with them at night and spread your unworthy Iraqi semen all over them?" Raaghib scoffed. "I don't think so." He pressed a button. The window slid down and warm desert air blasted his face. The stars were invisible, hidden by the haze of drifting oil fires. He hit the button till the window rose halfway and sat back in his seat. They were making good time. The army was moving well on this beautiful road, speeding home to barracks at Basra. The attack on Kuwait had been brief—a blink of an eye compared with his father's war with Iran. But the Americans were a different kind of foe. They fought with weapons fired from the other side of the world. With secret, invisible planes that couldn't be shot down. Or with helicopters and other aircraft that turned tanks into flaming torches. Even the American soldiers he had seen looked more like robots than human beings. Perhaps Amjad was right. Saddam shouldn't have taunted the Americans.

Major Emmet Portman banked the A-10 Warthog gently away from the tanker's left wing while "Razor," his wingman, edged his Hog forward and connected to the boom just vacated. This CAS—Close Air Support—airborne alert shit had been dragging on for what seemed like hours. Portman hoped they wouldn't get the call. The weather down on the deck was crap: gusty winds, rain, and thick smoke haze from blazing oil wells.

The only reason they were flying tonight at all was that General Glosson had made it clear to the wing king that weather aborts were no excuse. Buster Glosson had also made it abundantly clear that ground forces were to be supported at all costs, and the wing commander knew better than to do anything other than salute smartly and say, "Three bags full, sir."

The VHF crackled to life: *"Slam Two-One, Moonbeam."*

Damn it—Moonbeam. The A-B-triple-C, the airborne battlefield command and control center orbiting down near Q8. He and Razor were getting the call. The command informed them that they were in for a little BAI—Battlefield Air Interdiction, an attack against hostile land forces not in contact with friendly troops, but close to them.

Razor backed down and away from the boom, his off-load complete, then maneuvered onto Portman's left wing to make room for the next flight in the line.

Minutes later, they were approaching the coast, passing FL 120, 12,000 feet.

Portman pushed the Warthog hard over when he judged the waypoint was reached, and began the descent through the undercast. He checked his airspeed. Somewhere below, approaching at around 320 knots, was the Iraqi Army, while behind and below him were probably Apaches, AC-130 Spectre gunships, more Hogs, Strike Eagles, Vipers. *Damn,* it could really be crowded down there if the target area was as lucrative as it sounded. No doubt other flights were already probing forward and engaging the head and the tail of the column. Those Republican Guards, if that's who it was, were in for a hell of a fright, and their nightmare was about to go from bad to get-my-precious-goddamn-ass-outta-here.

Portman played briefly with his air-conditioning controls before giving up, sweat rolling down his neck. The crew chief had sworn the problem was fixed, but it wasn't—one of those gremlins that came and went with no apparent cause. Emmet waited until the altimeter wound back through 5000 feet, and then did what he'd been doing whenever he drew this jet: opened the vents and unclipped one side of his oxygen mask. The air coming through the vents was refreshingly cool and damp, though it smelled of burning crude from the oil fires, something he wished he could get used to.

At 3000 feet, the flight broke through the haze. "Jesus..." Emmet said aloud, stunned by the unexpected spectacle below. On the billiard table of the Kuwaiti desert was a highway crammed with vehicles heading northeast; hundreds, maybe thousands of vehicles, their headlights burning bright holes in the night—a conga line of stars. It reminded him of the Vegas strip on Saturday nights.

The major continued the descent toward the brilliant column of moving light, leveled off 2500 feet above it, and selected the infrared display from the Maverick missile located on station eight under the right wing. The missile's imaging infrared nose camera magnified the picture on the road and delivered it in glowing white-on-black to the video screen on the upper right-hand side of the instrument panel. The picture on the screen was clear enough to make out individual vehicles from beyond 3000 feet. And the picture told him there were trucks and flatbeds that were obviously military down there. The overwhelming majority of the vehicles, though, were civilian.

So this was the Iraqi Army heading home, giving up on its occupation of Kuwait. It appeared that Saddam's finest had grabbed anything they could find to drive home in. They'd probably also stolen everything that wasn't nailed down to make the trip with them.

Emmet glanced behind his right shoulder and caught the glow of Razor's panelescents, which made the aircraft appear a ghostly green. He called the turn, then banked hard right and crossed the highway at right angles before banking again, another crisp 3g ninety-degree turn, heading for the section of road allocated to him and his flight by the "Moonbeam" folks.

Daleel saw the unearthly glowing green shapes moving low and fast against the black sky and wondered what they were, until a thunderous jet roar arrived a second later and overwhelmed the music blaring in his headphones.

"What was that?" yelled Amjad, peering up through the windshield.

Time to go to work. Portman reconnected his mask, pushing the bayonet firmly in place. He didn't want the mask sagging off his nose during the turns. Then he rechecked his weapons loadout on his knee card: four CBU-58s on TERS—triple ejector racks—on stations three and nine, AGM-65 Mavericks on stations two, four, eight, and ten. On station number one, outboard under the left wing, was the Electronic Counter Measures (ECM) jamming pod, and on the opposite side, the outboard station, was a pair of AIM-9 air-to-air missiles for airborne threats. He doubted the Iraqi Air Force would put in an appearance; so far, they were the only people in Iraq who'd shown a lick of common sense by staying home.

The allocated target was a stretch of highway choking with traffic, mostly of the expensive European variety, but interspersed here and there with military trucks and low-loaders. In this environment, the CBUs—cluster bombs—were out. With a fuse function height of 1800 feet, he could deliver them level, but he'd have to pass straight and level over the target, and that would make him and his wingman susceptible to ground fire. And any other kind of delivery would put him and Razor into the murk of those oily clouds. *We'll go guns,* he decided, *and break away at a mile to keep well clear of ground fire.*

After confirming intentions with Razor, Emmet performed a low-g one-eighty to line up on the target area. Razor did the same two seconds later, then pushed up the throttle to get himself into position off his leader's wing.

Rolling out of the turn, the pipper on the head-up display settled down and showed Portman what he wanted to see—a sea of targets. He took the ECM jammer off standby and onto active mode, and selected "Gun" with the Guns & Stores select switch. Master Arm—on. The light on the panel indicated that the weapon was ready to fire. A glance to his left revealed that Razor was where he should be, a thousand feet away and line abreast.

A heavy truck between three others sat in the middle of the pipper. Now all Portman had to do was gently caress the trigger, and the weapon around which the A-10 Warthog had been built, the fearsome seven-barrel, thirty-millimeter GAU-8 Avenger Gatling gun designed to stop a Soviet armored thrust into western Europe, blasted into action. A two-second burst roared out from the Hog's nose, and the cockpit filled with the familiar smell of cordite.

Within an instant, a hundred and four rounds of extruded depleted uranium alloyed with titanium and encased in aluminum, plus thirty-two rounds of HEI—high-explosive incendiary—smashed into the truck below. Gas and diesel fuel from the targeted vehicles combined with atomized human fats and other liquids, producing orange flowers that bloomed high over the desert, rolling into the night sky. The shells from Razor's volley struck home moments later to underline the point.

Emmet brought the Hog around for another run as the column of traffic, unable to stop, piled into the burning, twisted wreckage, adding to the carnage. Flaming vehicles continued to roll along. Soon, additional pileups blocked all lanes of the highway in both directions.

The fireballs could be seen for miles against the black sky, beacons of destruction, harbingers of the horror to follow.

"What's happening?" asked Amjad with a mixture of wonder and panic when he saw them.

"The Americans have found us." Fear cracked Raaghib's voice.

"But we're *retreating*—Why are they still fighting? They have won, *they have won*!"

The brake lights on the car in front suddenly lit up and its wheels locked. Amjad stamped on the pedal and wrenched the steering wheel to one side to avoid the collision. The Range Rover lurched into oversteer. Amjad caught the savage movement just in time and managed to bring the vehicle skidding to a halt. All around them could be heard the awful shriek of tortured tires as the column came to a panic stop.

Daleel turned when he heard the noise. It was an Audi, traveling fast and sideways, out of control. The car spun off the highway and onto the sand, where it teetered on two wheels and then flipped and rolled. And rolled again. It finally came to a stop, dented, rocking and steaming back on its wheels, one headlight still working, the inside of the cracked windscreen spattered with blood.

A whole series of explosions lit up the sky half a mile ahead and a couple of miles behind. Daleel glanced up as two jets flew low overhead, almost invisible against the sky. That's when he realized he was crying.

A long convoy of Army vehicles, pulled to the side of the highway, unable to move forward or backward, came into Portman's view. Many were trucks covered by tarpaulins. They were troop carriers, thoughtfully illuminated by all the headlights of the stalled traffic jam around them.

On the cockpit video screen, the major could see the hot images of men sprinting from the trucks as his trigger finger sent more 30 mm rounds of DU—depleted uranium—on their way. Within moments, the troop carriers, as well as the troops themselves, were minced, shredded, and then blown to atoms. And then the heat generated by the fires consumed all the vehicles as well as the people running from the convoy in a massive and hungry conflagration.

"Fish in a goddamn barrel," came a burst of pointless chatter in Emmet's headset. The voice wasn't angry, not in the least triumphant. Just stating a fact.

"Razor, stay frosty," Portman reminded him, even though he agreed—fish in a barrel. Washington sure didn't want this army getting home safe and sound.

His wingman came back with a warning: *"Wino, tracer! Right, 3 o'clock!"*

Something clanged harmlessly off the titanium bathtub that enveloped the cockpit of Portman's A-10. If he'd been complacent, he snapped out of it instantly. There'd been sporadic small-arms fire, identified by its green streaks, shot randomly into the sky, but so far this mission really was a cakewalk. But it could turn ugly in a heartbeat if anybody on the ground had a trunkful of SAMs.

With the area now lit up by the fires, Major Portman reached over and selected the AGM-65s—the Mavericks—and went hunting along the road for large targets, Razor close behind. Thirty seconds later, he found them: fuel tankers, tanks, and artillery pieces—a column of maybe fifty vehicles—breaking out into the road's sandy verges, desperate to escape. Portman depressed a button on the base of the control stick grip, which enabled him to position the aiming gate. He settled the gate on an old Soviet-made T-72 main battle tank loaded onto a transporter, then released the button. It had a good lock, the missile's seeker head following the target. Portman tapped the trigger; the screen blanked—missile away. He thumbed the button again, moving the gate fifty meters down the road. He lined up on another target and released the button. *Shoot!* Again the screen blanked and the missile was on its way. Thiokol TX-481 solid propellant rocket motors accelerated the missiles to just under the speed of sound, while optical imaging guidance systems adjusted flight as the targets maneuvered. Portman had nothing to do except look for more targets. Moments later, 125-pound warheads smashed into metal with such heat and force that the surrounding sand was fused into glass.

"Amjad! Let's go, let's go!" Raaghib and Daleel urged. "Now! *Come on!*"

Amjad snapped out of his trance, jammed the gearbox into drive, and floored the pedal. The Range Rover leapt forward, charging through smoking debris, knocking it aside. Two armless men, blackened and bloody, suddenly appeared in the headlight beams, staggering from the burning wreckage of their vehicle, a Mercedes with a twisted fridge hanging forward over the hood. The young soldier stamped his foot on the brake pedal to avoid hitting them.

"*Yebnan kelp!* Son of a dog!" Raaghib swore. "Amjad—we can't do anything for them. Go! *Go!*"

The Range Rover accelerated. Men were wandering everywhere in shock. A truck ploughed through a cluster of soldiers, tossing them aside like mannequins. It didn't slow.

Portman was all out of missiles, except for the two air-to-air AIM-9s and the IR Maverick he now only occasionally needed to see with.

He pulled up into a shallow climb, re-engaged the Avenger Gatling gun, and gave it a quick test, tapping the trigger. The airframe shuddered the way it always did. Yep, still good. Leveling off, he glanced below and saw a cluster of vehicles still moving, just begging to be obliterated by DU.

Amjad saw an armored troop carrier two hundred yards ahead being pounded by an overwhelming force that seemed to push it into the ground like a bug mashed underfoot. Whatever was hitting the vehicle sparkled briefly before metal panels and chassis and engine simply burst into flame, just like the tanks he'd seen from that slit trench. Cars on both sides of it were instantly flattened by this same sparkling force before erupting into cones of fire. Another armored carrier seemed to crush itself into a ball a quarter of its size before a geyser of flame shot from its side. Men caught fire and ran around with their arms outstretched until they ran into each other or could run no more and dropped to the sand and continued to burn, screaming.

The air coming through the A-10's vent smelled like a mixture of burnt diesel, human flesh, and scorched French perfume. Portman had never smelled anything like it before. He gagged and instinctively flipped the oxygen to 100 percent. Only the perfume was familiar, like what was handed out on cards by pretty saleswomen in cheap department stores.

He flipped the switch back to cabin air, but left his mask in place. The road disappearing over the horizon was a string of bonfires. His eyes swept the instruments: temps and pressures all normal. Plenty of fuel and the Avenger's hoppers were still just under half full of ammunition—480 rounds. He had his orders, and there was plenty of equipment down there still reasonably intact.

Portman rolled into a dive, heading for a brace of trucks trying to make a run for it. He depressed the trigger for two seconds. The volley of DU lifted the first truck off the deck, causing it to turn in on itself like a snail curling around a hot match. The second truck was sawn completely in half, its tires blown out and its steel body panels on fire. The third, fourth, and fifth trucks seemed to be pushed beneath the desert sand before explosions ripped them apart.

A rush of heat and dust shot through the A-10's vents, enough to cause a tickle in Emmet's throat that resulted in a coughing fit. He banked away to find some clean air. *Fucking air conditioner.*

And that's when he saw the speeding vehicle, lit up in the glow of the fires. It was a Range Rover—a new model. Somehow it had managed to get away from the road. Now it was heading due north, bouncing across the sand at high speed.

Portman dived low and flew over the vehicle's roof. Then he executed a climbing turn to bring the 4×4 into the Avenger's kill zone. The Hog came around, and Emmet lined up the Range Rover on the HUD.

He compressed the trigger for a half-second. A whirring vibration rattled up through the seat as a stream of molten orange fire shot from the nose of the aircraft, slicing through the night.

Amjad and Raaghib heard the plane's engines before they saw its green glow through the windshield, passing low and fast overhead. But, Amjad reasoned, the Range Rover was black—in such darkness, surely they had a chance . . . ?

"Where is it?" Daleel screamed, searching the night sky. "Where is it?"

"Shut up!" Amjad snarled, wrestling with the steering wheel through a patch of soft sand. He needed every ounce of concentration to drive with the lights off across the desert at this speed.

Daleel looked back behind them at the highway and saw a ribbon of fire that stretched as far as he could see. He was about to say something about this when thirty depleted uranium and HEI shells drilled into the Range Rover, bringing it to an instant stop. The staggering kinetic energy released by the impact caused the DU and titanium alloy to ignite. They burned at 6000 degrees Celsius—the surface temperature of the sun—vaporizing parts of the vehicle in a swirling cloud of superheated uranium aerosol.

The major's descending turn brought him back over the burning Range Rover, now reduced to a blob of liquid metal in the sand. That smell came through the vents again—the awful sweet perfume smell. And this time, Emmet Portman threw up.

Three Days Ago
Bebek, Istanbul, Turkey

Emmet Portman, U.S. Air Attaché to Turkey, was beginning to feel a little more relaxed. If they intended to kill him, surely they'd have wrapped it up by now.

Portman had discovered the truth, and the fuckers had eyes everywhere. That he was still alive surprised him—not that he was going to complain about it. These people were ruthless. Just look at what they'd done in Kumayt. Perhaps the insurance he'd sent off on its round-trip had been unnecessary after all, but it had been worth doing, even if only for his own peace of mind.

The colonel sank into the antique gilt chair. Or at least tried to. He had a lot on his mind, and it wasn't the most comfortable place to sit. He let his head fall back. A knot of carved wood dug into the base of his skull. No, not the most comfortable place to sit. He considered moving, going to bed. Maybe in a few minutes.

Portman felt his muscles relax as he took a deep breath, letting it out with a hiss. The manila folder on his lap dropped to the carpet, the loose sheets inside sliding over each other and spreading across the carpet like splashed water. Portman sighed, too tired to bother doing anything about gathering them up.

The clock on the wall chimed. A quarter to two—0145 hours. His eyes wandered to the ancient Roman carved marble, panels of intertwined leaves and grapes, trophied for the room's doorway.

Colonel Portman had liked the idea of being posted to Turkey as the United States Air Attaché. It was a plum post. Turkey was a major ally in the global war on terror: a secular Muslim country, friendly to Washington and Israel, and strategically placed with its southern border snuggling up to Syria, Iraq, and Iran. And the Turks were investing big-time in American technology. TEI—the huge high-tech manufacturing consortium down in Eskisehir making turbofan jet engines—was a prime example. The F-16 Falcon upgrade program he was involved in with TEI might have been painful, but it was mild compared with that other business down in Kumayt, southern Iraq.

Portman took another deep breath. Time to get back to more pleasant thoughts, such as this house in Bebek. It even came with a manservant. *In a house like this, maybe Lauren and I could... No, don't go there....* Anyway, living in a place like this was a style to which he could become accustomed. Colonels, even full bird colonels, didn't ordinarily rate this kind of accommodation. It was more a general's gig, or an admiral's.

His eyes wandered to the concave ceiling, where seventeenth-century Ottoman craftsmen had executed an exquisite mosaic of bewildering geometric complexity. He'd read this apartment had been built and owned by a rich sea merchant back in the 1600s, and if he gazed at the swirling patterns of red, blue, and green tiles long enough, they reminded him of rolling ocean swells. From past experience he knew that if he looked too long, those patterns would make him queasy, the way a trip in a boat always did.

It was time for bed. He'd spent so much time thinking through the implications of the Kumayt mess that his brain was in danger of turning to mush. The conclusion he'd come to was this: The scandal hanging over Washington and Jerusalem was big enough to bring down the governments of both countries.

Portman closed his eyes again. Of course, blowing the whistle would also wreck his own career, but there was no way he could keep quiet about it—not once he'd seen the ugly truth. All those sick and disfigured children... A lot depended on State. Would they stand with him shoulder-to-shoulder when the secret was out and the shit came down?

He opened his eyes and saw a smiling face above him. Its sudden appearance startled him. There was enough time for Portman to register that he knew this face, and to ask, "What are you doing here, B—" before a cloth covered his mouth and nose and pressed down, hard. The attaché took a sharp breath, and his head swam with an acrid chemical smell—a hospital smell. Fumes filled his brain.

Another man leaned over the colonel, his face protected from blood spatter by a plastic shield. He held up a long, thin instrument: a wood chisel. Portman flinched as the tool dug into his eyeball.

Emmet Portman slid deeper into a tunnel of dull pain. Suddenly he was in the Philippine jungle, in the south of the country, looking at a man without legs or arms. Surgeons were trying to save him, a terrorist insurgent training in a nearby camp that had been surprised and ripped apart by a U.S. Marine Recon unit. The man's screams filled his head but, in fact, it was a scream torn from Portman's own throat. He gasped, sucking down more of the chemical that sloughed the skin off the back of his palate, sending a surge of blood into his mouth and nostrils. Portman was choking, drowning, unable to move. And then his remaining eye mercifully turned back in its socket like a ball rolling uphill as he slid into unconsciousness.

The hand held the gauze pad over the colonel's mouth a few seconds longer. Just to make sure. Then, satisfied that the victim was anesthetized, the man the colonel had recognized left.

Two assailants dragged the attaché's body from the velvet-upholstered chair and laid it out on the floor. His clothes were cut away with a surgeon's scalpel, revealing a forty-seven-year-old white male. The killers surveyed their victim. There was a hint of a tan line around his waist and middle thighs, suggesting that he wore boxers around the pool. The waistline was thickening. The chest hair was turning salt-and-pepper. There was an appendix scar, a significant one, which indicated that he'd been cut many years before anyone cared about the cosmetics. A hairline scar running down the outside of the left knee pointed to an operation on the cruciate ligament. The colonel had once been an athlete, or maybe a skier. No other scars or identifying marks, except for the fact that the man was circumcised.

The killers went to work. A large, dark-olive-colored plastic trash bag was set beside the body. Assailant number one pulled a couple of pairs of disposable paper coveralls from the bag while assailant number two straightened the victim's arms and legs. Next from the bag came a wooden mallet, a wood chisel larger than the one already used, and a battery-powered jigsaw. Tools ready, the killers put on the coveralls.

Placing a knee on the man's hand, assailant number two picked up the mallet and chisel, and laid the honed steel blade across the first joint of the attaché's thumb. Its edge was so sharp it cut through the skin under its own weight. The chisel was given a solid tap with the mallet, and the end of the thumb separated easily from the rest of the digit. The killers noted how surprisingly little blood flowed from the stump, and how the victim's remaining eyelid barely fluttered.

Two and a half hours had been allowed for the work ahead. A clock on a side table read 2:47. Plenty of time.

ONE

They weren't fooling anyone. The place was called the Hotel Charisma because it had none. I sat in the lobby and passed the time with a pencil, using it to reach down into the fiberglass cast on my left hand and scratch an itch on my wrist. The bellhop at the front door pored over a few curled brochures for a cheap local belly-dancing joint while he chain-smoked something that smelled like horse blanket. I wasn't sure which one of us was more excited. I watched this spectacle as I waited for Special Agent Masters. She was upstairs, doing whatever she was doing—washing the flight out of her skin, I supposed. There was no hurry; even if he was important, the victim had been dead three days: He wouldn't be drumming his fingers, impatient for us to get on with it.

A guy wearing baggy MC Hammer pants, a waistcoat that would have been small on a ten-year-old, and a red hat the shape of an ice bucket wandered in off the street past the bellhop. He saw me and came over to sell me a glass of something out of a polished metal urn strapped to his back. He insisted. I resisted harder. Eventually he gave up and wandered off to pester a couple of tourists standing around outside with their snouts buried in a guidebook. I went back to scratching with the pencil and staring absently out the window at the parade of stragglers coming and going. It was a new day in Istanbul, and outside, things were starting to liven up.

While I waited, I recalled the victim's particulars. His name was

Colonel Emmet Portman, and he was six foot two, eyes of blue, and just a little too perfect to be true. Well, maybe not perfect. According to his medical records, Portman's sperm count was down to a handful of stalwarts. Basically, the guy went to his grave shooting blanks. I was surprised to find that bit of information in his file. I wondered what interesting details *my* file might contain, but then I reminded myself that I didn't have to wonder. I knew what was in there: several hand grenades that would ensure I retired as the Air Force's oldest major, if I chose to stay on to the bitter end.

Where was I? Yeah, Colonel Portman, U.S. Air Attaché to Turkey, who now resembled a human being in kit form prior to assembly. The colonel was divorced and childless; his ex lived in Van Nuys. Aside from that, Portman was so perfect he could have stepped straight off the production line. He'd been third in his class at the Air Force Academy in '79; he completed the Fighter Weapons School at Nellis Air Force Base in '81; there was a stint in West Berlin during the height of the Cold War; he'd helped put together Reagan's bombing raid into Libya in '86; a conversion to A-10 Thunderbolts came next, just in time to bust Iraqi tanks in Gulf War I; then it was on to a posting to Lakenheath, England, where he commanded the 493rd Fighter Squadron—"the Grim Reapers." The job of Air Attaché to Turkey followed. Along the way, he'd collected a number of medals including the Silver Star, the Legion of Merit, and the Distinguished Flying Cross: valor, achievement, and flying ability. No doubt about it, the colonel already had a gold star on his forehead. General's stars on his epaulettes were just a matter of time. Only he got himself murdered, and pretty messily murdered, judging by the snapshots doing the rounds.

"Let's go," said Special Agent Anna Masters as she walked past. She was wearing a pair of faded jeans and a leather jacket, a New York Fire Department cap, and Ray-Ban Aviators. The Ray-Bans weren't necessary—it was cloudy and the sun was a long way from clearing the buildings. Most likely, Masters just didn't feel comfortable with eye contact. Eye contact with me, at least. I stood and followed her out onto the narrow hillside street.

OK, perhaps I should bring you up to speed.

My name is Vin Cooper, aged thirty-four. If you guessed from the name that I'm male, congratulations. Maybe you're in the wrong job. I'm also Caucasian, currently around 215 pounds, and closing in on six foot one inch. My hair is brown, eyes a murky kind of green. No distinguishing marks on my face, though, as I already mentioned, I'm currently wearing a cast on my left arm, from elbow to knuckle. I hold the rank of major in the AFOSI, which is the acronym for the following mouthful: the United States Air Force Office of Special Investigations. I'm a "special agent," which is a fancy title for an internal affairs cop. There are roughly 310,000 personnel in the USAF, give or take, and some of them need weeding out, particularly the murderers, deserters, extortionists, and rapists. We transfer those guys to the Army.

We've got all kinds of criminals in today's Air Force, committing all the crimes that make it worthwhile getting out of bed, seizing the day, and locking it up. At least if you're a cop.

Anyhow, somewhere along the way I seem to have earned a reputation for solving the more serious of these crimes. At the moment, what the people back in D.C. are hoping is that I'll—or, should I say, *we'll*—figure out who murdered our Air Attaché. We know someone broke into said attaché's house, sliced him up into bite-size pieces with a battery-powered saw, and laid him out on the carpet in all his sectioned, jointed glory. But we're hoping for a few more details.

Back to Special Agent Anna Masters. You could say we've met. In fact, until recently, Masters and I were an item. That is until she told me she was swinging from the chandelier for some attorney from the JAG corps. A little less than twenty-four hours have gone under the bridge since she delivered this news flash. In fact, she gave it to me an hour before we boarded the flight to Istanbul together. With timing like that, she should do stand-up.

"Did you say something?" Masters asked, turning those piercing Ray-Bans of hers on me.

"No," I said.

"Oh. I could have sworn you said something."

"You imagined it," I informed her.

"Are you going to say something?"

"No."

"Are you giving me the silent treatment here?" she asked.

"I don't talk to exercise my mouth. When I've got something to say, you'll hear it with your ears."

"Hmph."

A cab mooched by, the driver hustling for a fare. We took it.

"You are Americans?" asked the driver after Masters gave him the destination. He was looking in the rearview mirror and lighting up a cigarette.

Not a bad guess, given that we were headed for the U.S. Consulate-General.

"Yes," said Masters.

"I like Americans."

Masters nodded.

"I like Americans. And Japanese."

"Why's that?" I asked.

"Because you are rich."

"No . . ." Masters said, shaking her head. She leaned forward to check the meter was running, concerned this guy might also be taking us to the cleaners. Relieved to see the glowing numbers tick over, she sat back and stared out the window.

The rear seat of the cab was uncomfortable, but nowhere near as uncomfortable as the flight over, and not because we were sitting in economy. The problem arose because the flight was packed, and that forced us to sit *together*. Shoulder to shoulder. For more than twelve hours.

"Do you think this guy knows where he's going?" she asked suddenly, as the cab turned down a narrow cobbled street.

"Beats me. Why don't you ask him?"

Masters leaned forward again. "Excuse me, sir. Is it much farther?"

"No. We are here," he said, pulling over.

I glanced out the window. Where were the security cameras and the bulletproof glass? This didn't look much like a U.S. Consulate-General-type building, unless it was running a little tourist souvenir business on the side.

"You come and see Turkish rug," said the driver, turning around. "They are the best—double knotted." A guy trotted out from the shop with a smile that reminded me of a Chrysler's grille and opened Masters's door.

"What? No! We don't have time," Masters replied, angry, not moving from her seat.

"But my cousin has beautiful rug. You must see," the driver pleaded.

"No!" Masters grabbed the front seat with both hands. "We want the U.S. Consulate-General and we want you to take us there *now*. Do we need to take another cab?"

"No, no. It's OK. Please . . . we go now. Maybe you come back after."

The driver snapped out a few words at the guy holding Masters's door open. The guy nodded, confused, then closed the door.

"Can we get going, please?" Masters requested. Then she turned her anger on me. "Feel free to step in any time, Vin."

I shrugged. She was doing just fine.

The driver mumbled something that sounded vaguely like "U.S. Consulate" said backward, followed by a bunch of sounds that could have been words or could equally have been him clearing a nasty knot of mucus from the back of his throat. He wound down his window and spat, which solved that particular puzzle.

Masters read the address off a printed sheet of paper. "Kapli-calar . . . Mevkii . . . So-kak, number two."

The driver suddenly roared with laughter.

"I think you just told him that his camel's toenails needed clipping," I said.

Masters pursed her lips and handed the driver the sheet of paper with the address on it. He scanned it, nodded in a way that implied he had in fact misunderstood her, passed it back, and returned to that knot in his throat for a second helping.

I went back to the view out the window. We'd get to where we were going eventually. I caught a glimpse of a building way off in the distance. Lots of domes and minarets. A voice boomed from nearby speakers, punching through the cab's windows with a squeal of feedback: *"Allah-u-Akbar. Allah-u-Akbar. Allah-u-Akbar. Allah-u-Akbar. Ash'hadu an laa ilaaha illallaah. Ash'hadu an laa ilaaha illallaah . . ."*

I'd heard the refrain enough times in Afghanistan to know what was being sung: "Allah is most great" a bunch of times run together, followed by, "I bear witness that there is no god but Allah . . ." etc.

It still made the hair on my arms stand on end. The faithful were being called to prayer, the dawn prayer, or *Fajr*. It was the first of five times they'd be called to profess their faith during the day. Just in case they were inclined to forget who was boss.

We flashed past a shop, and inside I saw men rolling out their prayer rugs. It was Friday, the holy day. A little farther down the street were several young women wearing hip-hugging jeans that barely cleared their pubic line, showing off flat stomachs and pierced belly buttons. Accompanying them were two males around the same age. I didn't see them hurrying to lay out *their* rugs. They were all on their cell phones—maybe they were texting the Big Guy their prayer. On the other side of the street lumbered a couple of ample old women whose head scarves covered their hair in such a way that not a single lock would escape and, presumably, drive men to the heights of sexual frenzy.

The cab sped up a ramp to a highway heading north. The city of Istanbul quickly gave way to rock, scrub, and high-voltage electricity towers. The cab's wheels were out of balance, making the seat vibrate like a Las Vegas honeymoon special. The driver turned up the radio. As far as I could tell, it was a woman singing. She seemed to be having difficulty deciding which notes to hit, and so was hitting them all at once. I glanced at Masters.

"Where we headed?" I asked. "Bulgaria?"

"Istinye."

"Istinye! Istinye!" confirmed the driver, nodding.

I sat back and counted tenements. Twenty minutes later, we pulled off the highway and drove down through some low hills that gave way to a protected inlet. A road sign read ISTINYE. The place appeared to be a weekend retreat on the water for Istanbul's middle class.

The cab doubled back and headed inland. "There!" said the driver suddenly, pointing through the windshield. "U.S. Consulate."

He was indicating a sprawling building made from prefab slabs of concrete, perched up high on the hill like a castle and ringed by a twenty-foot-high concrete wall enclosing the entire ridgeline. It looked like the place had been positioned for a siege. The building was painted peach—maybe they were expecting a siege of home decorators from the eighties.

The cab driver delivered us close to the front door, which was a bunker wrapped in bulletproof glass and swept by surveillance cameras. Masters paid for the ride.

Two women wearing head scarves stood behind the security bunker's bulletproof glass. Masters took my passport, added it to hers, and slid them beneath the glass. "We have an appointment with Ambassador Burnbaum," she informed the women.

One woman checked the passports, scanned the biometrics, and consulted a computer screen. Her makeup was immaculately applied to flawless pale-olive skin. It was the only skin open for viewing, so maybe she figured it was worth the effort. She was wearing a short-sleeved shirt, but flesh-colored Lycra covered her forearms. White gloves hid her hands, black smudges on their fingertips. Her colleague was similarly sealed. The woman returned our passports with a vague smile. "Go through there," she said, indicating the metal detector and X-ray machine.

As we completed the preliminaries and walked across the open space toward the front door, the heavy steel gate to the parking lot opened and a vehicle pulled in. It looked like a cop car—dirty and scuffed, like all cop cars are, no matter what the country. Two males got out. They wore clothes freshly pressed by a park bench. I took a guess and pegged them as homicide—the local guys. I took a further guess and assumed their boss was riding them to get the mess with the dead attaché sorted out and fast. A U.S. Air Force colonel murdered in your country was just plain bad for the national image.

The two men eyeballed us, frowning. But then I realized they both had those solid mono-brows and were probably just born scowling. They walked like their shoes were lead ballast. If I read these guys right, the day was young and already it had gone bad. They got to the door before us.

I caught it before it closed behind them and held it open for Masters. "Judas first," I said.

Masters replied with a lift of her chin.

Up ahead was a window—more bulletproof glass—behind which sat a blonde in a blouse covered in big, bright menopausal flowers. The cops showed her their credentials and I heard Ambassador Burnbaum's name mentioned. The blonde passed them a clipboard under the glass and had them fill it out before handing them a couple of clip-on visitor's security passes and directing them toward an elevator.

She smiled helpfully as we stepped up. "How can I help you today? Visas? Passports?" she chirped with an American accent.

Masters flashed her shield. "Actually, I think we might be with them." She tilted her head toward the two cops. "Special Agents Masters and Cooper. We have an appointment with Ambassador Burnbaum."

I pressed my shield against the glass. As I did so, I caught a whiff of the blonde's perfume, which was sweet and powerful—had to be; there was a sheet of glass half an inch thick between us. A bee arrived and bumped into the pane, trying to get at the source of the bouquet.

"My, the ambassador *is* busy today," she observed. "Name, agency—I'll fill out the rest." She slid the clipboard through a slot at the bottom of the glass.

Masters filled in the details for both of us.

"There you go," the blonde said as she pushed a couple of passes beneath the glass. "Go around the corner, down the hallway till you get to the elevator. Fourth floor. Someone will meet you. Just follow those men."

"And try not to lose them, Special Agent," I added.

"Don't start with me, Vin," said Masters under her breath as she strode away from the counter.

TWO

An older woman, hair tied up in a gray bun and glasses on a chain swinging from her neck, met us when the elevator doors opened on the fourth floor. She led us to a large, sun-drenched room and closed the door behind us. The room was crowded with people standing around, deep in conversation. I took the opportunity to absorb the surroundings.

It was a modern white box of a room with recessed low-voltage spots burning bright holes in the ceiling. Natural light flooded in through two large southeast-facing windows. In contrast to this modernity, the furnishings came from a century long gone. A lush Turkish rug featuring what appeared to be foliage in rich reds and blues covered much of the floor. In one corner of the room stood a large antique desk heavily inlaid with mother-of-pearl in intricate geometric patterns. Gold-framed chairs upholstered in red velvet were arrayed around it. On the wall behind the desk hung an enormous painting in a heavy gold frame. And it was some painting. It showed a battle in progress being fought by soldiers wearing turbans, brandishing bloody curved scimitars and hauling an enormous cannon. In the background, the battlements of what appeared to be a Roman city were breached in a tumble of shattered stone blocks. In the foreground of the painting, beneath the feet of the victors, was a thick layer of diced body parts in a blood sauce. Reminded me of something.

My eyes met those of a trim guy in late middle age with styled gray hair, wearing a pin-striped suit. I recognized him from file photos—Ambassador Burnbaum. He excused himself from a conversation and came on over. "Ah, you must be Special Agents Cooper and Masters. Excellent!" he said. "We can get started."

I handed him a copy of my orders.

"No need for the formalities, Special Agent. Thank you for coming over so promptly. We're between Consulate-Generals at the moment, so I'll be standing in, shuttling between here and the embassy in Ankara. I hope that won't impede your investigation."

I gave him a nod, sure it wouldn't, and shook his outstretched hand.

"Pleased to meet you, sir," Masters gushed, on the verge of a curtsy.

Ward Baxter Burnbaum, United States Ambassador to Turkey. The guy was quite a legend. During the Cold War, the story went, he'd spirited a number of high-ranking Soviet military defectors out of East Berlin. On his last mission there, his cover blown, wounded and chased all the way to the barbed wire by a Trabant full of Stasi—and, did I mention, while dragging a similarly wounded defector to freedom?—Burnbaum had relieved an enemy soldier of his Kalashnikov and shot his way out to the West. Supposedly, as he lay bleeding in the arms of a fellow CIA agent, and moments before he slipped into unconsciousness, he announced that he had a couple of cartons of eastern bloc cigarettes to declare to Customs. Oh, yeah, and one KGB general.

Burnbaum shifted across to State and lay low for a couple of years. When things calmed down a little, after the East Germans had paid us back with a few shoot-outs of their own on our turf, and the scorecard had worked itself out about even, he came back to serve. These days, though, Burnbaum was heading for retirement. This gig in Turkey would be his last post.

"First, allow me to introduce General Zafer Mataradzija," he continued. "And this is his adjutant, Lieutenant Colonel Ozden Gokdemir." Burnbaum's lips tackled the Turkish officers' names like a blindfolded SEAL assembling an M4—that is, expertly. "General, Colonel, this is Special Agent Cooper and Special Agent Masters from the United States Air Force Office of Special Investigations."

While the colonel was of average height and build with no particularly distinguishing features, the general was short. Actually, I thought he was seated until he took a step toward us and put out his hand. His fingers were large and dry, and as rough as hand-rolled cigars. In halting but rehearsed English, he said, "A pleasure to meeting you in this unfortunate occasion."

"Yes, sir," Masters and I replied, almost in unison.

All by the book. An Air Attaché, especially one serving in a significant strategic partner-state like Turkey, was an important member of our diplomatic mission. His murder was a big deal for both the Turks and us.

Burnbaum moved on, sweeping us along with him. "This is Special Agent Seb Goddard and Special Agent Arlow Mallet." Masters and I nodded at Goddard and Mallet, who nodded back. "They're up from Third MP Group, out of Kuwait."

I wondered what they were *up* for, exactly. This was an OSI case, and although CID was a police organization working for the same country we were, that didn't mean we got along. In fact, it guaranteed we wouldn't.

Mallet said, "Y'all need U.S. Army CID resources on this one, you just holler."

"Here to help," Goddard echoed.

"We'll be sure and do that," I told them, lying. Goddard was a pinup for steroid abuse, with a neck so thick his earlobes probably had jock rash. Mallet was all ropy sinew with hollows for cheekbones and black eyes that reminded me of watermelon pits. Both MPs were in their mid-twenties, which meant they were most likely warrant officers—doers, not thinkers. Masters and I moved along.

"And these are the police officers who've done such a wonderfully proficient job of handling the case thus far," said Burnbaum, radiating the detectives we'd seen earlier with his warmest smile. Yeah, Burnbaum was good; the two cops had no idea they'd just been slandered by a pro. I wondered why the ambassador didn't think much of them. "This is Detective Sergeant Umit Karli," he continued, "and Detective Sergeant Baris Iyaz, both from the Turkish National Police, Homicide Division."

Masters and I said hello, and we all shook hands and exchanged business cards. I had the feeling we were returning to our corners before coming out to fight. There's nothing like the spirit of international cooperation.

Burnbaum glanced up, distracted by the door as it swung open. "Ah, General. Come right in, please."

"Morning, Mr. Ambassador," said a U.S. Army two-star. I wondered what his unit was and what his interest in the case might be. Maybe it was just that because *they* had a general here, we had to have one, too. He went straight up to his Turkish counterpart and shook the man's hand. Like the Turkish general, ours was short. In addition to that, however, ours was narrow-shouldered, bald on top, and wearing specs with thick, square green plastic rims. If this guy had a wife, I bet her name was Edna. I'd also bet it was the pressure of Edna's thumb that had worn the bald spot on his head. "So, you're what Washington has sent us?" he asked, his eyes bouncing between Masters and me like a pinball trapped between rebound cushions.

"Yes, sir," said Masters. She introduced us both by name, leaving out the rank.

"Don't you people ever wear a goddamn uniform?" he asked, pursing his lips.

Masters and I let it go without an answer. The general would've known that we rarely wear uniforms for a reason—the reason being that when we were in civilian clothes, officers who outranked us figured there was a chance we might outrank them, and so they wouldn't pull the I-outrank-you bullshit when we questioned them. And even when we did wear ABUs—airman battle uniforms, the standard Air Force combat camos—we wore them devoid of rank for the same reason. The general was just flexing his muscles, marking his territory, getting us back for having to wake up beside Edna.

The pin on his chest introduced him as Maj. General Buford Trurow. I'd never heard of him, but then I guessed he'd never heard of me either, so we were starting out even, more or less.

"Don't have to worry about introducing me to everyone, Ward," said Trurow, bursting with impatience. "If no one else is joining us, let's just get on with it."

Before Burnbaum could respond, the door opened. In walked a young captain juggling a bundle of satchels and a briefcase.

"Cain," snapped General Trurow. "Where the hell've you been? *You* might have all day, but if you do, son, I'd like to know why."

Refusing to be flustered, Captain Cain said, "Sir, the medical examiner has just finished the autopsy."

Trurow grunted and sat on a chair with his arms folded, doing his best to appear put out by the captain's uncommon gall at arriving in the room after him. The ambassador went through another round of flawless introductions.

I knew from the briefing we'd received in Washington that Captain Rodney Cain had been called in as the scene officer on the Portman case. Aside from supervising the crime scene and managing the USAF's interest in the murder of one of its own, he would also have to liaise with the local authorities, in particular, as he'd said, the local medical examiner. From the looks on the faces of Detective Sergeants Karli and Iyaz, there wasn't a lot of love lost between them and the captain. I guessed because Cain was doing his job. And maybe some of theirs, too.

I looked around the room. There were quite a few people here, plenty of us and plenty of them, but I couldn't shake the feeling that someone important was missing.

With one hand in his pocket and the other on his desk, and with the slightest movement of his head, Burnbaum conveyed that we should all pay attention to something he wanted to say. "I don't have to remind anyone here about the sensitivity of this investigation. The human side of it is tragic enough. We've managed to keep the press out of it—and for that we have General Mataradzija to thank." He nodded at the general. "The reason for this get-together today is to introduce you to the special agents Washington has sent to help the local effort, to share with them any developments in the case, and to give Special Agents Cooper and Masters the opportunity to ask any questions that may have occurred since they were briefed on the case yesterday in Washington. So... Where shall we begin?"

"Mind if I fire up my laptop, sir?" asked Cain.

"Please," said Burnbaum with a nod.

"I also have a projector here. Would you have a power outlet I could plug into, sir?"

Burnbaum stood aside and indicated the area behind him. Captain Cain squeezed past and fumbled around on the floor.

Projector. I had the feeling we weren't about to view holiday snaps.

"Can we just get this show on the road?" demanded Trurow, giving his wristwatch a double take.

OK, General, I get it—you're a busy man. I bet myself twenty bucks

Trurow would be the first out, just so everyone in the room would know his time was the most valuable.

I sat with my legs stretched out in front of me, crossed my feet, and got comfortable. "The show," as Trurow called it, would take as long as it took. If Trurow had better places to be, he'd be there. As for the Turkish police, I could see they were uncomfortable with the situation. This was their town, and the murder had happened on their soil. It would have been a different matter if the attaché had been killed within the grounds of the embassy or the consulate—technically speaking, U.S. sovereign territory and thus out of their jurisdiction. But he'd been murdered, according to the brief, in an apartment in the upmarket Istanbul suburb of Bebek, wherever that was.

"Of course, General," said Burnbaum, as smooth as shaving cream in response to Trurow's impatience. "Perhaps our Turkish friends would care to go through the facts of the case."

Detective Sergeant Umit Karli volunteered, taking half a step forward. The DS was five ten and built like a bag of dirty washing—narrow at the top, wide and round at the bottom. I pegged him as being around forty-five years old, but he could have been older. He was sporting a dark brown comb-over, the kind that'd make Donald Trump nod with admiration. The guy's front bangs had been carefully arranged to hide the sparse turf on the crown of his head, and stuck in place with some kind of goop. Classy. His pants were hitched halfway up his rib cage, the belt cinched tight. And I hate to go into details, but he dressed to the left—and with what I couldn't help thinking were a few pairs of socks stuffed down there for added stature. He stood with hands on his hips, which had the effect of pulling open his jacket, revealing an empty underarm holster, his piece checked at the front door. "Before I begin, have you read report?" he asked, addressing the question to me in heavily accented English.

Masters answered for me. "There was a report, but we don't know whether it was yours."

Karli glanced at his partner, Detective Sergeant Iyaz, who returned the look with the hint of a shrug. Iyaz, by the way, was around twenty-five. There was a deep five o'clock shadow across his cheeks and a brown spot in the center of his forehead, worn there by carpet rash from regular praying. His hair was jet-black, combed back, and as shiny as a beetle's carapace.

Karli put a mint in his mouth and cracked it between his molars. "We find deceased on the floor of his study."

"So, *you* found him?" asked Masters, jumping in before I could.

"No. A gendarme found him."

"Gendarme?" Masters was on a roll.

"Like a police officer, but also military," said Karli. From the look on his face I could see he couldn't quite work out what they were dealing with in Anna Masters. His simpering smile told me he'd already convinced himself she wanted to sleep with him and his socks. But the jury in his mind was out on the question of whether this American woman was plain dumb or just thorough. She was beautiful, so the odds on dumb had to be good. And not a Muslim, so also therefore of loose morals, right? Who was I to get in the way of his voyage of discovery?

"Who notified the gendarmes?" Masters asked.

"The deceased's manservant," Iyaz replied.

"He had a manservant?" My turn. "Did I miss something in the report?"

Karli spoke up. "No, the report we submitted contained what we knew after a few hours. There was pressure to get your embassy something. We were told to put down what we had. We did not have much."

Not unreasonable, I thought.

"We should tell you, we are no closer to solving this crime," Iyaz added.

Roughly seventy-two hours had passed since Colonel Portman's remains had been discovered. A stalled investigation would account for the obvious antipathy in the room—at least on the American side of it—toward Iyaz and Karli.

"You've seen the pictures of the deceased?" Karli asked.

"Yes," said Masters.

"A most savage murder. So much blood. We have not seen things like this before."

"I have," I said.

"You have?" Karli again.

Masters's face had the same question on it.

"Yeah, when I was a kid. The way he was laid out in pieces reminded me of plastic model airplanes, the kind you build."

"I'm not sure I get the relevance," said the ambassador.

"And I'm not sure I appreciate your sense of humor," added General Trurow.

"Actually, the consulting forensic psychologist agrees with you, Special Agent," said Captain Cain, stepping in.

"She does?" Trurow asked, not quite believing it.

"The way in which the attaché was murdered was plainly symbolic," Cain explained. "She made the same observation that Agent Cooper did about the similarity to those model planes."

Karli continued, checking with his notes as he spoke, stumbling over the pronunciation of some words, mispronouncing others. "The attaché servantman contact gendarme at eight on the morning of Tuesday. A police officer attend in fifteen minute later than that. Detective Iyaz and myself, we arrive after forty-five minute. The state of remains made time of death difficult to know. Forensics say he die around three A.M. No one in the street saw or hear this murder happening. We have no witness. But we have recover murder weapons."

"Excellent. Progress," said Trurow, clapping his hands together and then checking to see how far Mickey's big hand had moved around the dial on his wrist.

The Turkish general gave a satisfied nod, but about what I wasn't sure. It couldn't have been about progress because, quite obviously, very little had been made.

"Entry into the attaché home come through courtyard," Karli went on. "A window was smash. At first we thin the killer come in from house next door, over the roof. But then forensic people see disturb earth around drain cover in courtyard. We open this and follow drain to Bosphorus. In this drain we find plastic bag with . . . um . . . er . . ."

"Chisel," Iyaz prompted.

"Yes, chisel—many different-size chisel, a small knife like how you call scalpel, and a battery-operate . . ." Karli called Iyaz for assistance in frisking down this difficult sentence. The younger cop muttered something in reply, after which Karli continued, "We find battery-operate—we think you call it—*jigsaw*. It was blood all over."

"The drain explain why no one see anyone enter or leave," Iyaz added.

Maybe, but then so would apathy or fear of retaliation, I thought. "I read there was evidence of robbery."

"Yes. A wall safe behind a painting," replied Iyaz. "They use explosive on it."

"Explosives make a lot of noise," I said. "What did they use to kill the sound with?"

Iyaz checked his notebook. "Cushions."

"Hmm..." Pillows were designed for sitting on, not absorbing blast waves moving at the speed of sound.

"There was also a floor safe," he continued. "This was open, but not by force. We find nothing inside safes—the contents of both is removed."

"Do we know for a fact there were contents to remove?" Masters asked.

"We don't know, but why else have safes, no?" said Karli.

"What about fingerprints?" Masters wanted to know.

"We find fingerprints on floor safe. They belong to servantman and attaché."

"Any prints on the wall safe?" I asked.

"No, no prints."

"The wall safe had been cleaned out, Special Agent. By that I mean wiped clean," said Captain Cain, helping out.

"As in wiped down for fingerprints," Trurow chimed in, perhaps suddenly seeing himself in a trench coat.

"A little more thoroughly than that, actually, sir. It was cleaned inside most thoroughly—walls, ceiling, floor, and the inside of the door—using paper towels from the kitchen."

"If the killer was wearing gloves, which no doubt he would have been," observed Masters, "why bother?"

Cain shrugged. "Perhaps he was just being extra careful."

"The door of wall safe was... was..." Karli hesitated and again called his partner for backup.

"A shaped charge blow it," offered Detective Sergeant Iyaz. "Small but powerful."

"Forensics looking into the type of explosives used?" I asked.

"Yes."

"You'll copy us with the findings?"

"Yes, of course."

"So this manservant is a suspect," I said.

"Yes."

"Have you brought him in for questioning?"

"No." Karli shook his head.

"Why not?"

Karli again: "We cannot find him."

"He's missing?" I asked, attempting to clarify.

"Yes, we think so," answered Iyaz.

"What makes you think so?"

"He has not been back to his home," said Karli. "None of his clothes or personal effects are gone."

Iyaz: "He has just... disappear."

The double act was getting on my nerves. Any moment now I expected them to throw to sports.

General Trurow cleared his throat. "We've got a motive—robbery—the murder weapons, *and* a suspect. You people should have this all wrapped up in no time."

"So you found no prints on the wall safe, but you found prints on the floor safe." I spelled it out just to make sure nothing was getting lost in the translation.

"That is correct," said Iyaz.

"You found the attaché's prints on the floor safe."

"Yes."

"And the manservant's prints."

"Yes."

"But why would someone wipe down the wall safe and not bother doing the same with the floor safe?"

Karli and Iyaz stared at me.

"Maybe the killer didn't find the floor safe," I reasoned. "You're just assuming he did. For all we know, the manservant could have come along in the morning, found his boss dead, saw the wall safe emptied, and so went to the one in the floor and cleaned it out. Maybe the reason you can't find the guy is because he's sipping piña coladas from coconuts on Acapulco Beach."

The two homicide cops continued to stare in a way that suggested I'd lost them back at "Hello..."

"That's a lot of maybes, Special Agent," General Trurow said.

A lot? I counted only two. He was missing the point—that assumptions were no substitute for facts.

Masters jumped in. "Sir, with respect, when the clues are inconclusive, maybes are all you've got."

I glanced at her. The support took me by surprise. I thought, *It's going to take more than that to get back in my good books, sister.*

Trurow accepted Masters's comment with a grunt, which I took to mean he thought she was being a smart-mouth. "OK, so where do we go from here?" he asked.

"The crime scene would be a good place to start," suggested Masters.

I agreed. It wasn't that we expected to find anything—after three days of forensic teams dusting, taping, and luminol-spraying the place for blood-spatter patterns, the chances of us strolling on in and finding clues lying around were snuggling up to zero. But it might help us get our bearings.

Captain Cain cleared his throat. "Perhaps this is where I should come in. Unless homicide has something else to add?"

It was pretty obvious they didn't. Karli and Iyaz flipped their notebooks shut, took their seats, and feigned boredom. Iyaz put his hands behind his head and yawned.

"A number of things have turned up in the autopsy and in discussions with the forensic psychologist," Cain began. "If you don't mind, Mr. Ambassador..."

"Of course, please go right ahead," said Burnbaum. "I'll get the lights."

With the curtains drawn and the room darkened, the picture projected on the wall became sharp and bright. Cain clicked on an icon and a nightmare image flashed up. I'd seen this one before, but a five-by-eight in inches rather than in feet hadn't done it justice. The image showed a man, or what was once a man. His hand had been dissected and arranged on the floor. Each finger was separated from the hand and the knuckles individually jointed. The hands were removed from the arms, the arms from the body. The legs, feet, and toes had been given the same treatment. The torso had been flayed and the skin peeled back. The clavicles were laid beside the torso, as were the arms and each individual rib so that the body looked like an exploded diagram. The skin from one arm and a leg was neatly arranged beside the limbs it had been removed from as if it were a spare part in a catalogue. The head was separated from the neck. Blood was splashed everywhere.

"A couple of interesting facts have come to light from the autopsy," said Cain, unaffected by the image. "The first is that the attaché was alive when this was done to him."

A window rattled softly in its frame. I wondered whether the collective gasp might have been the cause. The blood—so damn much of it. The poor bastard's heart had simply kept pumping till it ran out of stuff to push through his arteries.

Cain continued. "The other point of interest is that twelve of the attaché's bones are missing."

THREE

Captain Cain clicked through other slides of the murdered attaché until he came to a view marked with various white circles. "There are two hundred and six bones in an adult human," he told us. "The medical examiner made an inventory of Colonel Portman's. The circles and marks you can see on these pictures indicate where the bones have been removed."

"Jesus..." Trurow leaned forward with morbid fascination.

Cain continued. "Working down the body, he's missing the C3 vertebra, the right clavicle, the left ulna, the manubrium of the sternum, a true rib and a floating rib, the proximal, middle, and distal phalanges of his right hand—the entire middle finger, basically—the right patella, the left lunate bone, and the right medial malleolus."

"How could the attaché have been alive when they did this to him?" asked Masters.

"Well, he wasn't breathing for all of it. The medical examiner's unsure about how long into this ordeal he survived," replied Cain. "But at least he was unconscious. Whoever did this put him under first with chloroform, and lots of it. The chloroform burned the skin clean off the roof of his mouth and the back of his throat. Cause of death was, in fact, drowning in his own blood."

"What does your shrink consultant make of all this—the way he was killed, the missing bones?" I asked.

"I have the doctor's notes to pass on to you, as well as a copy of the medical examiner's report. Dr. Aysun Merkit—that's the name of the consulting forensic psychologist, by the way—she thinks this appears to be a ritual killing. There's obviously a lot of controlled anger here."

"So, in other words, the shrink doesn't have a clue," I concluded.

Cain thought about this before answering. "You could say that pretty much nails it, Special Agent, except that she believes this one is probably just the first."

"The first?" Trurow said, horrified.

"Murder, sir. Someone with this much anger doesn't usually stop at one."

"So we might have a serial killer on our hands?" the general asked.

"There's a good chance," agreed Cain.

"Wonderful," Trurow said, throwing his hands up in the air.

I was tempted to say that one episode did not make a serial, but I kept it to myself. "Does Dr. Merkit have a view on why the attaché might have been broken down into bits?"

"No, although she thinks the airplane-kit symbology might well be significant. He was the *Air* Attaché, after all."

"And those missing bones? Any theories about why they've been taken?" asked Masters.

"Dr. Merkit believes they've been harvested."

"Harvested?" Trurow echoed.

"For later use, sir," replied Cain.

I looked at Trurow. He was peering out of those glasses with the concentrated frown of a man trying to see something way off in the distance.

"The doctor's certain they're going to turn up," Cain told us.

"With more victims?"

"More than likely, Special Agent Masters, yes. As I said, Dr. Merkit believes a killer with this much rage doesn't usually stop at one."

"Any theories about why *those* bones in particular?" I asked.

The captain shook his head. "No, I'm afraid not, though that's an angle we should look at." He made a quick note about it on a pad.

"And what about the *way* the body was cut up?" I pressed.

"Not sure what you mean, Special Agent."

"Does the medical examiner think it was done by an amateur or a pro?"

"Definitely by an amateur rather than by, say, a surgeon. And it would have taken the best part of two hours—even using a jigsaw."

I was now certain of two things. One, that this Q & A had been squeezed dry; and two, that I'd asked by far the best questions.

When he was sure there was nothing more to clarify, Cain turned off his laptop and handed out copies of the reports. Masters and I took one each, as did the Turkish flatfoots and the two Army CID types.

The spell broken, General Trurow stood up and informed us, "Well, a tragic and frightening business." He turned to Masters. "Keep me on top of your progress going forward. We need to effect a speedy resolution on this one." Handshaking followed, and then he departed.

First out the door. I won the bet. I took twenty bucks out of my right pocket and stuffed it in my left. "His work here is done," I muttered under my breath.

"What was that?" Masters shot back.

"I said, 'Isn't this fun?'"

She gave me the please-be-here-with-someone-else look. I obliged and made my way across to Cain, who was untangling power cords, packing up. "That was some slide show, Captain," I told him.

"Yeah," he agreed. "A nasty business."

"Did the attaché have an enlisted aide or an assistant?" I asked. "Was anyone handling his correspondence, keeping his schedule for him?"

"No. Apparently he was a hands-on kind of guy. Sent his own emails, answered his own phones, tied his own shoelaces."

"What about his office? He have one here?"

"Yes, he did. He also had one in the embassy at Ankara, though he seems to have spent as much time as possible here. He preferred Istanbul—liked his home in Bebek, from what I can gather. The office is down the hall, on the right. His name's on the door. It's all yours. I locked it to keep out the inquisitive."

He held out a key and then dropped it in my hand.

"There's not much there," he continued. "A few mementos, some vacation photos."

"Files?" I asked.

"Some, but from the looks of things, Colonel Portman was a believer in the electronic office."

"His emails?"

"Once you get settled, I'll forward the file to you."

Cain and I exchanged cards. "So why did Portman have a manservant if he was such a do-it-yourself kind of guy?" I wondered aloud.

The captain sucked air through a side tooth. "Don't know. Maybe he drew the line at housework."

I wasn't too keen on the dusting myself. "With a crime like this, I'm surprised there's so little forensic evidence. As in, none. Their forensics people up to the job?"

"Did they overlook anything, do you mean? Who knows? They use similar techniques to us. . . . You want my opinion? I think the killer was either real lucky or real good."

"What I'm not sure of is what we have here, exactly," I told him. "A murder with a robbery on the side, or a robbery disguised as a murder. What's your feeling about this manservant?"

"I like your theory about the fingerprints. If you're right, he's running because he's scared, not because he's guilty."

The captain had packed his gear and was about to leave just as Masters came over. I left them to it. I noticed that the CID guys had already slipped away. I also noticed that they'd asked nothing during the debrief. Was that because the only thing between their ears was white noise, or because they'd enjoyed a pre-brief?

I crossed the room to where Karli and Iyaz were eyeballing the exit, getting ready to leave. "Looks like a tough case," I remarked.

The older of the two, Karli, did the talking. "We will get there."

"Yeah, sure," I replied. Funny how two positives together can cancel each other out. "In the meantime, did this manservant of Colonel Portman's have any priors?"

"I'm sorry?" Karli scratched his cheek with a finger.

"A record? Previous arrests?"

"No. He had not before been in trouble from the police."

"You have anything on him?" I asked. "A picture, maybe?"

"Yes, we have pictures of him—we took from his home. We also took employment records, tax returns, bank account statements—"

"A photo would be useful, and a few other details like a name to put to the face."

"We will send these things to you here."

"You were about to tell me you have his cell phone records?" I prompted.

"Yes."

"So you have his number?"

"Yes."

"You tried calling it?"

"His phone?" asked Karli.

"Yeah."

Karli and Iyaz looked at each other with dumb smiles on their faces like I'd just told them that in the next life they were coming back as plastic surgeons. "No. It's a good idea. We will try it."

I didn't for a moment think this manservant guy would pick up, but in this game, you never know.

"Special Agent Masters and I are going to visit the crime scene this morning," I told them.

"The crime scene is . . . er . . ." Karli turned and said something in rapid-fire Turkish to Iyaz.

His partner gave him the answer. "Cleaned."

"You've called in the cleaners?"

"Yes."

I did a count-back. The timing was about right for the murder site to be returned to its former state. The weather was cool, but still, left any longer and the local insects would be busting down the door just to roll in the smell. I thought about all that blood splashed around—those cleaners would have some kick-ass spot removers. I was thinking this because I also just happened to glance down and notice a ketchup stain on my shirt, which I must have picked up on the plane on the way over. "How about late morning—say, eleven-thirty?"

Karli nodded. "We will meet you there at that time."

I like having my hand held, but only when it belongs to someone female, interested, and mustache-free. "No need. Just leave the key under the mat," I said.

"A gendarme will let you in," Iyaz replied.

"Fine." I looked around the room. Ambassador Burnbaum was shaking hands with the Turkish general. I walked over.

As I approached, I heard General Mataradzija say, "I must go." Then he saw me and said, "A terrible business. You catch these peoples, yes?"

"Yes, sir," I assured him.

"Good morning and good luck." He gave me a friendly smile, and I watched him and his adjutant head off in Masters's direction to say good-bye.

"The general's a good man and a fine leader," Burnbaum said, following my eyeline.

"Sir, I wonder if we could ask you a few questions in private."

"Of course. Captain Cain and the general are both on their way out. We can talk here."

I glanced up and saw Cain leaving the room with Colonel Gokdemir. Cain looked at me and tipped his forefinger to his head as if to say, *We'll catch up later.*

Burnbaum went to the door and closed it as Masters and I pulled chairs up to the antique desk. I sat down and again took in the massive painting on the wall, the one with the triumphant soldiers, the big cannon, the crumbling stone walls, and the mound of dismembered bodies and limbs under the winners' feet.

"Do you know what that painting's all about?" asked Burnbaum, noting my interest in it.

"No, sir."

"Special Agent Masters?"

She studied it. "I think the man in front leading his army over the bones of the conquered is the first Ottoman sultan, Mehmet the Second, who took the city from the Byzantine rulers after smashing down the walls with the biggest cannon the world had ever seen."

"Ah, you're a student of history."

"Actually, a student of the Lonely Planet guidebook, sir. I spent some vacation time in Turkey three years ago."

I looked sideways at Masters and thought, *Lady, you just keep the surprises coming.* She'd given me no hint she'd been here before.

"Do you like Istanbul?" the ambassador asked her.

"Very much, sir. I met my fiancé here, in fact."

Like I said, the surprises kept coming. This day was getting better by the minute.

"It's a very romantic city—magical," Burnbaum agreed.

Yeah, and I was sure that wherever the attaché was, he was also thinking about what a romantic, magical city Istanbul was. Time to get back to business before Masters launched into her wedding plans. "Mr. Ambassador," I began, "do you know whether the attaché had received any death threats?"

"No, not that I'm aware of."

"Would he have informed you if he had?"

"I doubt it. Emmet was the kind who wouldn't have taken threats seriously."

"What was he working on?" I asked.

"What do you mean?"

"Mr. Ambassador, we both know the Air Attaché to a strategically vital country like Turkey is a handpicked individual with certain skills. What had he been up to that wasn't noted on his calendar? Specifically, had he been involved in anything clandestine?"

Burnbaum stroked his pink chin. Liver spots dotted the back of his hand. "Not as far as I know, Special Agent. He was primarily occupied with the job of facilitating the upgrade of thirty F-16 Falcons to a new Block specification for the Turkish Air Force. Emmet was helping the local industry navigate through the worst of the red tape so that the upgrade could happen with a minimum of fuss."

"Nothing else?"

"Well, he did express some concern about the case of a young Turkish woman allegedly raped by an Air Force crew chief down at Incirlik Air Base. I've seen the file. It's an open-and-shut case against our man, I'm sorry to say—right down to the DNA evidence. The only problem is that the woman has brothers, and revenge is a recreational activity in this country."

My face evidently betrayed the fact that I might've attached some significance to this last bit of information, because the ambassador added, "Emmet had only just pulled the file to go through it. I could be wrong, but I doubt he'd even begun the interview process before he was killed."

"So that's it?" Masters asked, back on the job at last.

Smelled like dead ends to me, but I said, "Can we get a look at the case file for the rape charge?"

"Of course. I'll have it ready for you in an hour. Also, you'll need a base to work from while you're in Istanbul, so I've arranged for you to have this office."

"Thank you, sir."

The sultan in the painting behind the ambassador, striding across all those dismembered bodies, distracted me. The scene reminded me of Captain Cain's photos.

FOUR

The Air Attaché's office had a view similar to the one we'd just left down the hall. It was roomy. There was a modern desk—nothing fancy—a water cooler, a couch, and a filing cabinet. On the desk was a thin LCD computer screen and keyboard, a laser printer, an older-style, well-worn fighter pilot's helmet, a Rolodex, a pad of Post-its, and three pens. I gave the Rolodex a spin. Next I tapped the keys on the keyboard, in case his computer was just sleeping. The screen stayed black.

The walls without the view were bare, except for one with a bulletin board. On the board were a couple of photos of the murder victim. One showed him with his oxygen mask hanging free, taxiing in or out—I couldn't tell—and another showed him shaking hands with an officer who, like Portman, was wearing a flight suit. Behind the two men was a crisp lineup of F-15 Eagles, the air-to-air model. Both men were smiling.

I checked the desk drawers, looking for his calendar. I didn't find it. All were empty except for one, which held various items of stationery—pencils, erasers, paper clips.

"Did Captain Cain say Portman spent more time here than at the Ankara embassy?" Masters asked, standing beside open filing cabinet drawers.

I could see they were mostly empty, except for two. "Yeah," I said. "He did." I scanned the folders. "You wouldn't think so." It felt more like a temporary office, an office Portman was either in the process of moving into or moving out of. Perhaps, as Cain had said, the Air Attaché was an electronic-office kind of guy. "Let's go," I said. "Nothing to see here."

A stiff wind had sprung up since Masters and I had arrived at the Consulate-General. We walked down to the water and took a cab from there. After twenty minutes of contemplation, we were back at our hotel.

As I got out of the cab, I watched a huddle of old women wearing black walking up the steeply angled street toward us. They leaned into the wind, pulling the corners of their scarves down over their faces for protection. Behind them were a couple of young women wearing microminis. The sky was a pale blue with fluffy, powder-puff clouds, the city's skyline clean and stark against it. Sheets of newsprint and torn paper bags danced and swirled with the last leaves in airborne eddies. I shivered in my T-shirt and jacket. It had to be less than 50 degrees. The middle fingers of my left hand encased in the fiberglass cast, my own personal weather forecasters, ached dully with the chill. I gave them a wiggle, just to make sure they still worked, then held them up to my lips and blew some warmth onto them. Life had not been kind to those fingers. They'd been broken twice within the last twelve months, the first time by a small-caliber bullet fired from a handgun at close range, the second when I fell on them during a mission in Pakistan—from a height of around 20,000 feet. But that's another story.

"You want a coffee?" I asked Masters. "I'm buying."

"Come into some money?"

"Yeah, I won a bet." I dug my hand into my pocket.

"I saw a place down there," she said, indicating the general direction with a nod. The road was lined on both sides by jumbled pink, cream, and tan buildings like shoe-box stacks about to fall into each other.

"Well, luck before experience," I replied, gesturing at her to lead on.

Masters stepped off the sidewalk and headed for a place with a couple of empty, windblown tables out in front, their white tablecloths snapping in the wind. I waited for an old guy the color of smoked fish who was trudging up the steep road toward me. He was bent double under a heavy load strapped to a wooden brace across his back. A BMW, a big new one, came up behind him and blew its horn. The old guy ignored it. If I were the sensitive type, I might have said that this city was engaged in a war between the new and the old, one that had probably been going on for a very long time. But I'm not the sensitive type, so I belched with mild hunger instead.

"Hey, Mr. Experience, you coming?" called Masters from the other side of the road, impatient.

The café was warm and filled with the aromas of scorched sugar and coffee. The décor was early nineties, the color scheme a mixture of orange, dark wood, and chrome. Only a few tables were occupied. We chose one beside a couple of Nordic backpacker types: blond hair, long-sleeved T-shirts, shorts, and hiking boots. They could have been brother and sister, though the girl was twice the size of her companion. She wore her hair in braids. I could picture her in a helmet with horns.

A waiter came over, took our order, then left. I caught the Nordic guy staring at Masters, watching her as she removed her N.Y.F.D. cap and shook out her hair. When he realized I'd busted him in the middle of performing a little eyeball striptease, he swallowed, turned away, and self-consciously pointed at something in the guidebook before Brünnhilde also caught him and maybe slugged him. She looked like she could pack a punch.

Masters missed all this, as she always does, completely ignorant of the effect she has on a room. The immediate important business taken care of, namely breakfast, I said, "I have a few questions about this morning."

"Me, too."

"You wanna start?"

"Ego before talent," she said.

"OK," I began. "Karli, the cop hung like a sock drawer, said something about following the drain all the way to the Bosphorus."

"So what's the question?"

"What's the Bosphorus?"

Masters scoffed. "You've never heard of the Bosphorus?"

"And what if I haven't?"

Masters shook her head. "It's only possibly one of the most famous stretches of water in the world."

"Because . . . ?"

"It's less than a mile wide, divides the continents of Europe and Asia, splits Istanbul in half, connects the Black Sea with the Mediterranean, and people have been fighting for control of it for more than two thousand years."

"I thought it might be related to phosphorus—its evil sister, maybe."

"I'll get you a guidebook," she said.

"I don't need one," I replied. "I've got you. I'll get *you* a stick with a little flag on it." I was going to say something about her fiancé, the JAG lawyer, but I let it go. We still hadn't had The Talk. The Talk would be when Masters filled me in on this guy that, I'd just been told completely out of the blue, she was going to marry; the one she'd apparently met in this city; the one she started seeing five minutes after we had stopped seeing each other. Or maybe I was being generous: There could have been a period of overlap. "So what did you make of the show put on for our benefit?" I asked.

"At the Consulate-General?"

"Been to any other shows lately?"

She shrugged. "The ambassador's charming, the local cops are barely adequate, Captain Cain seems on the ball, those CID guys really gave me the creeps, and the attaché's missing a few components."

"Where was CIA?" I wanted to know.

"CIA? Why did they need to be there?"

"Lots of reasons."

"Name one."

"Portman was an appi-eight."

"A what?"

"An A-P-I eight." I spelled it out.

"I didn't see that in his file."

"It wasn't in his file. I went online before we left Andrews. I was hunting around for background." The acronym API was short for Aircrew Position Indicator, a term used by the bean counters to describe flying status within the fighting machine collectively known as the United States Air Force. An API-1 was a pilot assigned to a squadron. An API-8, or "appi-8," was an officer above wing level staff who was permitted to maintain a basic level of currency, which allowed him or her to fly a particular type of aircraft.

"So what was he current on?" Masters asked me.

"Eagles."

"Portman flew F-15s?"

"Portman had a loose attachment to the Grim Reapers, the 493rd. They let him out in the sports car every now and then."

Masters gave the kind of nod that indicated she was impressed, just as I'd been. The McDonnell Douglas F-15C Eagle was a hell of a weapon. In the right hands, the plane was capable of killing the enemy in any number of ways. In the wrong hands, it would more than likely just turn around and kill the pilot. It was a very fast and very lethal front-line fighter that required a lot of skill to fly. Portman was pushing fifty, and there weren't many his age allowed in an Eagle's driver's seat. Yeah, Colonel Portman was special.

"You're thinking that CIA would have had a guy like Portman working on something?" Masters asked.

"I'd put money on it."

The waiter arrived with breakfast and we ate in silence. It wasn't a comfortable silence.

"So," I said, deciding to warm things up a little, "heard the one about the attorney driving down the highway in his brand-new Mercedes?" Masters gave me a blank look. "He loves it so much he's even making up songs about it. 'I love my new Mercedes. Mercedes, Mercedes, Mercedes . . .'"

"Do I really want to hear this?" Masters asked.

Yes, she did. "The guy gets so caught up in how much he loves this new automobile of his that he forgets to take the corner. He goes over the embankment, hits a tree, and smashes into a boulder. Luckily, the attorney's thrown clear just as his car bursts into flames. Meanwhile, the guy who was driving in the vehicle behind screeches to a stop, gets out, and runs down the embankment. He makes it to the lawyer and finds him on his knees, sobbing, 'My new Mercedes! My beautiful new Mercedes!'

"Horrified at the sight of the crash victim, the guy says, 'My god! You've lost an arm!' The lawyer looks down and notices for the first time that he has indeed lost his whole arm. Then he starts screaming, 'My new Rolex. My new Rolex!'"

Masters didn't say anything for a moment, just glared at me with those turquoise eyes of hers. And then she said, "If you're going to tell bad lawyer jokes, at least do ones I haven't heard."

I shrugged. "Then I guess you also know the one about the scientist who goes to the brain store to get some brain to complete a study?"

Masters gave me another burst of silence, which I took as a no.

"Well, this scientist in the brain store sees that there aren't any prices on the various types of brains on offer, so he asks the guy behind the counter, 'How much does it cost for dentist brain?'

"'Three dollars an ounce,' says the guy.

"'How much does it cost for doctor brain?'

"'Four dollars an ounce.'

"'How much for lawyer brain?'

"'Five hundred dollars an ounce.'

"The customer's amazed. 'Wow,' he says. 'So why's lawyer brain so much more expensive?'

"The salesman replies, 'Do you know how many lawyers we have to kill just to get one ounce of brain?'"

Masters was sitting back in her seat, her hands clasped on the table in front of her, not the barest hint of a smile on the horizon.

"I know, you've probably heard that one, too," I admitted, "but the whole cop-marrying-attorney thing... You know what they say, one good cliché deserves another."

"Maybe us taking this case together wasn't such a great idea," she said.

"I wasn't aware we'd been given the choice."

Her face flushed with anger. "This isn't easy for me either, you know, Vin. And why the big problem with attorneys? You studied law at NYU, didn't you, before you enlisted?"

"Yeah, but I saw the error of my ways."

"Which was?"

"The law might have everything to do with guilt and innocence, but the system doesn't. It's about who has the biggest wallet, or which party has the most power. The people who win nearly always have more of both than the people who lose."

"As a cop, you're still part of the system."

"I like being a bottom-feeder. Everyone's equal down in the sludge. Down here, the evidence is the only thing that matters—at least to me. And I know it's the same for you. So, are you going to tell me about this JAG lawyer fiancé of yours, or do I have to tell you the one about the attorney and the devil?"

"I wasn't going to, no."

"Why not?"

"Because it's none of your damn business."

"So, anyway, there's this lawyer and the devil, and—"

"Vin!" Masters said it loud, to stop me. Both Brünnhilde and her companion turned their heads toward us. "You know it wasn't great between us," Masters said, turning down the volume. "It hadn't been for a long time. You were in Washington, I was in Germany, and neither of us seemed willing to do anything about it. We agreed—you agreed—to call it quits."

I wasn't going to disagree. I couldn't. What Masters said was true. It did seem to me, however, that her reasons for wanting an end to our relationship might have had less to do with our forced separation and more to do with the fact that her former Istanbul romance was in town, sniffing about. "Where's your fiancé based?" The guy was JAG, which meant he could be stationed anywhere.

Masters shifted uncomfortably in her seat.

"You going to plead the Fifth, Anna?" I asked.

Masters sucked in her top lip and her eyes shifted back to the view outside. "He moves around a lot."

"Where's he stationed?"

"What difference does it make where he's based?" she snapped, picking up a salt shaker and fidgeting with its top.

"Maybe it doesn't make any difference at all. It's just that you keep saying that distance is what killed us. I'm assuming this JAG guy is waiting for you back in Germany, at Ramstein." I could almost understand that. Getting together for a week here and there was frustrating and difficult and—

"He's in D.C., OK?" Masters blurted. It came spurting out like I'd just lanced a boil.

"Washington?" I said, uncertain I'd heard what I thought I'd heard. "He's at JAG? *At Andrews?"*

Masters thumbed the top right off the salt shaker, and fine white crystals sprayed across the tabletop.

"Jesus, Anna..." I was prepared to accept that Masters and I were finished. But now the reason for the ending was sounding more like an excuse. If, like me, he was also based at Andrews AFB, then what was all that crap she'd given me about the physical distance between us being so goddamn destructive? Masters busied herself with the mess she'd created, probably thankful for the diversion. Her fiancé was at Andrews Air Force Base? The asswipe could be sitting in an office just down the hallway from mine. There was even a good chance I knew the jerk.

Masters screwed the top back on the shaker and rubbed the palms of her hands together to brush off the salt.

"What's his name?"

"No, Vin."

"So anyway," I began, "the devil visits this lawyer's office. He rests his pitchfork on the desk and says, 'Hey, Mac, why don't you let me organize a few things for—'"

"Why don't you ever let up?" Masters interrupted.

"Your fiancé's working out of an office in D.C. and you're at Ramstein. Say, this sounds familiar."

"He's leaving the Air Force—joining a private firm—so that we can be together."

"He's moving to Germany so that you and he can—"

"No, Vin . . . I'm getting out, too," she said.

FIVE

So Masters was leaving the Air Force. Shit . . . now *I* wanted to get up and leave, even if it was just the coffee shop. But the reality was that, like it or not, the two of us were joined at the hip. Stuck in this country, investigating a high-priority case. I chewed without tasting anything.

"This is going to be difficult, isn't it?" Masters said.

"Nothing a lobotomy wouldn't fix. You first," I suggested.

"You and I need to forget we have a history."

"Like I said, you first."

Masters wiped her lips with a napkin.

"You met this fiancé of yours in Istanbul," I said. "When, exactly?"

"Vin, I'm not—"

"So anyway, the devil says to this lawyer, 'Yeah, I can fix things for you. Your income? I'll increase it tenfold. Your partners? They're gonna start loving you. Your clients will give you the respect you think you deserve; you'll get four months of vacation each year and you'll live to be a hundred, finally dying on the job with a young mistress—I'll find her, too.'"

Masters's arms were folded and she'd fixed me with that flat stare I knew so well.

"'In return, I'll just take your wife's soul, your children's souls, and their children's souls, and they'll all rot in hell for eternity.'

"To which the lawyer says, 'So what's the catch?'"

"You can be a real asshole, Vin. You know that?"

"This would be one of those rhetorical-type questions, right?" I said.

One of her hands balled into a fist. "OK, you asked for it. You already know I met him here in Istanbul. Three years ago. We were in a tour group. We started talking. He happened to mention that he'd just made lieutenant colonel. We were both in the Air Force—that gave us an instant bond. We hit it off, spent a couple of weeks together here. It didn't go further because he was involved with someone, but we kept in touch. Then, out of the blue, he turned up at OSI, Ramstein. Seems the Office of the Secretary of the Air Force volunteered us to help the JAG prepare a case for the Department of Defense. Things just happened between us, and they happened fast."

Again, I didn't say anything, because there was nothing to say.

"I'm sorry, Vin," Masters continued.

The door of the café burst open and a bunch of noisy people swirled in. From the way they dressed and from all the chatter and laughter, I pegged them as locals. I turned to face Masters. I wanted to get angry, but I didn't have the grounds. Apart from the fact that we had decided to call it quits before she'd reconnected with her JAG jerk, I reminded myself that I was also no angel. I'd only recently returned from Florida, where I'd been on a case and met a colonel of my own. She'd helped me nail a guy who'd cut a buddy of mine out of his parachute and let gravity do the rest. And things had happened pretty damn fast with the colonel and me, too.

"All right... you win," said Masters finally. "His name's Richard Wadding, OK? Lieutenant Colonel Richard Wadding."

The name of her fiancé caught me by surprise. "Sorry? I'm not sure I heard you right. Did you say 'Richard Wadding'?"

Masters nodded, relieved, perhaps because the secret was out in the open.

I wasn't so sure. That's because I knew the guy. Only I knew him by a different name—the one he'd been given by the Gulf War I and II vets flocking to join the growing class action against the military for exposure to depleted uranium ammunition. A buddy of mine by the name of Tyler Dean was one of them. Tyler used to drive an M1 Abrams tank and lived around the stuff in the Iraqi desert for eighteen months. A year ago he went to the doctor to complain about a sore throat and ended up in the hospital having most of his esophagus removed. While they were mucking around in his insides, they also found that one of his kidneys had died inside him. They stitched his stomach to his tonsils, removed the kidney, and introduced him to a dialysis machine. Tyler was only twenty-nine. Masters's fiancé was point man for the defendant, the Armed Forces of the United States of America, doing his best to see that the vets got nothing more or less than a kick in the keister. So, like I said, I knew this Richard Wadding by a different name. I knew him as Colonel Dick Wad.

"So you *do* know him?" she asked, exercising that annoying ability of hers to read my thoughts.

Before I could answer, the door opened and more folks surged in. Music blared and the party reached critical mass in an instant. A young boy crowd-surfed from the front of the café to the back on a roar of approval. An old guy with a five-day growth on his face and wearing a coat tailored from what looked to me like compressed lint materialized in front of Masters and pulled her up and out of her seat. He wanted to dance with her. She protested but gave up when it seemed he wasn't going to take no for an answer.

A large old woman came over to me, her hair clamped down by a colorful scarf tucked into a beige ankle-length coat buttoned to the neck. She was holding a plate of pastries doing the breaststroke in what I assumed was honey. "Here, here," she said, waggling the plate under my nose. I smelled nuts and cinnamon. "We cele . . . celebrate—you eat."

I gave her the only look I could manage, which was blank.

"Please, please . . ." she insisted, waggling the plate more urgently this time. I accepted one of the pastries because, like the dancing for Masters, following orders appeared to be the only option here. I took a bite.

"Very good," I said, because it was. The music and the laughter were loud enough to feed back through my ears like they were old speakers about to blow. "What are you celebrating?" I shouted.

She shrugged, unable to penetrate the language barrier.

"Married?" I yelled, holding my arms out to indicate the party. "Someone getting married?"

The woman frowned. And then what I was saying seemed to dawn on her. "No, no. No marry," she said, cackling, revealing the remaining three teeth still planted in her gums. "*Bir ca?* Um . . . circum . . . *Ünnet! Ünnet!*" And in case I still didn't get it—because I obviously still didn't—she used a couple of fingers to snip at the air.

"You're celebrating... a circumcision?" The kid did another turn of the café above the heads of the crowd and everyone cheered their approval.

"Yes, yes!" she replied, again using her fingers as scissors.

Masters managed to disengage herself from the dancing. "C'mon," she shouted. "Let's get out of here. This place has gone mad."

We stepped out the door and closed it, sealing off most of the noise behind us. The weather had warmed up a little and the wind had dropped. "Do you know what that was about?" I asked Masters as we stood for a moment to get our bearings.

"Yep," she replied, zipping up against the cold. "The boy had been circumcised. That's a big deal hereabouts." She threw me a wry smile. "You got a problem with that?"

"Me? Problem? I think it's great that the penis is celebrated. There should be more of it. There should be a World Penis Day."

I stepped off the sidewalk to hail a cab. It was coming up to 1100 hours—time to put in an appearance at the scene where Colonel Portman had been julienned by a crazed Veg-O-Matic.

Ten minutes later we were in a cab crawling along streets where the folks who were loaded lived—lawns and walls and towering gates with intercoms. Even the trees looked snooty. Overhead, a massive suspension bridge joining two continents blocked out the sun. I was busy making architectural comparisons between the homes on either side of the street when Masters spoke.

"So, you didn't answer my question."

"Didn't I?" I replied.

"No, you didn't."

"Hey, look at that pink building with the columns," I said, attempting a diversion. I knew where Masters was going. "You could cut that into slices and serve it at a wedding reception."

"I asked you whether you knew Richard Wadding."

The cab pulled to a stop. We paid and got out.

"Well, do you?" she asked again.

I compared the address of the residence in front of me with the one scribbled in my notebook. This was Portman's place, all right. How many others in the street were guarded by uniformed policemen behind portable bulletproof shields? I couldn't stall any longer. "Yeah, I'm familiar with a guy by that name. From a rich family been farming cotton down in Mississippi for half a dozen generations?"

"Yes, that's him."

"Then you're going to marry a known fuckwit," I informed her.

"What?" She was staring at me, her cheeks suddenly red and her hands moving to her hips, unsure about whether she'd heard it right. But she had, she knew she had, and she also knew she didn't want to hear me repeat it. "Jesus!" she said, and spun away like a twister off up the worn stone steps to the front door.

SIX

Masters flashed her badge at the two uniformed officers armed with weathered, early-model MP5 submachine guns who were holding the fort. The men discussed our arrival between them before unlocking the door. Masters stomped past them. I showed my shield and followed her in. One of the uniforms came behind me.

It was dark inside. A wide stairway with ornate carved banisters climbed upward. A radio was playing somewhere. I did a circuit of the ground floor, which was empty, and arrived back at the stairway. From information I'd already seen, I knew this to be a three-story house that was three centuries old, arranged around a central courtyard. The house was cool and still and smelled of various chemical solvents doing battle with aromas that most people fortunately never have to experience. I followed those smells up the stairs to the top floor. They grew stronger with each step, along with the radio's volume.

I heard laughter and voices. A woman was singing along tunelessly to a radio, or maybe it was the tune that was tuneless. I went down a wide hallway, walking on a dark red Turkish runner that turned my footsteps into whispers. The rug was laid over ancient black floorboards, the walls a light green color and hung with paintings—old paintings of sea battles and landscapes and portraits of mostly Asiatic faces with wide, high cheekbones.

As I moved through the house, the aromas that smelled industrial were winning. I turned a corner and saw a set of double doors that had been thrown open. Masters came around another corner and arrived on the other side of the room. Behind me, I sensed the uniform from the front door. Yellow crime-scene tape, which had, until recently, sealed the double doors shut, was rolled into an untidy ball and left on the rug. The radio, the singing, the voices, and the smells were all coming from inside this room.

Masters didn't acknowledge my presence, still annoyed at me for calling her Dick Wad a fuckwit. She kept walking into the scene of the crime. I completed the pincer move. Our arrival stopped the singing and the talking. The uniform accompanying us said something in Turkish, and I picked out the word *"Amerikali"* a couple of times. The cleaners gawked at us like we were from another world, which, I guess, we were.

The cleaning detail was a three-man team, two of whom were women. They all stood and continued staring at us. Both women were middle-aged and about as shapely as a couple of concrete mixers. Both wore black head scarves. The guy was older and bigger, with a broad face and a thick salt-and-pepper mustache twirled at either end like an old-fashioned villain's. We needed an ice-breaker. I went up to one of the women and presented her with the ketchup stain on my T-shirt. I gave her a shrug that said *What do I do here*?

"Oh," she exclaimed, and said something that made everyone laugh.

The uniform surprised me by speaking English. "Ha, ha . . . she says Istanbul has already left its mark on you. She doesn't want to take it off."

Nevertheless, the woman walked to a bucket, took out a bottle, and squirted a clear liquid over the stain, which made it instantly disappear.

"Thank you, ma'am," I said.

She smiled—they all smiled—and went back to what they were doing, including the singing. I should join the UN.

The room was a mess. I thought about Captain Cain's happy snaps. The chair the attaché had been sitting in when his attack began, the one I'd seen in Cain's photos and read about in the report from forensics, had been removed. The square of pale green carpet over the floor safe was also gone. The safe's door was open. I squatted beside it for a closer look. The door, lock mechanism, and internal walls were still covered in fingerprint dust and prints were clearly visible. The safe was empty.

The rest of the carpet had been ripped up in one corner and rolled back almost to the center of the room, where the safe was set into the floor, revealing the old floorboards beneath. I could see that attempts had been made to get the attaché's blood out of the carpet pile, but these had obviously failed and there were several large black stains spread into wide circles by the cleaners' labors—which, I assumed, marked out the area where the victim had been dismembered. There was the smell of decay in the air, as if an animal had recently died in a nearby wall. The women were scrubbing at blood spatter on the upper walls with bristled brushes on the ends of poles. Their efforts were simply moving it around. The guy with the mo was mixing paint in a two-and-a-half-gallon drum. The stains they couldn't remove were going to be painted over.

"The wall safe is this way." Masters nodded back behind her, the way she'd come in, and moved off, leading the way to an adjoining room. It was some kind of sitting room with more old paintings of people long dead and gone—longer gone than the attaché perhaps, but by no means more dead.

Crime-scene tape stretched across the painting of an elephant being attacked by a party wielding spears. The beast was on its knees, a bloody gash in its gut. Something that looked like a large sausage hung from the gash. Guys wearing turbans appeared to be cheering from atop another elephant nearby. The uniform cop interrupted my viewing pleasure, peeling the tape away from the painting.

"Behind here," he told us. He pulled one side of the painting away from the wall and it swung open, revealing a small safe recessed into the masonry. The door, which was steel an inch and a half thick, hung from a single hinge. Some seriously powerful explosive had done that. The door was powdered in the fine, light gray fingerprint dust, as were the safe's inside walls, ceiling, and floor. No prints had been revealed.

"Whatever did that to the wall safe was probably military," I observed.

Masters nodded.

"C'mon, let's go play in the sewer." I wanted the snooping around over and done with before Istanbul's Starsky and Hutch turned up.

According to the briefing notes supplied to us back in D.C., local crime-scene investigators believed that the killer's movements had been limited to just these two rooms on the second floor. Nevertheless, all the doors and doorframes throughout the place had been dusted for prints. Good and thorough.

We made our way down the stairs to the ground floor and the door to the courtyard. I unlocked it, opened it wide, and examined the frame—no jimmy marks in the woodwork, though a pane of glass had been punched out of a window beside the door. Smashing the pane, reaching in, and unlocking the door was a simple matter. Forensics had gone crazy in the area around the broken window; the framework was wearing more powder than a Colombian drug lord's nostrils.

Outside, winter sunshine washed over half the courtyard while the other half remained in shadow. Ancient tiles paved the ground and lime green moss filled the spaces between most of them. There was sea salt and mildew and cat's urine in the air. A birdbath sat in one sunny corner, a couple of pigeons copulating in it. Our arrival startled them and they flew off. I felt momentarily guilty, but then I thought, what the hell... I wasn't getting any, so why should they?

The manhole cover mentioned in the case notes was easy to find, on account of the fact that a couple of pieces of outdoor furniture had been dragged over it and lassoed together with yellow crime-scene tape. I shifted one of the chairs to get at the cover.

"How're we going to get that opened?" Masters asked.

"Room service," I suggested.

"What?"

Just as I said this—and as I expected—the uniform shadowing us stepped up with the appropriate tool and began putting it to use.

"See?" I told Masters.

I wasn't sure whether to thank the guy or give him a tip. I also wondered whether being so helpful to us wouldn't get him into trouble with Karli and Iyaz. I was more familiar with police cooperation delivered with a snarl than with a smile, but I wasn't complaining. Maybe the watchword on this case really was "cooperation." Or maybe these uniform guys just hadn't yet learned to be assholes. Whatever the reason, our number-one helper spat on his hands, rubbed them together, and then, with a grunt, hoisted the metal plate out of its seat.

Masters and I peered down into the hole. There was a vertical shaft of maybe a couple of feet opening out into a pipe that was around a yard and a half in diameter—wide enough to crawl through at a crouch. I could see some sort of trickling fluid at the bottom. I doubted it was Perrier.

"Well," I said to Masters, indicating the way down with a gentlemanly sweep of my hand, "zeal before flair."

"Thanks, Cooper. I didn't expect you to throw your coat on the ground, but I thought as the senior investigator you'd—"

"What?" I said. "Let my subordinates prove themselves? Thrust them forward into the limelight? Revel as they snatch the initiative?"

"I was going to say, 'lead by example.'" Masters stood to one side to give me room.

This was one I wasn't going to win. I lowered my body down into the drain and dropped the last couple of feet. I spread my feet, trying not to land in whatever was making its way to the sea, but my boots slipped against the walls, and I went down on both my good hand and the fiberglass cast, my face inches from the stinking, running flow. "Shit," I said, pushing myself up and getting back on my feet, my right hand and the cast greasy with pipe slime. I crouched and backed away from the overhead hole to give Masters room. A ladder came down the shaft, followed by Masters's Nikes.

"Where did that come from?" I asked, annoyed.

"The ladder? Found it propped against a wall. I figured people had been going in and out of this pipe for days."

Grinding my teeth, I turned around carefully and followed the pipe, using a small LED on my key ring to light the way. The air in the pipe smelled like you'd expect the breath of a two-thousand-year-old city to smell.

Wide cracks fractured the pipe in numerous places and the occasional tree root hung down into the cold, moist air. There were other manhole covers overhead indicated by keyholes of white light—openings to more courtyards and gardens.

Soon enough, the downward angle of the pipe increased and came to a junction with a bunch of other pipes. We climbed down into it and found a tangle of crime-scene tape marking the spot where forensics had found the murder weapons. I decided I'd be surprised if tests on the recovered articles revealed anything of interest about the person who'd left them behind. The murder seemed to have been too cold-blooded, and too meticulously planned and executed, for anyone to have made any obviously dumb mistakes. So why leave anything behind at all, I wondered—especially the murder weapons—when it would have been just as easy to disappear without a trace?

Other than the tape, there was nothing to see in the junction box. We continued for another thirty feet or so, working our way toward the light at the end of the tunnel. As we came around a kink, we surprised half a dozen black rats having a meeting. One of them was the size of a rabbit. It shrieked aggressively and sat up on its hind legs and sniffed the air, its grimy pink snout twitching and quivering at us, brown teeth gnawing at our scent. The other rats joined in. I heard Masters gasp. She tried to grab my arm and slipped. If we'd had a kitchen chair handy, she'd have jumped up on it.

"Christ!" she said as she slipped, stepping into the rivulet of effluent. Her turn to go for a paddle.

The rats stood their ground.

"I hate those fucking things," Masters muttered hoarsely, steadying herself.

A couple of the animals scampered forward a few feet toward us and squeaked. Masters flinched. "You just hurt their feelings," I told her.

With a final chorus of rat noises, the rodents retreated, disappearing into a crack.

"Ugh . . . disgusting," Masters said with loathing.

"I thought they were kinda cute."

She shivered. "Can we get out of here?"

So Masters didn't like rats. I was learning so much about her on this case. "In a minute."

"You doing this to be a jerk?" she snapped, exasperated.

"*Moi?* Actually, I want to see where this comes out—see where the killers came in."

Another thirty feet of bouncing along on our haunches brought us out into the cool bright sun and a vast expanse of water: the Bosphorus. The far shore was momentarily obscured by an orange-painted container ship sliding past, the low throb of its huge engines pulsing up through the pipe and into the soles of my feet. A small, rusty oiler chugged in the opposite direction, heading north. The pipe exited a yard or so above the waters of the Bosphorus slapping at the concrete wall. I grabbed hold of one of the remaining corroded iron rods that had once secured the end of the pipe. The concrete holding it in had been freshly broken. The rod came away from the crumbling masonry, slipped from my grasp, and fell into the water with a splash.

By the time we made it back to the ladder, my quads were burning from crawling along inside the pipe. Masters went up first, happy not to be left down here alone with King Rat and his subjects a moment longer than necessary.

Shadows had claimed more of the courtyard. The uniform was standing in the remaining island of sunshine, smoking, enjoying a three-way discussion with Detective Sergeants Karli and Iyaz—if being chewed out was his idea of enjoyment. From the hangdog body language, I didn't think it was. He threw his cigarette on the ground.

Iyaz saw us. He nudged Karli. They left the uniform mid-sentence and walked over to us. Karli hitched up his pants higher than usual as he led the pair toward the manhole. Maybe he was worried that Iyaz was going to pull them down.

"Hey, guys, great to see you," I called. "What's happening?"

"We said we would meet at eleven-thirty," Karli replied.

It was just after noon. I shrugged. "You're late."

"We wait out the front for you," said Iyaz.

"If you'd asked your people at the door, they'd have told you we'd come inside," Masters said.

Karli and Iyaz glanced at each other and frowned harder.

"OK, so we've had a look around. We agree the killers came and went through the pipe. Most likely there'd have been a boat somewhere out in that strait. It would have been three or four hundred yards out beyond the wall. Far enough away so as not to attract attention, but not far enough out to get mowed down by a supertanker.

"That's too far to swim with the gear they were carrying. Scuba gear would have been used. The water's close to freezing, which means they'd have used full dry suits. Along with keeping them warm on the swim, the suits would also have guaranteed the killers left nothing—not even hairs—at the crime scene. So, it might be an idea to get some divers out in the channel there to see if you can't find anything useful they might have left behind."

"Dry suits, swimmers, killers... *they*?" Masters asked me. "Plural?"

"Yeah, well, that's the other point I was going to make. We're looking for *two* killers. Whoever did it wasn't working alone."

SEVEN

The sightseeing tour over, we left Karli and Iyaz in the courtyard. On the way out, we said thanks to the uniform at the front door. I slipped twenty bucks into the guy's jacket pocket. I figured he'd earned it. He'd probably caught himself a night shift or two by being so helpful to us.

Just then, a cab pulled up out in the street. The rear doors opened and out stepped the two Army CID agents we'd met earlier that morning, Goddard and Mallet.

"What the hell are they doing here?" Masters inquired under her breath.

"Beats me. Let's ask them."

"Hey," Masters said as Mallet ambled toward her.

"Hey," he replied. "How you doin'?"

"Oh, you know, taking in the sights," she said. "How are you doin'?"

"What she means is what the fuck are you doing *here*?" I translated, keeping it light.

Mallet blinked, those little watermelon-pit eyes of his all but disappearing, the cogs in his brain jammed momentarily. "Well, y'all know how it is . . ." he drawled when things started to turn again. "For all we know, there could be a dead body in a cupboard you haven't thought to look in. I've heard you Air Force types have difficulty finding your own assholes on the toilet."

"Yeah, no need to be unfriendly, Special Agent Cooper," Goddard said. "We're just familiarizing ourselves with the case. Taking a look around, is all."

"This *is* me being friendly, Special Agent Goddard," I replied. "It's just that your partner reminds me of something I once saw in a museum formaldehyde bottle. Disturbing to see it walking around, is all."

"Any time, Cooper . . ." Mallet pushed out his chin.

Goddard put a hand on his partner's shoulder, then turned to face me. "Well, that's OK, then. I wouldn't want there to be any friction here." The smile stitched on his face strained at the sutures.

"Me, either. Just so long as we understand each other," I said, stepping past him. "Oh, one thing . . . ?"

Mallet paused on the steps leading up to the late attaché's house.

"You didn't ask any questions at the briefing this morning. Why not? You and Dr. Watson here got the answers figured already?"

"Had none to ask, Cooper. None that weren't plain dumb, like the ones you and Masters wasted everyone's time with."

"Oh, so it *was* white noise, then," I said.

"What?"

I didn't answer. Masters and I walked half a block in silence to a main road that looked like it might spring a cab. One came along pretty much immediately. Masters asked the driver to drop us back at the Charisma.

"You handled that well back there," she said.

"You think?" I asked.

"No."

"Maybe you didn't notice it, but those guys aren't exactly in the diplomatic corps."

"And I'm not sure you noticed it, but *you* started it."

"Well, you know what they say—first in, best dressed."

"What the hell does that mean?"

"Don't know, but they say it."

Masters shook her head and took to staring out the window.

"Goddard and Mallet started it off just by hanging around," I said. "I don't know what CID is doing here looking over our shoulders. I just let those guys know in the politest way possible that we can handle this. I don't want them trampling over this case, getting in our way."

She gave me a listless nod that lacked conviction. We sat in silence for a few blocks.

"So, we're heading back to the hotel," I said, implying we had a lot of work to do and all of it was in another direction.

"After that drain, I need a shower," she replied. "And trust me, so do you."

"Surely you're not suggesting we have one together?" I asked, as I examined the palm of my hand. It was brown. It smelled brown, too.

"No, I'm surely not. And don't try your anti-charm bullshit on me, Vin. I'm impervious to it."

"Anti-charm?"

"Making non-PC propositions of a sexual nature—which could be considered harassment, by the way—in the mistaken belief that I might somehow become attracted to your caveman-like persona."

"Sounds like you're coming down with something nasty," I said. "Lawyeritis, maybe. I didn't know it was contagious."

Masters sighed, the sort of sigh you might give a child who won't stop asking you to do something you've said no to at least a dozen times already. "Take me through your two-killer theory. What makes you so sure?"

"The wall safe. Some pretty powerful explosives were used to blow it. That means a lot of noise in a nice quiet neighborhood populated by rich, helpful, community-minded, law-abiding citizens. And yet no one heard a damn thing. Forget cushions. Something far more effective was used to eat up the noise, something designed for the purpose. I'm thinking blast protection blankets—three, maybe. Those things weigh thirty to forty pounds apiece, so that's a hundred-plus pounds right there. Add them to the weight of the hardware store used to dismantle Portman, getting up and out of the pipe with that heavy manhole cover... it says two assailants—one to pass the chisels, one to do the deed."

"Not three?"

"Overkill. You could do it with two, and three's a crowd, unless two of them are wearing negligées."

Masters ignored the wisecrack. "Why wasn't the other safe blown? And why weren't any fibers from the blankets picked up by forensics on the cushions?"

"Forget the cushions. They went nowhere near the safe or the blast blankets. And perhaps the blankets themselves weren't fibrous. As for the floor safe, I still think maybe the killers just didn't know it was there."

She nodded, coming along for the ride. "Everything else was meticulous . . . the planning, the execution. Is it likely they'd have made such a blunder—missed that floor safe entirely?" She chewed on her bottom lip and turned to face me. "Unless . . . what if Portman had it installed recently? If he had, the safe wouldn't have appeared on any plans or drawings of the property."

Good point. No, it wouldn't have.

"And what if the killers had gotten hold of these plans from somewhere so they could case the place before they broke in?" she continued. "Given the meticulous nature of the crime, that's something I think they might have done." She sat back in her seat and watched the traffic flash by. "Might be an idea to find out who the leasing agent was."

Yep, it might at that. "Any thoughts on why the killers might have left the murder weapons behind?"

"Maybe they plain didn't think the local cops would find them."

Karli and Iyaz weren't NYPD, but they weren't Keystone Kops either. The killers had to be working on the cache getting discovered. "I think the killers *wanted* their tools found," I said.

"What purpose would that possibly serve?"

"I asked you first."

"I have no idea."

"Maybe they wanted us to find their gear so we'd think they weren't as proficient as they obviously were," I suggested. "And I don't think they left *all* their gear, just selective bits of it."

"OK . . ." Masters said, letting the thought sink in.

Our hotel lay across the water—not the Bosphorus, some other strait. I leaned forward and pulled from my back pocket a map supplied by the concierge. The Charisma was in the area called the Sultanahmet, the quarter occupied by the old kings of this joint, the sultans. According to the map, this stretch of water was called the Golden Horn. Sounded like a euphemism if ever I'd heard one.

We crossed the bridge lined with fishermen trying to pull their dinner from the soup churned up by the incessant ferry traffic, turned right at a mosque, and climbed the hill. The cab did a few lefts and rights and pulled up outside the hotel. I gave the driver a handful of notes and asked for a receipt as Masters got out. She leaned on the roof and put her head back in the door. "And just a suggestion, Vin. After you've had a shower, you might think about a change of clothes."

"What have you got in mind? Something tight?" I asked.

"No, more like something without holes in it."

She gestured at my midriff. The miracle stuff the cleaners had used had removed the stain on my T-shirt—along with half the shirt.

EIGHT

I took a shower, changed into chinos and a clean shirt, threw on my green MA-1 bomber jacket, and was back in the lobby thirty minutes later, as agreed. During this interlude, I thought about what Masters and I knew so far. Problem was, we had nothing more than what Karli and Iyaz already had. All we could offer was perhaps a new way to look at what was there on the table: that Portman had been murdered by two assailants, not one, and that they swam out and back to a boat using scuba gear. We had no suspects—though there was a question mark on this manservant guy—and no evidence that provided any leads.

I thought about the way Portman was killed. Dismemberment was murder's equivalent of a nudist street parade. Obviously the perpetrators were either deeply disturbed or a couple of show-offs. Or were there aspects to this that I just wasn't seeing?

Ten minutes late, Masters breezed into the lobby wearing faded low-slung jeans with a tooled leather belt, a navy T that showed off her flat stomach, black Converse sneakers, a leather jacket, and the Ray-Ban Aviators. The N.Y.F.D. cap had been replaced by a Yankees ball cap. Her hair was tied in a thick ponytail that bounced as she walked. Traffic? Hell, Masters could stop a tank.

"You're late," I said.

"Phone call. And before you ask me any questions about it, it's none of your business." She tossed a brown paper bag at me.

"What's this?"

"A present."

I opened it and removed a red T-shirt.

"To replace the one I hope you've just thrown away," she said. "Wear it with pride, partner."

There was a graphic on the back of the T-shirt: the white crescent moon and shield of the Turkish national flag. On the front, printed in large white letters, was the word TURKEY.

"When you wear it, think of it as a caption," said Masters with a smirk.

"Turkey?"

"One good insult deserves another, Vin. Payback for the insults about Richard. And what's with the character assassination anyway? You don't know him. You don't know anything about him."

Masters was right; I didn't know him, not personally, but what I knew of his reputation was enough. "I was just passing along the opinion of several hundred vets suffering from various forms of cancer, or whose babies have been born with three eyes and extra sets of legs. They refer to your future husband as 'Colonel Dick Wad,' and they call him that because he's doing his best to make sure the system screws them. So, were you helping Colonel *Wad* put evidence together for the class action he's defending, the whole depleted uranium mess?"

"Need-to-know, Cooper—and you don't. I feel sorry for those people, but DU has proved to be safe. And his name is Colonel Wadding, OK?"

"Try convincing the grown men and women with leukemia hoping to get some compensation for doing a job no one mentioned would kill them slow. I think they'd probably prefer to keep calling him names."

Masters folded her arms tight. "Like always, you're real quick to judge. Oh, and I was late because I was on the phone to Richard. He has to go to Incirlik. He'll be in Istanbul the day after tomorrow. He said he wants to meet you—don't ask me why. Then you can see for yourself how wrong you are." She stomped across the lobby toward the door.

So Dick was coming to town. I could barely contain my excitement. I left the T-shirt she gave me on the couch and followed her toward the exit. I wondered if Masters really knew this guy she was going to marry. She said she'd met him on vacation, and then he pops back into her life years later with a proposal. Who does that?

As the revolving door released me onto the street, I saw a cab pull away. Masters was in the backseat. Her hand was up against the glass, giving me the bird.

The sudden boom of loudspeakers informed me that the faithful were again being called to prayer. Or to lunch, if, like me, you happened to be an infidel.

Cabs were queued out in front of the hotel. I picked one at random and settled into the backseat.

"Where you going?" The driver was a guy around forty years old with a black mustache the size and shape of a hair comb. He opened his door and threw his cigarette butt on the road.

I'd climbed in through a haze of secondhand smoke mixed with a strawberry air freshener. The seats were encased in a thick clear plastic embedded with yellow flowers that squeaked as I moved. Various trinkets—a golf ball, a crescent moon, a miniature plastic queen-of-hearts card, and a tiny metal horse—swung from the rearview mirror. Tobacco-colored carpet covered the dashboard. A couple of purple velvet cushions trimmed with gold tassels sat on the rear deck. This guy was driving around in his living room.

"The U.S. Consulate-General. You know where it is?"

"Yes, yes . . . I know it. U.S. Consulate—Kaplicalar Mevkii Sokak, Istinye."

"If you say so," I replied. Whatever he'd just said looked like it might line up with the words on the card Burnbaum had given me. Close enough, anyway. "No rug shops, no stop-offs, OK?"

"Sure. OK."

I glanced out the window. The hill off to my right was dominated by a building with a large dome surrounded by spires—minarets.

"The Blue Mosque," announced the driver, his eyes darting back and forth in the rearview mirror from me to the road ahead. "Most beautiful building in all of the world."

It was imposing, I had to give it that.

"Where you from?" he said.

"Depends on who you ask."

"Not *Amerikali*?" he asked, puzzled.

"Yeah, American."

"You like Istanbul?"

"Like it . . . ?" I said, leaving the options open.

"How long you stay?"

"Long enough."

"It is never long enough if you must one day leave. You need a driver while you are here. My name is Emir. I take you everywhere you want to go. You come to Istanbul alone?"

"No."

"That's good. Istanbul is city for lovers."

I glanced out the Renault's window. So I'd been told.

"I stop talking. You enjoy Istanbul," said Emir, reading the mood of his passenger like I was a street sign, one that said: *Shut the fuck up.*

I felt like sightseeing as much as I felt like talking. I wanted to say to Masters that her fiancé had come to embody the blind obstinacy of a government policy that was cold, heartless, and unjust. I thought about my buddy back home who'd be spending the rest of his shortened life bouncing in and out of medical centers, reduced to eating what he could suck through a straw. Outside, the high-voltage electricity towers and tenements drifted by beneath a chill blue sky. In the distance a low gray line of cloud hung like sludge above the horizon, threatening.

"OK," said Emir, pulling over. "We are here."

It had been a quick drive. I read the fare off the meter and pulled out my wallet.

"So, how about it? You want driver for your stay in Istanbul, sir?"

"Can you give me a receipt for that?" I asked as I handed over the cash.

"Yes, my cell number is on the receipt." He scribbled the fare paid onto a pad, tore off the sheet, and handed it to me. Then he began fishing around for change.

"Keep it," I told him. I climbed out of his living room and strolled over to the boom gate. In the reflection of the security glass beyond, I saw Emir waving me good-bye like I was headed off on a long trip and he was going to miss me.

Masters didn't even look up when I walked in. She was on the phone saying "Uh-huh" and doodling stars on the pad in front of her. I took a seat behind the mother-of-pearl desk, beneath the painting of the guy striding over a trash heap of body parts stewing in blood. The painting gave me the creeps.

The desk was sparsely populated with a flat computer screen and keyboard, a phone, a Rolodex business-card holder that appeared to be full, a manila folder, a pen, and a pencil. A handwritten note signed by Rodney Cain told me the Rolodex was Portman's. I swiped my common access card and the computer screen came to life. Apparently, I had mail. I clicked. The mail was from Cain.

I clicked again. Masters had been copied. The email read: *Here you go, Special Agents. Just click on the link. Warning—there's a lot here to go through. One thing I haven't sent you is a link to the electronic calendar Colonel Portman kept. I tried to open it and the file is corrupted. I spoke to IT services about it and they said there's nothing they can do to fix it. If you need any help at all, just holler.*

The news about the calendar was disappointing. Knowing where Portman had been recently and who he'd been with might have been an asset. Nothing we could do about it.

"Shame about the calendar," Masters commented from across the room.

I nodded as I clicked on the link to Portman's email box. While I waited for the file to open, I wound through a turn or two of the Rolodex. Most of the recent email traffic seemed to be between Portman and various people at an organization called TEI, the local aerospace company making General Electric jet engines for Turkish Air Force F-16s, and General Electric in the States. That seemed reasonable given the Air Attaché's main focus before his murder, which was working on the Turks' F-16 upgrade.

Next I opened his phone records. Captain Cain had attached names to the numbers. At some stage, I would have to take a couple of days to go through both files properly, but not today.

Masters put her hand over the mouthpiece. "Where you been?" she asked.

"Istanbul," I replied.

She glanced at the ceiling like she was hoping to find strength up there, then held the handset away from her ear, her hand still covering the mouthpiece. "Got the leasing agent here," she told me. "Portman had that second safe installed without informing them."

"So it definitely wouldn't have shown up on any plans." Masters's hunch had paid dividends. If I didn't smarten up, she'd become the brains of the operation.

"They want to know when they'll be able to re-rent the residence."

I thought about my T-shirt. "Tell them after the cleaners have finished dissolving it."

Masters went back to saying uh-huh. I flipped open the folder in front of me. Inside was a bunch of official OSI forms outlining the charge of rape against Staff Sergeant Mort Gallagher, the case down at Incirlik Air Base that Portman had, according to Ambassador Burnbaum, intended to look into. Beneath these was the original employment form filled out by Adem Fedai, manservant to Colonel Portman. Fedai was thirty-three, single, five eight, and 150 pounds. If he were a boxer, he'd be a junior middleweight. I looked at the photo. Eyes: brown. Mustache—of course. I copied his home address into my notebook.

"There's also this," said Masters, done with her phone call. She slid a couple of sheets of paper across the desk toward me.

The one on top was a letterhead with a shield and the words *Istanbul Emniyet Müdurlügü*—Police Administration. I couldn't read the contents as they were written in Turkish, but stapled to the letter was the translation: It was a report from Istanbul police forensics. I scanned it. Apparently, tests had determined the makeup of the explosives used to blow Colonel Portman's wall safe: HMX mixed in with some LX-14, a plastic bonded explosive that'd stop the HMX blowing up if the handler happened to sneeze. This kind of explosive was used in high-performance anti-armor warheads rather than heists. "So it was military. They got a spectroscopy analysis?"

"Yeah." Masters held up a couple more sheets of paper. "And if you're asking because you want to send it on to the FBI—done it. It'll take them a few days to get back to us." She raised an eyebrow, daring me to say something.

"Good," I said.

"Good," she repeated.

"Good," I repeated back.

"OK, then . . ." she said.

I left the field of battle and toyed with the scene-of-the-crime report. Each explosive has its own distinctive spectroscopic signature, its own chemical fingerprint, which could be cross-referenced with the FBI's explosives database. Not only could the database confirm the type used on the attaché's safe as being military, but it would also tell us whose military used it. And, of course, who manufactured it.

The door swung open and a man strode in, a big, round man. "You must be Special Agent Cooper," he said, holding out a hand the size of a Christmas ham to shake on the fact. "I'm Harvey Stringer, chief political adviser hereabouts. Ambassador Burnbaum asked me to come on over. I believe the OSI is now leading the investigation into Colonel Portman's murder."

"Yes, sir," I replied.

The translation for "chief political adviser" was CIA head of station. Harvey Stringer was three hundred pounds, in his mid-fifties, and balding, the remaining hair as fine and white as gossamer. It wafted about, catching the light from a window behind him like flares off the sun. He wore wide suspenders spotted with pink and blue polka dots. They held up loose-fitting pants big enough to pitch and sleep four in comfort. His head was big and round, too, with small, snug-fitting ears and a large red nose. Maybe he'd just come off working undercover at the local circus.

"And you must be Special Agent Masters," he said. "I'm pleased to meet y'all, though I'm sorry it has to be under such disturbing circumstances."

Stringer took Masters's hand within his and it disappeared, swallowed whole. His accent placed Harvey Stringer from down Alabama way. I wondered if maybe he'd shared a bucket of fried chicken with Special Agents Seb Goddard and Arlow Mallet.

"The ambassador told me you good people wanted to talk a few things over. So here I am. Let's talk. Mind if I sit?" He let out a grunt as he lowered himself into a worn leather armchair.

"Thanks for stopping by, sir. At the moment, because we don't know what we're looking for, we're checking on everything—the deceased's recent movements, people who worked for him, people he would have met. Sir, we noted from his flight record that he was an appi-8. He was a unique individual, and this is known to be a pretty hot part of the world. Put the two together, and we imagined there might have been some call on the attaché's time from certain quarters."

"So, you think Portman might have been working on . . . special projects. Is that what you're sayin'? Something that might account for the way he was killed?"

"In a nutshell, sir." Masters nodded.

Stringer shook his big head. "Sorry, can't help you there. I can assure you that Colonel Portman was not on the Company payroll, though I can honestly say we'd have welcomed his input on a couple of things. He simply didn't have the time. Too busy with the Turkish Air Force, I believe."

"We know about that," Masters confirmed.

"Had he ever done *any* work for the Company in Turkey?" I asked.

Stringer massaged his chin. "Well... over a year ago, he helped us out with an operation to find an al Qaeda terrorist cell looking to cause some mischief around Incirlik Air Base."

"But nothing more recently?" I asked, pushing. "Seems odd to us that a guy like Portman wouldn't be involved in, if not black ops, then at least something brown."

"No, nothing." Stringer sounded irritated. "On official business or otherwise." He glanced from me to Masters, waiting for a question. When none came, he stood. There was no grunt this time. He got to his feet light as a blimp and almost as big. "Well, if there's nothing more...?"

How much of this guy's mannerism was theater—maybe he'd just been putting on a show. It was my experience that clowns didn't usually make it to the corner offices in the Company's executive structure.

"I very much hope y'all catch this killer," Stringer added, adjusting his suspenders. "Like I said, if there's anything I can help you with, you got my full cooperation. So, if you'll excuse me, I have a luncheon engagement."

In fact, there was something the Company could help us with, but I knew that before a man like Stringer would give, he'd have to receive. "Sir," I began, "we're checking out a theory that there might have been two killers."

"*Two* killers..." he repeated, nodding, considering the possibility, accepting the gift of information. "What makes you think that?"

"When the assailants blew the attaché's safe, we believe they used blast blankets to deaden the sound. Those things are heavy. Add to that the rest of the stuff they left behind in the drain."

"I've seen the inventory," Stringer agreed. "So, more than one person could carry. Makes sense."

"Special Agent Masters and I also believe they may have had a boat moored out in the Bosphorus as their base—used scuba gear, floated everything in, and maybe sank everything they didn't need or want to leave behind on the way back out."

Stringer nodded again. "Still making sense."

"We'd like to know if the Bosphorus happened to be under any useful footprints on the night in question," said Masters, cutting to it.

"Hmm . . ." He pondered the request as well as its implications, drumming his huge fingers on the desk. While satellite photographs might allow us to identify such a boat, perhaps even helping us identify the killers, the downside would be—if it ever got out, and most likely it would—an admission that we were spying on Turkey, which was supposed to be an ally. "I'm not sure I can do that," he said finally, "even if there was a bird overhead at the time. Which I doubt," he added for safety.

Stringer was backpedaling fast enough to win the Tour de France sprinter's jersey.

"Have you considered that they could also have been dropped off and picked up by legitimate vessels?" he asked.

"No, we hadn't, sir."

"Something to think about, maybe." He cracked a knuckle. "Anyhow, I can certainly put your request to the people who decide these things. Y'all just let me know if there's anything else I can do."

"Yes, sir," I said.

"Well, it's been great to meet you." He gave us a wave and closed the door behind him as he left.

"Y'all just let me know if there's anything else I can do," Masters mimicked, ". . . so as I can just sit on it."

"Where it'd have no chance of ever seeing the light of day."

"So much for the full-cooperation bit. Especially when it comes to satellites."

I sat on the corner of the desk, picked up a pen, and used it to scratch the itch down inside my cast. Something was bugging me. I knew if I thought about it too hard, I'd lose it permanently, so I let it go. Maybe it would hit me over the head at three A.M.

Stringer. If *I* was head of CIA operations out this way, I would probably be pretty interested to know why a serious embassy asset was chopped into snack-size pieces, wouldn't I? That got me to thinking: If I was Stringer, and he was me, the only reason I'd play dumb would be because I had something *I* didn't want *me* to know. That made me wonder what I knew that I wasn't telling myself, and why the hell I'd allowed myself to put on so much weight.

The photo of Portman's manservant, Adem Fedai, caught my eye.

Fedai had a pleasant face, but it was a head-and-shoulders shot. The guy could have been smiling sweetly while, unseen and out of frame, his hands held a little girl's pet rabbit as it struggled under water. Jeffrey Dahmer had a pleasant face, too—

A rolled-up ball of paper pinged off my head. "Cooper, you still with us?" It was Masters, on the phone, her hand over the mouthpiece again. "It's Cain. We've got another murder."

NINE

The plant room was not much bigger than a phone booth, or maybe I just thought of it that way because of the number of people trying to squeeze into it. The room was on the bottom floor of the Istanbul Hilton parking lot, which was underground a hundred or so yards away from the hotel itself. We were all there to see the one person who didn't mind being crammed into the small space, on account of the fact that his head had been removed from his neck with a saw.

An ambulance had been called to the scene. A man I took to be the janitor was sitting in the back of the vehicle, attended to by paramedics. The guy, an old man in faded gray coveralls with a blue Hilton logo on his breast pocket, was sucking oxygen from a mask attached to his face. He kept shaking his head and gesturing as he talked to the uniform cop taking his statement.

Masters and I had been called to the scene not because the victim was an American. And it wasn't because he carried a California driver's license, either. The clincher was that he appeared to have a finger inserted in his anus. Someone else's finger.

"Looks familiar," said Captain Cain, stepping out of the plant room. "They were right to call us." The parking lot filled with silent lightning as the forensics team took their digital snaps. "It's similar to the Portman murder, but different. A variation of the MO—no systematic dismemberment this time, but the same casual überviolence. Along with the decapitation, both hands were severed. Smells like chloroform was again used to subdue the victim."

"Any bones missing from this one?" Masters asked.

"No, they all appear to be present and accounted for." Cain rubbed the top of his head.

"Maybe the killer was disturbed," Masters ventured.

Yeah, "disturbed" was one way to put it.

"I'm going to step way out on a limb here," Cain said, "and say the finger they found in his ass is one of Colonel Portman's."

Exactly how many human bones were out there doing the rounds in this city, being passed from one murder victim to the next? "What's the janitor's story, Captain?" I asked.

"As far as I can make out, he'd come to the end of his shift and was locking up for the night. He found the door ajar, Goldilocks inside, and the porridge all gone."

Dropped on the floor beside the open plant room door, I noticed, was a broom with a wide bristle head. "Did the janitor leave the door unlocked?"

"Must have," said Cain. "The lock wasn't forced or drilled out."

"What about the murder weapon or weapons—anything other than the saw left behind again?"

"They've searched. Nothing else has been recovered."

"So what's the connection between the victim and Portman, aside from what we already know?" Masters asked.

"You mean, aside from the fact that he worked for General Electric and was helping Portman with the F-16 upgrade?" I said.

"How do you know that?" Masters turned to face me.

"His driver's license says his name's Dutch Bremmel. There's a Dutch Bremmel, a retired U.S. Air Force lieutenant colonel, working for TEI. Bremmel was General Electric's man working with the Turks. There were emails back and forth between him and Portman. And his business card was in Portman's Rolodex." Could be a coincidence, but I doubted it. "You didn't happen to notice Bremmel's name on Portman's computer, did you, Rodney?"

Cain looked sheepish. If a tin can had been lying around on the ground, he'd have probably kicked it. "To tell you the truth, I haven't managed to spend too much time with the attaché's files."

I wasn't trying to break the captain's balls here. It wasn't necessarily his job anyway. The one reason the name Bremmel had been fresh in my mind was that I'd just finished browsing through www .recentlybutchered.com—Portman's email correspondence.

Meanwhile, people were coming and going, making like sardines in Bremmel's little booth. Any moment I was sure someone from Guinness World Records was going to arrive and make the record official. Masters, Cain, and I were standing around watching everyone else get their hands dirty. This wasn't our country and it wasn't our crime scene, but Bremmel was American. He was also ex-USAF, so arguably one of ours—OSI's. It was an argument we'd lose, though, because of the "ex." Bremmel was a civilian, which took him outside our purview. "So we got Portman laid out like an Airfix model. And now Bremmel, a heavy hitter at TEI, the guy Portman was dealing with on a day-to-day basis, is sitting around with something that used to belong to the attaché hidden in a very dark place. Do you think the killers are maybe trying to tell us something?"

"Did you say 'killers'?" asked Cain.

I forgot I hadn't brought the captain up to speed on our recent brainstorm. I was halfway through filling him in when Detective Sergeants Karli and Iyaz arrived to take control of the crime scene. They ignored us. The uniform taking tickets at the door for the show going on around Bremmel saluted and let them pass. Two minutes later they emerged and wandered over.

"Thank you for being attending." Karli tucked a clear plastic bag containing what I assumed were Bremmel's effects under an arm while he loaded a mint into his mouth. "This one and the other one . . . we thin they are related."

"Yeah, maybe," agreed Cain.

"Are you going to impound his vehicle?" I asked.

"Whose vehicle?" Karli appeared confused.

"The victim's." We were in a parking lot. The most likely scenario was that Bremmel was down here about to either get into his car or leave it parked for the evening. If he was attacked near his car, there might be vital clues in the vehicle or around it. Frankly, I doubted that, but in this game you have to have the bases covered.

Karli and Iyaz looked around, overwhelmed. They were surrounded by automobiles, most of which looked like they might have been driven by rich American executives like Bremmel.

Masters gave a helpful smile, reached across and, through the plastic evidence bag held by Karli, pinched the remote attached to a bunch of keys. An alarm chirped on a nearby late-model Lexus SUV, and its indicators flashed twice, zapping the cold cement cavern around us with bursts of orange light.

Iyaz immediately yelled at a uniform and pointed at the vehicle excitedly, as if concerned it might try to flee the scene. Uniforms began running toward the SUV until Iyaz started shouting at them some more to stop. One of them turned and raced back to an equipment bag, grabbed a roll of crime-scene tape from it, and sprinted back to the Lexus to start wrapping it up.

"So when do you think we could see the movie?" I asked the two detectives.

"Movie?" said Karli.

I tilted my head at the round surveillance camera pod wedged into a shadow like a large bug trying hard not to be seen.

"Yes, yes. We know this," Iyaz informed me.

Sure you do. What the hell . . . I told myself to ease up on these guys. Just because the local flatfoots spoke English like three-year-olds didn't mean they were. To be fair, it took more than a couple of minutes to get your head around a crime scene, particularly one as bizarre as this. Bremmel's body was seated, propped against the storeroom wall. His head was sitting beside him, resting on the clean-cut stump of his neck, one eye open and the other half closed as if he'd drunk a bottle of something on an empty stomach and was now paying for it. This lopsided stare was one I'd seen many times—like any moment the deceased would maybe snap out of it. But they never do. A moth had become helplessly trapped in the crimson pool of sticky blood and was beating a wing furiously. A tree saw, most likely the instrument used for the heavy work, was embedded in the flesh below Bremmel's collarbone as though the person sawing off his entire shoulder and arm had had a change of heart. Maybe, as Masters suggested, the killer had been disturbed. Bremmel's severed hands were also sawn off his wrists. One was beside the body's feet, the other had come to rest in a far corner among a collection of brooms, mops, and buckets.

Iyaz stood beside me, looking around, hands on hips, while the teams that descend on a dead body got on with earning their pay. He walked off to have a word with one of the forensics guys.

"What do you think?" Masters asked me.

"I'm not sure what I think," I said.

"I don't believe it. Are you the Vin Cooper I know, or has an alien snatched your body?"

"We're not going to find anything the killers don't want us to find, is what I think. There are no signs of a struggle, no witnesses, no easy clues like footprints or tire skid marks or handy buttons from the killer's unique and expensive coat clutched in one of the severed hands."

"OK, I get the picture. What about the surveillance TV footage?"

I saw that Iyaz had moved on to join a huddle comprising a couple of corporate types and a hotel security guy. One of the corporates pointed at the camera. "I don't think we should get too excited about it," I told Masters. "This ain't exactly post-9/11 downtown New York. I'll bet that half the cameras in this place don't work and the other half haven't been switched on—or the tapes are so old and worn, all they capture is snow."

"Nothing like a bit of positive thinking, Vin," she said.

I shrugged. Maybe I was just getting tired of hanging around a parking lot that stank of blood, dust, old exhaust fumes, and cold concrete. I needed to go get something to clean out my insides, perhaps a couple of nice, clean blocks of ice wrapped around two fingers of single malt, then get some shut-eye and put this day in the trash.

I caught Karli as he strode past, his pants hitched so high they looked like his butt cheeks were slowly eating them. "Detective Sergeant?"

Karli raised his eyebrow at me in the universal *can-I-help-you?* gesture.

"Do you know why the deceased was down here?"

He gave me the puzzled look that was starting to get on my nerves.

"The deceased, the dead guy—Bremmel," I tried again. "Why was he down here in the garage?"

Karli called Iyaz over and the two went into a huddle. Eventually they came out of it. Iyaz said, "Mr. Bremmel made a visit here."

"Who was he visiting?"

"A woman. The hotel says Mr. Bremmel came every second Friday afternoon for months to visiting her."

So, every other Friday at the Hilton for a little afternoon delight. Dutch Bremmel had made a tradition of it.

"Do you know who she is?" I inquired.

"It is Mrs. Bremmel."

"His wife?"

"Yes."

"You sure it's not his niece?"

"I am sorry?"

"Never mind." Men didn't take their wives to hotel rooms during business hours to do the business. They didn't take their nieces either, come to think of it. I knew very little about Bremmel beyond his connection with Portman, but I was learning fast. I knew, for example, something about his character. I also knew that somewhere he *did* have a wife, otherwise there'd be little use for the dishonesty. "Where is the alleged Mrs. Bremmel now?"

"She has left," Iyaz replied.

"What?"

"Yes, gone." Iyaz didn't seem to be getting my drift.

"Do you have an address for her, aside from the one that came with her husband's credit card?"

Iyaz caught on, suddenly looked nervous. "No. But we will find her."

"Uh-huh," I said. They'd turn up with her just like they were turning up with Portman's hired help. Which reminded me. "You managed to track down Colonel Portman's manservant?"

"Who?"

"Adem Fedai."

"No. Still we cannot find him."

"And you tried calling him on his cell phone?"

"Yes, we tried. No good." He shook his head. "We checked with phone company. The phone was switched off."

I shrugged. "Worth a try. And the surveillance footage?" I clarified my meaning by pointing at the camera wedged up high where the wall met the ceiling.

"Yes, yes..." he said. "We will see tomorrow. We will call you. We need time."

Time to what? I wondered.

The gathering was thinning out. The paramedics were pushing their gurney slow, unhurried, toward the plant room. An empty body bag was laid out on top. If they somehow managed to get their trolley into that small space, *I* was going to call the people at Guinness. I turned to leave.

"Where're you going?" Masters said.

"Bed. Wanna join me?"

She shook her head. "Don't you ever give up?"

TEN

Turkey is a Muslim country, so I wasn't expecting big things from the bar fridge in my room. I was rewarded, however, by a row of Johnnie Walker Black miniatures lined up along the door shelf like ducks at a shooting gallery. I cracked the seals on a couple of bottles and poured them together into a glass with ice, and drank half in a gulp. The slug of whisky felt good.

I lay back on the double bed and stared at the ceiling. It was just past eleven, but it felt later than that. It'd been a busy day. Two murders, obviously related; no witnesses and, so far, no real clues. I downed the rest of the Scotch and put the glass on the carpet beside my bed. I told myself I really should get up and have something to eat.

The room was dark and quiet when I woke, still fully dressed. The itch down inside the cast on my left hand had been my wake-up call. The bedside clock showed 5:10. I sat up, swung my feet over the side of the bed, and kicked over the glass tumbler I'd placed on the carpet.

I rubbed my face with my good hand, turned on the bedside light, and went to the john. Afterward, I reached for my suitcase, a small Samsonite. I unlocked it and pulled out Nikes, shorts, and a red Che Guevara T-shirt. A run would do me good, help me get things in some kind of order, even if it was only just to put one foot in front of the other. I'd started running a little over a year ago to help me recover from a case that had been bad news for me and worse news for the guy I ended up planting in the ground. It was the case on which Masters and I had met, one that had also nearly killed her. After I'd been released from the hospital, I'd started shuffling, which had eventually turned into running. Pounding a few regular miles had helped my body heal faster—or it could also have been all the sex with Anna that had done the trick. As I remembered it, getting regularly horizontal over that period hadn't exactly been bad for her recovery, either.

I changed and then used a knife from the kitchenette to move the spiders I was convinced had taken up residence between the cast and the skin on my wrist. Then, pocketing the room's card key and a small wad of cash, I made my way to the elevator but decided to use the stairs instead, just to get things moving.

I walked through the lobby. The guy at reception was looking pasty with sleep deprivation. He tipped his forefinger at me. I knew what he was thinking: another crazy jogger—had to be American. Or maybe he was just thinking about the sack.

Outside the front door, I got a surprise. Masters was bent over, stretching her hammies. She was wearing black Skins with yellow stitching. I admired her legs. Her ass was hot enough to steam collars. I leaned against the wall. Why spoil the moment? Masters had gone back to the N.Y.F.D. cap, her hair in the usual ponytail. No makeup. Those eyes of hers didn't need any.

"Morning," I said finally. The air was cold without being freezing and the wind had died down. Perfect running weather.

"Oh..." she said, surprised, looking around. "You been standing there long?"

"Long enough."

"Long enough to what—or shouldn't I ask?"

I countered her question with one of my own. "When did you start running?"

"A few months ago. Took your advice. I hated it at first, but I've come around."

It would have taken Masters a while to get used to running without a big toe, something she'd lost in a car accident, the one that had nearly killed her back in Germany. At the time, we'd agreed that the toe was a fair trade for her life. "You should take Uncle Vin's advice more often," I told her.

Masters smiled and replied, "Where you headed?"

"Thought I'd wing it. You?"

"The concierge gave me a map." She pulled it from the pocket of a fleece vest. "Want to join me? We can sightsee before the crowds arrive."

"Slow before steady," I said, indicating for her to lead on. Loud hailers burst into life nearby with the day's first call to prayer.

Masters shook her head at me before breaking into a jog, loping toward a collection of stone towers lit by yellow spotlights. I caught up and settled into a rhythm beside her. "So, this Stringer guy . . . I trust him as much as I trusted the last CIA guy I worked with."

"You know what they say about judging a book by its cover, Vin?"

"Stringer's got a lot of covering."

We paused at a corner for a tractor making its way to a road crew digging up the streetcar lines in the middle of the street. Masters led off again, picking up the pace.

"You trust him?" I asked.

"Innocent until proven guilty, I think is how it goes."

"The U.S. Embassy has lost a full bird colonel to killers who could've taught Jack the Ripper a few tricks, but Stringer seemed more interested in dinner."

"I think it was lunch."

"Whatever."

"How should he act?"

"*Very* interested."

"Cooper, you don't like the CIA, never have. In your eyes they're always guilty of something. He could be just like the rest of us—stressed out, staying one step ahead of the meat grinder, doing too much, and never getting enough of it done."

Masters was right. Harvey Stringer was probably just like the rest of us, or maybe just like the rest of three of us put together.

We ran up a steep hill behind an ancient building and took the path around the front of the building along flagstones worn smooth by over a thousand years of footsteps. We stopped to take it all in, breathing hard. Across the square, another giant mosque sat bathed in warm orange spotlights. Behind it, against a luminous dark navy sky, hung the burnished fingernail clipping of a crescent moon.

"You know, Caesar could well have stood in this very spot," said Masters, a look approaching rapture on her face.

"The guy who put croutons in salad? He stood here?"

"Jesus, Vin..." Masters sighed, turning away and breaking into a trot. I caught up. After a while she said, "So what do you want to do first? We've got the surveillance footage at eleven forty-five."

"Set up interviews," I replied. "We should talk to this forensic shrink ASAP—Cain's contact."

"Dr. Merkit."

"If you say so." I didn't have my notebook on me to check the name. "I want to get her reaction to this latest murder, see if she can weave some of that profiling magic for us." The cast on my hand was getting sticky with sweat, the spiders scurrying about. "I also want to follow up on Portman's appi-8 flight status, see if he'd been doing any flying in this part of the world."

"We can access that stuff through flight records back at Andrews." Masters timed the words with her breathing. "And maybe we can talk to someone down at Incirlik about this rape case—clear it off the board if we can."

"Yep."

We were heading up another hill, a steep one—like they had any other kind here. Both of us were feeling it, but neither of us was willing to show it. Masters broke first.

"You mind if we can the chitchat for a while?" she asked, breathing hard.

I took the lead and pushed the pedal to the floor, not that I'm in the least competitive or anything. I slipped into a good rhythm, watching the waves of cobblestones rush by beneath my running shoes. The hill plateaued in the courtyard of some ancient mosque—another one.

After a while, the fact that I was running disappeared and I was left with just my thoughts. I was thinking that if what we had here were serial killings, I had no experience with that kind of crime. What I did know was that making a breakthrough would revolve around finding the connection between the victims. From this knowledge could potentially spring a lead to the killers. Only we already had the connection between the victims, didn't we? Portman was the U.S. Air Attaché handling any government issues between Washington and Ankara with the

F-16 upgrade, and Bremmel was his opposite number at TEI, the program's engine supplier. Simple. Or was it? Burnbaum, Stringer, and Portman: an ex-spy, a current spy, and an appi-8 action man. I'd had enough experience with Washington's notion of team-building to know that people like this were put together for a reason.

Twelve bones had been removed from Portman's body. The phalanges of his right hand recovered from Bremmel accounted for three of them. If Masters was right and the bones were taken to be left on future victims, there could be as many as nine more murders to come. Adding Portman himself and Bremmel, the body count would be eleven. Was the number meaningful? Was the interval between the murders—three days—significant? Were the *types* of bones taken from Portman relevant? What about the bones removed from Bremmel's butt? Were the killers really saying *fuck you* in a playful, psychopathic let's-have-fun-with-the-flatfoots kind of way?

I went through all these questions so many times I started to feel like I was running in circles. At that point I realized I probably was. I stopped, opened my eyes to the world around me, and found I was looking out across the Bosphorus. I leaned on a rusted railing and scoped the surroundings to get my bearings. The sun was due to rise, Masters was nowhere in sight, and I was completely lost.

A horn tooted and a cab drove up. The driver leaned across and shouted out through the passenger-side window. "Taxi!?"

I recognized the guy and hadn't expected to. I walked over. "Emir, right?"

Hearing his name surprised him. "Yes, sir, how do you know this?"

"You took me to the U.S. Consulate-General yesterday, remember?"

"Oh yes, that was me, sir. Where you going now? The consulate?"

"You following me?" I asked. I didn't think he was. I could see from his face he had no recollection of the fare. Probably all we non-mustachioed Americans looked alike to him.

"No, sir." Then he thought about my question and said, "Unless you *like* me to follow you."

I climbed in the backseat.

"You know the Hotel Charisma, in the Sultanahmet?"

"Yes, I know it. It is far," he replied. "You came from there? You have run a long way. Do you mind putting on the seat?"

Putting on what? I wondered.

Emir passed back a green towel, solving the mystery. "I want to keep taxi nice for tourist."

I shrugged. My legs were sticking to the thick, shiny plastic encasing the seats. I sat on the towel.

"American?" he asked, leaning back.

"Uh-huh."

"Americans—good people. You like Istanbul?"

"Emir. You got any Turkish music?" If I didn't shut the guy up, he was going to tell me again that a stay in Istanbul was never long enough if I ever had to leave, and I could do without the déjà vu.

I was starting to cool down when Emir pulled up to the Hotel Charisma, just as Masters stepped out the door and checked the street for cabs. She waved at Emir as he pulled over. I handed him a ball of money, forgot about the receipt, and hopped out.

"Where have you been? I've had breakfast and a shower. And getting a cab ride . . ." She shook her head and *tut-tut*ted. "You must be really out of shape," she said as she made Emir's day and climbed in.

I was maybe forty minutes behind Masters by the time I made it to the Consulate-General, but she wasn't there. I killed a half-hour chasing up Portman's flight log from Andrews AFB Flight Records Office. They said it was going to take them some time to get back to me. How much time did it take to punch a code on a keyboard, copy the information, and send it online? Days, apparently.

I dialed the number Cain had given me for Dr. Merkit. Her secretary answered. From the sound of the voice, it was either a guy who answered or an old lady who chain-smoked. This being Turkey, my money was on the smoker. She told me the doctor wasn't in, but I was happy to settle for an appointment with her in the mid-afternoon.

Next, I sniffed around TEI, otherwise known as Tusas Engine Industries, where Bremmel worked as General Electric's point man on those engines. Bremmel wasn't a resident of Istanbul. According to records accessed with a little local police cooperation, he lived with his wife in Eskisehir where TEI was headquartered, a city more or less 120 miles southeast of Istanbul. I also knew from his email exchanges with Portman that Bremmel spent a fair bit of time at the Incirlik Air Base, close to the border Turkey shared with Iraq, where the work of those F-16s was being performed. "Bremmel" wasn't exactly a common name in Turkey, and I located his home phone number through an online directory. A maid at his home informed me that more than two weeks ago, Mrs. Bremmel had gone home to Seattle to visit relatives—which was a long way from jumping on her husband in a room at the Istanbul Hilton.

I went back to skimming through Portman's emails. An hour and a half later I pushed back from the desk for a breather, no closer to any kind of breakthrough. From the thousands of items, I could see that Emmet Portman and Dutch Bremmel were reasonably friendly, though not overly chummy. The relationship between the U.S. government, TEI, and the Turkish authorities, which included its Air Force and various government ministers, was a gauntlet of protocol issues, complicated by the usual supply-and-demand headaches—the wrong parts in inventory, aircraft with incorrect serial numbers delivered for upgrade, and so on and so forth—and every one of these stumbling blocks and hiccups was accompanied by at least thirty to forty email exchanges. There were hundreds of emails between Ward Burnbaum, who represented the interests of the U.S. State Department, and Portman. I skimmed through a few dozen at random and found nothing I wouldn't have expected.

Masters walked in with red circles on her cheeks, blowing into her hands to warm them. I closed the link. I'd find time to come back to the emails later.

"Jesus, the weather has turned. It's freezing out there. You ready to go?" She was waiting at the door, holding it open.

The clock in my head said it was just after eleven, confirmed by the time displayed on the computer screen. We had an appointment to review the surveillance footage. I took my jacket off the back of the chair, put it on, and zippered it up as we walked toward the elevator. "Where you been?" I asked.

"Got a call from the leasing agent. Not the person I spoke to yesterday—the general manager. He told me they'd had a break-in at their office about a month ago. I went to see him. They had computers stolen, files broken into, and papers strewn about. Some keys were also taken. One of them was the front door key to Portman's place. Also, the manager went to check on Portman's lease yesterday after I called, and the file's gone. He doesn't know whether it was stolen during the break-in. Seems he didn't believe our call about Portman was a coincidence."

"My kind of guy," I said. "Did the police pay them a visit afterward and dust things down?"

"Yep."

"And found absolutely nothing?"

She shrugged. "Lifted plenty of prints, then fingerprinted the staff for comparison purposes. They said it would take some time to identify whose prints belonged to whom, there being plenty of staff pawing the files. There might be unidentified latents among them, but, you know—it's the usual story."

The usual story was that unless those unidentified prints came with a police record, they'd most likely stay unidentified. "Did the missing file include floor plans of Portman's place?" I asked.

"Yep."

"They lost anyone else's plans?"

"He doesn't think so."

"And someone in the office hasn't just mislaid Portman's file?"

"Not a chance. I was there this morning. The boss runs a tight ship. The staff have to sign for every pencil they take from the supply cabinet."

"So the front door key was stolen. If we believe the killers did the break-in, why didn't they just use the key instead of coming in via the drain?"

Masters shook her head.

The elevator was waiting on our floor. As we headed down, I watched the floors peel off on the overhead digital display.

"There was a lot of premeditation, a lot of planning going on before the murderers struck," Masters noted. "If these are serial killings, is that level of preparation and plotting usual?"

"Don't know. That's one for the forensic shrink. We're seeing her this afternoon at fifteen hundred hours, by the way." Masters was right, though. There didn't seem to have been a lot left to chance. "We know what Bremmel was doing in the Hilton parking lot," I went on, "but I'd like to know whether he was keeping to a schedule and whether the killers caught him trying to keep it."

Outside, it was cold. My breath steamed in front of my face.

"Over here! Over here!"

I recognized the voice, which gave me the opportunity to ignore it and head in the other direction.

"Vin," Masters called out after me. "Where are you going? I've hired us a driver."

I knew he'd be standing by his cab, waving. I turned. Yep. Emir.

"Hello, hello. Please to get in where it is nice and warm."

I slid in beside Masters, where it was still chilly, and a long way from nice.

"Where to, lady boss?" said Emir, his mustache pawing at the air beside his cheek as he spoke.

"Lady boss?" I inquired.

"You'd better believe it," replied Masters. She gave him an address.

Emir headed north across town, through a network of backstreets, then onto a highway and over a bridge spanning a wide estuary to another area of the city entirely. Once into the rhythm of the journey, he felt the need for conversation. "Are you married?" he asked.

"To each other?" Masters was waving in front of her face like she was brushing away an unpleasant smell. "No, no . . . but I'm engaged. Not to *this* guy . . . Actually, I met my future husband right here in Istanbul."

"Istanbul is the city for lovers," I said, intoning it in unison with Emir so that Masters received this well-known fact in stereo. My reward for this was The Look.

"And you, my friend sir?"

"Me? Married?"

"Yes, sir."

"Do I look married?"

"Yes, yes!"

"There goes your tip."

"I would like to have many, many wives," Emir announced, "like the sultans."

"You would, huh?"

"Many," he said, nodding vigorously and rolling his eyes like he was seeing himself surrounded by a bevy of Barbara Eden lookalikes.

"Should I spoil it for him now?" I asked Masters.

"There you go, Vin. Proving to me again why *we* were never going to make it."

"'Cause I think that having one wife is tough enough, and that a nag of them—or whatever the collective noun is—might possibly be the worst idea anyone ever came up with? And I thought it was because I lived in Washington and you lived in Germany."

"No, it's because you're damaged, Vin," she shot back. "You see everything through the prism of your own experience, and assume that's just how it's going to be for everyone else."

I could have bitten, could have told Masters that you had to learn from something and that experience was as good a teacher as any—and probably better than most. But I let it slide. She was younger than me and yet to sit in Experience's classroom on marriage. Emir started giving us a guided tour of the sights. But neither Masters nor I was listening. We'd retreated to heal our cuts and bruises in silence.

ELEVEN

The Istanbul Police Department was housed in a sullen poured-concrete building slapped together in the sixties. Grime sweated from the pores of its flaking surface, the decades of ugliness accumulated within seeping out. Bare trees lining the road shivered in the cold breeze. Beside the main entrance, a Turkish flag the size of a basketball court executed a lazy roll around the flagpole.

Emir pulled up as close to the entrance as security allowed—around a hundred yards away. Traffic bollards prevented a closer drop-off, thwarting truck bombs and other special deliveries from being left at the front gate.

Captain Cain arrived as Masters and I walked to a brick bunker in front of the courtyard. We handed over our shields for inspection to a couple of swarthy uniforms with MKEK submachine guns slung over their shoulders. Their peaked caps would have given a South American dictator a hard-on. They examined our credentials minutely.

"Morning," said Cain.

"Morning," Masters replied, providing enough of a greeting for the both of us.

The captain nodded, then said, "Cold, isn't it?"

"Freezing," agreed Masters, blowing into her hands.

The guards raised the boom and cleared us through. We followed Cain, and about five minutes later arrived at a reception desk on the second floor occupied by nothing but a small silver bell, outside a wood-and-frosted-glass partition. The bell gave a *ping* when Cain tapped it. The place reeked of male sweat, urine, and the memory of disinfectant—basically, like every front-line police department anywhere in the world.

Detective Sergeant Iyaz appeared around a partition and gestured to let us know that he'd be with us in a few minutes. There were no chairs to sit on, so Masters, Cain, and I milled around while we waited for Iyaz's return, watching various unsavory characters come and go. And a few crooks, too.

Karli and Iyaz collected us and led us to another office. It was small: room for a desk, a chair, a corkboard, and enough oxygen for maybe one person at a time. Handwritten and typed notes, Post-its and scraps of paper scrawled with phone numbers and/or addresses, photographs of dead people and mug shots of others who looked like nasty pieces of work all fought for space with children's paintings. On the desk there was a photo of a couple of smiling kids—the suspects responsible for the artworks, most probably—trays, accordion folders, and a huge, old-fashioned computer monitor running a Tetris screensaver. Detective Sergeant Karli stood beside the desk, hands on his wide hips, sucking on a mint, chasing it around his mouth with his tongue. He gave us a nod.

"Did you get much from the cameras?" Cain asked as the show got under way.

Iyaz opened the tray on the CPU humming away beneath the desk and inserted a disk. "No," he said, shaking his head, disappointed. He tapped a couple of keys and the desktop's DVD player came up. "Only three cameras work."

I awarded myself a little I-told-you-so moment even though I'd have preferred to be proved wrong.

The computer ran the footage as we crowded around the monitor. The cameras were old, and the resolution was so bad it looked like the lenses had been covered with nylons. The pictures were actually a series of greenish black-and-white stills, one taken every half-second, so that the resulting footage was grainy, dark, and disjointed. A time code showed the date and time and counted off the seconds.

"Did the hotel put this together?" I asked.

Iyaz took a second or two to get my drift, then said, "No. We do it. We have all surveillance tapes. The pictures are bad."

From what I could gather, the three working cameras were positioned at the entrance to the parking lot, on a ramp, and on the level where Bremmel was found. The camera at the entrance showed an old, dark-colored Fiat driving past; the second camera caught it on its way down, as did the camera on the parking level. A view of someone in dark clothing and ball cap followed, the cap's brim shielding the face like the person knew not to look up. The figure was carrying a soft bag, walking beneath the third camera. Was this one of our killers? The time code jumped forward twenty minutes, and someone wearing a cap and dark clothing walked back, head low, retracing their steps. There was a cut in the footage—the Fiat climbed up the ramp, blowing a little smoke, and exited the way it had come in. With a little enhancement, the vehicle's number plate would be clearly visible.

"The license plate," said Cain, nodding at the screen, making the same observation out loud.

"Yes. We checked. The car is stolen." Iyaz tossed a couple of screen shots of the Fiat on the table, the now reasonably sharp license plate having been worked over by a computer.

There were probably half a million Fiats identical to this one running around Istanbul—same model, same color, same year of manufacture. Were we really looking at the vehicle used by Bremmel's murderer? I thought about it. Forensics would have been able to nail a fairly accurate time of death for Bremmel by measuring the decrease in his core body temperature. The timing of the car's arrival and departure would have to have tallied with that. But was it just a coincidence that this automobile was stolen? There had to be plenty of auto thieves who weren't butchers. . . . "Were these the only working cameras? Or were there others still taking pictures?" I asked.

"Yes," said Iyaz. "There were other cameras."

"And none of them caught anything at around the same time? No other cars came and went? No other foot traffic?"

Iyaz knitted those brows of his together while the translator in his head went to work. "No," he replied eventually. "There was nothing else."

"OK," I said, thinking aloud. "So there is a good chance these are our suspects."

"Suspects? I'm only seeing one suspect here," Cain objected.

"No," said Masters. "You're seeing two."

"How do you figure that?"

"The first time we see him, he's carrying a bag," Masters explained.

"The second time we see him, he's not carrying a bag. But no bag was found at the scene, therefore someone else is carrying the bag out, someone outside the camera's range." The disk ran the footage again. "See? They're wearing the same clothes and the build is roughly the same, so it just *looks* like it's the same person—one killer—but, in fact, it's two."

"You searching for this Fiat?" I asked Iyaz.

"Yes, of course."

And when they happened to find it, I was pretty sure the vehicle would yield three-fifths of nothing, if our killers remained true to form. So far, the bad guys had been so calculating, I wouldn't have been surprised if they'd staged the parade in front of the surveillance cameras to confuse the investigation.

"So a guy gets sliced to pieces in the early evening in a very public place, and no one notices?" said Captain Cain.

"Yeah, just like back in the States," I replied. "You're making me feel homesick."

Iyaz cleared his throat like he was making an important announcement. "We have found the woman Mr. Bremmel was to meet at the hotel."

"Good work," Masters said.

"She identify the corpse for us."

"Have you questioned her?"

"Yes."

"Who was she?"

"She was Bremmel's assistant."

"She was the guy's secretary?" I was feeling a cliché coming on.

"Yes," Iyaz confirmed.

"Does she know who did this to her boyfriend?" I asked.

"No."

"The real Mrs. Bremmel, maybe, after finding out what her husband had been up to," Masters offered.

I remembered the time I found my own ex-wife in the shower buffing our marriage counselor's dick with her tonsils, and the subsequent beating I gave him. I wouldn't have killed the guy—my ex wasn't worth it—but I'd had firsthand experience with stuff like this, and I knew it could get the blood circulating a little faster than normal. "How long had they been doing each other?" I inquired. Iyaz knew what I meant.

"For six month."

"Where is she now?"

"We have asked her to stay in Istanbul. Her mother lives here."

"Can we question her?"

Karli tick-tacked on this with Iyaz before answering. "Yes. It's OK."

"Has the real Mrs. Bremmel been informed of her husband's death yet?" Masters wondered.

"That is being handled by your ambassador," Karli answered.

It seemed the bones recovered from Bremmel's one-way street were reason enough for the case to be dumped in our current basket of goodies after all.

DS Karli wrote the name and address of Bremmel's secretary on a slip of paper and handed it to Masters.

"Based on previous experience around here," Cain noted, "there should be a Turkish police forensics report available on Bremmel's remains tomorrow, though DNA tests on those finger bones will probably take another couple of days, depending on the backlog. We should see if we can't get someone to give us an estimation for the size and weight of the two suspects on the tape."

"Yes, we can do that," offered Iyaz. "Also, we have begun a search in the water outside the attaché's residence. It will take time. The area to search is very big."

"OK," I said, satisfied. We were all in danger of being professional.

TWELVE

It was nearly two-thirty by the time we left the police building. The wind had risen again and plastic bags were drifting around on its currents like jellyfish. I pulled the zipper on my jacket up to my neck. As the three of us walked beneath the boom gate, Captain Cain said, "By the way, I sent Dr. Merkit a brief on the Bremmel murder."

"Good." That would save time debriefing her. I glanced at my watch. "We have an appointment with the doc in thirty."

"I'm heading down to the water for a snoop around," he announced. "Thought I'd see how big the police search area really is." With that, Cain peeled off to hail a cab.

I turned to Masters. "You want to go talk to Bremmel's secretary while I go see the shrink?"

"If it's OK with you, Vin, I want to hear what Merkit has to say about the killer's profile. I already know what the secretary's going to tell us."

"And what's she going to tell us?"

"What married men have been saying ever since they crawled out of the primordial slime to set themselves up with a piece on the side—that Bremmel's marriage was unhappy, that his wife didn't understand him, that he was going to leave her when the right moment came up, et cetera."

A tooting horn interrupted Masters's words of wisdom. It was Emir, a hundred yards down the road beyond the bollards, leaning on the Renault's open door, waving like an idiot.

Dr. Aysun Merkit's office occupied the ground floor of a pink three-story shoe box in the heart of Beyoglu, a hillside area of contrasts: consulates at the top, citizens near the gutter at the bottom. In the middle of this layer cake, the quarter had been claimed by TV soap actors, pop stars, artists, and various professional people. The street in front of the doctor's office looked like a Mercedes-Benz concession. Shrinking murderers' heads must be a good business in this neck of the woods.

Masters rang the security intercom at the front door and announced us. The lock buzzed and she pushed open the door. Sitting at a sleek stainless-steel desk with matching laptop sat the doctor's receptionist. It was a guy, which meant I'd lost money backing the old lady with throat cancer. He was the sort of guy I imagined rich, bored ladies in Palm Springs would hire to clean their pools—deep tan, slick black hair, piercing blue eyes. His smile was so perfect it could have been a retouched magazine photo. The one Masters gave him in return was bright enough to have been plugged into a wall socket.

Give me a break.

I badged the guy. "Special Agents Cooper and Masters for Dr. Merkit."

"Yes, yes, the doctor is expecting you. Follow me, please."

His accent was vaguely American, most likely picked up at a local international school. The guy got up from behind the desk and walked to a set of double doors like he was modeling something. He pulled them open and announced us.

We walked into a large white room featuring polished floorboards, dark Turkish rugs, and a large, modern, chocolate-colored couch with matching chairs. Bright modern art hung on the walls, the marble head of what looked like an ancient Roman senator sat on a black marble plinth, while books—hundreds of books—were piled into teetering stacks on the desk and on the floor, and crammed into bookshelves.

"Thank you, Nasor," said a woman sitting on the couch, her legs curled beneath her. She gently closed the book she'd been reading and placed it on the floor. At that moment the phone rang and Nasor glided out, leaving the doors open. "My nephew," explained the doctor. Something in my face, or maybe it was in Masters's, made her add, "It is true. He is my brother's son. Filling in. My regular secretary, she is sick today."

Actually, now the doc mentioned it, I could see the family resemblance. She had the same black hair, same blue eyes, same olive skin, although on her the combination worked somewhat better for me. My turn to smile. "I'm Special Agent Vin Cooper and this is Special Agent Anna Masters."

"Yes, I know," she said, getting up to close the doors. "Sit, please. Nasor will get us apple tea."

I was about to tell her not to worry about it, since tea, especially made from apples, didn't sound all that appealing, but I was enjoying watching her walk across the floor. The doc was somewhere in her thirties—it was hard to tell exactly where. Good genes. She was five eight, 140 pounds, twenty of those pounds filling her shirt, which was white, silk, fitted, and sleek. She wore expensive black tailored slacks. On her feet were simple leather sandals featuring a small turquoise rock between the first and second toes, the nails of which were painted red. Her eyes, when they caught the light, were the color of the sea. They were eyes a guy could get shipwrecked in. I took a seat beside Masters on the couch.

"So, you are here to discuss these murders?"

"You've had time to study this latest one?" I asked in reply.

"Yes, I have received some notes from Captain Cain this morning."

"He sends his regards, by the way."

The doc purred. "The captain is sweet."

I hadn't noticed. I wondered whether Rodney Cain and the doc had something cooking. "Special Agent Masters and I read your report on the Portman case," I said. "You believe it was some kind of ritual killing?"

"Yes, that was my opinion." The doctor had a formal way of speaking. I liked it; reserved, professional, but at the same time friendly.

The double doors opened. Nasor appeared with a silver tray that swung as he carried it, balancing a silver bowl of sugar cubes, three delicate bellflower-shaped glasses containing tea the color of dark honey, and a small silver spoon. He set the tray down on the table in front of us and left.

"*Was* your opinion?" echoed Masters. "You've changed your mind, Doctor?"

"Let me explain. I have done some work for your FBI in the past. My specialty is serial killers. The manner in which your Air Attaché was killed, it fitted the profile of a serial killing, which was why I was called in. But until several murders are committed that share a similar signature... well, it is not a serial killing."

I knew that.

Dr. Merkit leaned forward to put a lump of sugar in her glass, and as she did so I caught a glimpse of her bra—light blue and lacy. It was a half-cup number and those cups were seriously runneth-ing over. "What do you know about serial killers?" she asked us.

Masters shrugged. "Not much."

"I saw *Silence of the Lambs* once," I said.

"I am what your FBI calls an 'inductive profiler.' I look for patterns that give indications of the killer's personality—racial background, habits, anything that will help with the murderer's identity and, with luck, arrest. Until the killer strikes a number of times, no pattern exists that allows me to present a viable deductive profile, something the police can use. Just the one murder does not give me very much to work with."

"So this second murder should help," suggested Masters.

Merkit nodded. "You would think. First, Colonel Portman. He was murdered in Bebek, an affluent area. The way the killer came and went suggests he knew his way around. Did he live there? Does he live there still? Or did he simply study his prey?"

I made a mental note that Dr. Merkit hadn't been informed on the latest developments. She was in the dark about the break-in at the leasing agent, for example.

"There was also a robbery at the murder scene," she continued, "and a sophisticated one. Should the police search their records for a wealthy robber with a knowledge of explosives?" Merkit shrugged at her own question.

I nodded, and hoped she'd reach forward for another lump.

"Of course, there were other factors around this first crime that are worth consideration. There was nothing spontaneous about the method of killing; no aspect of the murder appeared to be improvised. It seems even the killer's tool kit left behind was done so intentionally. Perhaps it was a taunt? Also, there were no fingerprints at the scene, no glove-pattern indentations. There was the use of chloroform to restrain the victim. And, of course, there was the most striking and dramatic aspect of the killing: the presentation of the dissected corpse. Finally, there was the collection of twelve bones."

Masters and I listened and sipped tea. It was sweet and yet had a sour kick to it. Reminded me of someone.

"The killer was practiced and thought much about the execution of the crime," Doc Merkit continued. "Perhaps he had been caught in the past and learned from his mistakes. That could account for the great care taken at the crime scene. And so, from all of this, I have nothing the police could not conclude for themselves with access to the same statistics I have: The killer is most probably a Caucasian male, probably lives locally, is around thirty-five years old with above-average intelligence, might have a record for cruelty to animals—a not uncommon trait among serial killers—comes from a middle-class family, and so on. But then there was this latest murder." The doctor paused. "It's this second murder that makes me unsure about what we are dealing with."

"And why is that?" Masters wanted to know.

"As I said, almost always, serial killers follow a pattern." Merkit sat back and swung her hair away from her face in the one fluid motion. I noticed the buttons on her shirt were valiantly taking the strain from the pressure of those breasts, holding firm. "The way they kill is full of meaning to their subconscious minds. Mostly, it has something to do with events that scarred them deeply as children, events most often of a sexual nature—unfortunately and sadly, sometimes even when they were babies. Perhaps they were repeatedly molested, sometimes molested and tortured. The murders they commit later in life can often be explained in the context of this early developmental experience. Often, the reasons for the bizarre behavior become understandable only when the killer is caught and interviewed."

"So they're trying to resolve the issues and tensions buried deep within their subconscious minds," said Masters.

"Yes, exactly. However, these murders are not following the rules as they are generally understood. Colonel Portman was cut up into pieces and displayed like a child's airplane model. Did the killer have some frightening experience as a child with these models that we can't even guess at? Certainly this murder implied a deep and tightly channeled rage within the killer. I believed the motivations for this rage would emerge when a second murder was committed. It certainly seemed to me that such a killer would not stop at one, and the pattern would be revealed when the second victim was taken. But then this murder last night... Most definitely, the crimes are linked—the planting of the first victim's bones in the anus of the second puts that beyond doubt. Perhaps this is meant as another taunt. But where is the pattern within the murders themselves? It should be there, but I cannot see it. It is as though the killer has two completely different personalities and motivations."

Masters glanced at me.

"What if we told you we believed there were two killers working as a team?" I said.

Dr. Merkit sat back, genuinely surprised. "I had not considered this...."

"Maybe they're taking turns," I added. "Tossing a coin to see who kills next."

"Perhaps," said the doctor. "Yes, it's possible. Different rules apply when there are two killers at work. But it is unusual. There's not a lot of experience with this kind of partnership. Two killers—do you know this for sure?" The doc seemed almost excited by the prospect.

"We're reasonably sure," said Masters. "We believe one killer on his own would not have been able to break into Colonel Portman's residence. We also have surveillance footage from the Hilton that pretty much establishes as fact that we're looking for a couple of killers working as a team."

"The surveillance camera pictures. I read about this in the notes from Istanbul homicide, which Captain Cain forwarded to me. They did not include this conclusion."

"Also, we're reasonably sure the killers obtained a floor plan of Colonel Portman's house from the leasing agent, as well as a key to the front door."

"Yes, yes," said the doc to herself, nodding slowly. "Premeditation, planning . . . I thought this. . . ."

"Both murders were extremely violent and sadistic in nature, and both victims were dismembered to a greater or lesser degree," said Masters. "From your professional point of view, can you tell us why you think the second murder was so different from the first?"

"Yes, of course. Both murders were full of symbolism, but symbolism of a completely different kind. The first, with its unusual dismemberment, could, as I said, have something to do with aircraft, or models, which suggests something from childhood. But the second slaying is full of Islamic ritual: the cutting off of the hands representing the guilt of a thief, and then the beheading, which implies that the victim was an enemy of Islam. The two murders seen together are what you might call a mixed metaphor, a muddle, a riddle. That there are two killers working together explains so much, and yet . . ."

"Might a third murder reveal the pattern?" Masters suggested.

Hoping someone would get horribly slain so that we could stop people being killed defied logic. But I had to admit at the same time it made a weird kind of sense.

"Hmm . . . perhaps yes, perhaps no. I would be hopeful of that, but you must understand, forensic psychology is not an exact science. It is also not a crystal ball. The murders might even stop—but I doubt it. If the killers took the bones from Portman for the purpose of placing them in the bodies of future victims, we are quickly going to have a pile of corpses, and a very frightened city of Istanbul to go with it." The doctor crossed her arms like she was reassuring herself with a hug.

If I wasn't mistaken, her nipples had stiffened through the fabric of her shirt. I didn't know where to look. Actually, that's not true. I knew exactly where to look, but I didn't want to get caught at it, especially not by Masters. "Assuming the killers will kill again," I said, "any ideas on whether that'll be sooner or later?"

"Sooner, I think. Definitely sooner," Dr. Merkit replied confidently. "Serial killers usually strike when the pressure rises within them to do so. And usually the manner in which they kill gets bolder. Our killers are already bold, and there was just three days between Portman and Bremmel. I would say that we can expect another victim to turn up within the next couple of days."

So, the killers would strike again soon and in a potentially even more bizarrely cruel and bloodthirsty way. The doctor leaned forward and put her empty glass on the tray. Masters and I didn't really need someone telling us that the sun was going to rise in the east tomorrow, but damned if the doc didn't look great letting us know.

THIRTEEN

It was only 4:45, but night was falling along with the temperature. The sludge I'd seen on the horizon was now overhead and it smelled like snow, a fact the fingers in my cast were confirming with an ache more reliable than any weatherman.

Out on the sidewalk, Masters turned and waved at Merkit's nephew and said good-bye a third or fourth time—I'd lost count. Emir pulled up behind us, raced around the vehicle, and opened Masters's door. If he had a tail, it would've been wagging. The guy was a human puppy dog.

I opened my own door and climbed in. The cab was warm and it reeked of tobacco smoke. Emir bounced in the front seat, clapped his hands together a couple of times, babbled something about Istanbul weather, and then lit the butt between his lips. I was tempted to ask him not to, but changed my mind. Everyone smoked around here. Maybe smoking was the Turkish national sport.

"You want to see Bremmel's girlfriend now?" Masters asked.

The mistress wasn't going anywhere, and I didn't think she'd have much for us anyway. And I wanted to spend some more time going through Portman's emails, phone recs—the boring but necessary minutiae of investigating. "Let's do it tomorrow. We can double it up with a look around the residence of Portman's servant. Meanwhile, what do you make of all that?"

"All what?"

"What Doc Merkit had to say?"

"I'm surprised you heard anything. You spent the whole time taking the woman's clothes off. I thought you were going to jump on her when she leaned forward over the sugar bowl."

"Oh, right... And how about *you*? 'Thanks *so* much, Nasor. The tea was *wonderful*. Do you know where I can buy some? I've never tasted anything so *good*. Maybe it was just the way you made it....' What would Colonel Wad say?"

"Where would you like to go, please?" Emir interposed.

"The hotel," Masters snapped, the tips of her ears like hot coals.

"The consulate-general," I said.

I put the difficulties about working with Masters out of my head and got on with the case. Thus, I found myself still up at three in the morning, going through Portman's emails. I didn't find anything I hadn't already seen. The relationship between Bremmel and Portman was cordial, bordering on friendly. Each had a grasp of the pressures the other was under, and there was a lot of pressure. But nothing I found suggested the end they were both headed for.

I read the security file on Bremmel, looking for those patterns, and noted that both he and Portman had marriage problems. So? I said to myself. Didn't everyone?

I flicked through the attaché's phone records and found the number for his ex-wife, Lauren. I checked the clock on the wall and did the math. The West Coast was ten hours behind. That made it early evening in Van Nuys. I dialed. After eight rings, I was about to hang up when the call was answered.

"Yes, hello?" said a woman's voice.

"Lauren Portman?"

"No, her sister. To whom am I speaking?"

The woman was older, and spoke with the hint of an English accent. I pictured a headmistress type with kneecaps like pork chops.

"This is OSI Special Agent Vin Cooper, ma'am. I'm investigating the murder of Emmet Portman. If Mrs. Portman's at home, I'd appreciate asking her a few questions."

"The name is Morgan."

"I'm sorry?"

"After the divorce, Lauren reverted to her maiden name—Morgan."

"Mrs. Portman hasn't remarried?"

"No, *Ms. Morgan* hasn't. . . . Listen, how do I know you are who you say you are?"

"Why would anyone say they're me when they're not, Ms. . . . ?"

"Dorothy Morgan, and I don't know, but I felt I should ask. You never know these days."

"Yes, ma'am, it can get tricky," I conceded.

"So, three questions, Mr. Cooper."

"I'm sorry?"

"You said you wanted to ask a few questions. 'A few' equals three. The point is, I think more than three questions would probably exhaust her. Lauren is ill as a result of this rather unfortunate turn of events."

"Unfortunate turn of events" was putting it mildly. I heard another voice in the background asking who Dot was speaking to. All sound was blocked off for an instant—a hand over the mouthpiece.

"Hello?" came a new voice.

"Mrs. Portman?" I asked.

"Speaking. You're investigating my ex-husband's death?"

"That's correct, ma'am. Special Agent Vin Cooper."

"Apologies for my sister, Mr. Cooper. Dorothy's only doing her best to shield me."

Shield you from whom? I wondered. And then it occurred to me: from people like me. "I'm sorry for your loss, Mrs. Portman," I began. The way Portman checked out would have been a hell of a shock to a spouse, even an ex.

"How can I help, Special Agent Cooper? If you're going to ask me if Emmet had any enemies, or if there was anyone I might have known who could possibly have wanted to kill him, I can't help you."

"You've just answered two of the big ones for me, Mrs. Portman." Actually, it wasn't *the* big one. I'd intended to slide into it with a little shallow chitchat, but she'd left me no choice but to be blunt. "What about *your* relationship with your husband, Mrs. Portman?" In other words, if you and your ex didn't get along, there might be cause to be suspicious of you. I heard the woman breathing. She was going to hang up on me for sure.

"Are you going to ask me where I was on the night in question?"

"No, ma'am."

"Are you married, Special Agent?"

"Divorced."

"Did you end up enemies?"

"Ma'am, we don't exchange Christmas cards, if that's what you mean."

The memory came back to me—the final straw with the former Mrs. Vin Cooper: the shower scene. It didn't have the same cutting power it once had, time having blunted the emotion to a point where it was just, well, water down the drain.

"Emmet left me," she said. "I thought we had a reasonably happy marriage. And then one day he came home and said he didn't love me anymore. In fact, he said he'd decided he hated me, and that the last thing he wanted was to have children with me. Said it just like that—no warning that anything was wrong. He wanted to hurt me."

There was something here I was missing. What was the business about him not wanting to have children? Portman was sterile—it said so in his file. Maybe he just wasn't aware of it at the time. And if he was, the colonel must have had his reasons for not letting the wife in on his sperm count. I decided not to pass on this information.

"I was thirty-five, he was forty-five, Special Agent," she continued. "I had five years left before my body clock—well, we divorced soon after. He just walked away from our marriage; asked for nothing, took nothing. . . . We kept in touch. I don't know why—we just did."

I heard Dot in the background telling her sister to hang up the phone.

"I loved my husband, Special Agent, only he didn't love me—end of story."

There was bitterness in her voice, but I couldn't hear any murder in it. Not that I was expecting to. Interviewing Portman's ex was just tying up a loose end. "Mrs. Portman, do you know what your husband was working on when he died?"

After taking a moment to think about it, she said, "No. Even when we were married, I didn't ask. I'm sure your ex-wife learned the same lesson."

Yep.

I heard Dot in the background getting more insistent.

"I'm sorry, Special Agent. I must go now. I—"

"You obviously can't count, can you? I said *three*."

Dot. The line went dead. The damn woman had grabbed the phone, then hung up on me. I was tempted to call again just so that I could return the compliment, but I let it go. Lauren Portman had nothing helpful to add, unless I was just asking the wrong questions. Maybe if the battle-axe sister had given me permission to ask four, I'd have hit the jackpot. I thought about the reason behind the Portmans' separation. Children. My ex and I never got around to having them. Would she end up having them now with her new husband, her shower buddy and our former marriage counselor? Last I heard, they were expecting a BMW.

Back to Portman's in-box. I decided to concentrate on Ambassador Burnbaum's emails to the attaché, printing out the lot. An hour later, much of it spent figuring out how to print on the network, I hadn't found anything to change my mind about the association between the two men. They seemed to get on OK. I sent an email to the IT department to get me a stand-alone printer before my i-rage got the better of me.

There were at least a hundred exchanges with old Air Force buddies, particularly with pilots from the Grim Reapers, both serving and retired. Quite a few emails had bounced around between Portman and a Lieutenant Colonel Chip Woodward, call sign "Block." From these I gathered Portman had flown with Block and his squadron on several training missions, something I was expecting would be confirmed by Andrews once they stopped playing interoffice Doom (or whatever was soaking up their time and bandwidth) and responded to my inquiry.

I saw that Stringer and Portman had been out for drinks on a few occasions. Other meetings had been postponed or canceled due to work. Nothing there, though I wondered what the two of them would have talked about. I found myself wishing I had that damn corrupted calendar of Portman's to cross-check. Padding out the remainder of the electronic communications were dozens of miscellaneous emails from various people and companies—including spammers peddling the usual crap—nothing to do with anything relevant that I could see.

I moved on and reread the forensics report on the Portman crime scene, hoping for a revelation. None came. Then I switched to the phone records—and absolutely zip leaped out of there, too.

I woke up on the office couch. My tongue felt furry, but that had as much to do with there being a cushion pushed into my mouth as anything else. I got up slow and glanced at my watch. It was nudging eight-thirty.

I had time to visit the head and wash my face and hands before Masters breezed in, by which time I was gazing out the windows waiting for my brain to clear. It was gray outside. Snow had fallen overnight. Not much of it, just a dusting. An oil-green tanker glided down the Bosphorus toward Istanbul, dirty black smoke chugging from its exhaust stack and blowing forward across the sprawling deck. A small rust bucket bounced around in its wake, heading north in the opposite direction, toward the Black Sea. It looked cold out on the water, probably because it was.

I tried not to notice the fragrance of lavender soap mixed with arabica beans as Masters strolled past with coffee for us both.

"Consider this a peace offering, OK?" She set the mug on my desk.

"That depends."

"On what?"

"On who you think won last night," I said.

Her hands were wrapped around the mug to soak up its warmth. "Oh, right. Well, actually... to be honest, I think *you* won."

"Really?"

"Vin, you push my damn buttons. And you know you do. You joke about everything, mostly to annoy me. Anyway, I figured it out."

"Figured what out?"

"I keep wanting you to get bogged down like the rest of us. I want you to get stressed out, hit a brick wall, come across something that really gets under your skin. But it rarely seems to happen. And when it does—you joke about that, too!" She peered at me. "There's the shape of a button pressed into the side of your face. Did you sleep here on the couch?"

"It was more comfortable than the floor," I said, rubbing my cheeks. Masters knew that I wisecracked about things that got under my skin. She'd already learned that from prior experience. No, something else was going on here—this mood swing of hers into the agreeable zone made me suspicious. "So what's going on?" I asked.

"What do you mean?"

"The whole you-win thing."

"Nothing's going on."

"No, it's definitely something. . . ." And then I remembered. "You're in a good mood because a certain Colonel Wad is coming to town today."

Heat flooded her features. One hand went to her hip, the other stabbed at the air in front of me. "No, Vin. Here I am trying to smooth things over with you and . . . Jesus, I don't know why I care. He came *last* night, not that it's any business of yours. And you'll be pleased to know, so did *I*—several times."

I felt something tighten inside. The door to the office opened before I could respond, and an unfamiliar head popped in. "Busy?" the head asked.

Masters whirled around. "Darling!" she exclaimed. Then she cleared her throat and continued in a more inferior-officer tone. "Colonel, I thought you were going to stop by later."

"My meeting got moved forward, so here I am."

The head had a body attached and all of it decided to come on in. I read the name off the tag on the chest, not that I needed to. "Lieutenant Colonel Wadding," I said.

"And you're Special Agent Cooper, of course," he replied.

We shook on the fact that I was me and he wasn't. Eye to eye, I noticed the Wad was slightly taller than me, as well as being slightly older, slightly better looking in that incredibly clichéd *Men's Health* kind of way, and, of course, a rung farther up the promotion ladder. His hair was dark and vaguely foppish, cut in a way that goes with a riding crop, a country club membership, and a score of slaves to pick the cotton. His eyes were light blue to gray, his skin tanned which, given that we were now just into February, was probably from a tanning salon. The guy looked every inch the successful attorney, like he'd been delivered into this world ready to take a deposition just in case the attending obstetrician slipped up.

"Anna told me a couple of your lawyer jokes last night when we were lying in bed. Very funny."

We were lying in bed. . . . I wondered what Masters had told Wadding about our history. And why were they both so keen to inform me they'd been climbing the hairy pole recently? Whatever the reason, Masters's fiancé obviously wanted to come out fighting from the bell. Who was I to deny him a round or two? "I've got one you might appreciate, Colonel," I said.

"Bring it on. I think I can take it," he said. The smile was glued to his face.

"So there's this old lady having her will drafted. The attorney charges her a hundred bucks. She agrees, gives him a C-note, but fails to notice another hundred-dollar bill stuck to the back. Seeing the two bills stuck together, the attorney puts the ethical question to himself, 'Hmm . . . Do I tell my partner?'"

Wadding chuckled without a shred of warmth "That's very funny, isn't it?" he said.

"If I laughed any harder I'd be coughing up lung," I replied, deadpan.

Masters wasn't happy. She mouthed the word "Enough" at me, but I wasn't finished.

"Colonel, Special Agent Masters tells me you're heading up the DoD's depleted-uranium class action defense. That must be a pretty tough gig."

"Tough? Well, no, not really. Like many of these things, mostly it's just a case of rampant opportunism on the part of a small percentage of people with too much time on their hands."

"Really?" I said. "I heard there were more than a thousand of those so-called opportunists lining up to take a swing at the department, and more joining in every day. One of them is a buddy of mine."

"What's his name?" he asked. "I might know him."

"Tyler Dean."

"Dean . . . Dean . . ." Wadding appeared to be having trouble placing him.

"You would've heard of Tyler, Colonel," I said. "He drove an Abrams M1A2. Went to Iraq with the First Armored. Slept with DU ammo for most of his tour. Twelve months ago they took half his insides out. He used to bench-press two hundred twenty pounds; now he takes a crap and barely has the strength to lift up his pants."

Wadding's smile had gone on vacation and left a nasty frown to house-sit. "I think if you reviewed the evidence that's readily available, Special Agent, you would come to think, as most reasonable, *informed* people do, that depleted uranium ammunition is perfectly safe and not in the least harmful to human life. There is no evidence to support your friend's assertion that DU is the reason for his illness. Have you read the Capstone report on the subject?"

"Hasn't everyone?" I said, making a mental note to find out who the hell this Capstone was and what he'd said in this report.

"Then you know the score. There are probably other reasons for your buddy's troubles. He could just have been unlucky genetically."

Wadding and I looked at each other. His smile was back, a hint of victory in it.

"Richard, I might have to catch up with you later," Masters interrupted, before I could regroup. "Special Agent Cooper and I have a witness to interview."

"No problem," he said. "Well, pleasure to meet you, Special Agent."

I wouldn't have called it that.

FOURTEEN

"I don't know what you see in this jerk," I said as we went down in the elevator to the parking lot. Masters didn't answer. "Can I ask what you see in this jerk?"

"No, you can't," she replied.

"The whole depleted-uranium mess he's involved with doesn't trouble you at all?"

"Richard is doing his job, just like you and me."

"No, nothing like you and me."

"Really. And why do you think we're so different?"

"Because if we do our jobs right, there's no question about guilt or innocence. The suspect either is or isn't. Guys like Wadding are the Uri Gellers of facts. They twist them up so that guilt looks like innocence. Tyler Dean—my friend? I don't believe your fiancé has never heard of him, because he is, in fact, the pinup boy for the plaintiffs—their front man."

"What about Capstone?" Masters asked.

"What about it?" I said.

We climbed into Emir's home-away-from-home. Masters read him the address for Ms. Fatma Zerzavatci from the note Karli had given her.

"If, as you say, your friend Tyler is the point man, he'd know about the Capstone report," Masters continued, unwisely. "And if he hasn't filled you in on the report's findings, then it's probably because he didn't want to put any doubt into your head."

"So why don't you? Fill me in, that is."

"The Capstone report was compiled for the government on the effects of depleted uranium ammunition, in response to claims that it was carcinogenic. The report found that the health risks of depleted uranium oxide were comparable to many other battlefield materials; that it was no more and no less lethal to our people than anything else out there in the Iraqi desert."

"And who put the report together?" I asked. "One of Mr. Geller's people?"

"You'll believe what you want to believe, Vin, as you always do."

Masters turned away and watched the people on the sidewalk huddle along in the cold. Conversation closed. Suited me. I didn't want to get into an argument I didn't know enough about to win. I made a mental note to give Tyler a call and get some background on Colonel Wad.

Fatma Zerzavatci, alias Mrs. Bremmel, Dutch Bremmel's personal assistant and the woman who assisted him personally at the Istanbul Hilton on a regular basis, was a tall, slender woman of twenty-seven with skin the color of cream. Her eyes reminded me of honey, or at least one of them did—the other being bright red with burst capillaries buried in a puffy purple-and-black bruise that spread down her left cheek like an advancing electrical storm.

Usually a resident of Eskisehir, the headquarters of TEI where she and Bremmel worked, the woman was in town until the Istanbul police said otherwise. So she'd moved in with her mother, grandmother, and two unemployed brothers for the duration. From the outside, the house looked like it'd been built by one of the three little pigs, the one who'd used sticks, or, in this instance, old blackened fence palings. Geographically speaking, the street was close to Beyoglu, the affluent area where Dr. Merkit had her practice; socioeconomically, however, the place's closest neighbor was skid row.

A young man of around twenty-five, who I figured was one of the brothers, answered the door when we knocked. He opened it angry, and his demeanor went downhill from there. I saw Fatma behind him, head bowed. I showed him my shield and he reacted by yelling at us in Turkish, shaking his fist and smacking his open palm against the doorjamb hard enough to shake the floor. I noticed he'd lost some skin from two of his knuckles—probably somewhere on his sister's face. He banged the door shut.

A couple of seconds later, after more shouting, the other, younger brother tag-teamed, opened the door, and took over the yelling, then slammed it in our faces again.

Masters and I stood our ground.

Next, Mrs. Zerzavatci, who wore what appeared to be a black tent, opened the door. Was this the mother or the grandmother? I've always found a beard on a woman confusing. Fatma Zerzavatci stood impassively in the hallway, head still bowed, while the emotional storm raged around her.

We showed our shields again. Masters took half a step forward and asked, "Fatma, do you mind if we come in and ask you a few questions?"

Granny put her hand out and pushed Masters back. I took that as a yes, she would mind.

"It is all right, Mooshie," Fatma told her, attempting to soothe the old woman. "I have to talk with them."

Even if Zerzavatci the elder didn't understand the words, she picked up on the tone, standing aside reluctantly. The old lady shook her finger at us and appeared to be threatening dire consequences if we did whatever it was she didn't want us to do.

"Please come in," said Fatma.

The old woman muttered at us as we squeezed past. Once we were inside, one of the angry brothers stuck his head out of a room at the end of the short hallway and shouted at us some more.

"Please . . . in here." Fatma indicated a room with a sweep of her hand.

The house might well have come down with a huff and a puff, but inside it was spotlessly clean, at least this room was. A huge fifty-two-inch flat-screen plasma sitting on a designer stand dominated it. The box seat was provided by a designer tan leather couch covered in plastic, like the seats in Emir's car, partnered by two leather armchairs also wearing furniture condoms. Scattered across the couch and armchairs were purple silk cushions embroidered with a silver pattern. A collection of plastic flowers stood in a cut-glass vase positioned on an expensive iron-and-glass stand. The walls were covered in soft blue-and-green-striped wallpaper, and framed photos of old people hung here and there. Dark

Turkish rugs covered the floor. To say the décor was a lot more than I expected was the day's understatement.

Fatma took one of the armchairs. Masters and I sat on the couch.

"Did your brother do that?" asked Masters, indicating the young woman's shiner.

"It is nothing," Fatma said, touching her cheek self-consciously.

"Where did all the loot come from, Ms. Zerzavatci?" I asked. I knew the answer, but I wanted to see how candid the woman was prepared to be.

"Dutch and I were lovers. He bought me things," she replied.

OK, I thought, she passed that test. "Is that why your brothers are so upset? Because the presents have dried up?" I asked.

"I have dishonored my family."

"We can organize protection, you know," Masters said.

Could we? I wasn't so sure about that. I cut in before Ms. Zerzavatci decided to take us up on the offer. "How long had you and Mr. Bremmel been lovers?"

"We started seeing each other six months ago."

I flipped open my notebook. "And you started working for Mr. Bremmel seven months ago."

"Yes, we were lovers almost from the start. He was unhappy, lonely. His wife didn't love him anymore. She went back to America. They were husband and wife in name only. He told me he was going to leave her for me."

I glanced at Masters and caught the slightest arch of an eyebrow. Her turn for an I-told-you-so moment.

"You met him at the Istanbul Hilton every two weeks?" I asked.

"Not always. Sometimes we missed the appointment. Dutch worked very hard."

"Did you meet anywhere else?" Masters asked.

"No. The Hilton was our special place—our reward, he would say."

And Dutch sure collected it, I thought.

"Had you told anyone about your affair? Your brothers, perhaps?" Masters asked.

I knew where Masters was going, and it was a reach. Two brothers, two killers—plenty of passion. I didn't buy it for a second, but she was right to tick it off the list.

"No, we were careful," Fatma said.

Not careful enough. The killers, whoever they were, knew of their regular sausage sizzle at the Hilton. "Did Mr. Bremmel make it up to the room, Ms. Zerzavatci?"

The young woman's chin quivered. "No, he didn't. I was waiting for him. I was getting worried because he had not called to say he would be late. And then the police came with the hotel security man and another man—I think it was the manager. I was very worried. I knew something had happened, something bad."

And now for the question I already knew the answer to. "Do you know of anyone who might have wanted to kill Mr. Bremmel, Ms. Zerzavatci?" Aside from, as Masters had suggested, the real Mrs. Bremmel? Fatma was a looker—beautiful in that pouty Mediterranean way. She was the kind of woman who, in my experience, most other women feel threatened by, especially older women, and especially older women whose husbands had them for assistants.

Fatma Zerzavatci answered the question like I expected she would. She shook her head. "No. I can think of no one."

"Did Dutch Bremmel have good relationships with everyone at work?" Masters asked.

"Yes, yes," murmured Fatma, head bowed.

"So, no threats from anyone? Arguments? Heated discussions?"

"You ever see him push in front of someone at the staff canteen, maybe?" I asked.

Masters looked at me, her eyes narrowed to slits. Ms. Zerzavatci did likewise, only without the eyelid theatrics, unsure about whether she'd heard me right.

I explained: "At this point, Ms. Zerzavatci, we need to check up on just about anything."

"No. Everyone liked Dutch. He was funny. He made people laugh—always telling jokes."

I recalled how close I'd come to a horrible death myself the other day when telling Masters my lawyer jokes. Maybe that's what had happened here—Bremmel had simply told the wrong joke to the wrong person at the wrong time. Only that didn't explain the finger up the guy's emergency exit: the Portman connection.

I had no reason to doubt this woman's story. The facts were straighter than Hugh Hefner. She was having an affair with the boss, and someone stalked him and killed him for reasons that had something to do with

Portman, reasons she knew nothing about. All we were going to squeeze from Bremmel's girlfriend were tears, which I noticed had started to flow down the peaches-and-cream cheek, as well as the one that reminded me of stewed fruit. We still had nothing besides two very dead bodies—no leads and no suspects.

FIFTEEN

"It is a beautiful day to be in Istanbul, no?" Emir lit a Camel as we pulled away from the curb.

"No," I answered, agreeing with him.

"What did you think of that?" Masters asked.

"Of Fatma?"

"Yeah."

"I felt sorry for Mrs. Bremmel—against someone like Ms. Zerzavatci she didn't stand a chance. I also think the girl knew about as much as we did. Less, even, if that's possible. I hate to say it, but I think Dr. Merkit's right. We're going to need another murder before any of this makes sense."

Masters sighed. "Where to now?"

Adem Fedai rented a room in the suburb of Fatih, west of Sultanahmet and across the Golden Horn. I used the drive time there to go back over in my head what we had, hoping to find something I might have missed, even if it was a question we hadn't asked that might yield a useful answer.

Right now, the killers were probably closing in on someone else connected with the F-16 upgrade. There was a pattern here, but not the kind Dr. Merkit was used to working with.

Masters's cell rang. She answered it, said hello to Captain Cain. She said "Uh-huh" half a dozen times, a "No way," and a "You're kidding, really?" before ending the call.

"What gives?" I asked.

"Two pieces of news. You were right about those blast blankets. The Istanbul police divers just recovered three of them stuffed in plastic bags four hundred yards from the Portman place, weighed down with dive belts. There's also evidence to suggest you were right about there being two killers. In the bag, with the blankets, were two disposable coveralls."

If I was right about the blankets, I also had to be right about there being a boat positioned to drop the killers off and pick them up.

"Excuse, please . . . we are here," said Emir, interrupting my train of thought. "I cannot park on this road. I will have to drive around."

"What about that car there?" I asked. Up ahead, a Fiat was stopped half on and half off the road.

"Oh, that is *polisi*. They can park where they like."

The police were staking out Ocirik's, waiting for Fedai to return to his digs above the café, and advertising the fact. Emir was in the process of extracting a Camel, so I got out of the car before he had the opportunity to share it with me.

It was sleeting pins and needles of ice. I jogged over to an awning outside a local fast-food joint and took shelter beneath it, Masters a couple of paces behind. Inside the shop, a guy was cutting meat from an enormous cone skewered in front of a vertical grill. It made me hungry until I saw the ash from the cigarette in the corner of his mouth fall off into the shaved meat and get rolled up in the flat bread. But I decided I was going soft and ordered two, one each for Masters and me. My turn to make a peace offering.

"So I think, along with two killers, there has to be a support crew." Masters pushed her hands into a pair of fur-lined gloves. Her nose was red at the tip with cold, her eyes full of blue-green fire.

"Looks that way," I agreed. Perhaps we were making progress after all, even if the going was slow. I heard the call to prayer. A sprawling white marble mosque crowned the hill a couple of hundred yards farther up the road. A streetcar rocked by in the middle of the street, almost empty.

I got a tap on the shoulder, bringing me back to the here and now. "Did you buy this for me?" Masters asked, peeling the paper off the kebab. "The guy in there just handed it to me."

"Yep."

"Thanks," she said, and handed me mine. "I accept your apology, by the way."

We ate in silence, scoping the premises diagonally across the road.

Ocirik's was a water pipe and tea joint that put on belly dancing for the tourists at night. Ocirik himself was a famous Turkish wrestler, according to Captain Cain. A steady stream of local guys strolled into the place along with a smattering of tourists. Adem Fedai, the servant who came with the house Portman leased, kept a room on the second floor at Ocirik's when he wasn't at Portman's beck and call.

Before I realized it, I'd finished the kebab. It was good. Maybe the tobacco ash was a secret-herbs-and-spices thing.

"Mmm . . . delicious," said Masters, putting the wrapper in the trash. "Let's go."

Ocirik's was accessed down a narrow pathway that opened out into a sheltered courtyard dominated by a large leafless tree and a greenhouse. Most of the patrons sat outside, under the shelter of awnings from surrounding buildings, warmed by gas heaters scattered here and there. A large crowd of prelunch smokers sucked on hoses that snaked down into bubbling water reservoirs. If my nose wasn't deceiving me, the air was thick with the smell of tobacco-flavored coffee. Waiters wearing blue-striped jackets with "Ocirik's" stenciled on the back wove among the crowd, babysitting the pipes, popping red coals onto this one, restoking that one. Other waiters moved between the tables delivering tea and coffee on those swinging trays.

Tucked under the awning beside us was a photo gallery featuring wrestling bouts as well as various large-breasted belly dancers. They were big and hairy and oiled up. So were the wrestlers.

"Can I you help?" came the voice behind me.

Something was blocking the light. I turned and saw the biggest man I'd ever laid eyes on. Ocirik. The guy was a monster. I pulled my shield from my back pocket and gave him a good long look at it. "Mr. Ocirik, do you speak English?"

"A little," he said, demonstrating by holding his thumb and forefinger together. His thumb was almost as thick as Masters's forearm.

"I'd like to ask you some questions about Adem Fedai. You know this man?"

Masters pulled a small snapshot of Fedai and showed it to him.

"Yes, he live here."

"Does he still live here?"

"Yes."

"When did you last see him?"

"I see him in one week."

"You saw him a week ago?"

"Yes. He give money for the room. I tell you this already."

"You told who? Us?"

"Polisi."

"Would you mind showing us his room, Mr. Ocirik?" I asked.

"I show *polisi* already."

"We are different *polisi,* Mr. Ocirik," said Masters.

"There is nothing to see. He has only a bed."

"Has he taken his clothes?" asked Masters.

"No. His clothes are there."

"Has he gone away before? Left for a week or more?"

The overhang on Ocirik's bus-shelter-sized brow furrowed with confusion. Masters repeated the question a couple of times in different ways until the meaning sank in.

"Yes, sometimes he go away."

"When does he need to give you more money for the room?" Masters asked.

"He must give money in three weeks."

"Did he always pay rent one month in advance?"

Ocirik shook his huge, bony noggin. "I no understand."

"Did he always pay rent by the month?"

Ocirik shrugged. It was clear this was one three-hundred-pound language barrier we weren't going to push through.

"I couldn't help but overhear," said a man who'd been sitting nearby sucking away on a water pipe. "Perhaps I can help?"

"That depends," Masters said. "You speak Turkish?"

"Yes, of course," he replied with a smile, indicating his Turkish newspaper and tucking it under his arm. "What do you want to know?"

"We want to know if his lodger always paid rent a month in advance."

"OK," said the impromptu interpreter. He put our question to Ocirik, and Ocirik gave him an answer. "He says no—the man usually pay his rent after two weeks."

"Thanks," said Masters.

"Anything else I can ask him for you?"

"Ask him whether he'll change his mind and open up the lodger's room for us," I said, giving Ocirik my public-relations smile.

The stranger translated.

"Ocirik says he'll change his mind if the lodger doesn't return and his rent falls due."

"Fair enough," I agreed. Masters and I had no legal means of forcing him to comply anyway.

Another man almost as big as Ocirik, but maybe only half his age, came up and tapped him on his shoulder. This had to be Ocirik's son. The younger man—K2 to the old man's Everest—pointed impatiently to a couple of crowded tables across the courtyard. Ocirik said, "I must go now."

"Anything else?" asked our interpreter.

"Well, we'd like two apple teas and a water pipe with cappuccino-flavored tobacco," Masters told him.

"Sure. I get for you," said Ocirik, there being nothing wrong with his menu English.

"Before you race off . . ." I said to him.

Ocirik grunted.

"You see Fedai, you call." I held out my card.

Ocirik examined the card before slipping it in his pocket. "I call," he promised, walking off into a cloud of tobacco smoke.

Masters thanked the stranger for his assistance. He gave us a nod, deposited a couple of notes on his table, and left.

"Cappuccino-flavored?" I asked her.

"Can't you smell it? The tobacco's flavored here. You can get all kinds."

"So this is what, a carcinogenic Baskin-Robbins?"

"When in Rome..." Masters shrugged.

"I didn't know you smoked," I said, taking a seat.

"I don't. The last time I smoked was when I was last in Istanbul."

"When you met the colonel."

Masters ignored the comment. "So, what do you make of Fedai?" she asked instead.

"I think he's lying low somewhere. Maybe he got scared and thought someone might want to hang Portman's murder on him. I think he's coming back here, or intended to come back. Otherwise, why bother paying a month's rent in advance? He'd have just skipped."

Masters thought about it, then said, "He might have paid to give himself a head start and make everyone think he was coming back."

"Yeah, maybe."

Ocirik's gargantuan offspring brought the water pipe and picked at the nuggets of burning tobacco with a long pair of tongs. Masters sucked on the pipe so that its water reservoir bubbled away and the tobacco glowed orange and then red. The tea appeared, brought by another waiter.

"If it's OK with you, I want some time off tonight," she said, blowing smoke at the empty table beside us.

"I'm not your boss," I informed her. I sipped the apple tea. It reminded me of Dr. Merkit.

"No, but I'm giving you the courtesy of letting you know."

"Fine by me," I said. It wasn't, but there was nothing I could do about it anyway. If Richard Wadding was what Anna Masters wanted, then I'd misjudged her. I doubted that, but my options on that score had been cut to zero.

"So, that means you've got the night off, Vin. What are you going to do with it?"

"Pack."

"Excuse me?"

"We're going to Incirlik Air Base."

"Why?"

"We've done all we can here. Maybe the people Portman and Bremmel were dealing with can throw some light into the darkness for us. The upgrade on these F-16s seems to be the only real link between them."

"Agreed," said Masters with a nod.

"What's that like?" I asked, gesturing at the water pipe.

"Like inhaling cappuccino-flavored smog on a cold day."

"He's not right for you, Anna."

"And I suppose you are?"

SIXTEEN

It had stopped sleeting by the time we left Ocirik's. The lunchtime crowds were out in force now, huddling against the cold and dodging occasional sheets of water thrown across the sidewalk by vehicles driving through puddles. The cop car had gone.

Masters, I noticed, had turned a shade of green that didn't go with anything except maybe a toilet bowl and a nap. "You OK?" I asked.

She nodded unconvincingly. I checked the street for Emir, but didn't see him or his Renault anywhere, so we headed to the point where he'd dropped us off, a short distance down the road.

Two guys walking out of a shop with their heads down bumped into us. I was about to apologize when I recognized one of them—the interpreter from Ocirik's. He gave me a clear view of the butt of a handgun, removing it partially from his jacket. This told me an apology for bumping into him was probably unnecessary.

A van pulled up beside us, the door flew open, and Masters and I were hauled inside by half a dozen hands. The door slid shut as we were shoved onto the floor, the muzzles of various pistols thrust into our faces as the van accelerated away with a lurch and a squeal of wheelspin.

"What the hell—" Masters demanded.

"Shut up," came the reply, from someone out of sight behind me.

"What are you doing?" she said, ignoring the advice.

We'd been abducted, obviously, but by whom and for what purpose

I had no clue. I counted seven faces behind the guns. All had dark Mediterranean-type complexions, all were male, and all were as relaxed as if kidnapping was something they did every day of the week. "You going to tell us what this is all about?" I asked the interpreter.

"Like he said," he whispered, gesturing at the man behind me with a flick of his weapon, "shut the fuck up."

A man beside him raised his pistol, backhand, coiling for a downward strike into my face. The interpreter put his hand on the guy's arm to stop the follow-through. Something told me I should not misconstrue this as an indication that the interpreter was in any way an ally. The something telling me this was the silencer he had begun twisting onto the end of his H&K Mk 23.

I felt a couple of hands searching my pockets. Masters was getting the same treatment. They found what they were looking for and began passing around our shields.

"I told you they were OSI," said the interpreter once the wallet had gone around the van. Masters's credentials were tossed back on her chest. Mine were kept.

"Wimps," spat someone else.

"Yafa is going to love this one," said someone, leering at Masters.

"I hope she let us watch," added another.

Their accents were thick and varied. I wondered whether they spoke English because it was the common language among them. So what did that mean? That they were some kind of mercenary militia?

A few of the men began to chuckle, though none of the weapons were removed from our faces. The interpreter took out his cell phone and dialed. He spoke to someone in a language that didn't sound like Turkish. After a brief conversation, he ended the call. The van took several violent lefts and rights, throwing all of us around. Then it suddenly slowed; I felt the van sway and bump like it was going over a gutter. It sped up briefly before coming to a stop with locked wheels and a crunch of gravel and earth.

The door slid back in its rails, letting in the gloom of the day, as well as a little rain. Masters and I were pushed out of the vehicle. I recognized the Bosphorus and the smell of seawater and diesel oil that came with it. The cloud cover was now low enough to reach up and touch, and the city skyline had been consumed by it. I looked around. We'd been driven into a kids' playground, the swings and various monkey bars empty and silent in the steady drizzle. Nearby rose the gray marble wall of one of the many mosques that crowd Istanbul like Starbucks do American cities.

Another car was parked nearby, a large black Jaguar, a man and a woman leaning on it. There was no sun and yet the guy was wearing sunglasses, which meant he was either a rock star or an asshole. My money was on the latter. He was also wearing hiking boots, black cargo pants, and a Yankees hoodie. He moved like a pro boxer approaching the ring—slightly stooped, with ropy shoulders that rolled as he walked. A silver matchstick protruded from his tight lips.

His partner was a woman, a brunette, and way better dressed. She carried a small black umbrella to keep the rain off her shoulder-length dark hair. She wore a fitted black leather jacket zipped to the neck, expensive jeans, and black leather boots. Her fingernails were painted to match her Ferrari-red lipstick; her eyes were large and black with no discernible pupil. I could imagine her hanging out in a Victoria's Secret catalogue. For a reason I couldn't put my finger on, she also looked by far the more dangerous of the two.

"What have we here?" asked the man as he and his companion circled us like a couple of hungry sharks.

"You've got trouble," I answered.

Beside my ear I heard the double *click-click* of a pistol's slide being pulled back and released. "Shh," said a voice close enough for me to sense warm breath against my neck, smell the garlic on it.

One of the men passed my ID over to the guy with the toothpick.

"So, you are American. OSI. You are Air Force."

I said nothing.

"You may answer."

"This guy wants me to shut up, and you want me to answer. I wish to hell you people would make up your damn minds," I said.

Someone slapped the side of my head—hard. Once the marbles between my ears stopped rattling, I turned to the guy who did the slapping. "Do that again, Mac, and I'll stop your heart."

A couple of his buddies responded to my apparent foolhardy attempt at machismo with an appreciative smile and a nod.

"What is your interest in Adem Fedai?" asked the man with the toothpick.

I noticed his woman taking a special interest in Masters. She buried her nose in Anna's hair, inhaled deeply, and then raised her head. Her eyes were closed like she'd breathed in the intoxicating scent of heaven itself.

"I told you Yafa would like her," said one of the men to a buddy.

"Who the fuck are you people?" I demanded.

The next slap nearly took my head off. I turned. The guy smirked, daring me. I opened and closed my mouth to clear the ringing and lifted my shoulders up and down—keeping the motion slow and painful. Then I whipped back around and snapped out a short, sharp punch, aiming for the soft flesh an inch below the man's ear. I drove a cocked knuckle into it. The asshole immediately fell to the ground and began to convulse, the whites of his eyes showing in their sockets. A cold steel muzzle jammed into my nose, pushing my head back.

The guy on the ground began frothing at the mouth as a couple of his buddies dropped to their knees to check him out. They were swearing in a mixture of languages, wondering what the hell had happened to their pal.

"What have you done to him?" the interpreter yelled.

"Kept my word."

"You have stopped his heart?"

If they wanted to save the guy's life, I knew what they had to do. I also knew that they'd better hurry up and do it. I heard one of them say the magic words "heart attack."

"You might try CPR," I suggested.

"Shut you face," said the toothpick guy.

One of the men took my advice anyway and began administering mouth-to-mouth. The patient responded pretty quickly. He groaned and moved his arms and legs. Within a minute, he was sitting up, back from the dead, tears pouring down his cheeks.

"Not bad for a wimp," Masters said under her breath.

"So, you are a tough guy, eh?" the woman whispered in my ear.

I said nothing, mostly because I happened to note the set of brass knuckles now gracing her right fist. One of the men covering us pressed a steel barrel across my ear so that I could feel the cold metal. Satisfied I'd received the message to do nothing other than flinch, the woman swung a punch into my ribs that sent a white ball of pain exploding into the space behind my eyes. I doubled over, gasping for breath that refused to come.

She bent down and hissed, "If you will behave, I will become playful, yes?" The woman gave my ear a lick. "Now, Adem Fedai . . . tell us why you are interested in this former Mossad agent."

The coughing I had to do to get my lungs working again hid my surprise. *Adem Fedai—an ex-Mossad agent?* I felt the warm comfort of Masters's hand on my shoulder and heard her ask our captors, "How do you know he's ex-Mossad?"

"Only we will ask the questions," the woman replied.

"Not if you want answers," I said, getting slowly to my feet, trying hard not to show the pain.

"Be careful, my friend," cautioned the guy with the toothpick. "Yafa does not like men, and you have annoyed her. I would not like to be you."

I hoped the bitch hadn't added another broken bone to my growing collection.

"We have been searching for this Adem Fedai for six months," said the toothpick guy. "We trace him to the water pipe shop and have been watching his home. We were about to move on him when he disappear. Then Turkish police watch his home. We did not know why. Then you came along asking questions. You are military police. What is your interest in Fedai?"

The police had managed to keep the Portman and Bremmel murders out of the press, so maybe these people didn't know shit. Or maybe they did know and were just spinning us a bunch of crap. The woman who slugged me because she didn't like men had now pulled out a compact and was touching up those lips of hers like she'd just ordered a drink.

"We are investigating the murder of a colonel in the United States Air Force," I informed her. "Fedai worked at the crime scene. But he has disappeared, as you said. We thought we'd see where he lived and smoke a little coffee-flavored tobacco while we were at it."

The Yafa woman and the toothpick guy exchanged glances. "Where else will you look for him?" the woman asked me.

"I don't know," I said honestly. "And if I knew, I wouldn't say."

"We could make you talk."

"Lady, making me talk is easy. It's making me shut up that's the hard part."

"True," said Masters.

"You will be quiet."

Toothpick and Yafa went into a huddle with the guy who'd been our interpreter back at Ocirik's. I used the opportunity to eyeball the rest of these guys. All were confident and cool, with the certain swagger that comes from killing enough people that you no longer think too much about it.

"We wish to offer our apologies for these methods," said the interpreter, suddenly all sweetness and light. "We will return you to the place we took you from."

I was about to tell them not to worry about it, that we'd catch a cab, when the Yafa woman walked up to Masters, took her in her arms, and kissed her hard and full on the lips.

SEVENTEEN

We watched the van move away from the café and merge into traffic. "I think she liked you," I said.

Masters was as angry as I'd ever seen her. "Fuck you, Cooper."

I went to put my hand on her shoulder but the move was a little too sudden for my rib. I winced.

"You OK?" Masters asked.

"No, as a matter of fact."

"Good."

"Thanks for your concern," I said. "How about you?"

"I don't want to talk about it.... Jesus, I feel like taking a shower. One day I'm going to even the score with that bitch."

"A little tit-for-tat?"

"What did you say?"

"Forget it," I replied. I pressed the bruise on my side to see how bad it was. The rib wasn't broken, but maybe it was cracked.

"That punch of yours, how'd you do it?"

"There's a thing right here," I touched the skin on her neck below the ear, "called the vagus nerve. Runs from the brain stem all the way to the heart. Hit it just right, or squeeze it with a certain wrestling hold, and the heart stops. Dead, if you're not careful."

I could see the pulse in her neck and, despite the cold, her skin was smooth and warm. A couple of fine hairs waving in the breeze curled around my finger.

"It was a lucky punch. I've tried it a few times in the past and it's never worked."

"Well, it worked this time," she said with a smile.

A car honked close by and spoiled the moment. I looked up and saw Emir's Renault weaving toward us through the traffic. He pulled to a stop beside the curb. I opened the door for Masters.

"Where have you been, Emir?" I asked as I went in behind her.

"Looking for you, sir," he said, instantly on the defensive.

"You didn't see us get muscled into a van?"

"What is 'muscled'? Sir, I cannot stop here. I have been driving round and round. But I could not see you."

"Don't worry about it, Emir," Masters said. To me, she added, "What could he have done about it anyway?"

True, we couldn't exactly expect Emir to be the cavalry.

"So what do you think those assholes wanted?" she asked.

"You mean aside from Fedai?"

"Did you buy the whole we're-after-an-ex-Mossad-agent shit?"

"No," I replied.

"If Fedai were ex-Mossad, you'd think the CIA would've picked that up when they ran the guy's background. They'd have put him through the wringer for sure before they let him butler for Portman."

"You'd think so, only you're assuming the CIA wasn't busy someplace else, shooting itself in the foot," I said.

"So let's say they are Mossad."

"Then the whole hunt-for-a-rogue-ex-agent thing might explain them stomping around with guns in a foreign country, abducting and smooching beautiful military policemen. . . ."

"Vin—shut up," snapped Masters.

"Sorry. OK. Whether Fedai is ex-Mossad or not, the fact remains that those people—whoever they are—obviously want to get their hands on him."

"Could it be that he has something they want?" Masters wondered.

"Such as?"

"Well, take your initial hunch, the one about Fedai coming home to find Portman murdered, seeing the wall safe blown, opening the floor safe, and taking off with whatever he found inside it."

"Right, that hunch."

"Which brings me back to wondering who those people were," she said.

Whoever they were, they were interested in Fedai, interested enough to push us around. And that made me interested in them.

"Excuse, please," Emir interrupted. "But I think someone behind follow us."

"What . . . ? Where . . . ?" Masters said as we both turned to check our six.

"A white Hyundai," Emir said. "Can you see it?"

"I can see about thirty of them," I replied.

"This one is clean. I turn here, you will see."

Emir swung into a narrow side street. Several vehicles followed. One of them was a late-model white Hyundai. And it was dirt- and dust-free—something I had to admit was unusual on the streets of Istanbul.

"You got it?" I asked Masters.

"Yep."

The car was too far away for us to see who was behind the wheel.

"What do you want me to do?" Emir asked.

"You want to lose them, Vin?" Masters said.

"No, let's talk to them. Emir?"

"Yes, sir."

"Turn into the next main street. Don't drive fast. Take it nice and easy."

"Nice and easy. Yes, sir."

Emir did as I asked and turned into the next main street, easing off the gas.

"Did the Hyundai take the turn?" I asked him, not wanting to look around and, potentially, give the game away.

"Yes, he turn," Emir replied, squinting into the rearview mirror.

Up ahead, a streetlight turned red, bringing a block and a half of the traffic behind us to a stop.

"Let's go," I said.

Masters and I jumped out and ran through the crowd of stopped vehicles. The Hyundai was thirty yards back. As we approached it, I saw two silhouettes inside. I took the driver's door, Masters the passenger's.

"Hey, look. It's my favorite crime-fighting duo," I said as the window came down.

"You think you're so goddamn smart," drawled Special Agent Arlow Mallet.

"And you need to be smart when Howdy *and* Doody are on your tail," said Masters through the other window.

Goddard and Mallet looked angry and self-conscious.

"You want to tell us why you're following us?" I asked.

"We weren't following you, Cooper," said Mallet.

"C'mon, fellas. You were either following or blundering—take your pick."

"We don't have to explain anything to you, Cooper," Mallet replied.

"We think you do. You keep showing up just a little late. We want to know why."

"Blow me, Cooper."

"Say, Special Agent Masters. That was quite a show you put on in the park," said Goddard with a leer, switching to the offensive.

"Yeah, who'd have thought you swung both ways?" Mallet sneered.

"So you *have* been following us," I said.

"Just happened along, Cooper." Mallet smiled. His face reminded me of a deflated football.

"You saw all that going on in the park, but you did nothing about it?" Masters was pissed.

"Next time you're thinking of putting on a show like that, lady," sniggered Goddard, "give us a little advance warning and we'll try and get a webcam on it."

Masters's hands balled into fists.

Mallet inched the Hyundai forward. "Now, if you don't mind, step back from the vehicle," he said.

The blaring of horns suddenly entered my consciousness. I hadn't noticed the traffic snarl we'd caused. Up ahead, the traffic light was green, and Emir was parked in the middle of the road swearing at the motorists hurling abuse at him for refusing to move.

EIGHTEEN

Harvey Stringer, CIA station chief, Turkey, filled his chair like the breasts in a fat girl's bra. His huge stomach rolled over the edge of his desk and advanced and retreated with each breath. He glanced up from his laptop as Masters and I appeared at the door, and beckoned us in with one enormous hand while he continued tapping away with the other, a large index finger stabbing the keys one at a time.

The office was devoid of any touches of a personal nature. Not a single photograph, desk ornament, plaque—nothing—was on display. It was the office of a guy who wanted his private life to remain that way. Maybe he didn't have one to display.

"And . . . send," he said aloud for our benefit, clicking the mouse on an email. Job done, he leaned back in his chair. It groaned, probably in pain. "Afternoon, y'all," he greeted us. "Sit, sit. How's the investigation going?"

"We're making some progress," I replied, sitting.

"Yes, I heard they pulled some potential evidence from the Bosphorus. Blast blankets. Everyone's coming on board with your two-killer theory, by the way. That's good police work, Special Agents."

Enough with the pleasantries. "We met some folks just now staking out Adem Fedai's house," I said.

"Fedai?"

"Portman's servant."

"Yes, yes—Fedai," he said, the name clicking.

"Do we have any people out there working freelance on this?" I asked.

Stringer didn't ask for elaboration. He knew exactly what I meant. "No. What did these folks look like?" he asked in reply.

"Middle Eastern. We've passed the descriptions on to the Turkish police."

"Well, I guess you have to tick that box," he said dismissively. He sat forward, his elbows on the table, hands clasped in front of his chin, studying us like he might ponder the next move in a game of chess.

"These people claimed Fedai was ex-Mossad," Masters said. "Were background checks performed on Fedai?"

Stringer now leaned back in his chair, the evaluation continuing. I couldn't read him. Finally he said, "Of course we checked him out. Fedai was definitely not ex-Mossad. Fedai was a Kurd who belonged to a sect known as the Yezidi. You know who they are?"

"No, sir," said Masters.

"The Yezidi is a sect that worships the devil—Satan."

Masters and I shared a glance.

"Yeah, you heard right—Beelzebub. Last I heard, Mossad was basically a Jewish organization, and they worship the Big Guy *upstairs*. Though, from my experience with Mossad, I doubt many of its agents believe in anything other than doing whatever it takes to stomp on threats to the Jewish homeland."

"Would it be possible to see your file on Fedai?" Masters asked, pushing her luck.

"I will make it available," Stringer replied, surprising us.

"Also, sir," I said, "we're being tailed by a couple of U.S. Army CID types. Has the Company got anything to do with that?"

Stringer smiled with half his mouth. "If we had an eye on y'all, you really think you'd know about it?"

"No, sir."

"Well, then, you've just answered your own question, son. Can *you* think of any reason CID would put a tail on you?"

"To learn how it's done?" I suggested.

Stringer smirked. "You happen to ask them?"

"Politely, sir."

"Yeah, I'm sure you did, Cooper." Stringer scratched an earlobe. "Sorry, can't help you with that one either. Anything else?"

I thought about revisiting the subject of the assholes in the park. I wasn't so much annoyed about being abducted or having pistols waved in my face. What did bother me was that the people doing the waving were hot for what was most probably the last person to have seen the attaché alive, the only person who might be able to give us some kind of lead or insight into what happened on the night of his murder. It seemed to me that Masters and I were now under the gun to reach Adem Fedai first—assuming Fedai was still alive.

The more I thought about it, the more I decided to change the subject, maybe bring up the weather. I didn't want to show Stringer my cards. I figured he was keeping his hand under the table, too. After all, he was CIA.

We stood. I said, "Well, sir, thanks—"

"Oh, and before you two go..." Stringer opened his desk drawer. "I got this for you. I'll also forward you a soft copy." He dropped a stapled wad of laser printouts on the desk in front of me.

"What is it?" I asked.

"I was thinking about your request for satellite imaging of the Bosphorus on the night of Portman's murder. That there's the next best thing: the shipping schedule for the night in question. Every boat coming up and down that stretch of water is logged—the time, its flag, last port of call, cargo, and so forth. It covers the night of the murder from midnight to five-thirty A.M. Perhaps you'll find what you're looking for in there, Special Agent Cooper."

"What do you think?" Masters asked.

"That he needs to make friends with Jenny Craig," I said.

"You know what I mean."

I was thinking about the fact that there hadn't been a lot of trust making the rounds lately. But maybe that was changing. "Stringer didn't give us a copy of this log just so we'd drop it in the recycling trash."

"What about this Satanist angle? What are they called—the Yezidi? We've got a guy cut up into little pieces, blood everywhere. Could all this have something to do with some kind of weird ritual?"

"I don't think so. No, there's something else at work here," I said. "But, like Stringer said, it does eliminate the ex-Mossad claim."

"What about Mallet and Goddard?"

"What about them?"

"We are looking for two killers. . . ."

I'd had the same thought, briefly. Those guys kept showing up and, as Masters had said, there were two of them. "Our killers are smart," I reminded her.

"Perhaps Mallet and Goddard are just playing dumb."

"No one can act *that* good," I said. But could we really discount them?

"Ah! There you are. Just in time," said Colonel Wadding, catching us off-guard as we walked into our office.

"Richard," exclaimed Masters, practically bursting with excitement.

I repressed a sigh.

"I was just admiring your painting here," said Wadding.

He was standing in front of the horror I'd renamed *Conquest. With Body Parts,* tilting his head one way and then the other as he regarded Mehmet II and his army trampling over all those corpses like they were grapes in a wine press. "They don't paint 'em like this anymore, do they? I find it quite uplifting. How about you, Vin?"

"Uplifting? How do you get that, Colonel?" Maybe I was missing something. All I got from the painting, aside from concern that it might leak, was the confirmation from another age that the human thirst for other people's blood and misery was something embedded in our genetic code.

"Oh, I don't know." Wadding was doing that head-tilting thing again. "I'm hardly an art critic, but to me it says . . . it says . . . winners are grinners."

Winners are grinners. Wow. I wondered if this guy had ever done any of those Rorschach ink-blot things. Maybe he had. Maybe some law faculty had tested him and found deficiencies in certain fundamental areas of humanity and streamed him straight into litigation. The Wad was made for it.

I happened to catch sight of Masters. Her head was on a tilt, too, but looking at her fiancé rather than at the painting, perhaps seeing him in some new light. Perhaps it was something admirable she saw: Maybe, like me, she saw a man insulated from other people's dreams and hopes by an upbringing that had instilled in him an isolating class superiority. Or perhaps that's what I *hoped* she saw. I was rapidly coming to the conclusion that I couldn't read Masters at all. But then, what the hell—it was just a goddamn painting, and I was beat. Outside, it was already dark.

There was a tap on the door. "Come on in, Rodney," I called out.

"Richard, this is Captain Rodney Cain," said Masters, playing hostess. The Wad and Rod shook on it.

"You're JAG," Cain observed. "Here on a case, Colonel?"

"No," Wadding replied. "Just paying a social visit."

"The captain's our local liaison, working on the Portman murder with us," Masters explained.

"Great. Well, sweetheart, ready to go?" the Wad asked.

"Um . . . well, it's pretty early," Masters answered, glancing sheepishly at me and then Cain, and then back at me.

"I'm sure Vin won't mind. Vin, you don't mind if I steal the special agent for the rest of the day?"

In fact, I did mind. We had work to do. But I wasn't Masters's boss, so I said, "Sure. Captain Cain and I were only going to sit around here flipping cards into a hat. You go, sweetheart. We'll see you tomorrow."

Masters gave me a pinched smile. "You sure?" she asked.

"Sure I'm sure. Don't forget we're headed to Incirlik tomorrow," I reminded her.

"What time?"

"See you downstairs at seven."

As I turned away, I could see her indecision out of the corner of my eye. She wanted to stay. And go. I asked Cain, "You got those cards handy?"

He looked at me funny.

"See you at seven," Masters repeated, dragging it out. Wadding waited impatiently for her at the door, drumming his fingers against it.

"Yeah, tomorrow," I replied, giving her a wave without looking up.

After another few moments of second thoughts, Masters finally picked up her jacket and walked out.

"What's going on between Masters and the colonel?" Cain asked.

"Marriage," I said.

"Oh."

"What you got for me?"

"I don't have any cards."

"Forget the cards."

Cain opened his briefcase. "Local forensics pulled an all-nighter on the items found in the Bosphorus. Unfortunately, everything had been in the water too long, and Portman's blood drove the fish and the crabs crazy. There wasn't much left."

"Which leaves us with?"

"Three blast blankets and two coveralls. I think that means we can say two people really did carve up Colonel Portman."

"Can we? I'm not so sure." Doubts about my own theory rushed back at me. I hit command-print on an email from Istanbul homicide on their Bosphorus discoveries. IT had delivered a printer, but a box popped up on-screen to inform me that it was low on toner.

"What? You don't think that firms things up at all?"

"I don't know," I said, shaking my head, preoccupied. The damn printer. Couldn't they have checked the thing before they brought it over? I shot IT a note to come and replace the cartridge. "Maybe, maybe not. We've got two murder victims. There's the theory that two killers were caught on camera in the Hilton parking lot, but it's hardly conclusive. And the blast-blanket theory at the Portman scene only *suggests* more than one killer."

"And now we have proof of that."

Something was bothering me. Maybe they wanted us to find those blankets. Maybe the killers were just stringing us along. "No we don't," I told Cain. "All we have *proof* of is that blast blankets were used on the Portman job and that two coveralls were dropped in the drink along with them. What size were they?"

"The coveralls?" Cain flipped through the findings to check. "Two size L for large."

"Could have been one person wearing both suits, couldn't it?"

"I guess so," Cain admitted, "but I doubt it." He threw me a raised eyebrow.

I let it go. "Anything come back on the two suspects caught on camera down at the Hilton?"

"Just heard before coming over. Istanbul police found the stolen Fiat. Burnt to its axles. Forensics have told us to expect nothing of value from it."

"Why am I not surprised?" I said. The killers were maintaining their unblemished record for thoroughness. "Anything from the surveillance tapes?"

"No, not much there either, I'm afraid. The clothes they wore were loose-fitting and black, which apparently made it impossible to be certain of anything other than that the killers were a pair of adult males."

"At least we know not to be on the lookout for a pair of female chimps. Can I read the forensics report?"

"I'll send you a JPEG."

"A hard copy would be better. My printer has decided it would like to be thrown out."

"Take my copy," he said, getting up and putting the printout on my desk. "I've had it translated."

I flipped through the pages. The Istanbul forensics team again seemed pretty thorough. "Have Karli and Iyaz received this, too?" I asked after a while.

"I think so," Cain replied.

I nodded. I wanted the local folks to keep an eye on these crimes. Maybe the killers were Turkish. There was always the chance that Istanbul homicide would come up with something useful if they stayed on the case.

Resting my head in my hands and staring at the forensics report, I tried to concentrate on putting the pieces together, taking them apart, and then reassembling them in a different way. But I kept coming back to the same point, which was that I didn't like Wadding, mainly because the guy was distracting me. "Cain. Got a joke for you," I said.

The captain looked up from his laptop.

"So an attorney says to a judge, 'Your Honor, I must appeal my client's case, on the basis that I have discovered important new evidence.'

"To which the judge says, 'And what is the nature of the new evidence?'

"'Your Honor,' says the attorney, 'I have discovered that my client still has five hundred dollars left in his wallet.'"

Cain gave me a smirk. "Don't like Special Agent Masters's fiancé much, do you?"

"What's not to like?" I said.

"Rumor has it he's the infamous Colonel Wad."

I nodded. "You know much about him?"

"He's supposed to be a legendary asshole. I heard about him through an ex-girlfriend of mine. She's suing the government over DU."

"Really. You up on the class action?"

"She's an ex, not a current. All I know is that the defendant, the DoD, believes depleted uranium oxide—that's the stuff left after a DU penetrator burns—is safe enough to sprinkle on your Cheerios."

"That's almost funny," I said.

"Yeah," he agreed. "Almost."

"What's your ex got?"

"Actually, it's what she hasn't got," said Cain. "Two kidneys. One of them died—necrotized, I think they call it. They had to cut it out. The one remaining only works at fifty percent. She hangs out on a dialysis machine most of the time these days."

"What'd she do in the life?"

"Spent a year in one of those cleanup teams the Army sent in after the Warthogs, Apaches, and Abrams stopped shooting shit up. Afterward, she believed she was pissing pure uranium. Back when we were an item and she was on active duty, I remember her saying she wore protection on the job, but not a lot of it and not always. Only wore a T when the temps climbed past a hundred, which in summer was every damn day. You got any friends taking on Washington over this stuff?"

"Yeah. And you've just reminded me to give him a call."

"Y'know, it's none of my business, Vin, but I thought *you* and Masters had something special going on," he said as an aside, going back to his laptop.

I was going to say he was right—it wasn't any of his business. But I was curious. "Where'd you get that idea from?"

"Beats me. Just an impression, I guess."

The phone on my desk rang. I didn't recognize the caller ID, but I picked up anyway. Cain was getting a little too close for comfort. "Cooper," I said.

"Special Agent Cooper?"

"That's right, ma'am." I knew the voice, but couldn't put a face to it.

"This is Dr. Merkit speaking."

I remembered the Dr. Merkit face. As faces went, it was a damn attractive one. "What can I do for you, Doc?" I said.

"Special Agent, I have been studying the reports on the two crimes prepared for me by Captain Cain. And I would like to talk to you a little more about your theory."

"The one about there being two killers?"

"Yes."

"You got our office bugged, Doc?"

"I am sorry?"

"Never mind. What are you thinking?"

"If it's possible, I would rather meet to discuss," she replied.

"It's possible, Doc, only Special Agent Masters and I are leaving for Incirlik in the morning."

"Well, perhaps it can wait, but it would be better to talk soon, I think."

"Then that just leaves tonight," I said.

"If you and Special Agent Masters are not busy, perhaps we could meet for dinner? I will bring my nephew."

"Sure," I replied. "But Special Agent Masters has another engagement."

"Well, then, Nasor can find someone else to have dinner with," she said with the hint of a laugh. "Perhaps I can show you a little of Istanbul also. Do you know our city at all?"

"I know the murder here is spectacular."

"We do other things here besides that."

We agreed to meet outside a mosque called the Aya Sophia later that evening. If I didn't know better, I'd have said I'd just scored a date. I tried not to think about it, because I still had some chores to take care of. Like book a couple of seats on a plane to Adana, which was the city in the far south of the country close to Incirlik Air Base—the sprawling NATO facility used by U.S. forces traveling to and from Afghanistan, the place where both Portman and Bremmel had worked together on the Turkish Air Force F-16 upgrade.

"You need a hand with anything here while you're out of town?" Cain asked as I finalized the tickets. He'd camped over on Masters's desk and was now closing the lid of his laptop.

"Yeah. You could do my job for me," I said.

"Sure, especially if it means standing in on all outstanding dinner engagements with beautiful doctors."

"You've just reminded me—are you and the doc seeing each other?"

"I wish. Been trying to make that happen, but it hasn't so far. Why?"

"I think you've got a fan there."

"Really?"

I handed Cain the shipping schedule. I told him I had no idea whether it would prove in the least bit useful to us, or what to look for when he went through it. But he understood the relevance, particularly now that the killers' bits and pieces had been pulled from the Bosphorus. They'd come and gone by boat. Just maybe, that boat was on the schedule.

After I'd finished briefing Cain, I still had half an hour to kill before my rendezvous with Doc Merkit. I checked the clock. The time difference with Ocala, Florida, made it just after midday there, so I decided to put in the call to Tyler Dean that I'd been meaning to make for a while.

Their answering machine kicked in with a recorded message from Tyler's wife, Katie. Behind her voice were the screams of a couple of toddlers—twins. *"Hey, great to hear your voice. Can't come to the phone right now, diapers to change and all. But we're five minutes away. Leave a message and we'll call you right back. Promise."*

I left a message, just to say I'd called, and gave the number for the cell I was carrying.

NINETEEN

I made it with ten minutes to spare, enough time to stand around stamping to keep the blood circulating and watch the floor show. The puddles on the sidewalk were frozen, the procession of people walking past seeming to break-dance as they slid around on the black ice, their feet suddenly running on the spot before they half-fell, grabbing for partners who then broke into similar routines as they struggled to stay upright.

A sign said the mosque I was loitering around was called the Aya Sophia, so I had the right one. It was familiar—I'd run here with Masters yesterday morning. The vast area dedicated to buses indicated that the mosque was a popular attraction. Its many domes and walls were flooded with yellow light, and from across the road in the park, regular flashes pinpointed tourists taking artsy night shots. I couldn't see what the fuss was all about. To me the place looked like a giant clump of mushrooms.

"She is beautiful, isn't she?" asked a woman's voice.

I didn't recognize the triangular shape standing in front of me, on account of the fact that it was dressed all in black, with a black veil over the head, covering most of the face, and a black coat that brushed the ground around the shoes. "Who is?" I replied.

"Aya Sophia."

"That you in there somewhere, Doc? I asked.

"Of course. Who did you think it was?"

"I wasn't sure. Not every day I meet a shadow that talks."

"Yes, it's me." She pulled the fabric away from her face. "See?"

Yep, it was her all right. I hadn't pegged the doc as a Muslim fundamentalist. In fact, I'd have been less surprised if she'd turned up in a bunny suit with a drink on a tray. "So," I said. "Where to? Are you hungry?"

"Yes, but first I want to show you some of Istanbul's attractions."

I'd seen Doc Merkit without the veil and the coat. As far as I was concerned, she headed the attraction list.

"Have you heard of the Aya Sophia before?"

"No, I haven't."

"But it is famous. . . ."

I didn't need to see her face to know my ignorance took her by surprise. It couldn't have been that famous, otherwise there'd be an Aya Sophia near the Eiffel Tower in Vegas. I kept this to myself.

She continued: "It was built by the Emperor Justinian more than fifteen hundred years ago. When he came inside for the first time, they say he cried out, 'Oh, Solomon, I have outdone you!'"

"Who was Solomon?"

The shadow turned to face me. Again, I didn't need to see the expression on her face.

"Just kidding, Doc," I said.

I heard her give a small laugh. "You do not like to be serious."

"I guess not."

"Why is that?"

I shrugged. We began to walk.

She said, "Perhaps you have too much to be serious about."

"Maybe," I agreed.

"People say I am too serious. Would you like to hear a Turkish joke, Special Agent?"

"That depends. Is it funny?"

"Yes, very."

"OK, let's hear it."

"Temal and Akasma are newly married. On the wedding night, Akasma says, 'Temal, if I gather up my hair, it means I don't desire whoopee. If I gather my hair up halfway, it means if whoopee happens that's OK, and if it doesn't happen that's also OK. But if my hair is completely down, that means I definitely desire whoopee.'

"Temal thinks about this and says to Akasma, 'Akasma, if I drink one glass of raki, I don't desire whoopee. If I drink two glasses, then it's OK if whoopee happens, and if it doesn't, that's OK, too. But if I drink three glasses, I don't really care which way you wear your hair.'

"That's funny, isn't it?" The doc was laughing.

"A rib-tickler."

"So, we can go inside if you like. I have a cousin who runs the security here."

"Do you have a cousin who could sell me a rug?"

"Do you want to buy a Turkish rug?"

I was about to say that I was only fooling around, but then I thought, What the hell... Perhaps it was the thing to do in Turkey after all. "I've been thinking I might," I replied.

"Yes, when visiting Turkey you should buy a rug. I can arrange it," she said. "Everyone in Istanbul knows someone who sells Turkish rugs."

"Really? I never would have known."

"Shall we go to see inside?"

"Perhaps some other time, Doc."

"Yes, in the daytime would be best. You can miss much in the dark."

I had to agree there. I was almost missing her in the dark. We crossed the road where the buses parked, and walked toward another mosque, a newer one lit up like night roadworks.

"Looks like Sophia's younger, prettier sister." I gestured toward the building.

"It is much newer, built only five hundred years ago. Tourist books call it the Blue Mosque."

It looked white to me. "Why is that?"

"Inside it is covered in many beautiful blue tiles."

"Like a giant bathroom."

"No, nothing like a bathroom!" She gave a sound like she didn't know whether to gasp or giggle.

"Sorry, Doc," I said. "Didn't mean to give offense."

"Your humor... sometimes it makes me want to run away."

"I'll try to keep a lid on it."

"No, it's OK. I like it... I think."

I became aware of the ache in my fingers, the ones encased in fiberglass. "We should find someplace to eat and talk," I suggested. "I think it's going to snow."

"Oh no, I don't think so. It is too cold for the snow. But yes, let's go. I know a restaurant near here."

Ten minutes later we were sitting at a table in a tourist joint half a block from the Hotel Charisma. Doc Merkit had removed the veil so that I could see her face. I left the ordering to her. After she was done, I got things rolling. "So, Doc, these two killers . . ."

"Yes. As I said on the phone, I've been going over Captain Cain's reports, and having two killers makes more sense than one, but—"

"But you don't think that's what we've got," I finished.

"No."

"I agree with you. I've been thinking about those patterns. The only consistent element seems to be the use of chloroform to disable the victims. But the amount of chloroform used to knock Bremmel out was much less than Portman had pushed down his throat. At first I thought this wasn't significant, that the accomplice with the anesthetic would have been the same person involved in both crimes. But now I'm thinking it's possible that two *different* people administered the stuff—someone who knew what they were doing with Bremmel, and someone who didn't with Portman."

I continued: "I'd thought perhaps the person who did the cutting and the person who splashed around the anesthetic simply traded places, but, as you rightly pointed out, the MO of each murder was so different."

"Yes, you and I have been having similar thoughts," she said. "The Portman murder and the Bremmel murder were both bizarre and ritualistic, but the manner of each murder and the nature of each ritual were *so* different. . . . I am now thinking it is more likely there were two *teams* of killers—four or even five murderers."

The more I thought about it, the more I thought the doc was on to something. The fog surrounding these cases seemed to part a little. "It's possible."

"Whatever is going on here, it is something I have no experience with," she confessed.

I told her about the items pulled from the Bosphorus—the blast blankets and the two disposable coveralls.

"What size were the coveralls?"

"Large—which doesn't mean a hell of a lot. Gives us no real clue to body size. As you know, we believe the killers wore them over Gore-Tex dry suits, and they could have worn them tight or loose, or maybe one wore it tight and the other loose. They also could have chosen the same size so as not to give us any leads. Forensics couldn't narrow the description on the suspects from the Hilton surveillance footage either—'a couple of adult males' was all they're willing to say. The Fiat the killers used has turned up but, like everything so far in this case, it's taking us nowhere. The vehicle was thoroughly torched."

The waiter arrived with dinner. We both picked at it. I noticed a table of tourists sitting at the window pointing at the street outside, excited. It was snowing.

"See?" I said to Doc Merkit when she turned to observe what the commotion was about. "My fingers are never wrong."

"How did you break your arm?" she asked.

"My knuckles, actually."

"What happened?"

"A friendly reminder from my last case."

"Do you always get injured on these investigations?"

"Lately, I've been unlucky." Or lucky, depending on how you looked at being cut out of a parachute and surviving the fall.

"Oh," she said, stifling a yawn. "So, you and Special Agent Masters are going to Incirlik tomorrow?"

"Yes."

"I wish you better fortune there."

"Thanks, I hope you get your wish."

"Where is Special Agent Masters tonight? Nasor was disappointed."

"Her fiancé's in town."

"She is getting married?"

"Uh-huh."

"Please give her my congratulations."

"I take it you're married, Doc?"

"No. In this country the husband must provide a dowry. I could not find one with enough goats and camels to satisfy my father." She laughed. "Why do you think I am married?"

"The veil. Isn't it something married women wear?"

"Yes, and no. And in Turkey, what you call a veil we call a *türban*. Wearing a *türban* can mean that you are married, or engaged, or widowed, or devout, or old, or any reason you choose."

"By 'devout,' you mean fundamentalist?"

"Yes."

"And you are devout?"

"Yes."

"I'm surprised," I told her.

"Why?"

"Because, in the West, we view Muslim fundamentalists in a certain way."

"You don't have to worry—I am not wearing a bomb," she said, then sighed. "The West has much to learn about Islam. And perhaps it also has much to learn *from* Islam. Turkey is a secular Muslim country. If you are in the public service, for example, you cannot wear a *türban* to work—it is against the law. Sometimes, when I am feeling close to God, I wear a *türban* while I am working, because I am not in the public service. When I met you the first time, I was not wearing it. I did not think it was something I had to warn you about."

"Not at all, Doc. Just curious, is all."

"Turkey is still an Islamic country, and most Turks follow the teachings of the Prophet Mohammed, may his name be praised. My father and brothers are religious, and my wearing the *türban* in public does them honor. So when I am out walking, I always wear a *türban*."

"You don't find the whole veil/*türban* thing a little, y'know—anti-woman?" I felt uncomfortable asking the question, but Doc Merkit just didn't seem to fit the mold.

"Anti-woman? You are sounding like one of your feminists!"

"Just trying to get in touch with my X chromosome, Doc."

"The *veil*, as you call it—it liberates me. I am a rich, educated, professional woman. Istanbul is a modern city, but independent career women like me are still unusual and there is some prejudice. So this is another reason why I wear the *türban*. Men do not harass me; they think I am either married, or devout, or perhaps both. I can come and go as I please, unnoticed."

"So it's a kind of camouflage," I said.

She thought about that before answering. "Yes—but it is also more. I *am* one of the faithful."

The waiter arrived and asked if there was anything else we wanted.

"Look at the time," said the doctor, suddenly aware of it. "You are getting up early tomorrow. You should get some sleep. I must go."

I wondered why the sudden rush. "Sure," I replied. "The minibar back in my room is probably wondering where I am." The doctor began fishing around in her bag, I guessed for her wallet. I said, "Let Uncle Sam get this, Doc. It'd be his pleasure."

"Are you sure?"

I nodded.

"Thank you. Well, then . . . shall we go?"

We stood outside the restaurant, beneath its awning, and looked on a changed world. Everything was covered in a layer of white. The flakes floating down were smaller than I'd seen falling earlier, but there were infinitely more of them. Cars were marooned on the streets, which had mostly disappeared beneath the snow. A motorcycle parked nearby had a pillow of snow on the tank and seat at least three inches high. A cab down on a far corner tried to move but instead skidded into another parked car, the deadened sound of the impact reaching my ears as a brittle *crunch.*

"How am I going to get you home, Doc? The only things moving out on the roads are idiots, and walking a few miles in this doesn't seem such a good idea, either."

"Yes. I don't know," she said, neck craned, checking up and down the street.

I could only think of one solution, but even as I voiced it I wasn't exactly sure of my motives. "My hotel is near," I offered. "We could go there for a while."

"And if the weather doesn't improve, yes, I will take a room for the night."

"Good idea, Doc," I said. There you go, problem solved."

We were standing outside the Hotel Charisma minutes later, brushing the snow from our shoulders and stamping it off our feet. The flurry was getting heavier. The lobby was empty. A handwritten sign explained that the front desk would be unattended for twenty minutes. I wondered when the sign had been placed there.

I went around behind the bench, took the key to my room from its hook, and led the way to the elevator. No one saw us going through the lobby, which was a relief. Being seen by any locals heading up to my room wouldn't have looked so great on the doctor's résumé, blizzard or not. As the elevator climbed, we stood like a couple of strangers, watching the floors light up one by one on the control board, both of us suddenly quiet.

My room was mostly bedroom, with a large king-size bed dominating the space, a bathroom off one corner, and a sofa bed in the corner opposite. There was enough room left for a small table with two chairs, a television cabinet, a closet, and a kitchenette in the short hallway to the front door. But it was warm and free from snow, unlike the street outside, which was now totally obscured. I told myself that having the doc stay over was legitimate.

"If you want to freshen up, the bathroom's in there," I said, giving its location a nod. "There are plenty of clean towels."

"Thank you." She headed toward it.

"I'm going to fix myself a drink. Can I get you a soda?"

"Yes, please. Coca-Cola, if you have it."

"We have it," I confirmed as the door closed. Then, a little louder, I said, "I'll also call down to the lobby and book you that room for the night, just in case."

I made the call; it went to voice mail. I left the booking, went to the minibar, freed a couple of Johnnie Walkers, and poured them into a glass over rocks. I took care of the doc's drink, too. Then the cell in my pocket started ringing. The number on-screen told me it was the United States calling. It wasn't a Washington number, nor was it any of the numbers my ex-wife or her lawyers hide behind, so I pushed the green button. "Cooper."

"Vin, it's Katie—Katie Dean."

"Katie. Hey..."

The doctor came out of the bathroom. I pointed to her soda on the table, put my hand over the phone, and told her, "Sorry, gotta take this. Make yourself at home." I sat on the end of the bed. "Katie! How you doin'? How's Deano?"

"Vin, I've been trying to reach you. Tyler's..."

I knew what the problem was even before she managed to get the words out, but the news still stopped me like a bullet.

"Vin—he died four days ago."

"Katie... What happened?"

"Complications from the last surgery, they say."

"But he was doing fine."

"No. He wasn't. He was just tough."

"Jesus."

"The hospital's not ready to make any kind of official statement yet—because of the lawsuit. One of the doctors told me, off the record, that when they did the esophagectomy to remove the cancer, there might have been a small tear in the suture line. Tyler went back into the hospital ten days ago, but he just got worse. I don't think there was anything anyone could have done. I overheard one of the nurses talking about massive infection."

"Christ..."

"He didn't suffer, Vin. He was unconscious or asleep most of the time."

There was a pause and a rustling sound. I pictured Katie gripping the phone, her eyes squeezed shut. After a moment, she spoke again. Her voice cracked now. "We buried him today, Vin. It was a good service." In the background, I heard one of the twins crying and another woman's voice giving comfort—Tyler's sister, probably. Katie and I talked for another twenty minutes, mostly about how much we both loved her husband.

The call ended, I dropped the cell on the bed beside me and raised an empty glass to my lips. I'd drained it during the call. Another tumbler was pressed in my hands. Johnnie to the rescue.

"Medicine," Dr. Merkit said.

"You're the doctor."

"Yes, I am the doctor. Do you want to talk about it?"

Tyler had been a friend—as good as they came. I had a soft spot for Katie, too. Things would be tough for her and the kids.

I told Doc Merkit about meeting Tyler when we were both stationed Stateside, back before someone decided Saddam was mixing WMD cocktails for his neighbors. Tyler was with the 1st Armored Division. He scared the crap out of me when his tank accidentally ran over the front of a Humvee I was a passenger in and squashed it flat.

I told her about how he met Katie. In response to a dare, he'd filled in for one of his crew who had part-time employment as a male stripper. The job that night was to entertain a bridal party and Katie happened to be one of the bridesmaids. Tyler decided to ignore the bride and was all over Katie like hives instead. The bride-to-be complained. The crew member he was filling in for got fired; Tyler got laid. He and Katie were married within three months.

Then I told her about Tyler's cancer and the fight with the DoD over the claim that his condition was a direct result of long-term contact with depleted uranium, the ammunition his tank fired in Iraq.

It was well past midnight when the Johnnie ran out. Outside, the snow was still falling. I called down to the front desk and finally managed to raise someone, who informed me that the hotel was booked solid. Dr. Merkit and I were snowed in.

"I'll take the sofa bed, Doc, you take the bed," I said, pulling it out.

"No, you are the man. You must take the bed. And I think you need a good sleep after this sad news."

"No, no, I—"

"*I* insist."

I gave her a shrug. "Well, Doc, if you insist."

"I do. I will take the sofa."

"So, my comfort comes first. I could get used to this country." I was slurring my speech, and the words ran into each other like a pileup on a foggy interstate. "Thanks, Doctor."

She smiled. "Please, can you call me Aysun? That is my name, you know."

"Sure, Doc—I mean, Aysun. Do you want to take a shower or something?" I asked, sitting down heavily on the bed.

"You go first. I will make up this bed and tidy up a little."

"OK." I was beyond arguing. *Make the bed and tidy up a little...* "How many goats and camels are needed for that dowry?" I asked.

"More than you have," she replied as she grabbed a handful of Johnnie Walker empties and placed them in the trash.

Ten minutes later I'd showered, brushed my teeth, and even sobered up a little. But when I came out of the bathroom, all the lights were off and Doc Merkit was lying in the sofa bed, breathing steadily, asleep. A shoulder was uncovered, along with a bra strap. The veil was gone. I pulled the sheet over her, Aysun's breathing staying slow and deep.

"Night, Doc," I said quietly. I sat on the side of my bed and listened to the night. All sound seemed to have been vacuumed out of it. The falling snow also took the electronic edge off the light from the street and turned it golden, shafts of which slanted up through the windows.

I thought about Tyler and Katie as I climbed between the sheets. My head hit the pillow, but it might as well have been a blackjack.

I woke up suddenly and for no reason. Or so I thought. The numbers on the bedside clock told me I should still be asleep. I wondered what had awakened me.

"Are you all right? You were yelling in your sleep."

It took me a moment to remember where I was and whose voice the accented English belonged to. Doc Merkit... Aysun. I peered at the sofa bed in the corner. There was enough light to see that the doctor wasn't in it.

"You were yelling," she continued. "You said, 'There! Shoot! Shoot him! They'll cut his head off!'"

I couldn't see her, but from the direction of her voice, I knew the doctor was standing in the darkness over by the kitchenette.

I rolled over so that I was facing her. "It's a dream I have every other night. Something that went on in Afghanistan. But it's OK—I know what happens in the end."

"What happens?"

"I live."

The doctor came out of the shadow. Her skin had taken on the golden color of the light coming up from the street below. I remembered how she'd worn a blue lace bra the day Masters and I had called in at her office, but now her underwear was plain, conservative. Maybe the formal approach also extended to her underwear when she left the house. "I cannot sleep," she said.

The light played across her upper body as she floated across the room. For sure, a crazed Taliban fighter was going to step out of the bathroom any moment and prove this was just another dream. "What's the problem?" I asked.

"I have been thinking... there is a reason I am here."

The light moved up to her breasts. She knew how to walk, a hip thrusting gently forward with each step, swaying on a waist on the narrow side of slender.

"A reason for what?"

"I am a thirty-one-year-old virgin," she said.

"You're kidding...."

"You do not believe me?"

"I've just never met one before."

The doctor stopped beside my bed. My eyes wandered down the length of her body to where the light peeked through the wide gap between her legs.

"It is still snowing. We are here and cannot leave. Do you know what *'Insha'Allah'* means?" she asked.

That there was a good chance I was about to get lucky? I thought.

"It means 'God has willed it.' But if you do not want me, I will understand."

I understood enough to peel back the covers.

She slid in beside me, her legs cool and smooth against my skin. We kissed, tentative and slow at first, but then the fire kicked in. We broke and came up for air as her hand moved down my belly. Her fingers wrapped around me and squeezed playfully. She whispered, "I *know* all about this, but I have never felt it. It feels good." Her fingers then proceeded on a voyage of discovery. "And big."

"You say all the right things, Doc," I said.

"Aysun, remember?"

I went on my own reconnoiter and slipped a hand beneath her bra. I peeled back the cotton cup and ran the tip of my tongue over one nipple before circumnavigating the other, and she shivered. I ran it down her belly, up the inside thigh of one leg and then the other, teasing her. She pushed her groin toward my face. I took the hint and hooked a finger inside the elastic of her underwear where she was warm and wet, and pulled the fabric aside. The tip of my tongue touched the skin of her perineum and Aysun went crazy, grabbing my hair and pushing me down into her. I didn't resist; I buried my tongue between the lips of her vulva. She tasted sweet and salty. Her hips began to thrust, driving my tongue deeper inside her. She was in control at first, and then her rhythm became ragged, and her breath caught in her throat. Then Aysun suddenly shook and wrapped her legs around the back of my head until the current ran from her limbs and she quivered with the echoes of the orgasm racking her.

I lay down beside her, breathing deep and slow and staring, unseeing, at the ceiling.

"Not bad for a first-timer, Aysun," I said.

"I have practiced."

"Practiced?"

"Yes. I have . . . toys."

"They must come with some pretty explicit instructions."

I propped myself up on an elbow and tickled her stomach, following the muscles with my fingers. I tried to forget that in the shadows she reminded me of Anna. "Be honest, Doc," I said. "This has to be sympathy sex."

"Sympathy sex? What is that?"

"You feeling sorry for me."

"No . . . that is not the reason. I believe there's an expression you have that goes something like: 'It is now, or never'?"

"Something exactly like that."

"That is how I felt. Being here, the snow, the tragedy of your friend, the murders—all brought us together. I am not married and I do not know any men. I have been thinking for some time, Who wants to be an old woman making love to an old man for the first time?"

Seemed like a hell of a good reason to roll in the hay. But then, no reason at all would have been reason enough for me.

"I always imagined Americans would be selfish lovers," she said.

I was about to defend the reputation of the American male when she added, "Now, it is your turn."

I woke to a soft hum, opened an eye, and tapped the button to kill the sound. The numbers on the clock were a little more reasonable this time—5:45. Doc Merkit lay curled into a ball, facing me, with the sheet pulled up under her chin, asleep.

I edged out of bed so as not to wake her and walked to the window. The falling snow had turned to rain, which meant Istanbul had begun to move again. I hoped Aysun wouldn't wake with regret about what had happened between us.

I examined my bruises in the shower. I thought of the woman on the other end of those brass knuckles. *Yafa.* She enjoyed dishing it out. I'd like the chance to see if she'd be as happy receiving it. Masters and I could take turns.

When I opened the bathroom door, Aysun was waiting, a towel around her waist and her nipples pointing in the general direction of heaven. She pressed a small cup into my hand and said, "Good morning, Vin. Try this. Coffee, the way we Turks drink it."

"Thanks." The coffee was black, the right color at least. I had a sip and had to stop myself spitting it straight back out. "How many lumps you put in here?"

"Five," she replied.

"Is that all?"

"So, you like Turkish coffee?"

"'Like' doesn't quite cover it," I told her, dodging the question.

"Vin, I wish to thank you for last night."

"So you're OK with what happened?"

"Yes. Why would I not be?"

"Can't think of a reason, Doc."

She was about to set me straight on the first-name thing again when I put my finger against her lips, setting the cup on the bedside table. My towel slipped to the floor and I pulled Aysun's away. She came into my arms, turning so that her bare ass rubbed against me, a deep sweeping curve in the sway of her back. I reached around for her breasts as she raised her leg, took me in hand, and guided me down the slippery slide.

The *türban* was folded and packed in her bag. Aysun said it would've been hypocritical to wear it, given what she'd lost between the sheets. I didn't argue. Morality was a subject I'd failed from the age of sixteen.

She opened the door and stepped out into the hall while I conducted a final check of the room.

"Anna. Good morning," I heard her say.

A chill suddenly blew in from the North Pole and ran down my spine.

"Dr. Merkit. What a nice surprise." Masters's sugary tone implied there was nothing in the least bit nice about it. "And here's Vin," she added as I walked out. "I'll bet you've been hard at work all night."

"We were snowed in," I replied by way of defense.

"I'm sure you were."

Colonel Wadding appeared in the doorway behind Masters, carrying their bags.

"This must be your fiancé?" Aysun asked, aware of the tension. "Vin has told me you are getting married. Congratulations."

"Thank you," said Masters. "Yes, this is my fiancé—Lieutenant Colonel Richard Wadding. Richard, this is Dr. Merkit. The doctor is helping us with our investigation."

"A pleasure to meet you, Doctor," said Wadding. "So you're the profiler. Anna's told me a lot about you."

I could see Wadding liked what he saw. His grin was so wide he was in danger of bending his bridgework.

As he and Doc Merkit shook hands, I allowed myself a sideways glimpse at Masters. If looks could kill, I'd have been playing a harp. Or maybe a pitchfork.

"I invited you and Vin to dinner last night to talk about the murders," Aysun said to Masters. "But Vin told me you were busy."

"I'm sure he did."

"I have studied the case notes," Aysun continued, "and I have a point of view about the killers. Perhaps Vin will explain it to you later."

"I'm sure he'll do plenty of explaining."

I was sure I was getting sick of Masters's bullshit.

We all made our way to the elevator. On the way down, Wadding and Doc Merkit chatted easily while Masters and I stared in silence at the numbers as they lit up. After what seemed like a month, the doors slid apart. I said to Wadding, "Remember I told you about Tyler Dean, Colonel?"

"No, I—"

"Tyler Dean," I repeated. "You know damn well who he was." I couldn't hit him, but words could still smack him around some. "He died. Complications from surgery. He had a tumor resected from his esophagus. The guy was twenty-nine. Left a wife and two kids. No doubt you'll be doing your best to see they get screwed."

No one moved to leave the elevator. I gestured toward the open doors. "Delusion before grandeur, Anna."

TWENTY

Snow and ice at Incirlik Air Base lay a couple of feet thick by the roadside. Snowfalls like that were usual here, but it had turned into that kind of a winter all over the northern hemisphere. The snow that had come down through the night and into the morning was still being cleared by heavy equipment from the last of the ramps, but the business of war was continuing unimpeded.

Masters and I were waiting out in the parking lot for the liaison, who was signaling at us through the building's window that he'd be out in a minute. Masters stayed in the vehicle, an Air Force–blue Ford Explorer. I chose to wait outside in the ice and snow where the air was less frigid. I leaned against the front fender and massaged my fingers, the ones in the cast. That didn't help their circulation much, so I breathed on them. The heat from my breath felt like a blowtorch.

We hadn't spoken much since leaving Istanbul. Or at all, come to think of it. I knew that she wanted to chew a piece out of me over my evening with Doc Merkit, but she had no right to and she knew it.

I watched a C-5 skim the main runway and then settle, its four engines screaming in full reverse. Blizzards of loose snow enveloped its drooping wings as it barreled along. Lined up behind it on final, I counted three sets of landing lights in the pale midday sky. Those farthest away quivered like stars seen through desert haze. I got back in the car.

The pre-fab's door swung open and our liaison, a civilian contractor in coveralls, bounced down the stairs and trotted toward the Explorer. "Johnny Oh," he said, offering his hand through the driver's window. "Sorry to keep you. Had to push some paperwork around. You know how it is. Shall we get a move on?"

"Let's," said Masters, from inside the vehicle.

"Either of you speak Turkish?"

"No, that's why we've got you," I replied.

"You're an American with Korean parents," Masters said.

"How'd you guess?" Oh asked in reply.

"She's a detective," I said, answering for her.

"My point was," Masters continued, "why Turkish? Seems like an unusual language choice for someone of your background."

He shrugged. "I saw *Sinbad the Sailor* as a kid—you know, the one where Sinbad battles with skeletons. I was hooked."

"I thought Sinbad was an Arab," said Masters.

"Don't tell me I got it wrong!" Johnny Oh grinned. "So, where do you good people want to go first?" he asked as he opened the rear passenger door and climbed in. I'd seen bigger hood ornaments than this guy. His body was concave, barely filling his clothes. He had a broad flat face and so many teeth packed into his small mouth that he didn't appear able to close it. The specialty badges he wore told me he had been in Air Force munitions.

"We want to go see someone at TEI," I told him as I belted in.

"They know you're coming?"

"Damn well hope not," I said.

"You want to keep it that way?"

"Habit," explained Masters. "The Special Agent hates dropping in invited, because people mostly don't want to see him." She threw me a fake smile.

Johnny Oh regarded Masters from the backseat. From the look on his face, and being a fellow male of the species, I could tell he approved of the package.

"Well, it's coming up on a quarter to one," he said. "People here tend to be at lunch in Adana about now. They've got a Burger King there, better than the one we've got here."

"OK," Masters said. "We'll leave it an hour."

"Anywhere else you want to go in the meantime, Special Agents?"

There was one person we were here to see who wasn't going anywhere.

Staff Sergeant Morton Gallagher was a handsome guy: green eyes, olive skin, sandy hair, average height and weight. His record said he was a farm kid from Muskogee, Oklahoma. His fingernails were gnawed down to bleeding quicks, and his knee jiggled like it was plugged into a wall socket. Gallagher wasn't behind bars. He'd been confined to base for his own safety, but that hadn't stopped him from looking over his shoulder.

He sat forward in the chair, his leg vibrating. His attorney, a JAG captain, had briefed him and was now leaning against the wall, out of the sergeant's line of sight.

"Just a few questions about the charge against you, Sergeant," Masters began. We'd both read the report in the kid's file. The local police had a DNA sample—Gallagher's semen. Young Mort here already had one foot in Leavenworth. Like Burnbaum had said, it was an open-and-shut case.

"I'm innocent. I never raped her, ma'am."

"Like we said to your attorney, we're not involved in the court-martial. We're here to establish whether or not a murder we're investigating is in any way related to your situation."

"Yes, ma'am."

"So, you want to tell us about the woman who filed these charges against you?"

"Ma'am, I believe she's scared—maybe more scared than me. Durhab Kalim Ali is her name, and she's the most beautiful woman I ever saw."

Masters didn't blink. She continued the questioning and established that Durhab worked in that Burger King in Adana, where Gallagher had met her one day while he was having lunch. The woman was serving at the counter. Morton started going there for lunch and dinner. Eventually, the ice was broken and they struck up a friendship that turned into several secret dates. One thing led to another and, being healthy adults, Durhab and Gallagher ended up where these things usually do. Stupidly, they hadn't used a condom and Durhab had become pregnant. "It was God's will," Gallagher said.

According to the sergeant, her family found out about it, as they were always going to. Then, in an attempt to reposition the pregnancy, they forced the girl to bring a charge of rape against Gallagher. The young woman's father, brothers, and uncles had also vowed to kill him for dishonoring their family. Of course.

I had to admit, Mort Gallagher's version fit the facts every bit as snugly as Ambassador Burnbaum's reading of them. But I hoped for the sergeant's sake that the sex was incredible, because he was sure paying for it. Whether or not he was guilty or innocent of the crime wasn't for us to say, but he must've had big bowls of stupid with his fries at Burger King. Forces coming into Turkey were fully briefed on the customs of this place: Messing with the local women was a one-way street to the land of Six Feet Under.

"Did you ever get a visit from a Colonel Emmet Portman, Sergeant?"

"Yes, ma'am, I did. Is that what you're investigating?" he said. "It's true, then—I heard on the grapevine the colonel was murdered." So, Portman was quicker off the mark than Burnbaum thought.

Masters nodded. "We want to know whether Colonel Portman might have talked with Durhab or her family."

Gallagher shook his head. "You think Durhab's brothers could have somehow done it? No, not a chance. I only saw the colonel for twenty minutes, max. He apologized that he wasn't able to spend more time reviewing my case—said he was flying down to Ali. I never saw him again. And then, like I said, I heard he'd been murdered."

"Ali?" I asked.

"Ali Air Base—formerly Tallil Air Base, in southern Iraq. The ragheads call it Ali, we call it Tallil. That's where he said he was going."

"So, as far as you know, after Colonel Portman paid you a brief visit, he flew to southern Iraq," Masters said, compressing Gallagher's story.

"Yes, ma'am."

"You know whether he was flying with the 493rd?"

"He didn't say, but heading down there with the Reapers? I don't think so. Far as I know, we don't have assets like F-15s flying around Iraqi skies. There's nothing there for them to shoot down."

The interview went backward and forward for another twenty minutes, but Gallagher was already cleaned out of anything useful. Ali Air Base—Tallil. I hadn't seen anything about either name in Portman's emails. I'd already written notes to self to again chase Andrews Flight

Records over Portman's file, as well as to put in a call to the squadron commander of the 493rd, Lieutenant Colonel "Block" Woodward. I opened my notebook and underlined the two reminders.

"We've murdered that hour," announced Johnny Oh, grinning, as we took our seats in the Explorer. "You wanna go call on your TEI person now?"

I told him we did.

"TEI. OK, so turn left out of the parking lot," our guide instructed.

Five minutes later, Masters and I walked into a building hot enough for the civilian folks within to be wearing T-shirts. We approached a Turkish Air Force guy sitting behind the reception desk.

"Artie Farquar," I said, using my polite voice.

The sergeant looked like he was going to discuss the request until he saw our shields. "Yes, wait for a moment, please. There is a seat there to take." He pointed a chewed pencil at a cluster of chairs.

Masters and I both passed on the seating arrangements. We stood.

Farquar arrived within a couple of minutes, power-walking into the area. He was short, American, and black. "Artie Farquar," he announced coming to a stop, hands on hips. "You're OSI."

Smart cookie. We showed him our shields anyway. "Mr. Farquar," I began, "we're investigating the deaths of Colonel Emmet Portman and Dutch Bremmel. We have some questions we'd like to ask you."

"We need privacy?" he asked.

Masters shrugged. "Up to you, sir," she said.

"Follow me." Farquar didn't seem to like wasting breath on unnecessary words.

He led us to his office in the building's south-facing corner. Immediately, three small glasses of tea arrived on the usual swinging tray, delivered by a young guy immaculately dressed in civilian clothes. I took a glass and had a sip. Apple tea.

"Now, how can I help you?" Farquar asked, lowering himself into an Eames chair behind an expansive designer desk.

"You worked with Mr. Bremmel on the upgrade program," Masters said.

"Yes."

"How's it going?"

"It's going OK. The usual glitches, but better than expected. I had two of your guys here only yesterday asking the same questions. Don't you people exchange notes or anything?"

"A couple of guys?" I glanced at Masters but kept talking to Farquar. "One tall and sallow with the bone structure of a sunken soufflé, the other like he belonged on the end of a heavy chain staked into the ground?"

"Well, I might have been a little more generous with the descriptions, but, yes, sounds like them."

Arlow Mallet and Seb Goddard. I wasn't sure what upset me the most: that our CID brethren were here, or that they were here before us. "Sir, if they come around again, be careful. They're with the enemy," I told Farquar.

"The enemy?"

"The U.S. Army."

"Oh, bit of inter-service rivalry—I see."

Masters threw me a can-we-get-on-with-this? look and continued. "How about Mr. Bremmel? Everyone get along with him?"

"Absolutely. Dutch was a great guy. A leader, great sense of humor. The kind of guy you'd follow up and over the trench wall. The way he died, the fact that he died at all... well, it's a tragedy. I still can't believe it. He had a lot of friends and—rare in a company the size of this, where there's a lot of competition—no enemies. We're all in deep shock here. I keep expecting he'll just walk in like he used to, sprawl on the sofa, and shoot balls of paper into my trash."

A picture of Bremmel as I had last seen him flashed past my eyes. That version of the guy could slam-dunk his own head. "Did you know he was having an affair?" I asked.

"Like I told the other two, that was an open secret, Special Agent. Dutch's marriage had broken down. He was involved with his secretary. You ever get to meet her, you'll understand why."

I'd met her, and I understood why.

"You mind if I ask *you* a question?" he said.

"Shoot," Masters replied.

"Office scuttlebutt says there's a serial killer at work, and that the murders have something to do with our F-16 upgrade. I have to say the line of questioning I keep getting tells me that's more than rumor...."

"What's *your* personal security like, Mr. Farquar?" Masters asked, giving him an oblique response.

"Why? Am I in danger?"

"To be honest with you, sir, we're not sure what we're dealing with. The scuttlebutt's reasonably accurate. Both victims were U.S. citizens, and both were involved in this upgrade."

"And I fit the victim profile?"

"We're afraid you do, sir," Masters replied.

"I appreciate your candor, Special Agent. Security here is good. But just in case, TEI has provided me with a personal bodyguard. He's a former Turkish wrestler, a real heavyweight."

Yeah, a wrestler would be a big help to Farquar if the killers came at him armed with headlocks. Maybe that's how they usually settled these things in Turkey—your wrestler versus mine. Only, if these were the rules, the killers who'd butchered Portman and Bremmel weren't playing by them.

"Can you think of anything going on between Bremmel and Portman that might have accounted for their murders?" Masters asked.

Farquar shook his head and rubbed his chin. "No, no, I can't. And that's a hell of a broad question. You people really are getting nowhere, aren't you?"

Neither Masters nor I was prepared to deny the plain truth.

A thought occurred to me, linked to the Air Attaché's corrupted electronic schedule. "How much time did Portman spend on this project?"

"Time? As in hours?"

"As in, how many days a week."

"Going by the amount of time *I* spend on this, probably—I don't know—around one to two days a week, max."

I chewed that over for a couple of seconds. "Any other Americans working with you on the upgrade?"

"As a matter of fact, yeah, one: a former U.S. Navy F-18 plane captain named Denzel Nogart. Everyone knows Nogart. They call him 'Ten Pin.'"

"Why Ten Pin?" I asked.

"When you meet him, you'll see why," Farquar replied. "You'll find him, easy—either down at the engine shop or out on the flight line."

"Do you happen to know if the other two military police interviewed him?"

"No, as far as I know, they didn't."

As we climbed back into the Explorer, I could tell from the look on

Masters's face that things weren't adding up for her on this case, either. Portman was a good man; Bremmel was, too. Both had plenty of friends and no enemies. The upgrade was going as smoothly as anyone expected. Black ops didn't appear to be involved, and neither did the business with the crew chief and the rape charge. There didn't seem to be any aggrieved parties circling either victim. And sex and/or jealousy weren't factors in their unabashedly gruesome deaths. We were here and we were chasing our tails. And I could just as easily have been back in Istanbul, chasing Doc Merkit's.

TWENTY-ONE

An engine shop is a place where the Air Force stores replacement engines. The floor of the one at Incirlik was big enough to land a jet on. Had to be. Thousands of NATO and U.S. planes flew in and out of the base and not one of them was a glider. Basically, they had to stock a lot of engines and parts.

When we arrived, the place was alive with activity that seemed close to panic: heavy forklifts shifting large wooden crates around, people shouting and rushing about, some whistling instructions, others dodging out of the way. Masters and I made our way around the perimeter of the space, accompanied by Oh and a woman who volunteered to be our human shield. She took us to an office looking out over the shop floor where knots of officers and enlisted personnel were huddled over computer terminals. None of them looked happy, so I guessed it wasn't to look at porn. There was panic in here, too, but of the white-collar variety: two guys pacing the floor, others making suggestions about possible software glitches, plenty of sweating and gnashing of teeth.

Masters stopped a Royal Air Force lieutenant on his way out with a page of printout clutched in his fist, and asked what the problem was. Before he could answer, an Air Force captain broke away from a nearby terminal, and said, "We've lost ten 129s, ma'am. You see 'em lyin' around, we'd sure appreciate you pointing 'em out."

"What's a 129?" Masters asked.

"A GE F110-129 F-16 replacement engine, ma'am."

"And you've lost ten of them?"

"Completely disappeared off the system, like they never existed."

Masters showed her badge.

"Here already?" the captain exclaimed. "Gee, you guys are sure on the ball."

"What would you say the engines were worth?" Masters asked him.

"Around seven million bucks a pop." I repressed a whistle. Seventy million dollars was a lot to misplace.

"When did you notice they were missing?"

"Yesterday. We figured it was just an error on the inventory, but now we're not so sure. We're turning the place upside down looking for them."

"At what point are you going to decide they've been stolen?" she asked.

"There's a way to go before that." He pinched his sinuses while he considered the question. "Those engines are big. Weigh a few tons apiece. Point is, you couldn't just walk out of here with a couple of them stuffed under your jacket."

"There a contractor by the name of Denzel Nogart handy?" I asked, interrupting the postmortem.

"You looking for Ten Pin? He's down on the flight line doing engine trials."

A brief exchange was had between Johnny Oh and the captain, there being several miles of flight lines at Incirlik he could have been down on.

"How long you here for?" asked Oh as we drove along a short row of RAF C-130 Hercules. The way he looked at Masters, or rather, the way he never took his eyes off her, told me the question was personal.

"The day. Maybe two. Depends," Masters said.

"What if I told you I happen to be available tonight? Might that convince you to stay around?"

"Sorry, might not."

"You know what they say, Special Agent—good things come in small packages."

"Really," she said.

"Beneath these ordinary clothes . . . Put it this way, my last girlfriend called me 'Disproportionate Man,' the superhero with a *really* special gift for women."

This one I'd have to remember.

"And under these ordinary clothes, Mr. Oh," Masters informed him, "I'm every inch engaged to be married."

"Yeah? I'm pretty sure I could change your mind about that, ma'am."

"And I'm pretty sure you're getting close to pissing me off. Say, are those F-16s?" she asked, diverting our attention to the neat row of fighters with a blue lightning bolt on their tail fins.

"Those? They're Cheil Ha'avirs," replied Oh.

"Israeli?"

"Yes, indeed, ma'am. They're the new F-16 Sufa. Don't look like your average F-16, because they're not. To start with, they're two-seaters. Those bulges on the fuselage above the wing root are conformal fuel tanks. Longest-range F-16 there is."

"What are they doing here, in Turkey?"

"Practice on the bombing range off to the north. Over Israel, those things can't get out of second gear before they run out of airspace and start bumping uglies with the Egyptians, Jordanians, Saudis, and Lebanese."

"That's neighborly of Turkey," Masters observed, "to let them drop their bombs here."

"Israel buys water from Turkey. The two countries are pretty chummy; at least, the governments are. There's a local group of religious nuts who don't like the Israelis bombing their land, so they regularly pay the base back with some incoming of their own."

"Those F-16s use depleted uranium munitions on the bombing range?" I asked.

"Can't say whether Israel uses DU or not, Special Agent. That's classified. But I'm not breaking any rules if I tell you that no one's *supposed* to use it on the bombing range—part of the agreement. DU's potentially bad for the groundwater and no one wants to take the risk. Incirlik's a pretty important air base round these parts. We've got aircraft here from all over. Right now we're playing host to a squadron of Australian F/A-18s, Polish MiG 29s, Saab Viggens from Sweden, a bunch of American F-15s out of England..."

"They wouldn't be out of Lakenheath, by any chance, would they?" Masters asked.

"Yeah, the 493rd."

"They in town long?" I asked.

"They're on the bombing range today and tomorrow, working in with the Israelis—those F-16 Sufas. So a couple of days at least."

"We need to speak to the squadron's commander. Can you set it up for us?" I asked.

"I'll make a few calls."

We drove past the end of the Israeli lineup, toward half a dozen slate gray C-17s and massive C-5 Galaxys. "You know how DU ammo works?" I asked Johnny Oh. From his badge, I knew he was a BB-stacker, a munitions specialist, which meant he'd have a pretty fair idea. Masters ignored us, choosing instead to stare out the window at the huge transports.

"Sure."

"Mind giving me the highlights?"

"Well, you take uranium, remove all the radioactive U-235 isotopes, and you're left with uranium that has been depleted. Simple. The U-238 that's left is around sixty percent less radioactive than naturally occurring uranium, because, as I just said, all the real bad stuff has been taken out. DU makes great ammo, especially for busting tanks, because the sabot does two things when it slams into armor: it self-sharpens as it penetrates, and it's pyrophoric, which means friction causes it to burn. So, basically, when it hits the tank, it burns a hole clean through, becoming a high-temperature aerosol along the way that blows on in through the hole, incinerating everything inside."

"Is DU dangerous to handle?" I asked.

"When it's just lying around?"

"Yeah."

"I know what you're trying to do here, Vin," Masters interrupted. "It's pretty damn transparent."

"Depends on who you ask," Johnny continued when Masters turned away. "Some people say no, some people say to the people who say no, 'Are you kidding?'"

"What do you say?"

He shrugged. "The experts believe at least three hundred twenty tons of the stuff was lost in the first Gulf War—turned into that aerosol I mentioned, and it's just blowing around out there. Uranium, even the depleted U-238 variety, is both chemically toxic and a radioactive hazard. The radioactivity means it decays, breaking down into isotopes like thorium and protactinium—things handled best by someone else wearing a lead suit. Me? I don't care what the Pentagon says. I give the stuff a wide berth, unless I can't avoid it. Then I go out of my way to make sure I'm protected. OK, here we are."

Johnny Oh pulled to a stop fifty yards from an engine test facility on the far side of the flight line.

"I should say about now that I've been instructed to tell you to be very careful in this area when the engine's turning over." He reached into his bag and handed each of us a set of muffs. He put on a set himself, leaving one ear exposed.

"We know about the dangers, Johnny. We're in the Air Force," Masters said, leaving the "duh" implicit, but quickly donning the hearing protection.

"Sorry if this sounds condescending, but I've got my orders. I've been instructed to inform—OK, *remind*—you that the F-16 engine is just about the most powerful vacuum cleaner money can buy. It'll suck the hairs clean out of your skin from twenty paces, even when it's just idling. To ensure your own safety, you must remain outside the yellow line painted on the concrete. See it?"

In fact, you couldn't avoid it, unless the paint was covered with ice, which a few of them in the vacant parking spots down the flight line were.

"Even though it seems a long way out from the air intake," Oh continued, "you do not, under any circumstances, want to venture inside that yellow semicircle."

As if on cue, the 129 on the test stand closest to us began to spool up, generating a moan that went through the Explorer's metal like an angle grinder. There were several vehicles parked away from the test stand: a couple of branded TEI trucks and a vehicle known as a "bread van," which was an all-purpose personnel-, tools-, and parts-carrying utility vehicle that didn't carry any bread unless the line supervisor happened to bring along a boxed lunch. Several technicians in puffy cold-weather gear and headsets or muffs milled around on either side of the facility. One of these technicians was positioned directly in front of the intake. He was well outside the yellow semicircle, talking to the console operator sitting in a bunker via a long cord. She had her head forward, buried up to her ears in her instrument display.

"The man you're after is the guy out front," Oh yelled over the now screaming engine.

"The fella who looks like a bowling ball zipped into a parka?" I yelled back.

"Yeah, that's Denzel Nogart—Ten Pin."

I was reluctant to get any closer to the engine. Even with ear protection, its naked shriek was causing me physical pain. Masters stood beside me, wincing like she'd just hit her thumb with a hammer.

"Let's go," I yelled at her. "We'll talk to him later."

"What?"

I was about to repeat myself when a blue bread van distracted me. It had detached itself from the stream of traffic moving along the perimeter road behind the flight line, and was motoring slowly toward us. It looped around the back of the facility and pulled up a safe distance behind Ten Pin, well beyond the yellow line.

Two men in ABUs got out and walked toward the guy we were here to see. One halted about four feet away from him; the other, a senior master sergeant, continued to approach. He stopped beside Ten Pin and appeared to tap him on the butt. Startled, Nogart turned, and, just as he did, the man who had held back hit him low with a running block. Ten Pin was no lightweight, but he was caught off balance. He staggered back, lurching several steps to recover himself. Those steps took him well inside the yellow line. And then he was drawn forward, arms flailing through the air, feet barely touching the ground, desperately trying to throw himself down. Suddenly, he was flying, like a superhero, more than six feet off the ground and traveling as fast as a speeding bullet straight into the intake of the F-16 engine, which swallowed him whole. Ten Pin was gone. Sucked in.

A loud *bang* immediately followed. A tremendous backfire with a few thousand pounds of thrust behind it shook the test stand viciously. White and black smoke rolled out of the exhaust, accompanied by a belch of fire. The engine's shriek faltered, there was a grinding sound, and then another belch of smoke. All around the back of the enclosure, the concrete and walls began to turn red as a mist bloomed from the engine's nozzle.

The technicians and engineers were frantically, helplessly, signaling the console operator. The woman lifted her head and looked around, bewildered, wondering why the engine had just hiccupped.

It had taken a few seconds for the reality to register in the part of my brain that wasn't frozen in disbelief. Someone had just deliberately fed a man into the whirling titanium blades of a 20,000-horsepower meat grinder, and had done so with no more compunction than that of a mailman delivering a letter. And now, like a mailman, he was just going to drive off. I started to run toward the bread truck.

"Hey!" I called out as the jet engine died. "Hey!"

The truck's tires spun on a patch of ice, then the van picked up speed and began to pull away. I ran harder, which made my cracked rib feel as though it was going to split the skin and pop out like a busted mattress spring.

A Hercules, heading toward the van on an intersecting taxiway, forced the vehicle back toward some parked aircraft. It spun suddenly sideways on another ice patch. The guy on the front passenger side stuck his head out the sliding door to see if they were being followed. He did a comic double take when he saw me running, arms pumping, gaining ground. His head disappeared back inside the van.

The vehicle sped up and lurched off in a direction that took it toward the Israeli F-16s. That was a mistake: I cut the corner, dodged between a pair of C-5s, and gained on it. The van slid on another patch of ice and whoever was at the wheel lost control. There was a shrieking skid to the left and then one to the right and then another to the left—I watched it clip the tail on one of the F-16s, which flipped the van completely sideways. It rolled, doors ripping open, equipment flying out. The van kept rolling. It ended up on its roof, skidding along on the ice. It slid right into an R9 fuel truck servicing an F-16 separated from the rest. The refueler rose up on its suspension then settled back, the van lodged against it. Fuel cascaded out of the ruptured gas tank.

I stopped, panting. Those guys weren't going anywhere.

The explosion that followed seemed to come from somewhere deep within the earth beneath my feet. The R9 jumped maybe a foot. Then it broke apart as flames tore through the fuselage of the F-16 beside it. The fighter's wings sagged and hit the ground; then they, too, exploded as the fuel inside them heated, vaporized, and ignited. Without thinking, I dove behind the heavy ramp of the nearest transport and buried my head under my hands as a huge fireball rolled through the air toward me. A wave of heat seared my throat and I smelled a sour mixture of burning kerosene and my own singed nostril hairs. Next, steaming, smoking pieces of aircraft began to rain down, pummeling the tail ramp I'd sheltered beneath. A large wheel hub thumped into the concrete not two yards away, cracking it. It sizzled as the ice around it melted into a pool of water.

TWENTY-TWO

I stood up, grabbing hold of the plane to steady myself. The world was swaying, but that could have been me. I must have been unconscious for a few minutes: Personnel were already rushing around with portable fire extinguishers. Fires were burning here and there for two hundred yards all around the main body of the inferno that was consuming the F-16's fuselage and wings, as well as the remains of the R9, the van, and its unfortunate occupants. Four hundred yards away, the main firefighting team swerved into view, lights and sirens blaring.

I turned around, feeling shaky. Several guys were on their knees pointing nine-millimeter Berettas at my chest. Their backup arrived next—a swarm of Security Force vehicles. Men in full combat gear with MP5 submachine guns jumped out and yelled at me. I stuck my hands in the air. Three guys rushed in. One hit me in the back of the legs with a nightstick to get me into the more respectful, on-my-knees position.

As far as pretty much everyone was concerned, I'd just destroyed an aircraft worth millions. Index fingers twitched outside trigger guards. Handcuffs tightened around my wrist. Two of the men hoisted me up, and I was led to a van and thrown in the back.

They took me to a cell block that was once a shipping container. My legs throbbed from the nightstick cracks while the dive to the ground was playing havoc with the cracked rib. A Turkish military policeman with enough food in his mustache to make a kebab patted me down and locked me in a cell.

Half a dozen of his buddies eyed me, frowning, cigarettes drooping from their mouths, one of them banging a nightstick against the metal wall. The guy with the smorgasbord above his lip pulled my wallet. His eyeballs bugged out of their sockets when he got a load of the shield inside it.

Special Agents Arlow Mallet and Seb Goddard mooched in and exchanged a few quiet words with a couple of the Turkish guards. Mallet cased the block and saw me behind bars, handcuffed to one of them. He came on over wearing an appreciative grin. "Finally achieved your level, Cooper?"

"Someone make a loud noise when your face was in the oven, Mallet?"

"Good to see you've still got your pathetic sense of humor, even when you're up to your eyeballs in shit."

"You guys went to see Artie Farquar at TEI. Looks to me like you're running a concurrent investigation. Who authorized that?"

"Blow me, Cooper." Mallet shook his head slowly from side to side. "Destroying an F-16? You're in no position to be asking the questions. They'll be taking this one out of your pay for the next three hundred years."

"Ask me to blow you one more time, Mallet, and I'll seriously start to think maybe that's why you keep following me around. I asked you who atuhorized your investigation."

"Y'all's in no position to be asking *anything*, Cooper. In fact, with you in there and us out here, I can't help feeling that a little natural order has returned to the good Lord's earth. Hey, Goddard," Mallet called out, enjoying himself, "come on over here and feed the chump a banana."

Goddard joined his partner. "So, Cooper, you get a look at the two in the van?" Mallet asked.

"How do you know it was two, and why should I tell you?" I said. Mallet just stared at me. "Hey, if double-barrel questions are too hard for you to handle, I can give them to you one at a time."

"Just answer *my* question, wiseass," said Mallet.

"For a moment I thought I was chasing the both of you."

"Us? What the hell gave you that idea?"

I shrugged. I didn't feel like explaining.

"So you didn't recognize them?" Mallet insisted.

"No," I said. The two CID special agents shared a glance. It was the kind of glance that clearly has meaning—only I had no idea what that meaning could be.

"Did you get a good enough look at them to be sure you *didn't* recognize them?" Goddard pushed.

"No, as a matter of fact, I didn't. I was chasing and they were running—in a van. Now give me a little quid pro quo and get lost."

"Innocent people have been known to rot in Turkish prisons, Cooper," Goddard remarked. "Have a nice life."

"Your knuckles are dragging, Goddard," I replied.

He tossed me a final glower before leaving, both men turning up their collars, bracing for the cold before they stepped out into the late afternoon dusk.

Masters arrived, suddenly appearing in the doorway, just as boredom had settled over my jailers. "Who's in charge here?" she demanded.

One man answered with a sneering lift of his chin.

Masters held up her shield, the exact same one as mine, and said, "This man is a special agent in the U.S. Air Force OSI. You need to release him. And you need to do it *now*."

She got more boredom mixed with noncompliance until Johnny Oh came in behind her, shouting in Turkish. Then everyone started yelling. But Turks seem to do that a lot, and I was getting used to it.

It took some Turkish colonel heading up the local investigation to finally make the call on releasing me from custody, and only after several witnesses confirmed our version of the facts. Namely, that I was chasing a vehicle driven by a couple of men who were trying to escape after murdering a U.S. contractor, and that the destruction of the Israeli F-16 was an unfortunate accident.

As we walked out of the makeshift prison into the cold evening air, Masters said, "Sorry we took so long, Vin. No one seemed to know where you'd been taken."

"Goddard and Mallet did. I hadn't even warmed up the seat before they arrived."

"Maybe CID is better connected than OSI. What did they want?"

"To gloat, mostly. They also wanted to know if I recognized the guys who took care of Ten Pin. I could be wrong, but they seemed surprised when I said that I didn't."

"What does that mean?" Masters asked.

"It means they know more than we give them credit for. But then, I wouldn't give them credit to buy a pint of milk, so that's not saying much. There's something going on with those two. And it'd be helpful to know what it is."

"Perhaps we could get Cain to run a check on them through their unit," Masters suggested.

"Good idea."

"So... how are you feeling? You were pretty close to the plane when it blew."

"OK, I guess. Sore ribs, is all."

"Someone up there loves you, Vin. When I saw that fireball roll over you, I thought your goose was cooked."

"And I thought that smell was my hair," I said.

Masters allowed herself the faintest smile. "Now that you mention it, it does look a little... crunchy." She seemed about to run her fingers through it, but changed her mind and buried her hands in her pockets instead. "You did get a look at the guys in the bread van?"

"I saw one of them—white male, around thirty years old, dark hair.... Nothing a police artist could use."

We'd arrived at the Explorer. Johnny Oh took the wheel. As Masters climbed in the back, she said, "Why do I get the feeling you don't think those guys in the van were the killers we're looking for?"

"Two of them, maybe."

"Just how many killers are we looking for?"

"We're not dealing with a couple of serial killers working in tandem."

"Then what *are* we dealing with?" she asked, confused.

"A hit squad."

"A what?"

"That's Doc Merkit's theory, the one I was going to tell you about," I said.

Masters didn't respond immediately. I wondered if perhaps she was weighing up whether to regress and give me a little more grief over my night with the profiler.

"So now two of them are off the team," she said. "Are we dealing with a beach-volleyball-size team, a basketball-size team, or something bigger? And while we're at it, did your doctor friend go on to have any theories about *motives*? Or did you have more important business to attend to by then?"

I was right about the grief. "We going to get anything out of the fire?"

Masters shook her head. "Forget it. I spoke to the fire investigators. They're saying there'll be nothing left for identification purposes. The plane burned too hot."

Her cell rang. It was a brief call. "That was the medical examiner looking at what was left of Ten Pin," she told me. "Says she's come across something disturbing."

Denzel Nogart, aka Ten Pin, had been reduced to just two pins, namely his legs, before the console operator could shut down the engine. An ear and part of a hand, which included the thumb and forefinger, had also come through the turbine. But everything else belonging to the technician above his navel had been chewed off and turned into spray.

Rivulets of fluids ran red, yellow, and brown from where Ten Pin's top half used to be, joined together in the central groove pressed into the stainless-steel mortuary table, and disappeared down a hole at the head of the table. During the pauses in conversation, the rivulet could be heard making a sound like someone had forgotten to turn off a tap.

The medical examiner had cut off the guy's pants as well as his underwear, and removed his boots and socks. Disconcertingly, there were still indentations ringing his dark brown ankles from the elastic in his socks.

The ME, a woman with an English accent, massaged her chubby chins while she regarded the naked remains. "Cause of death: massive trauma . . ."

"You said you'd come across something disturbing," said Masters, beating me to it. "You're going to tell us you found a human bone on the deceased's person."

"How on earth did you know that?" the ME asked.

"Educated guess," Masters replied.

"The last guy we saw kept someone else's bird up his anus," I added, holding up a middle finger and giving it a waggle so that the ME knew what species of bird I was referring to.

She pulled back a sheet of plastic on the adjacent cutting table, revealing a stainless-steel kidney tray. "I found this in his back pocket." The object was yellow, streaked with dried blood, and the size and shape of a squashed golf ball. "It's a patella."

"A kneecap," Masters said.

"Know your anatomy, huh?" the ME responded.

"The guy who lost it gave us a crash course," I explained. "Doc, you ever do anything for the living?"

"Rarely. What do you need?"

"A little help taping up a busted rib."

TWENTY-THREE

"The man who pushed Ten Pin toward the revolving steel blades tapped him on the ass first. That's when it must have been planted," I said as we walked across the parking lot toward Johnny Oh, who was keeping the motor running.

"There's absolutely no uncertainty about this murder being number three, is there?" Masters asked.

"The killings haven't made the papers, so it's not a copycat. But, like the ME said, DNA tests will prove conclusively whose kneecap it was. I don't believe we're going to be getting any surprises on that score."

"I feel like we know even less now than we did yesterday, even though we knew enough to be down here to witness Ten Pin's murder in the first place. Why is that? We must be close to *something*, Vin. I just wish I damn well knew what it was. Do you think those missing engines are somehow connected?"

"Maybe," I said without a lot of conviction.

"If your profiler friend hadn't come up with the theory about a hit squad, we'd be saying right about now that, with those two guys dying in the fire, the case is closed."

My gut told me Masters's frustration was peppering some kind of bull's-eye. She was on the verge of a breakthrough, of looking at the three murders in a different light. I just had no idea how to push her, us, through it.

Johnny Oh pulled up outside the engine shop, a line of articulated heavy vehicles idling in the slush, belching clouds of gray vapor into the evening. I lowered the window and called over a Security Forces non-com directing traffic with a clipboard. "You guys found those missing engines yet?" I asked.

"Yep. Look behind you, sir." He ran his eyes up and down the line of trucks. "Turns out some moron sent 'em to the wrong warehouse." He shrugged. "So now we can all live happy ever after."

I gestured at Johnny to drive on. "Where to now?" he asked.

"I don't know," I said. "Let's just drive around aimlessly. Seems to fit the mood of the moment. Even better—take us to the nearest bottle of single malt."

Half an hour later, Sergeant Oh had dropped us off at the officers' club. The place was quiet because the action, such as was available, was in Adana. A few groups from different countries and outfits occupied scattered tables, nursing drinks. Masters and I were one such group, sitting beneath a huge portrait of a guy called Atatürk. He'd been painted with a benevolent yet determined set to his jaw. Apparently, this was the guy who founded modern Turkey. He was also the owner of the most spectacular set of eyebrows I'd ever seen. The waiter brought my third and Masters's second.

"So, to sum up, we've got three guys brutally murdered and no hard forensic evidence," I said. "The killings are related. The victims knew one another, and as you've already pointed out, the trail, what little of it there is, has led us here."

"They look like serial killings, but the expert tells us we're after something different," Masters added.

"So when is a serial killing not a serial killing?" I asked. And it occurred to me like a hole in the fog had opened. "When it's something else entirely."

"I think you should lay off the sauce, Vin, you—"

"No, I'm serious."

"For once." Masters sipped her Bloody Mary.

"Hear me out."

She shrugged.

"Portman was hacked to pieces. The violence was extreme and unnecessary. It looked like it was done by a wacko, but his safe was cracked by someone who not only knew their way around explosives but had access to them. So we can be pretty sure Portman wasn't killed by some nutjob who got dressed in his mom's underwear and sliced up the neighborhood cats. What if it has all been just . . . theatrics?"

"Theatrics."

"To send us down a blind alley—all the way to Incirlik."

"So, where would that leave us?"

"Hanging around this here cul-de-sac, which is exactly where whoever is pulling the strings wants us. There won't be any more murders."

"And why not?"

"Because there doesn't need to be—if I'm right about the theatrics."

From the look on Masters's face, I could see she wasn't convinced.

"Look," I went on, "let's assume that the hit squad set up these crimes to look like they were perpetrated by two people. Two killers died in the fire, and with their deaths, the trail goes cold—a dead end. If this has all been an elaborate setup, the perpetrators can shut down the operation now and leave us wallowing down here with no leads and nowhere to go."

"Are you saying the two men who just died in the bread van were sacrificed? Or sacrificed themselves, intentionally?"

"No, they died accidentally. But their deaths provided their mission planners with a windfall."

"Then what about the rest of Portman's bones?"

"Red herrings."

"So only one of our three victims was murdered for a reason. Which means the other two were just window dressing to cover it up," said Masters, gesturing at the barkeep for a fresh round.

"That's what I'm starting to think."

"Unlikely, Vin."

"Why?"

"If someone wanted to remove, say, Ten Pin, and wanted to muddy the trail, there'd be a lot better ways to cover it up than the scenario you're suggesting."

"Such as?"

"Such as walking into a restaurant you know your victim frequents and killing everyone in it, waiters and cooks included."

"So the cops would conclude the restaurant was hit by someone who didn't like their entrée?"

"No, Vin, stay with me here—to hide the identity of the true victim by making him a statistic. Just one of a large number of deaths."

"That's a good plan, Anna. Remind me not to get on your bad side."

"Sorry, too late."

"Well, who knows why the serial-killer ploy was used by the guys we're up against, rather than the one you suggest? Maybe Portman was sick of kebabs, preferring TV dinners to going out, so they couldn't murder him in a restaurant."

Masters grinned. The waiter arrived with our drinks. I paid.

"Ten Pin wasn't the key," she said after a long sip. "He was too low on the totem. That leaves us with Bremmel and Portman."

"My money's on Portman," I replied.

"Based on . . . ?"

"Bremmel was having too much fun banging his secretary."

"I beg your pardon?"

"He seemed mostly preoccupied with his . . . secretarial affairs. There was nothing to murder him for, not from what we've seen. Which leaves Portman, the first and by far the most meticulous and bloodthirsty of our murders. And then there was the robbery. Neither of the other two victims had anything taken from them, except their lives."

"Any bright ideas on why you think Portman was killed?"

"No, but now that we're not looking for serial-killer types, we can look at his death as a straight murder case."

"And how might that change the way we're investigating these murders?"

"First, we need to go back to your room and get naked," I said.

"And after I slap you and then bring a sexual harassment charge against you?"

"We need to review what we have already—go back over the forensic report, revisit the crime scene, talk to the people we've talked to already, apply some pressure, shake the tree. There have to be details we've missed, or maybe previously meaningless items will suddenly become significant now we're looking at this through a different lens. In the meantime, it wouldn't hurt to find out who or what Portman was so interested in down at Tallil."

Masters and I had been allocated quarters on base separated by half a mile, a minor blizzard, and temperatures way below zero, if you took the wind-chill factor into account. I knew Masters well enough to figure she'd had a word in the ear of the folks who organized our lodgings.

Despite the ferocity of the nighttime weather, the morning broke to a pale blue sky with visibility CAVU, as pilots say when there's nothing to obstruct the view and no wind. I had time to fix myself a black coffee before Johnny Oh arrived at eighty-thirty sharp, with Masters already in the copilot's seat.

"Morning," she said as I climbed in the back. "Sleep well?"

Between the cracked rib, the bruises, and the cast on my arm, sleep had been a battle. "Like I'd been blown up earlier in the day," I replied cheerfully.

"Good."

"You're welcome."

"The Reapers have been out for a dawn run," said Johnny, who'd quickly learned to ignore the banter between Masters and me. "They should be touching down in around five minutes."

He took us down the flight line, past the wreckage of the destroyed F-16, which was now mostly blanketed by snow mixed with frozen white foam and surrounded by a tangle of yellow crime-scene tape. A couple of hundred yards away, Ten Pin's engine test bed was similarly ringed with tape. Several MPs stamped their feet on the ice while they stood guard around it.

We parked off the side of the tarmac allocated to the Reapers just as the first of four low-viz gray F-15 fighters touched down on the main runway with a scream and a blast of light powdered snow. The frigid morning air rumbled as if a major storm was brewing nearby, indicating that the remainder of the squadron was cruising along the downwind leg of the landing pattern not far behind.

Within minutes, the four-ship squadron was on the ground, taxiing toward us. The usual trucks and vans swarmed to meet the arriving aircraft, prompting a flashback to the gruesome events of the day before.

Masters and I stood beside the Explorer, trying to stuff the palms of our hands in our ears while the jets swung into positions dictated to them by the guys with the wands. The Eagles shut down one by one, stopping in a line as straight as a crease ironed into a pair of admiral's pants.

The name stenciled on the fuselage of the nearest F-15 told us it was flown by Lieutenant Colonel Chip Woodward, the man who'd replaced Emmet Portman as squadron commander. The colonel's helmeted head bobbed around as he performed various shutdown checks, and suddenly the engines cut, their shriek dying instantly. The ground crew moved in and a short while later "Block" was climbing down the side of his aircraft. As Masters and I approached him, I said, "He's the guy in the photo, the one on Portman's bulletin board."

"I thought he looked familiar," Masters replied.

"Colonel Woodward," I said, "mind if we have a word?" Masters and I both presented our shields.

The colonel gave us a small double take. "Jesus Christ! Can't that damn woman ever leave me the hell alone? I am getting tired of this goddamn BOHICA."

"I'm sorry?" said Masters, puzzled.

"BOHICA—Bend Over, Here It Comes Again," I translated.

"*She* didn't send you here?" Woodward asked.

"No, sir," said Masters, still a little confused.

"Well, that's a relief," he said, hands on hips, visibly relieved. "Thought she might have chased me all the way downrange. Wouldn't have been the first time." He pulled a pack of gum from a front pocket, pressed out a few pellets, and popped them in his mouth. "You married?" he asked, addressing the question to me.

"Divorced."

"Then you know the score. Met her on I and I. Then twelve months ago, she meets the love of her life, a saxophone player in a local jazz band, for Christ's sake, and expects *me* to goddamn pay for them to shack up together."

I chose not to throw my own tale of marriage woes into the pot. Instead, and before Masters could ask, I leaned into her ear and whispered, "I and I—intoxication and intercourse. Just like R and R, only more accurate."

Woodward turned to Masters. "How about you, Special Agent? You still a virgin in the matrimonial stakes?"

"Engaged, Colonel."

"Then you're standing on the edge of the precipice. Two words of advice, young lady: *Step back*. You're walking into a surefire Charlie Foxtrot."

"We're here to ask you some questions about Colonel Portman," Masters said, failing to keep the annoyance out of her voice—"Charlie Foxtrot" meaning CF for cluster fuck.

"Emmet? That's why you wanna talk? Poor bastard. I heard the guy was FUGAZI."

"FUGAZI?" Masters asked.

"Army talk for Fucked Up, Got Ambushed and Zipped Into a body bag. Give me a minute and I'll let the boys know I'll be getting a ride to the maintenance debrief with you."

"Can we stop off and get an interpreter for this guy?" Masters muttered under her breath as the colonel went to pull over a truck coming our way.

The truck wasn't a bread van but it still reminded me of the one that had stopped behind Ten Pin. Woodward went around the back and told his people that he'd be riding with us. The truck drove off and someone called out, "OK, see you back at the ranch, Block."

The colonel turned in time to see my smirk. "A name like Woodward and my parents have to go and call me Chip," he explained. "So for the rest of my life I'm a chip off the ol' you-know-what."

Masters held the rear door open for the colonel.

"Why, thank you, Special Agent," he said as he took a seat. Woodward was average height and weight, in his early forties, with light brown, close-cropped hair and tan skin. His eyes were a cool light blue—two chips of the winter sky.

"Where can I take you, sir?" asked Oh.

"Just follow that there six-pack," said the colonel, indicating the vehicle ferrying the pilots in his flight.

"Colonel Woodward, how long did you know Colonel Portman?" Masters asked, all business.

"A year or so, give or take."

"Did you know him well?"

"Well enough to have had a cordial friendship and, I hope, share a mutual respect. Emmet's were big shoes to fill."

"Would he have confided in you any troubles he might have been having?"

"Possibly—I don't know. We've all got our own crap, right? But as far as I know, he had no enemies. In fact, I honestly can't recall anyone having a bad word to say about him. Sure, Portman was ambitious, but he was also one of the good guys. What can you say about something like this besides FISHDO?"

"When did you last talk to him?" Masters persisted.

"A few weeks before I heard about his murder."

"And when did he last fly with the Reapers?"

"Less than two months ago."

"Was that instance a training flight?" I asked. "And have your training missions involved a turnaround at Tallil Air Base?"

"I can't talk to you about operational specifics, Special Agent."

"Well, then, what was the nature of the last training mission Colonel Portman participated in?"

"As in, what were we training for?"

"That'll do."

"I'll repeat my last answer, Special Agent. You think that kind of detail's going to help you solve his murder?"

"Maybe," I said.

"Tell you what I'll do, son. I'll clear your questions with the higher powers. And if they're OK with it, I'll get back to you."

"Appreciate it, Colonel. Can you tell me how many times Colonel Portman had flown with the squadron?"

"He flew a total of eight sorties with the Reapers."

"And do you know why Colonel Portman was interested in Tallil?" I asked.

A deafening scream filled the Explorer. I glanced out the window.

"Those Israelis," Woodward yelled, as one of the odd-looking F-16 Sufa variants roared past in the flare, a low-viz Star of David on its flank. "Just been having a friendly joust with our guys. I tell you, the Cheil Ha'avir's one Air Force I'd think twice about tangling with. Those Ha' Negev boys and girls can sure crank and bank."

Johnny Oh followed the truck ahead, turning us away from the flight line toward a dark row of nondescript 1950s-style brick buildings and old Quonset huts.

"What was your question again, Cooper?" Colonel Woodward asked.

"We know Colonel Portman had some interest in Tallil Air Base. Would you happen to know what that interest was?"

Woodward considered the question before answering, probably debating in his mind in what context he could talk about it. "I don't think it was the base Emmet was interested in," he began. "It just happened to be the nearest friendly facility to some town he had his eye on."

"Can you remember the name of the town?" I asked.

Again, he thought about it for a moment. "Kumbayah—something like that."

I made a note of this, and doodled a question mark beside it. "Did he happen to mention what was so special about this . . . Kumbayah?"

"Can't remember. Something about an infrastructure project being built down there. Something to do with water, or maybe it was a hospital. To tell you the truth, Special Agent, if it doesn't have flaps, I'm not interested. Most of what Emmet told me about things that had nothing to do with flying, or his days at the squadron, rolled in one ear and out the other." The truck ahead of us had stopped. "Just pull over there, son."

Johnny parked and left the motor running.

"Emmet was a fine airman and a good American," Woodward told us. "You folks got any further questions?"

"No, not for the moment, Colonel," I replied.

"Well, if I can think of anything, or if I get clearance from my superiors, I'll be sure to call you. Either of you got a card or something?"

Both Masters and I obliged. Woodward pocketed them, climbed out, and bounced up the steps. We motored off to join the base traffic stuck behind a snowplow grinding away at the roadside's ice shoulder.

"I know I said I had no more questions, but—FISHDO?" Masters asked.

From the front seat, Johnny Oh translated: "Fuck It, Shit Happens, Drive On."

"Thanks."

"How does that song go?" I said. *"Kum-ba-yah, my lord, Kum-ba-yah . . ."*

Refusing to join in, Masters said, "Sergeant Gallagher and now Woodward said Portman was interested in something going on down in southern Iraq."

"A Christian fireside song, perhaps?"

"Vin . . ." Masters snapped.

"You heard the colonel—if it doesn't have flaps . . . Who knows what the name of that town was? But there's nothing even vaguely like it mentioned in Portman's emails. And that's surprising if it was important to him," I reasoned. "For that matter, why would he talk about this project supposedly close to Tallil in a reasonably open way to Woodward and Gallagher, but say nothing to either Harvey Stringer, Mr. CIA, or Ambassador Burnbaum?"

"Or perhaps he did, but neither Stringer nor Burnbaum thought it worthwhile enough to pass on to us."

"Maybe we should give them both another opportunity to mention it," I suggested as my cell began to ring. The number on-screen had an Istanbul area code. "Cooper," I said, answering it.

"Captain Cain here, Special Agent. How you doin' down there? I heard about the F-16 going up in smoke. I also heard you lit the fuse. Any truth in that rumor?"

I put the phone on speaker to include Masters in the conversation. We gave him a rundown of recent events and asked whether any of the information we'd requested had come in.

"Yeah, that's why I'm calling. We just got the results back from the FBI on those explosives—the ones used to blow the safe in Portman's house. Thought you might like to know."

"We would," I said.

"The stuff was manufactured in the U.S.A."

"It's *ours*?"

"Apparently, we sold it to Israel. We shipped it to them in artillery shells—bunker busters. I checked it out with the people at military intelligence. According to them, the shells were fired into Lebanon during the September 06 rumble with Hezbollah."

Whatever I was expecting, it wasn't that. "Every last one?"

"Who would know? You think the Israelis would give us the specifics? Also, I've been breaking down that shipping register you left me. I think we might have something there."

"What you got?"

"As you know, over the five hours covered by the log, the period that spanned Portman's estimated time of death, there were thirty-six vessels transiting the Bosphorus. Twenty-four of them required pilots."

"And the twelve that didn't?"

"They're the smaller local ships. Only one of these stood out as being odd. A rust bucket of around ten thousand tons called the *Onur*—which in Turkish means 'pride,' by the way—registered out of Istanbul. She was carrying cooking oil. At 0217 she went up the strait, and she came back down again at 0502."

"What's so odd about that, Rodney?"

"I've been reliably informed that you either go up the Bosphorus, or you come down, not both—at least, not so quickly. Round-trips usually take more than a few hours, unless you're a public ferry. If you're lugging cargo, that means entering and leaving a port, and that eats up time. The round-trip usually takes you more than a day and includes either loading or unloading cargo, and lots of paperwork. So, anyway, at some point in the Bosphorus or up in the Black Sea, the *Onur* decided to come back to Istanbul."

"She would have been in the right place at the right time to make deliveries and pickups," said Masters, looking at me as she spoke.

I nodded.

"Yeah," said Cain. "Exactly. There were the usual radio calls logged between the vessel and shipping control confirming all of this, by the way. The *Onur* apparently went back to Istanbul because of engine trouble."

"A likely story," I cut in.

"Actually, I called around and the engine trouble checked out. Seems *Onur* was barely seaworthy. Anyway, I went down to the port this morning to see what I could dig up, and guess who I ran into?"

"Ramses the second?"

"You did ask for it, Cain," Masters said.

"Sorry. Try Detective Sergeants Karli and Iyaz."

"What were they doing there?" I asked.

"Investigating a homicide. It appears the *Onur* sank at its mooring last night. All hands were lost."

TWENTY-FOUR

Masters had called ahead, and Emir and his mobile living room were waiting for us at Istanbul's Atatürk Airport. He gave Masters a hug and then went for me. I warned him not to try it. The guy got even, smoking and chattering all the way to the docks.

I tuned him out and thought about Stringer and Burnbaum. We'd called the Consulate-General from Incirlik and learned that Stringer had left for CIA headquarters in Langley, and that Burnbaum was at the U.S. Embassy in Ankara. Neither was contactable.

When Detective Sergeant Karli saw me walking toward him along the dock, I caught him raising his eyes to heaven, as if asking his maker what the fuck I was doing there. Then he turned and walked off quickly, like he'd forgotten something. Maybe it was his desire to cooperate.

Rodney Cain met us on the dock. I saw him standing near a cluster of police vehicles, deep in conversation with one of the Turkish forensics people. He gave us a wave and came on over. "Morning," he said.

I checked my watch. He was right, it was morning. Only 11:45 and already it felt like late afternoon.

"They just pulled the last of the bodies out," he reported. "Ten of them. All drowned. The divers found them floating around in the mess. The hatch had been jammed shut—there was a piece of steel shoved in the mechanism."

"A great way to clean house—flood it," I said. "How'd they sink her?"

"It could have been done any number of ways. Until the divers have completed their survey, the general thinking is that someone blew off the engine cooling ducts."

"Have you informed Turkish homicide we were looking into the *Onur* as part of the Portman investigation?" Masters asked.

"Yeah. They're not happy about the connection, but I told them it wasn't exactly our fault. I think they just want the whole show to catch a flight home to the States, us included."

"No survivors, no witnesses," I said. "A person or persons on board met Portman's killers—maybe even handed them towels when they came back. Let's at least see how much they paid the ship's master for the pickup and delivery service."

"I'll get the master's bank records pulled," said Cain.

"Has anyone seen or heard from Portman's servant yet—Adem Fedai?"

"No. And while I'm on the subject of bank accounts, Fedai's hasn't been touched. I checked yesterday. I'm starting to think that more than likely he's out there somewhere"—Cain gestured at the rusting expanse of the port and the cold gray sea beyond it—"dusting Davy Jones's locker."

"I'd like to take the afternoon off, if that's OK with you," said Masters as we walked back toward Emir, who, as usual, was waving at us like he was stranded on a rooftop and we were a couple of rescue choppers.

"Again. To do what?"

"It's personal."

"We don't have any more time for personal crap, Anna."

"And I don't know why I even asked, Vin. I don't need your permission, and you know it."

I did know it, but I also knew a lot of people were dying long before they were supposed to and that Masters and I were the best chance any future victims had of not becoming one of them. Or was there another reason I didn't want to let her go?

Emir took us back to the Hotel Charisma. When we pulled up there half an hour later, I watched Masters step out of the car and into the arms of that other reason—Colonel Wad—who was waiting for her in the lobby.

Emir drove off. At the corner, I stopped him, got out of the car, and gave him the rest of the month off. He wasn't happy about it, so I told him to take it up with Special Agent Masters. I needed to walk, get a few things straight. I had paperwork to write up—the events down at Incirlik and a progress report on the case—but I put it all off. I needed some time to consider how I felt about Anna ending up with someone other than me. I also had a new thought on this hit squad theory.

I walked for thirty-five minutes, past the Blue Mosque, the Aya Sophia, down the hill, past two more mosques, across the bridge, and up the other side. At least, that's the route I must have walked. There was no other way I could have taken to end up outside Dr. Merkit's house. But that's exactly where I found myself when I finally stopped.

I could have walked up the steps to the front door, could have rung the bell, could have discussed the latest theories on the case with her, could have ended up naked for some skin-on-skin action. But instead, I hailed a cab and went to the scene of the original crime—Portman's place in Bebek.

Investigating crime can alter the investigator's perspective on time. A week can compress itself into a space that feels like a day, while a day can stretch on and feel like a week. I had to think about how many days or weeks had passed since Masters and I had first taken a look around the place where Portman died. I believed it was four days ago, but it could also have been months. But then I saw the familiar green van belonging to the cleaners parked out front.

They should have finished by now. Perhaps business was slow in Istanbul at the moment and they were squeezing every nickel they could out of the job. The police still had a guard on the place, but only one uniform now and not a guy I recognized. The portable bulletproof shields were also gone. But the uniform was still conspicuously armed, an FN FAL rifle slung over his shoulder, the stock and bluing so worn it looked like a family heirloom.

I took the steps to the front door and showed the guard my shield. He smiled, showing me a set of teeth held in place by wire thick enough to hang a coat on. He opened the door. I went in and heard the door close behind me.

The hallway was still dark, but the heating had been turned on and the place felt almost cozy. The smell of fresh paint was in the air, reminding me that Portman's blood had been impossible to clean off. That memory killed the cozy feeling instantly. I noticed an antique wood table by the front door, which wasn't there the first time I visited the place. A large and expensive ornate glass vase sat on it, filled with imported irises and poppies. The leasing agents must have been working overtime to fill the place with cheer for any potential renters.

I went for a lap around the ground floor to get my bearings. The door through which the courtyard and drain were accessed had a new lock. The key was in the lock. The smashed windowpane had been replaced and the fingerprint dust removed. I unlocked the door, opened it, and took the steps down to the courtyard. It was cold and damp, deep in shadow. I walked to the drain cover and looked down at it, hoping for some inspiration. None came. A couple of birds circled overhead, keening, disappointed. Perhaps because the water bed was dry.

I walked back toward the door, but something crunched underfoot. I ignored it and it crunched again. Lifting my boot, I saw that a wedge of glass was caught between the blocks of rubber. I pulled it out. It was about the right thickness—a sliver from the broken windowpane. My boot must have picked it up from a gap between the flagstones. *What's it doing all the way over here?* I wondered. I flicked it at the courtyard wall and it landed in a corner.

I went back inside the house, climbed the steps to the second story, and kept going up to the third. Halfway up the stairs one of the women I'd met when Masters and I had inspected this place—the one who'd dissolved my T-shirt with her miracle cleaning fluid—appeared on the landing. She was carrying a bucket, a mop, a couple of brooms, and a plastic trash bag. She said hello and followed up with a little Turkish, all delivered in a friendly manner, as we passed each other mid-flight. I gathered that her job here was finished at last, and that she was off to freshly bloodied pastures.

On the top floor, I made my way to the room where Portman died. I'd read the report on the crime scene so many times it was tattooed on my brain. The gilt chair upholstered in red velvet wasn't quite in the same position it had previously occupied, but it was no longer overturned, the claw feet pressing into the Turkish rug. Beneath the chair and rug, I knew, was the removable tile in the carpet and, beneath that, the floor safe, the one Portman had had secretly installed.

There was a small antique table in front of the chair. The room smelled of fresh paint and the chemicals released by new carpet. The Oriental faces that hung on the wall gazed out inscrutably, giving away nothing of the horror they'd witnessed here a week ago.

I had no good reason for returning to Portman's house. The Turkish forensic team had been as thorough as any I'd ever worked with. They'd done a great job, missed nothing, and yet I couldn't shake the feeling that *something* had to have slipped through our collective fingers.

I walked into the adjoining room, the one with the wall safe. I pulled back the painting with the guys in turbans bringing down their elephant. The original safe door had been destroyed in the explosion. This one was new, the combination dial gleaming with black and silver enamel, the handle a scratch-free matte black. I pulled on it and the door swung open. There was nothing inside, as expected. I closed it, replaced the painting, then wandered back to where the Air Attaché had been sitting on his last night on earth.

I shifted the chair and then the table, moving them back into their original positions, the ones they'd been in on that bloody night. Then I stood back and looked at the chair. Portman had been sitting right here when a pad soaked in chloroform had been pressed over his mouth and nose. Would he have seen the faces of his killers before he'd gone under?

I sat in the chair and tried to imagine the way it had gone down. We knew the killers had been wearing coveralls and dry suits. They would also have been wearing diving-style face masks. But were those masks pulled over their faces the entire time, or just while they cut Portman up, to make certain that his blood didn't splatter into their eyes?

I glanced behind the chair to the set of wide double doors on the far side of the adjoining room. It made sense that the killers would have crept up behind their victim. The murder took place sometime after two A.M.—maybe Portman was asleep or resting, his head already tilted back. I put my head back and looked up at the ceiling, allowing my eyes to follow the maze of intricate painted patterns, and tried to think what that elusive something we'd missed might be. The two safes? The use of chloroform? My thoughts drifted to the moment when the killers appeared in Portman's view—hoods over their heads, goggled up like bugs, one of them brandishing a jigsaw, perhaps? How long had the attaché's terror lasted before he'd slipped away on the chemical carpet ride?

The room was quiet and still, the only sound my own breathing. The top of the chair had a hard wooden knob that dug into the back of my skull, and the cushion was firm. Finding a comfortable position in this rack wasn't easy. The forensic report stated that up to the time of his murder, he'd been fully dressed, wearing suit pants, leather shoes, a white shirt, and a loosened tie. I sat up so abruptly I nearly toppled the chair.

There was no sound system in the room, no books on the shelves, no view—nothing. And this chair was no place to come to relax. So the question I was suddenly asking myself was: What was the attaché *doing* when he was sitting in this chair at the time he was killed? Who just sits in a chair and does nothing? Was he working through a crossword? Picking his nose? *What?* Something had to have been occupying the guy's time. Was he reviewing notes? Writing correspondence? Portman might well have been doing one, some, or all of these activities, or something else entirely. Except, according to the forensic report, there was nothing of that nature (or any nature) found with the guy's remains. According to the evidence, Colonel Portman had just been sitting in this gilt chair, twiddling his thumbs, waiting to be made into chop suey. If I didn't believe that, which I didn't, it meant a person or persons—possibly the killers, but also possibly someone else entirely—had removed something from the crime scene. If so, what? And who? Maybe the elusive, or equally possibly very dead, Adem Fedai?

I got out of the chair, tipped it back the way the Turkish police had found it, and rolled away the rug. The carpet tile was in place. I removed it and the floor safe was revealed, its door ajar. I opened it: empty. I had no idea what I might be looking for. But having no idea when I returned here to Portman's place had revealed *something*.

I closed the safe, replaced the square and the rug, and sat the chair back on its feet. The carpet was new and freshly nailed into the floor at the molding. A small antique cabinet was placed against one wall. I opened the cabinet doors—two shelves on each side, all empty. I leaned it back so that I could look under, behind, and beneath it. There was wicker bracing between the legs, which could double as a kind of shelf. Again, empty.

What had I been thinking? Forensics wouldn't have missed anything.

I stood, frowning. The picture of a plastic trash bag came to mind... Where had I seen it? And what was the significance? And then it hit me. Goddamn it—*the cleaners*!

I ran to the other side of the house, where I knew I'd get a view down into the street. The woman was talking to the uniform, bag and bucket in hand, saying good-bye, her other hand on the handle of the van door. I called out, but they didn't hear. I tried opening the window, but it had been painted shut. I ran for the staircase and took the steps three at a time, all the way down.

I hit the front door, fumbled with the lock, pushed it open, and jumped past the uniform and onto the sidewalk. Just in time to see the back of the van as it disappeared around a corner, a hundred yards down the road, in a cloud of exhaust. "Damn it!" I swore, maybe a little too loud.

The uniform scowled. I gave him a wave and fumbled for my cell.

"Captain Cain," said the voice at the other end.

"It's Cooper."

"Hey, Vin, what's—"

"I'm over at Portman's place, Rodney. Can you give me a number for the cleaners here?"

"Yep. What's the problem?"

"No problem—I just passed one of them on the way out of here. She was carrying a plastic trash bag. I want to know what she was taking out."

"OK. Call you back ASAP."

I rang off and stood there on the roadside, hoping for a cab to happen along so that I could follow that van, but the street was empty. An icy wind blast blew a handful of grit into my eyes. I took a seat on the front steps and waited. A minute later, my cell rang.

"It's Cain. OK, I got hold of her. She's on her way back to you at the house."

"You tell her why I wanted to see her?"

"No."

"Thanks, Rodney," I said, just as her van ambled around the corner down the far end of the street. "Can you hold?" I asked Cain. "I might need your language skills."

"Sure," came the cheerful reply.

I put the phone on speaker as the van pulled up. The woman opened the door and wheezed as she got out.

"Hi," I said.

She replied in Turkish.

"What'd she say?" I asked Cain.

"You don't want to know."

I could tell the woman wasn't happy. Plus, she had a way with chemical agents that I wasn't prepared to tangle with a second time.

"Tell her I want to have a look inside the garbage she just took from Portman's place."

"OK," he said before again breaking into Turkish.

The woman threw her hands up and spoke to someone above, and then turned and lumbered over to the van's sliding door.

Digging into a pocket, she fished out a pair of surgical gloves and thrust them at me. Then she dumped the contents of the orange garbage bag out onto the floor of the van. I picked through the heap with a bent wire coat hanger.

"What's going on?" Cain wanted to know.

"Just practicing for when my retirement benefits run out."

"What?"

"Never mind.... So, in the bag we've got some half-eaten tomatoes, a bunch of soiled rags, five empty water bottles, three Mars Bar wrappers, and what looks like—yeah, pages from a local newspaper used to clean the windows."

"So, nothing much," he summed up.

"Oh, I don't know. I missed lunch and those tomatoes look pretty appealing." I prised open the balls of newsprint. Nothing.

The woman's arms were folded and her face looked like a pair of old sneakers. She said something.

There would have been other bags of trash disposed of throughout the cleanup. I was wasting everyone's time here, especially my own.

"She wants to go," Cain translated.

"OK. Can you thank her for me? Tell her I think she has a camel's eyelashes or something—something nice." I grinned at her, nodding.

Cain took over. The woman grunted, turned her back, and heaved a buttock back onto the driver's seat. Then she drove off, the exhaust blowing smoke like a good Turkish vehicle should.

I turned and almost collided with an old guy wearing an official but shabby uniform. He pushed past. He had the determined walk of someone who did a lot of pushing all day every day. The old man stepped up to the door of Portman's place, where the police officer raised a cordial finger in his direction like the two were great pals. Next, the old-timer reached into the faded cloth sack hanging over his shoulder, pulled out a couple of envelopes, and pushed them through the slot in the door. Then he trudged back down the steps, off to the next house down the street.

I pulled out my cell again and hit the redial button.

"Captain Cain."

"Rodney, did you have Portman's mail rerouted to the Consulate-General as a matter of procedure?"

"Yeah, why?"

"Never mind." I cut the call.

I pocketed the cell and climbed the steps. The uniform opened the door for me again and I went back inside. Two envelopes lay on the tassels fringing the Turkish rug that ran the length of the hallway. I bent and picked them up, intrigued. Both were addressed to the leasing agent—which made sense. I wondered whether other letters had been delivered, but I couldn't see any. Maybe the leasing agent had already collected them. There was nothing on the side table and nothing in either drawer. I looked behind the vase and discovered a stack of mail. All bills. Except for one. Prickles went up my spine and played with the hair on the back of my neck.

In neat handwriting, the letter had been addressed to Sultan Mehmet II at 827 Tenth Avenue, New York, NY 10019. *Sultan Mehmet II.* The name was familiar.... Wasn't he the guy in Burnbaum's painting? The one standing on a mountain of body parts?

On the back of the envelope was the address of the residence I was standing in—Portman's—but no name. Predictably, given the letter's addressee, across the front of the envelope was scrawled RETURN TO SENDER. There were enough stamps to start an album, ensuring it made the round-trip. The postmark indicated that the letter's journey had begun just over three weeks ago.

The sender had to have been Colonel Emmet Portman. Furthermore, he must have addressed it the way he had to keep the contents out of circulation for a period of time—the time it takes a letter to make the trip from Istanbul to New York and back again. I tapped the envelope on my fingertips, considering whether to open it. After traveling thousands of miles and passing through at least half a dozen pairs of hands, one more set wouldn't compromise the envelope's forensic value, would it?

I took the letter to the kitchen, slit it open with a bread knife, and shook the contents out onto the counter. A single sheet of paper. On it, printed in neat black ink, identical to the handwriting on the envelope, was a single line of numbers and letters: *L12R25L36R19L51.* Goddamn it—the combination for a safe!

I raced up the stairs again, all the way to the third-floor sitting room, gripping the paper's corner between thumb and forefinger. I pulled the chair away, rolled back the carpet, and flipped up the floor tile. After pushing the safe door closed and spinning the knob left and right to lock it, I dialed in the combination from the letter...and the door popped open. *Je-sus!* I hunched down on the floor as another burst of those prickles ran up my spine.

Portman had known he was in danger. So he'd put...what? Evidence of some kind? Whatever it was, he'd put it in the safe and then mailed the combination to the U.S. and back. He'd locked something away, something to be found in case of his death, and it had been removed on the night he was killed.

TWENTY-FIVE

The cab pulled up outside Portman's place. I got in. The driver wanted to know where to, which was precisely the question I was wrestling with. The hours off that Masters had demanded had yet to pass. But enough afternoon delight was enough, especially when Colonel Dick Wad was the one giving it. The general X-rated nature of those thoughts had made me think of Doc Merkit. I needed to pay her a visit too, and even managed to convince myself that said visit had nothing to do with the potential of once again seeing her without her clothes on.

A short ride later, I pulled up outside the familiar pink shoe box in Beyoglu. The lights were on, holding back the mid-afternoon gloom. Wind whipped down the street in a sudden blast that turned a couple of umbrellas inside out. I huddled into my jacket, took the steps up to the front door, and rang the bell. I heard footsteps and then the door opened and I was looking into the doc's deep-sea eyes. She was smiling, pleased to see me. The feeling was mutual.

"Vin! You must come in. Hurry, it is cold out there," she said, scooping me in with a wave of her arm. The house was warm but the doc was dressed as if it wasn't, in a thick woolen sweater the color of cornmeal and a sea-blue scarf that covered her hair and framed her face. Beneath the sweater was a narrow sheath of dark blue fabric that forced her to take small quick steps. Her feet were bare. "You have caught me relaxing," she said.

"Sorry about that."

"Please, it is OK."

"Where's Nasor?" I asked.

"He has gone back to university, and my receptionist is still sick. I have no patients today, so I am closed." She shrugged. "I was making some apple tea. You would like some, too?"

"Sure," I said.

"I saw you outside in the street earlier—an hour or so ago. Was it you or is there someone else in Istanbul who looks just like you?"

"That was me," I admitted as I walked behind her to the kitchen.

"You left before I could invite you to come in."

"I walked here from the Sultanahmet. I had some things on my mind. The walk helped."

"Why did you leave?"

"I went back to Portman's home—to have another look around the crime scene."

"Oh," she said, pouring the tea into two bell-shaped glasses. "I heard from Captain Cain about the terrible thing that happened at Incirlik. He told me you were lucky not to have been killed." The doc was frowning. I couldn't help but notice she frowned sexy, too.

"Cain's prone to exaggeration." I was suddenly aware of my cracked rib. It was throbbing beneath the bandages. "You mind if we sit down somewhere? Been kind of a long day."

"You are injured. I was about to take a bath—*you* must have it."

I had a sudden image of the doc all soaped up and slipping around with me in the tub. It took an effort to wrench myself away from the happy thought. I said no thanks and meant to leave it there, but I heard myself add, "Maybe later."

She nodded as if that would be fine, and sat beside me on the couch. I did my best to try to stick to the point. "Did Cain tell you about the man killed down there and what they found on him?"

"Yes. Again, like the Bremmel murder. These murders are not happening for psychological reasons." She handed me a glass of tea.

"That's what I wanted to talk to you about. The other murders were just a smoke screen—a diversion. I think Portman was assassinated."

Aysun sipped her tea, giving herself a moment to consider it. "What makes you think this?"

I gave her a rundown on the significant developments, starting with her own theory that Bremmel's murder was too different from Portman's to have been the work of a serial killer. There was the FBI's confirmation that the explosives used to blow Portman's wall safe were military, made in the U.S.A.; the discovery of the blast blankets and other items in the Bosphorus; and the sinking of the *Onur* with the death of all on board. Then, of course, there was the mysterious presence of the supposed "agents" and their hunt for Adem Fedai, Portman's servant, the man I was certain had cleaned out the hidden floor safe when he arrived for work to find Portman in pieces on the floor. There were other factors, too, ones that didn't seem to fit any scenario other than that of a planned and systematic attack: the break-in at the leasing agent's offices to steal the floor plans for Portman's residence; the care with which the crime scenes had been managed to lead us down blind alleys; the letter containing the safe combination that Portman mailed to a phony address, proving he believed himself to be in mortal danger.

"Do you have any suspects?" she asked when I'd finished.

"No." The admission pricked the soap bubble, the feeling I had that this case was finally leading somewhere. *Pop.* I shifted on the seat and the rib hooked my breath, causing me to grit my teeth.

Doc Merkit looked concerned. "Please, Vin. Come with me." She got up from the couch, stepped over a pile of books, and helped me stand. She led me down to the back of her house and into the bathroom. "Here, sit." She indicated an old wooden chair.

I eased down onto it with a grunt that reminded me of the way the cleaner over at Portman's moved. I glanced in the mirror and rubbed the growth on my chin and cheeks. I was even starting to look like her.

The doc struck a match and lit two fat candles on the broad, white marble benchtop. Then she knelt in front of me and began unlacing my shoes.

"Doc, I don't have time . . ."

"You have never had a Turkish girlfriend."

"No."

"Turkish women know how to care for a man." She slipped off my boots.

"I'm sure that's true, Aysun, but . . ."

"Shh."

I put up about as much resistance as an old drunk with a fresh bottle.

Aysun stood and slipped off the head scarf. Her hair was tied in a ponytail. She slid the elastic from her hair and shook it out. The sweater came next. The blue sheath beneath it was a dress made from some fabric that followed the curves of her body, with low off-the-shoulder sleeves cut to accentuate the narrowness of her waist and the swell of her breasts.

She leaned over, unzipped my jacket, and helped me out of it. "Can you lift your arms?"

"Yep," I said.

"Show me."

I showed her and the doc gently eased the T-shirt over my head.

"These . . . need to be taken care of," she said, running a hand across the bandages on my chest. "A doctor must be good for something, don't you think?"

"Must be," I replied, by this stage not really caring what her prowess with a bandage was like.

She released the clips that kept the elastic tight around my ribs, and the sudden drop in pressure caused me to flinch. "I am sorry," she whispered.

"It's OK, doc, though I think I'm going to need a *lot* of sympathy."

TWENTY-SIX

The guy with the urn on his back was loitering outside the Charisma, plying the tourist trade. My cab caught his attention as it pulled up, but his eyes slid off my face when I got out. This was one ambulance he'd given up chasing.

I crossed the empty foyer to the elevator, which arrived with a perfectly timed *ping* as I stepped up to it. The doors parted. Lieutenant Colonel Wadding was staring at the floor as if a good friend had just been buried there.

"Special Agent Vincent Cooper," he said when he raised his head and saw me. "I've been hoping to run into you." His hair was wet.

"I'd like to say the feeling's mutual, Colonel, only I don't happen to be driving a bus."

Wadding bared his dental veneers at me. "You're a funny man, Cooper. Say, I checked up on your friend—Tyler Dean. Y'know, it's such a shame he's gone. As a good friend of yours, I'd have enjoyed...let's just say, I'd have enjoyed making his life even more miserable than it already was."

"You need to get out of my way before we both regret it," I told him.

"Unless you've forgotten, Cooper, I'm JAG, as well as being a superior officer—so, as they say: Go ahead, make my day."

"You're not worth the skinned knuckle, Dick Wad."

His eyes narrowed at the mention of his call sign. "You can refer to me as 'sir.'"

"I think that's unlikely."

Wadding gave a small snort, and a smile crept over his lips like something out of a hole. "Anna told me you and she used to be involved. Now that I know a little about you, I really do find it hard to believe. Y'all know what I love most about your ex-girlfriend?"

I'd changed my mind about wanting to hit the guy. My new problem was deciding where.

Wadding took half a step forward and whispered in my ear, "It's the way she shudders when she comes."

"Vin," said Masters, suddenly appearing on the stairs beside the elevator shaft. "Is that your foot jammed against the door?" She peered around the corner to confirm it. "So *you're* the holdup. You know you're keeping the whole damn building waiting?" She was smiling, but the smile faded when she caught the mood. "What's the matter?"

"Nothing, sweetheart," Wadding replied. "Vin and I were just exchanging pleasantries. Call you later." He kissed her on the cheek and strode off into the gathering dusk.

Emir was furious, throwing us around as he carved up the traffic. As for Masters, she hadn't said a word since we'd left the hotel.

"So, what do you see in this guy?" I asked, kicking things off.

"Which guy? Emir?"

"She speaks.... No, not Emir."

"Which reminds me. Why did you fire him?" Masters asked.

Emir's eyes were hot, flitting from the road ahead to the rearview mirror. He dragged on his Camel and the orange embers gave his features an evil cast.

"We die, Emir, and you're a dead man," I warned.

"Vin!"

"Forget Emir," I said. "I'm talking about Wadding."

"I won't have that conversation with you, Vin. Not here, not now. Maybe not ever."

"Over at Ramstein. You said you were helping Wadding. What were you helping him with?"

"I'm not a hundred percent certain, but I think that's classified. And if it's not classified, it's privileged."

"You're not a lawyer, so privilege doesn't apply. Quit stalling."

Masters turned away, adjusted her jacket, thinking about it. "I was his liaison."

"His liaison for what?"

"There were experiments with armor on the base—old tanks. They shot them up with DU."

"What did the tests show?"

"Look, I can't—"

"What did they show, damn it?"

"What do you think they showed, for Christ's sake? You subject anything to a hard rain of depleted uranium ammunition, and what's left is radioactive and stays that way for four and a half billion years."

"And the guy who's going to twist that up so that the men and women who fought our wars lose their battles with cancer—*he's* the guy you're going to spend the rest of your life with?"

"Oh, come on. . . ."

"Well, aren't you?"

"Look, I'm sorry about Tyler—"

"Then why don't you call his wife?" I challenged. "Her name's Katie, by the way. Yeah, why don't you just call Katie and let her know just how sorry you are for her and the twins—their names are Talia and Montana. You've known Wadding for maybe six weeks. Do you really have any idea what you're letting yourself in for with this asshole?"

"He's a lawyer, Vin. Lawyers sometimes take unpopular cases, root for what seems like the wrong team. That's the system, that's how it works. You can't hate him for it."

No, now it was a lot more than that. *It's the way she shudders when she comes.*

Masters folded her arms tight like they were secured that way with straps. I went into a huddle with the door. Emir swerved into Kaplicalar Mevkii. The asphalt snaked up the hill toward the peach Consulate-General building lit up bright enough to be seen from space.

"Stop the car!" Masters snarled.

Emir hit the brakes.

"What?" I asked, thrown hard against the seat belt.

"Look . . ."

She was pointing at a human column standing in the parking lot. It was Ocirik, the wrestler. He was waiting for something, maybe for us.

"Ocirik!" I called as I got out. "What brings you all the way out here? Changed your mind about letting us search your place?"

"I bring message," he said, pulling on a cigar big enough to hit a home run with.

"Who for?" I asked.

"For you. Adem Fedai ask me."

OK, now the guy had my full attention.

"Why us?" I asked.

"You give me card, I give to him. He scare."

"He's scared?" Masters interpreted.

"Yes. He trust America."

"Now I *have* heard everything," I said.

"Vin!" Masters was annoyed. "Go on, Ocirik. What's the message?"

The big man took a cell phone from his pocket, dialed what I took to be his message bank, then put it on speaker. "You listen," he said. He puffed on his cigar, then blew more smoke than an old Turkish Fiat.

A small, frightened voice began squeaking from the palm of Ocirik's immense hand. *"My name is Adem Fedai,"* it said. *"I worked for Colonel Portman. I know you are looking for me. You must know I did not kill him. I have something you want. I took it from the colonel's safe. I will meet you. You come to Ephesus—I will meet you at the top gate tomorrow, half an hour from closing. Before you come, you must look at the town of Kumayt in Iraq."*

The number that Fedai had called from to leave the message was unlisted. We couldn't find him, but he could find us—tomorrow, sunset, at the top gate of a place called Ephesus.

We thanked Ocirik and raced inside the building or, at least, I raced. Masters took it slow. As we stood in the elevator, I said, "Ku-may-et, my Lord, Ku-may-et . . ."

"Sounds like Colonel Woodward was listening harder than he thought after all," Masters said.

She was pale. "You OK?" I asked.

"I'm fine."

"You don't look it."

"I'm *fine*."

I shrugged. Normally, the deeply sensitive guy that I am would have been more concerned. "This is the break we've been hoping for," I told her.

"Yeah, sounds like it could be," came the reply.

"I went back over Portman's place today."

"Why?"

"No reason. Just went to have another look around. Something interesting turned up."

"What?"

"The mailman." I reached into my jacket, pulled out the letter, and handed it to her.

"And here I was thinking you might have grabbed the opportunity to pay a house call on the good doctor."

"Nope, *way* too busy for that," I replied.

"Sultan Mehmet, eh?" She checked the return address. "So, Portman sent a letter he knew would get returned?"

"Yeah."

"Why'd he do that? What did he have to say to himself?"

"He wrote down the combination to his floor safe, which he then sent on a round-trip that'd take several weeks. I think the guy knew his goose was cooked, and he wanted this to turn up in any investigation into his death. This combination doesn't open the wall safe, so he wanted us to know there was a second safe. But we'd already found it." The elevator came to a stop with a jolt.

"Only Fedai got to it before us and removed the contents," said Masters. "Still doesn't take us anywhere new, though, does it?"

No, it didn't, but it provided a fascinating window into Portman's state of mind leading up to his murder.

We walked into the office, the one with the painting of Mehmet stepping all over people on his way to the top. The clock on the wall said eight o'clock. For us, however, the day was just starting. We both had catching up to do. I went to my desk.

"I'm just going to take a moment," said Masters. She removed her jacket and ball cap, lay full length on the sofa, and stretched. She was wearing a lowish-cut red T-shirt. If I looked, I could see the tops of her breasts straining against her white lace bra. OK, so I looked.

I tore myself away from the show and on to the package sitting on my desk. Further investigation revealed it to be a printer cartridge. The

IT guy must have brought it up. Maybe there was some union rule against him installing it.

I pulled out the old cartridge, unpacked the new one, and inserted it. After hitting the on button, I pressed print. I seemed to have several documents backed up in the printer queue.

A *ding* sounded, and a box appeared on the computer screen informing me that now the printer was suffering from a paper jam. I was on the verge of making the damn thing suffer a hell of a lot worse. I got up, opened the slot, removed the new cassette, and checked the rollers. Nothing. A little diagram on the unit's control panel flashed, telling me to keep looking. So I got down on my knees, opened another slot, and peered into the plastic bowels. There it was—a sheet of paper jammed below one of the rollers. I pulled it out, ripping the paper in half. Then I dropped it in the trash, scanning it as my fingers let it go. Something told me to retrieve it. I smoothed out the folds, and read it.

Goddamn . . .

I picked up the phone and called IT. Everyone had gone home. A recorded message provided an emergency after-hours number to call. This was an emergency. I dialed the number.

"Hello, this is Special Agent Cooper. . . . Do you know anything about a printer brought up to my office? . . . You do? Who had it before me? . . . Uh-huh . . . Uh-huh. OK, thanks."

Masters was frowning and her eyes were closed. I dropped the sheet of paper onto her stomach.

"What's this?"

"Read it."

She sat up and read it aloud. *"You know the score. We'll hold you to your promise that the mess down there won't sour our chances on future contracts. All the best, B.* What's this?"

"Part of an email."

"I can see that, but—"

"I just dug it out of my printer. IT services brought the printer up from *Portman's office."*

"This was Portman's printer?" Masters blinked. "So who's B? Burnbaum?"

I shook my head. "From what I've seen, and I've read hundreds of Burnbaum's emails to Portman, he always signs off 'Ward' when it's informal and 'Ambassador Burnbaum' when it's not. Also, that doesn't seem to be the kind of email you'd send to someone who works down the hall. So, I have no idea who this is from. There is something, though."

"What?"

"Like I said, I've been through Portman's emails. And funnily enough, I don't recall seeing this one."

"Which means Portman's email has been edited."

"I'd have said 'fucked with.' There's also Portman's conveniently corrupted electronic calendar. From the guy's service record—in fact, from everything we know about him—he's an overachiever, a workaholic. The biggest slice of work on his plate takes up one or two days of his working week, according to Artie Farquar at TEI. Allow around one day a week for official duties, plus maybe half a day for admin, and I can see Portman sitting around for fifty percent of the week twiddling his thumbs."

"Only he's not a thumbs-twiddling kind of guy," Masters mused.

"He doesn't seem to be a party animal, doesn't have a girlfriend... so what's he doing to keep himself occupied?"

Masters nodded.

"Let's speculate here and connect a few dots," I said. "What if 'the mess down there' was something at Kumayt keeping Portman busy? What if it's an infrastructure project, something to do with water or a hospital—like Block remembered Portman had told him."

"Go on."

"And let's also speculate that something about this project was tucked away in Portman's secret floor safe. Maybe it's a bit of a leap, but I'm thinking Portman duplicated this unknown information and put copies in *both* safes."

"So that if one set got stolen, there was always a copy in the floor safe."

"Exactly. And the killers fell for it. They murdered him, blew the door off his wall safe, and were happy enough with what they found to stop looking and swim back to the *Onur,* from whence they came."

"Fits the facts," Masters agreed, digesting the theory. "It certainly explains why Portman would mail that combination back to himself."

"Only Portman didn't take Fedai's actions into account. He arrived early for work, perhaps earlier than usual, found his boss in pieces on the carpet and saw that the wall safe was blown. And because maybe

Portman trusted him, Fedai knew about the hidden floor safe and had a combination to it. Maybe Portman confided in him. So he opened it, took whatever he found inside, and split."

"And then a few days after the murder, we're looking over Fedai's home and we get jumped by a bunch of thugs who are after him," said Masters. "*They* have to be our hit squad, our team of assassins." She was leaning forward—excited, but avoiding eye contact.

"What's wrong?" I asked. "Out with it."

She wrung her hands together. "We've got problems."

"More than the ones I'm aware of?"

"Kumayt. I already know a lot about it."

TWENTY-SEVEN

"You want to fill me in?" I said. At least the reason for Masters's sullen demeanor was now out in the open. A knock on the doorframe distracted me.

"Ah, the sleuths are in." It was Ambassador Burnbaum, back from Ankara. He was beaming, dressed in an immaculate tailored Italian suit, white cotton shirt, and red silk tie. A Stars and Stripes pin adorned one lapel.

"The New York City Ballet is in town. I'm off to the preview," he announced. "Just let me know if you want tickets, OK?"

"Thank you, Mr. Ambassador. I might take you up on that," I said, though I doubted it—men in tights only do it for me when one of them is Mel Brooks. "In the meantime, do you have a moment, sir? We'd like to bring you up to speed on the investigation and maybe ask you a few more questions."

Burnbaum checked his Breitling for permission. "Well, yes, I suppose, as long as you keep it brief."

"Do our best, sir," I promised as he took a seat on the couch and crossed his legs.

Masters got up, walked to my desk, and leaned against it.

"To start with, Mr. Ambassador," I began, "we don't think Colonel Portman was the victim of a serial killer. We believe he was assassinated by a hit squad, possibly one with military or Special Forces training."

Burnbaum's mouth dropped open. He eventually got control of it. "But what about the other killings?"

"We believe they were a false trail, designed to lead us away from the real reason that Portman was murdered."

"Do you have any evidence to support this theory?"

"No, nothing hard," I said, but maybe that would change tomorrow at Ephesus. I took the crinkled email from B off my desk and passed it to him.

"What's this?"

"We think Colonel Portman was involved in some way in an infrastructure project at a place called Kumayt, down in southern Iraq. Would you know anything about that?"

Burnbaum shook his head slowly, frowning. "No, no. I don't. Where did you say? Iraq's not exactly my turf."

"You don't know who this B could be, sir?"

"Well, it's certainly not from me, if that's what you're thinking. Frankly, I have no idea. Where did you get it?" He handed back the ragged sheet of paper.

I filled him in on its discovery, then said, "Mr. Ambassador, I've gone through Portman's correspondence and I can't find the rest of this email. Or, in fact, any email that refers to events or projects he might have been involved in."

"So what are you suggesting, Special Agent? That Portman's email folders have been tampered with?"

"Is that possible?" I asked, putting it back on him.

"I wouldn't have thought so." The ambassador stood. "I don't have to tell you both that your allegations are grave."

He was right—he didn't have to tell us that.

"Do you have any suspects for these murders?" he asked.

"We're looking at a few people."

"Are they part of my mission?"

"No," I said, telling him what he wanted to hear.

"That's something, at least." He shook his head, dismayed.

"That's all we've got for the moment, sir," I said. "We've been hoping to catch you and bring you up to speed."

"I appreciate the heads-up, Special Agents. You're both doing great work here. Now, I'm going to be late—"

"Just one more thing, Mr. Ambassador—would you know if Harvey Stringer's in the building?" I asked.

"I think Harvey's still in the States."

"Thanks."

"Well, keep up the good work," he said, giving us a few more words of motivation. They weren't necessary, nailing up the bad guys being the fun part of the job. He gave us a nod and departed.

And after he was gone, I was back where I started: circling Masters for an opening. "You want to play twenty questions?" I asked.

Masters returned to the couch and sat heavily.

"What did you make of Burnbaum?"

She shrugged. "I think he's about ready for retirement."

"I know what you mean," I said, sitting beside her. "So, here we are... a little spot called Kumayt."

"Maybe you'll understand how difficult this is for me once I've told you."

"Just tell me what you know before I go get a crowbar and jimmy it out of you," I replied. Silence. I sighed. "Something tells me this is going to be a long night."

Masters turned to glare at me. "Richard asked me to help compile his case for the DoD," she began, "which meant I got to see a lot of sensitive material—facts, figures, depositions. The arguments and counter-arguments about aerosolized DU oxide and its effects on the human body aren't neatly balanced. For every scientist or expert who's anti-DU, there are half a dozen who are pro."

I nodded. Not surprising.

"But if you dig around, what you find is pretty ominous. When Richard came over this afternoon, he spent most of the time in the bath..."

I chose that moment to tactically retie a shoelace.

"And I know I shouldn't have, but while he was out of the room, I went through his notes."

"Is that why you're upset? You feeling guilty?"

"That's exactly what I'm feeling. I'm upset because I'm betraying a trust."

I wasn't going to argue with her.

"I wrote down some stuff," said Masters, opening her notebook.

"Twenty-eight percent of Gulf War veterans have suffered chronic health problems loosely called 'Gulf War Syndrome.' That's more than five times the rate of Nam vets."

"What?"

"Yeah, I know." She referred back to her notebook. "How about this: Over seven thousand soldiers were reported as having been wounded in Gulf War I. But over *half a million* vets have received disability compensation. That makes the number of vets disabled since that war finished *seventy times* the number wounded in the conflict itself."

"Shit! Because of DU?"

"That's what this class action's all about—the people sitting on the other side of the courtroom from Richard believe it's a big part of the reason why they're sick, and that it's being covered up. And then there's Capstone. The full title was *The Capstone Depleted Uranium Aerosols Study and Human Health Risk Assessment*. The report cost six million dollars and was prepared by a company called Battelle. Battelle is a major nuclear contractor to the U.S. government."

"Call me cynical, but a company like that is hardly going to bite the hand that feeds it."

"It's unlikely," Masters agreed. "From what I can make out, one of the main arguments against these claims that DU is harmful is that there are no results from studies done on the long-term effects of exposure. Could be that the people with the money to spend on that kind of research... they don't want it done."

"You sound like you've changed teams."

"Plenty of questions have been asked about the validity of the report's findings. And yet so far there haven't been a lot of answers. It makes you think."

It did. It made me think about the way Tyler had wasted slowly away and the fight he'd put up—and the anger I felt about this was rising into my temples.

"So anyway," she continued, "back in 1979, this same company that now insists depleted uranium is harmless found that more than thirty percent of those aerosolized DU particles remained airborne until inhaled or rained out. And Battelle can't claim ignorance about how easily and effectively aerosolized DU can penetrate the human body, because it has a subsidiary that develops aerosol devices to deliver medications *through the lungs*. When they get into your body, these small particles emit alpha radiation that penetrates the cells around them, wreaking damage all the way down to the DNA level."

"Must have been a long bath," I said.

"What?"

"You've become an overnight expert."

"I'm an investigator, remember? I had questions—these are some of the answers."

"So what happens to those rained-out particles?"

"My understanding is that they end up in the groundwater or the food chain, or both. From there, it's only a short trip to your kidneys, which get necrotized—die, basically. And you know, at the end of the report, there's a disclaimer. I wrote it down because it made me laugh. Well, maybe not laugh, exactly..." Masters flipped through a few pages until she found it. *"Neither the U.S. government nor Battelle is responsible for the accuracy, adequacy, or applicability of the contents, or any consequences of any use, misuse, inability to use, or reliance upon the information."*

"Sounds like a sidestep written by someone like your fiancé."

"Whether you like it or not, Richard's just doing his job."

Of course he was. "Dick's not going to be real happy when he finds out you've been doing yours in his case notes."

"He already found out, because I told him."

"How'd he take it?"

"That's none of your business."

"Suit yourself. You still haven't told me what any of this has to do with Kumayt."

"I found a register in Richard's notes," Masters continued. "During both Gulf wars there were disposal sites for wreckage contaminated by DU—trucks, tanks, you name it. There's a rumor that Kumayt is one of the places where a dump is located. They trucked wrecks from the Highway of Death up there, dug a big hole, pushed everything into it, and buried it. According to what I've heard, that wreckage was over a hundred times more radioactive than the background radiation."

The Highway of Death. It was before my time in the military, but I remembered the pictures. The road out of Kuwait heading to Basra where, on a Sunday night early in '91, mile after mile of the retreating Iraqi Army was charred beyond recognition, shot up by DU fired from

Coalition aircraft back when DU was just a whispered half secret. I sat back and exhaled. Kumayt, the Highway of Death, the unresolved issues circling the use and effects of depleted uranium... "So what exactly have we got here now? A series of savage murders linked to a radioactive trash heap?"

TWENTY-EIGHT

Masters shrugged. "Maybe we should do what Adem Fedai suggests and put the place under the microscope."

"Well, don't let me get in your way," I said. I returned to my desk, ignored Mehmet on the wall behind me feeding the earth blood and bone, and fired up the Dell. My in-box was clogged with the usual office detritus plus two emails from Cain, one from the FBI with information about the explosives, another from someone in State I'd never met, and—at last—a note from Andrews Flight Records.

Before I opened any of them I sent an email to Cain, briefing him on the discovery of the email from B, and asking him to run a search on bids for reconstruction projects in the area of Kumayt, southern Iraq, over the last five years. I asked him to be especially interested in bids for hospitals and/or water projects.

Cain's first email to me was one forwarded from the Turkish police with the subject line "Onur." I skimmed it. Homicide—Karli and Iyaz's people—had found the vessel's master in his car. Someone had torched it: His charred head was found on the floor of the backseat. Two nine-millimeter holes above his left eye completed the picture. Most of the drowned men aboard the *Onur* had bleeding and cracked fingernails. There was also quite a bit of smashed furniture that had made no impression whatsoever on the steel coffin sinking into the Sea of Marmara, aside, that is, from a little chipped rust on the one door out. A couple of men had tried to make emergency calls on their cell phones, but the boat had gone down fast and panic had gotten the better of them. Forensics had come up with no leads. Nothing I hadn't expected: a bunch of ends, neatly pinched off with nothing left loose.

The captain's second email was another forwarded from the Turkish police. They'd failed to find any trace of the assholes in the park. No surprises there either.

Next, I clicked on the email from a Tracey Pratt, who, according to her email address, worked for State. I doubted that, if only because it was Pratt who'd forwarded both Masters and me a copy of the CIA background checks on Adem Fedai, the file promised by Harvey Stringer. "You got all these emails?" I called across the room. "Two from Cain, one from CIA masquerading as State, one from Andrews Flight Records?"

"Nothing from Andrews. Opening the others now," said Masters.

I clicked on the Flight Records email and read it. This one surprised me. "Hey..."

Masters looked up.

"I'm forwarding this one to you. Y'know how everyone—including me—keeps talking about how Portman was this incredible F-15 appi-8 warrior?"

"So?"

"So the guy was officially grounded a month before he died."

"Why?"

"Wasn't putting in the required hours."

"What was his last mission?"

I opened the PDF, a copy of a page of Portman's flight log, and translated the block of data. "With the Reapers. A training sortie out of Incirlik."

"Miffed" was the word that best described Emir when Masters told him we were leaving him and his secondhand smoke behind. The drive down to Ephesus, which turned out to be the site of a bunch of Roman ruins, would have taken around eight hours, give or take. I figured we were doing the guy a favor. He wouldn't have survived the trip, and I'd have been up for manslaughter. Rather than sharing Emir's company, we could catch a one-hour flight to Izmir, a city near Ephesus, jump in a rental, and drive the short distance remaining. The term for this alternative was "no-brainer."

So it was that Masters and I arrived at Ephesus around two hours before the appointed time. But I'm getting ahead of myself. I'll rewind.

We'd pulled an all-nighter, mostly reviewing our case notes, going back over interviews, reviewing the forensic notes, chasing Karli and Iyaz for anything new (there wasn't anything new), calling folks in the States, and spinning our wheels trying to get additional hard information about those pits holding radioactive wreckage in Iraq—in particular, the one at Kumayt. The Department of Energy had quietly consulted on the containment operations in Iraq, but calling from the other side of the world as we were, it was easy to be given the runaround.

The CIA background check on Adem Fedai was interesting. He was a Kurd. His family still tended goats in the mountains between Turkey and Iraq. Masters researched the Yezidi, the supposed Satan worshippers of which Fedai was allegedly a member. Apparently, the devil-worship thing was a label the sect had had for at least a couple of thousand years. Their religion was older than Islam, older than Christianity, and probably challenged Judaism in the most-ancient stakes. Yezidis believed that God had forgiven the Fallen Angel—"the Peacock Angel," as they called Him—after He refused to say some nice words about Adam. Other odd facts: Yezidis were forbidden to wear the color blue, they didn't believe in heaven or hell, and lettuce was off their menu. Lettuce? If they just added brussels sprouts to the forbidden list, maybe there was an opportunity to turn around the sect's slide into obscurity.

Fedai himself had never worked as a manservant before being hired by Portman, but he was educated and had no weird affiliations other than the one he'd been born into. Basically, the FBI and then the CIA had both done the bureaucratic equivalent of a shrug, said "What the hell, he's clear," and banged his forms with all the right stamps.

Moving on to Kumayt, research revealed it was a small Shiite town around 170 miles southeast of Baghdad and forty miles from the Iranian border. Two minutes on Google Earth put it roughly midway between Baghdad and Al Basra, around 160 miles from both. Tallil Air Base was 80 miles southwest of Kumayt, just twenty convenient minutes away by chopper. Someone in Portman's position would have been able to scoot down there fairly easily if he'd wanted to.

Kumayt itself was built on the dwindling marshland where the Tigris and Euphrates meet. According to the intel we had access to, in comparison with most places in the hornet's nest of Iraq, the town was a sleepy hollow. But something was going on there, and it was connected to Portman's dramatic exit. Adem Fedai, we were now reasonably sure, would lead us to it.

We had to wait two hours in the Ephesus parking lot. I spent them asleep, my head on my chest, drooling onto the seat belt.

My body clock woke me twenty minutes before the alarm Masters had set on her cell phone. I watched a tour bus disgorge its load in the light rain. The tourists hooked up with a guide and trickled slowly down the hill.

I pulled the photograph of Fedai from my jacket pocket and propped it on the dashboard. Another tour bus arrived and dropped off its passengers. I studied the photo. Fedai had a pleasant though ordinary face: brown eyes, olive complexion, dark hair, mustache. He was short, just under five foot seven, and had a slight build. It was easy to see how he could just vanish in a country like Turkey. He looked like every other guy you passed in the street. Fedai must have gotten the shock of his life when he came to work that morning and found the mess his boss had made all over the carpet. But somehow he'd kept his head, and he was still alive while others connected with this case were fattening up worms. He was smart. I wondered how smart.

I glanced at Masters. She was snoring softly. I wondered how things were between her and her fiancé. There were plenty of reasons for them to be going off the rails. Maybe that's why the guy looked like he'd swallowed a turd when I saw him in the elevator back at the Charisma. Masters took a deeper breath and shifted position, and her hair slid across her face. She was a hell of a lot easier to get along with when she was snoring. I decided to give her a few more minutes. But then I changed my mind.

"Anna." I shook her arm.

"Wha . . . ?" Her eyes opened, blinked a couple of times, then brought me into focus. "God, it's a nightmare," she groaned before turning away.

"Rise and shine. Fedai's here early." Like us.

The guy had suddenly appeared, standing under a black umbrella a dozen yards from the ticket box.

"Jesus, I fell asleep," Masters informed me.

"Yeah, that's unforgivable. Let's go." I cracked open the door and got out. I didn't bother with an umbrella because that's the kind of macho guy I am. Besides, it was only drizzling.

"You see him arrive?" Masters asked.

"No. The guy's scared. He could have been here all day, scoping the place out."

When Fedai saw us approach, he turned on his heel and joined a tour group heading off across the open ground to the ruins.

"Did you take a look at the guidebook?" Masters asked as we set off after him.

"Nope."

"This place was once the capital of the whole of Asia Minor."

"Wow," I said. "That's heavy."

"Thought you might be interested in a little culture. Ephesus was sacred to Artemis."

"The handbag maker?"

"That's Aramis, and *they* make perfumes. Artemis was the goddess of hunting, of the chase."

"I feel an omen coming on," I said, tuning out.

Adem Fedai appeared nervous, his head swiveling constantly. It was clear from his disappearance, the choice of this meeting place, and the way he moved, that Fedai believed he was in danger. I was pretty sure he was right. The guy slid away from the tour group as it loitered around a bunch of crooked columns and continued moving down the hill. We followed.

"He's heading to the library," Masters said.

I assumed Masters was talking about a columned façade at the foot of the hill, which reminded me of every modern government and municipal building I'd ever seen. But I'd seen this ruin before, on a postcard or stamp, or maybe in a history book.

Fedai glanced over his shoulder as he climbed the steps up to the façade's main entrance—a glance to check we were still in his shadow. Somehow we'd tucked into a gap between the tour groups: The forecourt was empty. Fedai stepped beneath the main arch and disappeared inside. We had one last look around before following. The coast, from what we could see, was clear. We took the stairs and went in. The room was small and open to the sky.

"You will turn around and face the wall," said the voice I'd heard coming out of Ocirik's cell. The speaker was the man in the photo, but he now seemed tougher, more determined than he'd been in his message, and the mustache was lost in a couple of weeks of beard.

"Why would we do that?" Masters asked, beating me to it.

"Because I said so," he replied, pulling a hand out of his coat. His fingers were wrapped around the familiar black plastic stock of a Glock 19.

We did as we were told and turned to face the wall. Graffiti had been scratched over the stone. Apparently, Guido was here in 1879, along with a bunch of other people who felt compelled to recall the event for posterity.

"You are armed?" Fedai asked.

"No," I said.

He frisked me with his free hand anyway, and gave Masters the same halfhearted treatment. He might have been familiar with guns, but not with hostage taking. "Show me ID," he demanded.

We pulled our shields and held them out.

"You're comfortable around firearms," said Masters as he examined our credentials.

Fedai shrugged. "I am Kurdish. My people live in the mountains. Saddam try to kill us. The Turks try to kill us. I cannot remember a time when I don't handle weapons."

"So much for the Company's background checks," Masters muttered under her breath.

"Hand over the gun, Fedai," I said. "We're taking you into custody." If I sounded confident, it was only because I believed that the last thing Fedai wanted to do was shoot us.

"No," he replied. "I do not think so."

"It's for your own safety."

"And what will you do? Sleep outside my cell?" He shook his head, pulling back his coat and burying the muzzle in his belt. "I trust *you,* Mr. Special Agent, but I do not trust the Turks. When I am finished here, I will trust the mountains. And also, I know you cannot arrest me. You are American. You have no powers here."

He had us there. "What did you see when you arrived for work that morning?" I asked, letting the whole arrest thing slide. Fedai had managed to keep himself alive till now. Maybe he knew how to keep doing so. And, as he and his Glock pointed out, what choice did we have?

"I did not see the killing. I saw blood and pieces of body. I have seen much death, but none delivered with such..." He searched for the word. "... such *pleasure*. Over the smell of death, there was another smell—sweet. I have been in hospitals. It was like that."

"Chloroform," Masters suggested.

"I like Mr. Portman. He was good man. We talk. We talk of many things."

"In your phone message, you said you had something for us," said Masters, suddenly impatient.

Movement out of the corner of my eye caught my attention. A posse of tourists was meandering toward us, picking its way across the flagstones.

"The safe in the floor was secret," continued Fedai. "No one know of this, only Mr. Portman and me. The safe in the wall—it was destroyed. I went to safe in the floor, open it. I took what was inside, and then I run." He reached down inside his coat, produced a large envelope, and held it out. "I think Mr. Portman, he want you to have this."

The package was heavy, had a bulge in it. I tipped the contents into my hand, leaving a wad of papers behind in the envelope: a USB flash drive and a small clear plastic bottle containing a liquid the color of orange Gatorade.

"On the flash drive is document," he explained. "There is a photocopy of this also in envelope."

"What's in the bottle?" I asked.

"It is water, and many other things—none of them good. You read document."

I passed the flash drive and the bottle to Masters. The envelope held ten or so pages, stapled together.

Masters squinted at the bottle. "Does this have anything to do with Kumayt?"

"Yeah, it does," I said, answering the question for Fedai. The pages were a report from some laboratory in California, its black-and-white logo on the top left of the page. "Apparently, what we have here is a sample of the water from Kumayt. You know what a becquerel is?"

Masters nodded, reading the report over my shoulder. "It's a unit of measurement—one becquerel equals one nuclear decay per second. *Jesus*... according to the sample tested, the water at Kumayt is seriously radioactive."

Two large women wearing floppy hats and clear disposable raincoats over their walking clothes came puffing in, recovering from the climb up the stairs. They smiled politely at Masters and began pointing at various items of interest, twittering in German at each other.

"I must go," Fedai said.

Two other tourists entered the rapidly shrinking room.

"You need to give us a forwarding address," Masters informed him.

"Where are you going?" I said, interpreting.

"I tell you already. The mountains. I have done all that I can. There are people who will kill for what I have given you. For this, they kill Mr. Portman."

"Do you know who killed him?" Masters pressed.

"You do not know?" said Fedai. "It was Mossad, of course."

TWENTY-NINE

We gave Fedai a five-minute start before heading back up the hill to our rental car, but a few moments was really all the guy needed to disappear completely, melting into one of the many tour groups. It was starting to pour.

"Mossad?" Masters asked.

"So he said."

"You're not so sure?"

"Last I heard, Mossad was supposed to be on our side. It's a stretch to believe the Israeli intelligence service cut up Portman and Bremmel, fed Ten Pin to the F-16, shot the master of the *Onur,* and then sank it with all hands. And let's not forget planting one on your kisser."

"No, actually, let's really try to forget about that. And thanks for reminding me," she said.

The light faded fast as the rain fell harder. We put our heads down and ran.

Masters took the driver's seat while I locked the flash drive and sample bottle in the glove compartment. "We're going to have to go to Kumayt," I told her. "Retrace Portman's steps."

"Yep," said Masters as she performed a one-eighty and hunted for the gate. The rain was now a solid wall of water.

"Mossad is Israeli, and the explosives used on the attaché's safe were sent to Israel," I said absently as I tried to read the report in the dim glow provided by the cabin light.

"The coincidence hadn't escaped me. And yeah, I know—you don't believe in coincidences."

I flicked back and forward through the first couple of pages. "What's uranyl fluoride?" I asked.

"I don't know. But anything with uranium in it is bound to be unhealthy."

"Maybe it makes your teeth hard *and* glow in the dark."

"I doubt it."

"Whatever, looks like they found plenty of it in that sample."

"Vin, you're going to have to douse the light," Masters said, distracted. "I can't see where I'm going."

The access road to Izmir snaked through hills that rose a thousand feet above the plain. They were covered mostly by slash pine. I remembered this because on the way up I noticed that some of the drop-aways were getting close to vertical, yet someone had still managed to plant trees in the ravines. I also remembered deciding the road would be treacherous in rain. I was recalling these earlier thoughts as we swung around a hairpin and saw a tour bus sitting astride most of both lanes, its front end hanging in midair over the edge and its hazard lights flashing. The driver was scratching his head, shining a torch on the tires, the rain hammering down, rivulets of water washing over everything. There was nowhere to pull over. I didn't have to suggest to Masters that she should go around the bus and find someplace farther down the road to park.

Except for the driver, the bus appeared empty. It was a big one, with a double-bogey rear end. As we drove slowly past, I saw what was baffling the driver: All sixteen tires had blown at once. A length of road spikes was mangled up with the rearmost pair. Masters, looking where the headlights swept the hillside, said, "Hey, guys with guns."

"Drive!" I shouted.

"What?"

"Step on it! *Now!*"

Masters hit the gas. The engine coughed then caught, jackknifing us forward; the car skidded sideways as the back wheels hunted for traction.

I twisted to look at the bus receding behind us, swallowed by the night and the rain. I was about to tell Masters about those road spikes when we hit a bump and all four of our tires exploded. The car slithered across the wet road. Masters fought the wheel, spinning it from one lock to the other. The car had a mind of its own. It kept going straight ahead as the road swung hard right. We left the asphalt and for a few long seconds everything went quiet. Our headlights played across pine trees. *Radioactive contamination.* Then the rocky ground between them. *Surface-water contaminants.* Nothing we could do. *Becquerels.* The hood dipped steeply as the ground fell away. And then . . . we slammed into something, bounced, hammered into the ground so violently that my seat belt crushed my chest. We rolled. The car came apart. And then we hit some—

Flashlight beams. Machine-gun stock. Blinding light. Even more blinding headache.

"This one is breathing," remarked a voice belonging to the MP5 beside my face. He slapped me around to make sure of it.

"Hey, don't do that—he will stop your heart."

I heard laughter.

Whoever it was who was enjoying himself so much slapping me slapped me some more.

"And the woman. She's alive, too," someone called out, not far away.

I was relieved to hear that. Hands began turning out my pockets. I had a pain across my chest, a different pain from the one radiating from my cracked rib. Probably from my seat belt doing its job. If it hadn't, I'd have left half my face on the windshield.

A couple of guys hauled me to my feet. There was blood in my mouth; my lip was bleeding. Several pairs of hands half pushed, half carried me up the hill, through the trees. The road was surprisingly close. Eight silhouettes stood waiting for me in the headlight beams of a vehicle parked in the middle of the road. The eight shadows became four when my eyes brought them into focus. My headache was subsiding to a dull roar.

Masters was pushed into the headlight beams. The crash had messed up her hair some. I doubted she'd broken a nail. A gloved hand under my chin lifted my head, and I looked into a familiar face. It was the guy with the silver toothpick from the park in Istanbul. He was still sucking on it. His sunglasses were pushed back on his head. "You have something we want," he said.

My brain must still have been bouncing around in my skull, because I wasn't sure what he was after. But whatever it was, I wasn't going to cough up. "Fuck you," I said.

The guy snapped. He grabbed me by the throat, stuck a fat black pistol barrel in my mouth, and pulled the trigger. *Click. Click. Click.* Just like that. My heart thumped, bounced off my ribs like they were turnbuckles in a boxing ring. Then he removed the weapon, slammed a magazine into the handle. "Next time . . ." He fired up into the trees. BANG! The boom reverberated through the ravine. "The sample and the flash drive," he shouted, shoving the muzzle into my cheek. "Tell us! Where are they?"

Now I remembered. The glove compartment . . .

"You have searched them? What about their car?" The new voice rang a bell. It was the sort of bell the village lookout rings just before the bad guys ride over the hill and begin an orgy of indiscriminate killing. In this instance, the bad guys were a single woman by the name of Yafa. I hoped she'd left home without her brass knuckles.

"We have gone through their pockets," replied a male voice. Again, I recognized the owner; it was the man we knew of as the interpreter from our visit to Ocirik's. "We should kill them. They killed Ben and Jonah."

"There's time for that," Yafa said, nice and cool. "What about their car?"

"Yes, it is being done now," the voice answered.

"So, you found Fedai," Yafa said, speaking to us now. "I congratulate you. Or perhaps he found you. But unfortunately you are too late to do him or yourselves any good."

The shock of the crash was wearing off a little. My vision was clearing. I could smell the wet pines, smell the slick road surface. A timid half-moon peeked out from behind the clouds. I don't know why it bothered me—the light it threw was sick and gray. I breathed in. It helped. I forced myself to stand up straight. Something in my lower back begged for mercy, maybe my spinal cord. Masters was pushed in beside me. She bounced off my shoulder. "You OK?" I asked.

She gave me a tight smile, which I took for yes, she was OK.

"Why is Mossad running an assassination squad?" I asked, Yafa's Ferrari-red lips close, her breath warm and smelling of coffee.

"You think we are Mossad?" scoffed Yafa. She clicked her fingers and made a dismissive *pff* sound, like Mossad were a bunch of featherweights.

The toothpick spoke again: "It does not matter who you think we are."

A young guy with close-cropped hair and a five o'clock shadow ran up and handed Yafa the specimen bottle, the flash drive, and the printed report. "In the glove box," he said. "They also had luggage." He dropped a couple of overnight bags on the ground at my feet.

"So, you and your partner were now going to a hotel room to make love, as you Americans say?"

I had to admit, in other circumstances it would have been a good idea, but I kept that to myself.

"You Americans are so hung up. It's just sex." Yafa took the pistol from the guy with the toothpick and pushed the muzzle into the hollow beneath Masters's ear. I felt Masters go rigid.

"Would you like to fuck this woman?" Yafa asked it pleasantly, like a waitress inquiring about whether I'd like the dessert menu now.

The men around us grinned. Yafa was putting on a show and they were enjoying it.

"*I* would like to fuck her," said Yafa, nodding, then jabbing the gun harder into Masters's neck so that she pushed her head over. "This one is beautiful, no?"

The question received unanimous nods.

"Do you think I am beautiful?" Yafa asked Masters. "Would you like to fuck me?" She grabbed Masters's hand, put it between her legs. "Have you ever had a woman?" she whispered. "You would enjoy it, I think. A woman knows what a woman wants, and how a woman wants it." She let Masters's hand go, but only so that she could unzip my partner's jacket and pull it back off her shoulders. Yafa worked her hand inside Masters's shirt, tore away her bra, and cupped her breast.

"OK, that's assault, lady," I said, snapping out of it. I tried to move, to step between her and Masters. A weight crashed into the back of my skull. I saw red balls behind my eyes that floated briefly before exploding like fruit hit with a baseball bat. I staggered to my knees. As I struggled upright, I saw a piece of my scalp with hair on it stuck to the butt of an MP5.

The guy holding the gun smiled. No doubt about it, they were a happy bunch.

Yafa ignored me completely. "Do not try to fight this yearning," she said to Masters, her breath quickening and her voice now husky with lust. Masters's shirt was ripped and her breasts were exposed to the cold, her bra pushed down and hanging loose around her waist. Through it all, Masters stared straight ahead, unblinking.

"Yafa, we have no time for this bullshit," said the guy with the toothpick, still wound tight, pacing back and forth. As if to confirm this, down the road a flashlight was waving back and forth—a signal.

Yafa got herself under control, cleared her throat, smoothed her clothes. "Such a pity," she said to Masters, walking behind us both.

I couldn't see her, keep track of her. That made me nervous. The asshole with the gun in my back pushed it harder into the base of my spine. Something was coming.

Beside me, Yafa suddenly grabbed Masters from behind and smothered her mouth and nose with a cloth pad. Masters's vacant eyes instantly rolled back and her knees buckled. The air was filled with a smell that reminded me of combat hospitals in the field, of hurried amputations, seeping wounds, and operations performed under fire. And then I knew what that smell was.

A sudden pressure over my nose and mouth, dragging me back. Fire in my throat. A wave of white noise wrapping me in its folds.

THIRTY

The light was soft and gray. I heard Masters's voice, but couldn't hold onto the words. They slipped away like a failing handhold on a cliff face.

I was thirsty. My tongue had swollen in my mouth. My teeth crunched. Masters hovered over me. "Vin..."

"Wa'er..." I gabbled. The back of my throat felt raw, skinned. I'd swallowed some dirt. Maybe that explained the thirst and the rawness, and maybe not. The sand crunched between my teeth like glass.

The water I asked for arrived in my own boot. That's when I knew we were in trouble. I drank from Masters's shoe next. The sound of dripping water echoed, disorienting. There was a small crack of sparkling white light in the ceiling and a cold gloom everywhere else. I felt Masters lay my head down, and I looked up into her face haloed with that light. Yafa was right—Masters was beautiful. I asked myself who Yafa was and found I couldn't put a face to the name. Maybe Yafa wasn't a who, but a what. The question drifted into the awareness that the floor beneath my back was rough and hard, rock-strewn. I drifted off again, unable to keep my eyes open.

The count I'd been down for was so long the arena had emptied, everyone had gone home, and I was still on the canvas. I had either a hatchet buried in my forehead or a bad headache. The jury was out on which. I was familiar enough with the symptoms of concussion to know I had it.

Masters was standing with her back to me, hands on her hips, looking up at the patch of light twelve to fifteen feet above her head, contemplating it the way a caged animal contemplates the bars.

"Hey," I said in a voice that sounded like it was someone else's.

Masters turned. "Hey, yourself. How're you feeling?"

"Not sure yet," I replied as I grunted, struggling up onto an elbow to get a better angle on things. "I'll let you know after you tell me where we are." The suspicion I had was that we were in a place known as Deep Shit. My throat still felt flayed, and the taste of copper—blood—was in my mouth. My head hurt, my ribs and chest hurt, and the arm in the cast had gone to sleep and hung heavy and useless by my side.

"I think we're in a cistern," she said. Frogs started up, a steady chorus of croaking.

"Isn't that another word for a toilet?"

"A cistern is what the Romans called a water storage tank."

"The Romans . . . ?" My eyes were adjusting to the twilight. We were in a rectangular room around ten yards long and six wide. Columns of various heights and thicknesses kept the vaulted roof in place. One near the center had collapsed, and a small chunk of the roof had come down with it, accounting for the light source. There'd been another collapse in the corner to my right, a pileup of rock and earth. There was something scattered across it. I peered into the murk. "Those things over there. They what I think they are?"

"Depends on whether you think they're human bones."

Masters came over and helped me to my feet. Once I'd steadied myself, she checked my pupils for dilation. "You'll live. And sorry for kneeing you in the head."

"Did I do anything to deserve it?"

"No. For once. They threw us down that hole. When I came to, I was lying on top of you."

"See, even unconscious I'm irresistible."

"OK, *now* you deserve it."

I ran my hand over my skull. There were more lumps than in a sugar bowl. There was also a large, crusty patch of dried blood. My feet were cold. I looked down at them. They were white, naked, and soaking in a pool of icy water. I wriggled my numb toes.

"I've put our shoes to better use," Masters said, gesturing at a far corner of our tomb where a tree root had broken through a crack in the rock facing. Water dripped steadily from the root's spidery fingers into Masters's Nikes. My boots were off to one side, full to the brim. I remembered drinking from them in a half-forgotten dream.

"If your dentist tells you you've got athlete's foot," I remarked, "don't blame me."

"Deal." She gave me a smile, but it didn't last long. "Vin, we're not going to survive very long down here. My cell battery is dead, and your cell doesn't work down here. I checked. We need to find a way out." Worry had etched itself into the lines on her face, and this partner of mine was not easily spooked.

I took an unsteady walk around the cistern's perimeter. "The stuff that bitch used on us was chloroform. Kinda closes the loop on our murders in a circumstantial way, doesn't it?"

"Kinda."

"And we're the only people who know about it."

One column had come down and the hole in the roof was the result. So what about taking out another column or two? I checked the condition of the ones still standing. A quick inspection told me all seven were in pretty good shape, and all were marble. Three were identical, probably pilfered from the same building. Constructed from five sections, each still had that just-quarried look. The four remaining columns were solid, each a work of art. And they weren't going anywhere either. Damn Romans.

I moved on to the walls and chipped at the joins between the stones with a chunk from the broken column. I got nowhere. The granite blocks had been keyed together with molten lead poured between the cracks. This cistern had stood for a couple of thousand years at least—unlikely it was going to come down in the next day or so. Made me wonder what'd be left from our own civilization a couple of millennia from now, aside from plastic bags, tires, and divorce statistics.

OK, so the one way out was up and through that hole; the only problem was that the roof was well out of reach. I squinted up at it. Maybe, if it rained enough, the place might fill with water and we could swim out. But the stonework was stained with mineral deposits up to my hip—a high-water mark that wasn't nearly high enough even if a convenient flood arrived before we died of starvation.

There were no doors. We had no tools. No food. No fire. No means of contact with the outside world.

Masters read my thoughts. "Yeah, I know. I've had most of the day to think about it, and I keep coming up with dead ends, too."

"Interesting word choice," I said. "What about Cain?"

"We told him where we were going but not when to expect us back. Might take a few days before he raises the alarm. And when he does, it's not like he's going to send a rescue team here. Hell, *I* don't even know where *here* is."

"So then it's up to us," I said, lost in my own thoughts. I found myself staring at the bones neatly laid out on the mound of dirt and collapsed stonework. A couple of frogs hopped between some ribs. Masters, despondent, went to oversee our water storage facilities.

I picked through the scraps of rotting clothing that remained. From the style and age, I figured that the skeleton inside them belonged to a guy who had fallen into this place around three years ago. The bones themselves were dry and clean, without being brittle. A farmer, or maybe a shepherd. The poor sap had landed hard and snapped his tibia and fibula. At least Masters and I had both been spared that kind of injury. I wondered how long he'd managed to hold on. Hopefully, he'd died quick.

I raised what was left of his jacket. There were other skeletons mingled with his—four, to be exact. I picked up one of the skulls for a closer look. It was small, the size of a large walnut, pointed at one end, with four yellow interlocking, chisellike teeth. "Rats," I said, thinking aloud.

"You say something?" Masters asked.

I looked up, dropped the skull into the muck. "What? Nope. Frogs, probably . . ." Given Masters's fear of rodents, my thinking was not what she needed to hear right at the moment. When this guy was dying—or if he was lucky, after he'd gone and collected his harp—rats had paid him a visit. Maybe like him they'd accidentally fallen in. I gave the hole above another glance. Maybe the guy's distress as he lay slowly dying had brought them running. Whatever, the animals had feasted on him.

I continued the walk around, doing it a step at a time like I was pacing out a crime scene. I found quite a few more bones belonging to critters that had probably just tumbled in rather than having been summoned by the prospect of fresh meat: the remains of a couple of snakes, half a dozen squirrels, a couple of rabbits, plus seven more rat skeletons. There was also a large mound of bat guano in one corner. It crawled with bugs. There were no bats here now. Maybe they made their home in the cistern during the warmer months. The whole pet cemetery thing didn't bother me much. What did worry me was that all these animals had died here, which meant they'd been unable to find a way out. And if snakes and rats hadn't been able to escape this place, what chance did Masters and I have?

We were cold and hungry. And both of us knew this would be just the beginning of the ordeal. Night had come down five hours ago. The stars were bright enough to throw a thin shaft of ghost light through the hole. We sat huddled together in the shaft for the meager comfort that being able to see our own noses by starlight provided. The rest of the cistern was immersed in a darkness thick enough to ladle into a bowl. Masters's teeth were chattering. "You mind turning the heater up?" she stuttered.

Gladly. I wrapped my arms around her and squeezed.

"I haven't th-thanked you," she said as we clung together.

"Thanked me for what?"

"Yafa. When that bitch was all over me. You tried to stop her."

"Sounds out of character," I replied. "I'm usually all for a little girl-on-girl action."

Masters punched me in the arm. After a while she said, "At the time, when it was happening, I felt angry and degraded. I just stood there, frozen."

"Try not to let it worry you. From what you've just told me, you played it smart, played dead."

"I guess... Now, in this place, the assault—the helplessness I felt—doesn't seem so important. But if I ever get my hands on that goddamn freak show..."

"Can I watch?"

I earned another punch. Masters's teeth stopped chattering. She was warming up, which was good. She was also wasting excess energy, which was bad.

I remembered the gun in my mouth and the shock of the *click, click, click*. "Did you get a good look at the odd-looking handgun I was chewing on?" I asked. "Ever seen one of them before?" It had been all angles and bumps—a distinctive weapon.

"No. You're right, though. It was an odd-looking thing."

"It was Israeli. A Barak. They designed it for their armed forces, but the weapon didn't catch on."

"Israeli," she said. "Now, there's a word that keeps popping up. And, while I think about it, so does the word 'Mossad.'"

Masters was right about that, but I still found it hard to believe those jerks were on its payroll. The Mossad I knew, Israel's secret external security agency, was the toughest and most determined organization of its kind in the world, their agents steeled by a fight to the death with neighbors committed to their homeland's destruction. They were hard-asses, not psychopaths.

"Hey, I've got one Jewish joke. Want to hear it?"

"Like I can escape," she grumbled, teeth chattering again.

"OK—so it's the close of the tax year and the IRS sends an inspector to audit the books of a synagogue. While he's going through them, he turns to the rabbi and says, 'I notice you buy lots of candles. What do you do with the wax drippings?'

"'Good question,' says the rabbi. 'We save them up and send them back to the candlemakers, and every now and then they send us a free box of candles.'

"'Really,' replies the auditor, disappointed his tricky question had a practical answer. 'What about all these bread wafers? You're going to have crumbs; what do you do with them?'

"'Ah, yes,' replies the rabbi. 'We collect them and send them back to the manufacturer, and every now and then they send us a free box of bread wafers.'

"'I see,' says the auditor, now determined to fluster this smart-ass rabbi. 'Well, Rabbi, what do you do with all the leftover foreskins from the circumcisions you perform?'

"The rabbi responds, 'Here, too, we do not waste. What we do is save the foreskins and send them to the IRS. And then they thoughtfully send us back a complete prick.'"

Masters got her teeth under control. "Please don't make this any harder than it already is. I can deal with hunger and exposure . . ."

"Y'know, seriously, and not that I'm going to send in a complaint about it, but I don't understand why those assholes didn't just put a bullet in our brains before dropping us down here."

"Vin, if we're still down here in a week's time, we'll wish they had."

THIRTY-ONE

We must have both dozed off eventually despite the cold and hunger, because when I woke, the darkness had disappeared and the rest of the cistern had materialized. Masters and I were spooning on the damp earth.

Through the hole above, morning delivered a triangle of sunlight that hung high on the wall. Masters had been calling out in her sleep, dreaming. I lay still for another twenty minutes, my joints locked up solid with the wet cold, thinking long and hard about Korean barbecue beef. I listened to Masters breathing and wondered how the fuck we were going to turn this one around.

She finally woke, stretched, and mumbled, "Jesus, I feel like shit."

"Shit we've got plenty of. Lucky you didn't ask for coffee."

She groaned and lay still—in my arms.

"What happened to Richard?" I asked.

"What?"

"You were dreaming. You kept repeating, 'It's over, Richard. Take a hike.'"

"Yeah, right."

"Seriously, you had a dream."

"I don't remember it."

"Just before you woke up, you were struggling with something, and it was making you angry. You called out Richard's name a couple of times. 'You lying fucker,' something like that. I think 'asshole' was in there somewhere, too. Sure sounded to me like you were talking to Richard. Who else could it have been? You can tell me. You know, Anna, dreams are a window into your heart."

"Jesus, Vin . . ."

"OK, then—into your soul."

"It's over."

"What's over?"

"Richard and I. Short and not so sweet."

"You want to tell me what happened?"

"No."

"Why not?"

"Look, my intention was to ride off into the sunset when all this finished. It's not like you'd have been expecting a wedding invitation. Anyway, as I think you guessed, not everything was happy in paradise. We had a fight. You were right—he didn't appreciate me looking through his case notes, going through his computer files. Caught me in the act, basically. Accused me of espionage—spying on him for *you* on behalf of the plaintiffs. We argued about the effect the case was having on so many people. Like your friend Tyler, for instance."

"What happened to all the crap about attorneys, the system?"

"I haven't changed my point of view, but there's a difference between defense and running interference. And, yes, you were right about Richard when you said I didn't know him. We had a fling in a beautiful city a few years back. That's all it was. That's where we should have left it."

I had nothing to say—at least, nothing she'd appreciate hearing. I was somewhere between breaking into applause and being angry at her for putting me through the mill. Her feelings weren't my fault, but her engagement to Wadding was nonetheless a kind of punishment directed squarely at me. And if she'd gone through with it, married the jerk, she'd have been stuck with him. I recalled the last time I'd seen Wadding, the confrontation we'd had when he was coming out of the elevator at the Charisma. *It's the way she shudders when she comes.*

Masters squeezed my hand. "Don't say anything, please, Vin. I'm annoyed with myself enough as it is. . . . Well, I suppose we should get up."

"You got a pressing engagement someplace?"

Masters shifted her arm beneath her head but otherwise didn't move.

"So why didn't *we* go the distance?" I asked. "The real reason. And don't give me any of that tyranny-of-distance bullshit."

Masters turned to face me. "You want the real reason, Vin? Because it was too intense. The way we met, the investigation at Ramstein, the shooting of the vice president, the car accident, and then the recovery."

I was about to interrupt when she held up a hand to stop me.

"Y' know, I've had a little speech prepared for this moment—so don't interrupt me. If you do, I'll forget it." She continued. "I lost myself when I was with you. I wanted to know what you were doing when we weren't together. And when we were together, I almost couldn't bear it—the tearing apart afterward. And then we'd be back on opposite sides of the planet again and all I'd be able to think about was you. I couldn't function, even after we'd agreed to call it quits. My feelings for you were destructive, and I needed to move on. I wanted *less* passion, Vin . . . and I wanted more control. Control over myself, mainly, but also over whoever I was with."

I let that sink in. She was right about the passion—the depth of feeling. It consumed a lot of my time and energy, too. And still did. "Can I ask you something?"

"I'll let you know after you've asked it," she replied.

"Why Wadding?"

"Honestly? I don't know. Because he was there, I suppose. He was good-looking, wealthy, great career. . . . He was the kind of guy I always thought I'd end up marrying. He fit the mold. My mom and dad were going to love him."

"What about you? Were you going to love him, too?"

"It was romantic. I felt secure with him. . . . I believed—I *wanted* to believe—that love would follow."

And then I kissed her. It was a small kiss at first, nothing passionate. But it was like a pilot light beneath the furnace because suddenly there was a *whomp,* and the main burners lit up and our hands began to move. Her fingers unhooked the buttons on my fly. I did the same to hers. Her shirt came out. Her tongue. I ripped the crotch from her underwear getting them off. An ear. Her hair. Her tongue. A handful of ass—hers. I wanted to eat her, climb inside her. She pulled my hair, cupped my testicles. An explosion built with each hurried breath.

I heard a splash. And then another. Ignored it. A third splash. Masters screamed. With ecstasy, I thought—until I got an accidental knee in the nuts a couple of seconds later. She was pushing me away, pointing in horror at something moving around in the water.

"Jesus, Anna, you really know how to—" I saw the eyes first, two red coals the size of cigarette embers swimming a figure eight in the gloom, getting oriented. Rats.

A black shape sat up on its scrawny hind legs in the shallow water and nibbled at something between its front claws. The animal sniffed at the air, ran around in a circle, then swam for the dead man's bones. It climbed onto the dirt and rubble, took up a position on top of the human skull, and crouched. It squealed next, a high-pitched sound like nails down a blackboard. Its buddies gathered around it, answering the call.

We glared at each other across the shallow lake: them and us. The fuckers appeared to be waiting for something. Probably for us to hurry up and die.

"Ever eaten rat?" I said out loud for their benefit as I stood up. "They say it tastes like rat."

One of them squealed. Masters had pulled her clothing together and was sitting with her arms wrapped around her knees like any moment she might start rocking.

I wondered what had brought the animals. Did they smell us or hear us? Or did they just happen to fall in, lemminglike, following the boss rat there perched up on the skull?

I had woken with half an idea in my head—a way to get out. The granite in the walls was harder than the marble columns. I walked toward the rats, which scampered back into the water before I had the chance to use one of them as a football. Then I picked up two of the broken granite blocks from the dead guy's final resting place and carried them over to the column. Using one block as a hammer and the other as a chisel, I started chipping away below the high-water mark where the stone might be a little softer. The outer layer of marble, about a quarter of an inch thick, flaked off reasonably easily but, like an onion, there was another layer beneath, this one not so compliant. "Anna," I called. "Need a hand here."

After a little consideration, Masters came over, wary, keeping a lookout for her own personal nightmare, but the rats were lying low, out of sight, biding their time.

Seven hours and six pulverized granite blocks later, what remained of the column where I'd been chipping away reminded me of an apple core. All we had to do was take out the center and the column should fall, bringing down enough of the unsupported roof and in such a way that we'd be able to climb out. Anyway, that was my theory. Of course, the whole roof might also collapse and crush the juice out of every living thing below it—a thought that had begun to dawn on me at about hour five.

When Masters was back hugging the wall farthest from the column, I started taking out the last three inches of marble, hefting rocks at it from a couple of yards away. I missed the target more times than I hit it. The light faded, leaving Masters and me with three rats that kept us awake all night with their inconsiderate squeaking and squabbling. Fighting, perhaps, over who was going to take that first irresistible bite.

This was our second night in the cistern, and it went by a second at a time, all forty-three thousand two hundred of them. And now each one of those seconds was like a splinter under the fingernails. Masters screamed when one of the rats jumped over her feet into the water. The scream sounded like an F-16. The rodents kept their distance after that, no doubt fearing permanent hearing damage.

The sun came out eventually, mercifully, and lit our tomb. I was up with the first rays, surveying the remains of the column. I chose five granite blocks I knew I could throw a couple of yards, lined them up, then waited for the light to increase. Masters took up her position against the wall.

I threw the first block. Missed. Second block struck a glancing blow, below the sweet spot. Third block missed. Same with the fourth block, disappointing my inner quarterback. I threw the fifth block. Bingo.

The top two thirds of the column dropped away, struck the base with a *boom,* rolled and splintered. The pieces splashed into the water with such force that the vibration came up through the rock floor. I reached Masters in two jumps.

"Shit..." she said with a cough, clearing the dust from her lungs.

"Yeah, shit," I repeated, looking up. There was a third option I hadn't considered: that the damn column would come down without any apparent effect on the roof whatsoever.

I crouched against the wall as the light was sucked from the cistern as if someone had flicked a switch. It was barely nine A.M., a whole day before sunset. The fingers in my cast were throbbing, providing a hint. Snowflakes began drifting down through the hole.

Skinned, rat looked like rabbit, but it tasted gamy. As I thought, like rat. After a couple of tries, Masters managed to keep the meat down with minimal gagging, raw hunger having finally overcome her revulsion. She gnawed on a thigh, stripping the tiny bone clean.

The two remaining survivors were out there, lying low, hugging the shadows, doing the rat version of drawing lots. It was better to keep the food supply fresh by letting it run around on the hoof—free-range.

I'd made a knife out of one of the dead guy's ulnas, splintering it and then sharpening one of the larger pieces on a granite block. The bone held an edge sharp enough to cut and gut. So, sharp enough. To skin the rat, I'd made an incision just above its shoulders and secured the carcass by tying a shoelace around its neck and looping the ends around the back of a heavy granite block; then I dug my thumbs under its skin and simply pulled it off like a tight-fitting sock.

Day five. Lucky we had water. With water, we could survive a long time down here on a diet that also included cockroach, frogs' legs, and tree root. In fact, the beardlike tendrils that also collected the water into our footwear were tender and filling. With a little imagination you could think of it as salad. OK, a lot of imagination.

Despite this smorgasbord, I'd lost half a dozen pounds at least. Masters was looking like a thirty-day contestant on *Survivor,* minus the plastic boobs. With the dank cold, pneumonia would eventually get us. It was just a matter of time.

So staying warm was the biggest challenge. I suggested to Masters that we should have sex, purely for survival reasons, of course. It would help pass the time, and it would be a hell of a lot more fun than running on the spot. She pointed out that as a survival technique, sex wasn't so smart, because it would burn up too much energy. Spooning was as far as she was prepared to take it.

What helped most was reviewing the current case, piece by piece, fact by fact, going through crime scenes, forensic reports, interviews.

Yafa and the guy with the toothpick were the killers captured on the surveillance TV footage in the Hilton parking lot—same build, same team, same loopy-nutcase thing going on. They probably did Portman, too, and I wouldn't have been at all surprised if they'd high-fived each other while they cut away. We'd killed their Incirlik team—Ben and Jonah—as the interpreter guy had told us. That slip of the tongue confirmed the hit squad theory. The fact that they were obsessed with Fedai convinced us that we were right about the other killings being diversions to throw us off the track. In Yafa's case, maybe they were also recreation.

So, we were solid on the "who." The "why" was the mystery. It had something to do with radioactive water in the southeastern Iraqi town of Kumayt. But what it had to do with Emmet Portman was the point at which we started scratching our heads.

Masters dropped her lunch scraps in the water—tidbits for tomorrow's dinner to munch on. Something wet had found its way inside my cast, next to my skin. I took the sharpened bone and reached down inside the cast to have a good scratch, shift the spiders around some. And suddenly I saw it, like a set of instructions had just been pinned on the notice board inside my head: *the way out*. "Jesus, Anna... give me a hand here."

"To do what?"

My plan contained a slight hitch—namely, blinding pain. "You're going to have to do something unpleasant if you want to get out of here."

"Vin, we've already talked about that, and the answer's no."

"Funny."

"Then what?"

I rested my cast on a piece of marble column. "You need to get a block of granite."

"Why a block of granite?"

"You'll need it to break my hand."

A couple of minutes later, I was biting down on a chunk of root, the block in Masters's hands poised about a foot above my hand. "Here we go," she said softly.

I closed my eyes, braced myself, and waited for the explosion of hurt.

"On three. One, two, three..."

I felt the pressure of the strike but the rock just bounced off the cast. I spat out the root. "Jesus, Anna..."

"All right, all right."

"You need to put your shoulder behind it, goddamn it."

"OK, this isn't so easy, you know."

I felt sorry for her, but sorrier for me... which canceled out my sorrow for her. "Just do it, for Christ's sake!"

She held the block over her head this time. I bit down on the root and watched with morbid fascination now as it smashed down onto the cast.

"JESUS CHRIST!"

"You OK?" said Masters. "Was that too hard?"

I paced the cistern walls, my knuckles throbbing, feeling like a bunch of smashed eggs. The fibers of the cast around my fingers were shattered. I closed my eyes tight and hoped this dumb-ass plan of mine worked.

"Ready for step two?" Masters asked.

I nodded, biting my lip, and sat down opposite her. I scooped up some mud and smeared it around my fingers—lubricant. What we were about to do would probably hurt more than step one.

Masters hooked her fingers inside the cast up around my forearm and buried a foot in my armpit. "You want me to apply steady pressure or give it one big tug?"

"Steady pressure," I grunted.

Her heel dug into the cracked rib, the worst possible spot. I felt something push into my lung. The cast squeezed against the newly broken knuckles, the bones sliding and grinding over each other with the pressure. "Do it!" I snarled, on the edge of passing out.

"I'm doing it, for Christ's sake. It doesn't want to come free."

"Pull..."

Masters dug her foot into my side and kicked.

"Agghh!"

The cast suddenly flew off and sailed across the cistern, landing in the water.

"Oh, God," I groaned, breathing hard, lying back on the ground, sweat beading my forehead. "That. Hurt."

Masters retrieved the cast.

"You're going to have to do the rest," I told her, nursing my unfortunate hand, cradling it carefully in the other.

"I know what to do," she replied, collecting the dead guy's bones.

I watched her go to work, feeding a femur into each end of the cast. She wedged them in place with smaller bones, hammering them in with a small granite block. Mud was then packed into the spaces that remained between the bones and cast so that nothing moved. Finally, Masters took her belt and slipped it around the cast.

"You'll have to test it," I told her.

She found a gap between two blocks, set the contraption between them so that it formed a bridge, stepped up onto the cast and bounced up and down.

Nothing broke.

On the cistern floor directly beneath the hole was a mound of mud and stone. Masters, standing on my shoulders Barnum & Bailey–style, pushed the cast-and-bone contraption up through the hole in the roof, using a fork made from the dead guy's ribs and tree roots tied together with shoelaces. Once it was through the hole, she simply turned the cast ninety degrees and lowered it. The ends of the femurs were now wider in this axis than the hole, and the end of her belt dangled within reach of her fingertips.

I stood and stared at the triangle of light overhead, at the belt hanging down. Somehow Masters had found the strength to pull herself up that belt, hand over hand, determined not to fail.

That was thirty minutes ago. Thirty minutes was a long time—too long. Maybe Yafa and Co. were still out there. Maybe they'd recaptured Masters. Killed her.

My knuckles throbbed. My ribs whined almost as much as the shoulder Masters had dislocated when she removed my cast. It wouldn't be long before all these complaints became a chorus and reminded me of my ex-wife's legal team.

"Hey, you down there! You OK?" came Masters's voice from above, her face suddenly appearing in the hole haloed by the white light. A length of cable came down.

THIRTY-TWO

I woke as we flew into Istanbul, the Turkish Airlines 737 sweeping low over the Bosphorus. The city felt like an old friend. I took in the view out the window as we broke through the sparse cloud. I could spot all the great monuments—the Aya Sophia, the Blue Mosque, the Topkapi Palace, the home of Dr. Aysun Merkit.

Barely a day later, the five days we'd spent in the cistern seemed almost unreal. After she'd pulled herself out, Masters had found a 4x4 belonging to some forestry workers parked among the pines, miles from anywhere. The keys were left in the ignition. Conveniently, it also had a winch and a hundred feet of steel cable mounted on the front fender. An hour later, we left it where she'd found it—the owners none the wiser—hiked down to the road snaking through the trees, and waited for a tourist bus. The newspapers would be all over the discovery of the cistern hidden between two small hills, so we decided to keep it under wraps for now. We had a little strategic advantage up our sleeves; it would be a shame to give it away instantly. Better to let Yafa continue to believe for a while longer that her lust for Masters would remain unfulfilled.

Codeine was taking the edge off the pain in my knuckles, which had been wrapped up temporarily by a quack back at Izmir. The guy had wanted to reset and recast them properly, but first he had to duck out and geld a horse for a neighbor. I decided to wait, get more specialized medical help at the Consulate-General, preferably from someone whose patients walked mostly on two legs.

The 737 landed, taxied, and pulled up with a jolt before shutting down. I saw that the terminal was across the ramp, way over on the other side of the airport. A buzz of concern rippled through the cabin at this, so I gathered parking halfway to Greece wasn't SOP.

"Please remain seated," said a woman in Turkish, followed by English, followed by a language that sounded like she had a sticky fly caught in the back of her throat.

The doors at the front of the aircraft and down the back opened simultaneously. And suddenly there was a rush of black. An anti-terror team swarmed aboard. They raced down the aisle in the familiar hunched crouch, MP5s raised to their eye goggles.

"Shit, it's—" Masters was suddenly jerked from her seat and dragged to the floor. Nice and efficient.

An instant later, I got the same treatment. They pulled and pushed until I was on the floor, nose flattened against the carpet. Expert hands patted me down, took my wallet. Handcuffs came next, steel jaws around my wrists. Then we were hauled to our feet and shoved forward past the terrified passengers to the front hatch.

Gathered around the plane's nose were various marked and unmarked Istanbul police vehicles, their lights all flashing. I was lifted down the stairs toward a couple of guys I was getting to know quite well: Detective Sergeants Karli and Iyaz.

"You are under arrest," said Karli, his pants riding especially high.

"Hey, Detective," I said, keeping it light. "I see you've dressed to the right today. What's the occasion?"

"You will be quiet."

"What's the charge?" Masters asked.

"We arrest you for the murder of Adem Fedai."

They had taken my belt and shoelaces, the bandages off my hand and chest—anything I might use to stretch my neck if I was so inclined. Standard practice. I sat on the cot and listened to the guy in a cell two down from mine try to knock himself out by diving off his cot headfirst. The jailers hadn't thought about confiscating gravity. I was surprised how many attempts it took him to succeed. They carried him out cuffed to a gurney, his face looking like Bolognese sauce.

I invoked Ambassador Burnbaum's name and got nowhere. We

hadn't killed Fedai, but I had a good idea who had. I thought we'd be released with apologies within an hour. But seven hours later, I was still sitting on the cot consoling my knuckles. Karli and Iyaz eventually strolled into my cell.

"I want to speak to someone at the U.S. Embassy," I informed them.

"When we are ready and not before," said Karli, which made me think perhaps the embassy wasn't even aware of our detention.

"Where is Special Agent Masters?"

"We are holding her also."

"If you're going to charge us, get on with it so as we can post bail, or however you do it here."

"Yes, it is different here. This is not the United States—you have the rights *we* are prepared to give you."

"If you like, we could make it worse for you," Iyaz contributed.

"You're gonna sing?" I asked.

"We found your rental car five days ago at the town of Kusadasi, near Izmir," said Iyaz, ignoring me. "Adem Fedai was found dead inside the car. He had been beaten and shot through the ear. We found your DNA in the car, and your partner's. Also, we have many eyewitness who saw you and Special Agent Masters with the deceased at Ephesus."

"You find anyone else's DNA lying around inside the vehicle?" I knew it was a dumb question the moment I asked it.

"Of course, it was a rental," said Iyaz.

"Don't you think that also accounts for the presence of our DNA?"

Both detectives were implacable.

I tried a different tack. "So tell me, do I look a little thinner than the last time you saw me? And Masters, too?" Karli and Iyaz looked at each other. "We've been on a rat diet for the past week. Karli, you ought to try it. By the way, your killer is a woman named Yafa. She's around thirty-two, five foot eight, 125 pounds, dark complexion, great figure, and sado-lesbian tendencies. She has a partner: male, dark, same age, five nine, 190 pounds. Has an appetite for silver toothpicks. They travel with a bunch of thugs I'd loosely describe as assholes. But you know all that, because I gave you their descriptions over a week ago. When you find them," I continued, "you should also ask them about the murders of Portman, Bremmel, and a guy called Denzel Nogart, otherwise known as Ten Pin, down at Incirlik Air Base. And while you're at it, you could drill them about the entire crew of the good ship *Onur*."

"So you do not deny that you met with Adem Fedai at Ephesus?" Karli asked.

"Of course not. Fedai picked the spot. He knew we were investigating his boss's murder. He wanted to tell us what he knew about the night Portman was killed."

"What did he tell you?" Iyaz asked.

"That he wasn't the one who did it," I replied.

"And that is all?" Karli asked.

"Pretty much." I wondered whether Masters had been interviewed yet, and if she had, what she might have told them. I gambled on as little as possible. "Fedai gave us a rundown on what he saw, what time he came to work that morning, the time he left—the details. It all added up, by the way."

"What about the safe?" said Iyaz.

"He said he opened it but there was nothing inside."

"Nothing?"

I shook my head and added a shrug, the disappointing-but-there-you-have-it combination.

"Did he see Portman's murderers?"

"No."

"He told you nothing else?"

"He said he wanted us to leave him alone, that he believed people were trying to kill him—Yafa and the creeps I just described to you—and that he would only feel safe back at his home in the mountains somewhere in northern Iraq. Seems his fears were justified."

Iyaz's arms were folded. He was buying this. "Adem Fedai made you go all the way to Ephesus to tell you nothing?"

"Like I said, the guy was scared. He saw what had happened to his boss. And after the little adventure Masters and I have just had, neither of us feels all that secure around here, either. Maybe once you let us out, we might head for those mountains, too.... Seriously, though, you guys need to put some manpower onto finding this hit squad running around your neighborhood."

Iyaz and Karli shared another glance.

"Tell us what happened to you and Special Agent Masters." Iyaz leaned against the sink, making himself at home.

I began with the meeting at Ephesus in the rain, leaving out—as I hoped Masters had done—any mention of a flash drive, water-quality report, radioactivity, the words "uranyl fluoride," and the town of Kumayt. Then I moved on to the shredded bus tires, road spikes, our subsequent off-road detour, the moonlight rendezvous with Yafa and her buddies, us waking up in the cistern and, finally, a rundown on our escape. When I'd finished, Karli came in for a close-up on my knuckles. They were badly swollen, the pale skin marbled with ugly bruising.

The two detectives talked between themselves for a moment. There was plenty of nodding. Karli told me, "The tourist bus you saw with tires blown. It was stolen. We found it in the valley near Ephesus. Burnt out."

"What about the Michelins on the rental?" I asked.

"They were all new. One was the wrong type—it did not match the others."

"So maybe the people I've been telling you about had difficulty locating a new identical set of four." And maybe Yafa and her team were starting to make all sorts of mistakes—not shooting Masters and me dead among them—that were going to snowball and run right over them.

I looked at Karli and Iyaz, and they looked back at me. There was a lot of looking going on. It occurred to me that these guys were so in the dark, it was a wonder they weren't bumping into things in broad daylight.

"Your story is the same as that of your partner," said Iyaz after he'd done enough looking. "We did not believe her, but now we are sure you are innocent of this crime. Also, your rental car. It had been in an accident—hit a tree. But there were no trees in the area we found it in. This confused our forensics people. Your story also explains it. We apologize for your treatment at the airport."

"Forget about it," I said, feeling benevolent. "Just let me out and we'll call it square."

"However, we are unhappy that you chose not to keep us informed of your movements. If you had done so, perhaps you would have been found and rescued earlier."

"Sure. When you're right, you're right." I stood up and gestured at the barred door. "Now, if you don't mind..."

"When you find new developments or evidence on this case, you will tell us."

"Cross my heart," I said.

Neither detective moved. I could sense some resistance to ending my incarceration.

There was a little more conversation in Turkish, punctuated by nods and smiles. A consensus between them had been reached and there was happiness all round. They walked toward the door, opened it, walked out, and closed it behind them. Through the bars, Iyaz said, "We believe your story ninety-nine percent, Special Agent Cooper. For this one percent we don't believe your story, we will keep you here overnight."

With a smirk Karli added, "Yes, seeing an American policeman in a Turkish prison. This is the occasion for which I dress to the right."

THIRTY-THREE

I was lying down, trying to sleep and hoping to wake and find this all a nasty dream, when there was the sudden sound of metal on metal and the heavy, gray-painted door swung open. Mallet and Goddard walked in.

I didn't sit up. "So let me guess. Masters entered me for an extreme makeover and you're here to start my transformation into Brad Pitt."

I got blank stares from both of them. "Let me take another guess. You two are playing Dumb and so far it's a tie game."

"A room with rubber walls, Cooper, that's what you need," Goddard said, pushing out his chin.

I hoisted myself up off the cot. My hand throbbed and my rib snagged on something, causing a spasm that stretched my lips tight across my teeth. I had a sudden loss of interest in sparring.

"For a cop, you seem to spend a hell of a lot of time behind bars," said Mallet. "Time to leave. Can you get up under your own steam, or do you want a hand?"

"Keep your applause to yourself. Where are we going and what's the catch?"

"No catch, Cooper. Holding you for an extra hour was Istanbul homicide's little joke. They called the embassy, who phoned us to come and get you. And here we are, fast as our little legs could carry us."

I managed to stand, feeling woozy. A strong hand under my armpit kept me upright.

"You've lost weight, Cooper," said Goddard. "We heard about your stint underground."

Was I mistaken, or were these guys playing nice? They weren't biting like they used to, but I knew how to fix that. "The people who killed Ten Pin at Incirlik—I think you knew who they were," I began. "That's why you came across Masters and me being heavied in the park. You weren't tailing us, you were following *them*—the woman called Yafa, the jerk with the toothpick, and their entourage of sociopaths."

"You're guessing, Cooper," said Mallet.

"I don't think so. At Incirlik, you wanted to know if I'd recognized the two guys in the van who died in the fire. You were fishing. You thought I might have identified them because *you* knew who they were and you wanted to know whether we did, too. Their names were Ben and Jonah, by the way. So, you want to come clean and tell me about the shit you guys are wading around in? And maybe while you're at it, you could drop the whole CID routine."

"Harvey will be seeing you later, back at the ranch," Mallet informed me, a slack smile on his face. It was like the guy had had a lobotomy. I think I preferred him mean. "You got questions, ask him," he continued.

Harvey Stringer. CIA. I might have known.

As I walked, the blood started flowing again and the muscles felt a little less seized. I collected my stuff from a bored guy behind a thick wire screen, stuff that included a box of bandages and the laces for my shoes. I checked my cell phone but the batteries had rigor mortis.

"Where's Special Agent Masters?" I asked.

"Outside," said Mallet, pointing me in the general direction.

Winter sunshine bathed the access road. I lifted my face to soak up some warmth.

A black Suburban idled, waiting. A young guy, trying too hard to look the part in Ray-Ban Aviators, jeans, and leather jacket, held open the rear door. Inside, I could see Masters dozing, her head against the window. I stopped and scoped the building behind me. Somewhere up there, Karli and Iyaz were having a laugh at my expense. Maybe we weren't so different after all.

There was a fully equipped OR in the basement of the Consulate-General. The doctor, a middle-aged woman with a crooked nose and a mole on her cheek sprouting hairs, took a look at my knuckles.

The X-rays came back and the picture said things weren't as bad as they felt, although it was back to square one on the original fractures. At least they wouldn't require surgery to line up the pieces.

The doc extracted half a syringe of reddish fluid from them and re-taped my rib. Being up-to-date on my shots, I passed on the hepatitis and tetanus boosters. She left to go stir a cauldron while I sat on the cot and waited for the plaster to dry out.

Not long after, Masters walked in with a glow, looking like she'd spent a week at a health farm. Rat apparently agreed with her. "How you doing?" she asked.

"I'll never play the violin."

"So we're all in luck. I just saw Cain," she said. "He thinks he might have struck gold on that email, the one signed by the mysterious B."

"Yeah?"

"More than likely it's B for Bob. Bob Rivers—CEO of Thurlstane's European operation. He's based in Paris."

Thurlstane Group, the U.S. civil engineering giant. I recalled the email: *You know the score. We'll hold you to your promise that the mess down there won't sour our chances on future contracts. All best, B.* "So what was the mess Bob hoped wouldn't curdle their reputation?"

"A little two-billion-dollar project."

"What does two billion buy you?"

"A big fat desal plant."

"Desalination . . ." Water. It fit.

THIRTY-FOUR

There were no cabs at Charles de Gaulle Airport, the drivers off striking for better pay. But a large number of enterprising locals had filled the gap, offering their private vehicles for a fare that was, ironically, double the usual going rate. We picked one of these at random from the lineup. As we rode into Paris, I was thinking that maybe it wasn't such a bad idea to get out of Dodge for a day or so—let everyone cool off.

"You been to Paris before?" I asked Masters as we motored away from Arrivals.

"As a matter of fact, I have. You?"

"Yeah, I've been to Parris."

"Really?"

"As in the island. Parris Island, Beaufort, South Carolina. Ah, those mad, impetuous Marines. What sweet memories."

Masters gave me a smile that did a better job of warming up the vehicle than the heating, and said, "On the way, why don't we detour and drive past the Eiffel Tower?"

"Only if you think we'll see some poodles with that funny haircut they give them."

Masters surprised me again by having a conversation with the driver in fluent French.

We saw the tower but no poodles. No guys with pencil mustaches wearing berets and striped T-shirts either. But we saw a lot of Muslims wearing head scarves and more than a few dressed in hijabs. Maybe East had moved West from Istanbul and was having a meeting here, too.

It was late by the time we arrived at Thurlstane, just after eight P.M. The conglomerate's European HQ was on the Rue de Rivoli, overlooking the Jardin des Tuileries—a classic eighteenth-century Parisian building washed and sandblasted so that it gleamed in its floodlights like a clean conscience. A block and a half away, various kings by the name of Louis had lived in a little outhouse called the Louvre. You could throw a stone into the front stalls of the National Theater from here, or maybe a tomato if you didn't like the show. Thurlstane had a reputation for buying its way into the local establishment. In Paris, cred was costing them plenty.

Masters and I were shown into a room lined with huge antique mirrors set in gold frames, portraits of Louis XVI and Napoleon staring at each other from opposite walls, and on the ceiling a bunch of Bonaparte's soldiers on horseback surrounded by naked flying babies with wings sprouting from their backs. The table was wood, enormous, and so highly polished that it seemed to be covered in a thin film of water.

Before we left Istanbul, I'd spoken briefly on the phone to Bob Rivers and pictured a big guy with a confident jaw. In person he was pushing five ten in lifts, was shaped like a football, and had a wandering eye, so that I wasn't sure which one to look at. He sat flanked on either side by an attorney, both of whom clasped their hands in front of them on the table. Rivers's eyes moved around like they were on stalks. Together, the three of them reminded me of a crab sitting on a mudflat at low tide.

"This is the second page of the email I told you about," I said, pushing the sheet across the table toward Rivers.

One of the lawyers intercepted it, picked it up, and read it. He nodded. *Yes, this is a sheet of paper. Yes, there are words on it. Yes, it is signed B. So far, so good.* He passed it to Rivers, who read it and put it down.

"What can you tell me about the desalination project at Kumayt?" I asked.

The attorney on the left answered. "Before we start, a few ground rules. We have instructed Mr. Rivers that you have no authority to ask questions and that, as a result, there is no need for him to provide you with answers on any matter. Most especially, do not ask about confidential business matters. Should you transgress on this point, the interview will be terminated immediately."

Attorney on the right piped up. "Our client wishes to inform you that neither he nor the Thurlstane Group, which will henceforth be called 'the company,' had any involvement whatsoever in the unfortunate murder of Colonel Emmet Portman, and so if you ask him questions on this matter inferring his or the company's involvement, this interview will be terminated. Furthermore, be aware that this interview is being taped for use in any possible proceedings that may arise as a result of this meeting."

I tried to connect with one of Bob's eyes and approach the issues from another tack. "Did you send Colonel Portman this email?" I asked Rivers.

He hesitated, then checked with the claw on either side to make sure this question was permitted. He received nods. "Yes. I wrote that email," he said.

"Did 'the mess down there,' as you wrote here, refer to a bid for construction at Kumayt in southeastern Iraq?"

More nods. "Yes," replied Rivers.

"A desalination plant?"

"Yes."

"Did 'the mess' you referred to have anything to do with radioactive contamination of the water supply?" I asked, fishing.

Rivers was about to answer when Attorney on the Left interrupted. "'The mess' was in relation to our concern about the way in which the bidding process was being conducted," he replied on Rivers's behalf.

Attorney on the Right chipped in: "This meeting is teetering on the edge of termination, Special Agent."

This meeting was teetering on the edge of making me want to punch the both of them.

Rivers must have felt the same way, because he shoved himself back from the desk suddenly and said, "This is pure bullshit."

"Mr. Rivers—sir. As we agreed prior to this interview, we recommend—"

"I recommend you go find a sock and chew on it. I'm going to speak for myself from now on," he snapped. "Emmet was a good man. I'll take full responsibility for any . . . ah . . . *transgressing*." Maybe Bob had a square jaw after all. He continued. "The mess, Special Agent, was simply that our bid was a farce from the very beginning."

Attorney on the Left got up from the table and walked to a control panel on the door. He flicked a switch. I guessed he'd had a change of heart about recording the meeting. He sat back down and said, "I'm sorry, Mr. Rivers. Please continue."

Rivers sighed. "A lot of money had been changing hands under the table. There was stuff going on you wouldn't believe. But there was two billion at stake, and that kind of money can warp the process, especially in a currency-hungry place like Iraq. I'd bumped into Emmet when I was in Ankara, looking into a highway we were building there. I hadn't seen him for thirty years, maybe more. We grew up together, kids from the same neighborhood.

"Anyway, we had lunch and I got around to telling him about the problems we were having in Iraq. He offered to look into it for us—said he knew some people who might be able to help out. As it turned out, there was not a lot he could do, but the project really fired him up. He started putting in a lot of time at some hospital there. Anyway, we—the Thurlstane Group and Portman—fought the good fight, but it was clear the project was always going to go to Moses Abdul Tawal. He—"

Masters cut in. "Who's he?"

"Moses Abdul Tawal. Fascinating character. I'd love to see what you people could dig up on the man. He headed up a joint consortium of Iraqi, Turkish, and Egyptian interests. Tawal won the bid. As I said, Tawal was always going to win the bid."

"What can you tell us about him?" Masters asked.

"That he's a crook. But murder?" Rivers shook his head. "I can't say if he would or wouldn't be capable of it."

"What can you tell us about the radioactive contamination?"

"The contamination was part of the reason for building the plant. An environmental statement went out with the bid that included a water-quality report. Traces of chemicals and low-grade activity indicated the presence of depleted uranium in the surface water. The groundwater was almost brine and undrinkable—the other reason for building the plant. The Iraqi government didn't want to make too many waves about the DU because of its reliance on Washington and its desire not to embarrass its biggest benefactor. Money was put up for the desal plant—so everyone was happy."

"Would you have a copy of the environmental statement?" Masters asked.

"Shredded," said Attorney on the Right. "One of the conditions of the bid."

"How did Colonel Portman think he could help you out?"

"We were getting raked over local politics. Emmet was going to dig around and find out who was pulling the strings."

Rivers snorted. "Y'know, my company can play hardball with the best of them, but these people operated on a whole new level."

I noticed that both attorneys had been getting increasingly restless—huffing, wringing their hands.

"I can tell you the plant they ended up building cost closer to three billion," Rivers added.

"That's a lot of overruns," I said.

"Yeah, either Tawal built more down there than was included in the scope of works, or big chunks of money went missing into someone's pocket."

"Mr. Rivers . . ." Attorney on the Left interjected. Attorney on the Right pulled the plug, ending the interview. Attorney on the Left claimed we were wading into dangerous, litigious waters. I hoped they both had cuts on their legs and that there were also piranhas swimming in those waters.

A multibillion-dollar desal plant, a missing billion, DU contamination, and a water sample that people were being killed over. These facts had caused a bell between my ears to ring, and it was ringing to point out that both Masters and I had missed something obvious and extremely dangerous.

Back on the street, the first thing I noticed was that our ride had disappeared. We had no choice but to head for the metro. A map informed us that there was a train line to Charles de Gaulle from the Châtelet metro station, a fifteen-minute walk away. Ten minutes if we hustled.

On the way, I told Masters about the uneasy feeling I'd had. "We've got a mole. Someone on the inside, working with Yafa."

"What?"

"We've got a mole. No doubt about it," I said as we broke into a trot. "Think about it. That floor safe at Portman's wasn't on the plans—not even the leasing agent knew about it. So Portman's killers cleaned out the wall safe, thinking they had everything there was to have, and split.

Then suddenly they're after Fedai. Why? Because someone told them about the floor safe, and that Fedai was the person who emptied it."

"Jesus... you're right. How the hell did we miss it? Any ideas about who it could be?"

"That's the sixty-four-thousand-dollar question. Could be someone within the Consulate-General. Istanbul police has access to the case notes, so it could be someone in Iyaz and Karli's department. Might even be Iyaz or Karli. Then there are the forensics people.... I wouldn't even know where to start looking."

We made it to the station in a little over seven minutes, took the stairs, and headed for the ticket office. It might have been the world's biggest subway station complex, but at nine-thirty at night, the place was a morgue. We headed down to the platform. We had a few minutes to kill before the next train arrived, so I took the opportunity to get something else off my chest. "You know, I haven't told you how much I enjoyed being stuck in a toilet with you."

"Like I keep telling you, Vin, a cistern isn't a toilet," Masters said, leaning over the edge of the platform, examining the tunnel at both ends of the platform. "And 'enjoyed' isn't the word I'd have used to describe the experience."

"No, I guess not."

"But I know what you mean. We nearly, um... all over again, didn't we?"

"We did." The breeze coming through the tunnel stiffened. "We should talk about it one day soon. Maybe over a bottle of moisturizer."

"Don't you ever give up?" she asked, raising an eyebrow.

"If you don't ask, you don't get, right?"

The platform was almost empty. Twenty yards to our left was a woman wearing a scarf over her head. She was looking straight ahead, toward the railway lines. In front of her was a stroller. Her baby was crying. To our right, two metro cops were walking the platform, coming toward us, chatting. There were also a couple of guys in hooded sweats, horsing around. The cops had words with them, which moved them on. One flipped the uniforms the bird behind their back. Something was giving me an uneasy feeling. I wasn't sure what it was. But then I realized: the crying.

I glanced back at the woman. She was doing nothing to comfort her baby. Nothing at all. It kept crying; she kept ignoring it. Odd. And then she turned toward us. Stubble. The woman had forgotten to shave. She reached into her stroller and pulled out an Uzi. I turned toward the cops, looking for assistance, only now they were behind us. Pistols jammed into our backs.

"We'll give you and your partner a choice, Mr. Special Agent," the man in the dress with the machine pistol called out as he strode toward us. His accent was heavy. "You can catch a bullet or the train."

The breeze turned into a wind and the light down in the dark end of the tunnel became the silhouette of a train. Rushing air tugged at my coat. The pistol dug harder into my spine. The cops braced. They were going to throw us both over the lip of the platform, straight into the path of the train. It burst through the tunnel into the station. We had one chance. No time left for alternatives.

Snatching Masters's wrist, I yanked her toward me, over the platform edge. She screamed. VOOM. The train thundered past inches from our heads, brakes screeching, wheels locked, the driver executing an emergency stop. I fought for breath, winded, my taped rib like a knife in my side. I wrapped Masters in my arms, pushed her against the ground, away from the rails, the wheels, the sparks. I lay over her, shielding her, pushing her down into the filthy concrete. Hydraulics hissed and the subway cars heaved to a crashing halt.

"Vin, Jesus, I—"

I put my finger against her lips. Somewhere close I could still hear that damn baby crying.

The train wasn't going anywhere. The driver was probably in shock. The carriages that nearly killed us were now protecting us from further attack. For all anyone up on the platform knew, we were crushed, dead. I was happy not to spoil the assumption.

I saw a service duct a couple of yards ahead, in the shadows. "Go," I said quietly, pushing Masters forward toward it. Above us on the platform, an increasing number of people were running about, shouting.

I joined Masters in the service duct. There was a door. It led to some stairs, which brought us to a maintenance elevator. My hand was shaking so violently I couldn't get a finger onto any of the buttons.

THIRTY-FIVE

Back in Istanbul the following day, we walked into the U.S. Consulate-General like nothing had happened. The mission had mostly decamped to Ankara anyway, and only the local staff had clocked in. We had a message to contact Captain Cain. I put in a request for a video chat.

"That was quick," Cain said, his face suddenly appearing on my desktop. "How'd you make out?"

I filled him in, leaving out the attempt on our lives.

"That tallies with the Request for Information I put in on the Kumayt project," he said, when I'd finished. "Got a reply this morning."

"Yeah? What'd it say?"

"Almost nothing you haven't just told me. Tawal sounds like a real piece of work."

"What do you mean, *almost* nothing?" I asked him.

"Might not be anything. The bids were made three and a half years ago, took six months to be awarded. One of the reasons Tawal's group seems to have won the project was that they promised to have the plant built inside three years. They're late, by the way. It's not operational yet. But something on the scale of that desal plant would normally take close to five years to build."

"So they're in a hurry," I said.

"I did say it might not be anything. . . . Oh, yeah. I read something online about two people jumping in front of a train at Châtelet last night.

The driver swears he hit them, but they never found the bodies. You were near Châtelet last night, weren't you, Cooper?"

"Paris is a big city," I told him. While he talked, I Googled "Moses Abdul Tawal." There were pages and pages on the guy. He was a playboy businessman who indulged himself in powerboat racing, Ferraris, and women who could get you into a lot of trouble. A potential role model for my next life.

"Just wondered whether you'd got caught up in it, is all. The station was closed for an hour," Cain rambled.

"Uh-huh. Anything been happening here?" I asked, changing the subject.

"As a matter of fact, yes. I ran that check on our friends Goddard and Mallet. They aren't CID."

"I know. They're CIA."

"Good guess."

"Not really. They pretty much told me."

"I called in a favor and had an Army buddy stationed over in Kuwait walk in off the street into 3rd MP. They've got a Goddard and Mallet there, all right. Only, guess what? They're both African American and black as Alaskan winter sunshine."

We batted around the small talk for a minute or two, then ended the call. I liked Cain. He was thorough, a good man to have on the team.

I leaned back in my seat and glanced at Masters across the room. She was tapping away on the keyboard. "You hear all that?" I asked.

"Yep. Not surprised."

"I'll shoot you some stuff on this Tawal character."

Masters sat back and exhaled.

"C'mon," I said, after pressing the send key. "Get your coat."

"Where we going?"

"To test this theory of mine."

We got into the elevator. "So where are we going?" she repeated as it bumped to a stop.

"Portman's residence. But first we have to call in at Doc Merkit's place."

"Merkit? Why her?"

"Because I don't want to ask anyone here if I can borrow their Geiger counter."

"Whoa... wait a minute," Masters said, holding the doors open.

"What's up?"

"Vin, maybe you should fly solo on this one. I've got plenty to do around here—keeping Stringer off your back, for one thing. And for another, I want to dig around in the DoE, see if I can't uncover a little more about those DU waste dumps."

The elevator doors buzzed, annoyed at the long delay. We stepped out and the doors closed.

Masters had her reasons for avoiding the doc. I guessed they were ones that lived in the same apartment block as my desire to practice a left-right combo on Dick Wadding's jaw. I wasn't going to push her any further. "If you're sure," I said.

"I'm sure."

"Well, if you're going to stay here, you might also have a look into the stuff Portman found in that water sample."

"Uranyl fluoride. Cain and I are already on it. You going to come back here?" she asked.

"Yeah, but give me a couple of hours."

"Hours, eh? You seeing Merkit for, you know, other reasons?"

"No."

"Vin, if there are other reasons, it's OK—really. But you'd better be up-front with me because, if you're not, I'll saw your testicles off with my nail file."

"Deal," I agreed with a smile and a twinge in my groin.

"I called Emir earlier—he'll be out front in the parking lot," Masters said.

"Then I'll sneak out the back—"

"C'mon, he's not that bad. And he'll save you time calling a cab."

Emir *was* that bad, but Masters had it right about the time—I didn't have any to waste sitting around.

I walked out into the failing afternoon light, a chill gathering in the air, and Emir leaning on the roof of his old Renault. The guy didn't look pleased to see me. There was a distinct lack of waving. He flicked his Camel into the wall hard enough to make it bounce in a shower of orange sparks, then hopped in his car.

I noticed he'd made some changes. The rear window was now framed by a line of small white pompoms, and a few additional items hung from his rearview mirror: a silver human skeleton, a pair of dice, and a line of gaudy silver coins that jangled over the bumps like a jogger with a pocketful of dimes.

"So, Mr. Vin, I hear you having trouble on the road when you go to Ephesus." Before I could answer, he added, "You would not have had this trouble if Emir had been driving."

"No, probably not," I agreed. "I'm going to Beyoglu and then Bebek. And if there's any trouble on the road, it's all yours."

Emir's head gave a tilt. He was happy with that. "Yes, OK. I have an uncle in Beyoglu. If there is time, I will visit him."

"Sure. And Emir, keep a lookout for tails, OK?"

"What is tails?"

"Anyone following."

"Yes, of course. I make sure no one is tails."

I was dead tired. I closed my eyes and tried not to think about my throbbing knuckles, the aching rib, or Masters's nail file separating Little Coop from his wingmen.

Too soon, Emir's voice penetrated my snooze. "No tails, Mr. Vin."

I opened my eyes. We were turning into Doc Merkit's street. It was just after four and dark enough for the streetlights to have come on.

I gave my face a rub with my good hand. I didn't have a lot of faith that Emir was equipped to spot a professional tail, but having him check the rearview mirror every now and then let me sleep easier. "Drive around the block," I told him. The business at Ephesus and Châtelet had made me jumpy.

Emir's shoulders hunched in a shrug. I scoped the parked vehicles, the usual lineup of Mercedes and a few Fiats. All were empty as far as I could see. I'm not sure what I expected to find but we made the circle anyway. "Pull over around the corner," I told him.

Emir drove past Doc Merkit's pink shoe box. The lights were on. We rounded the bend and stopped another fifty yards beyond it.

"I'll be an hour, max," I said, opening the door.

"I will take tea with my uncle."

"I'll see you back here."

"Back here," Emir repeated as he lit up. Sour tendrils of Turkish tobacco curled through the air.

I watched his taillights disappear down the street. There was no other traffic. Turkish folk music played in a house nearby. Three young boys laughed and squealed as they wrestled in the gutter; a large grandma type with legs thick enough to support coconuts and palm leaves sat in a nearby chair and kept watch over them. Lamb sizzled on a grill somewhere down the street, reminding me I was starving.

Knuckle dusters wielded by a psycho superbitch seemed a long way away from this scene.

"Vin! It is you! I have been so worried. Come in, come in, please," the doc said, throwing the door wide. On her face, I could see consternation and relief wrestling for control of her features.

I did my best to show her how remarkably fit and well I was, hopping up the stairs. The cracked rib did its best to spoil the show.

"Your hand!" She took the new cast carefully in her slender fingers. "I am just having a late lunch."

"It's four o'clock."

"Well, then, perhaps it's an early dinner. Have you eaten?"

"No, but I'm not h—"

"Vin, you must eat. And then you must tell me what happened."

The latter was the reason I was here, so I quit protesting. Over olives and cheese I filled her in on the past week: the meeting with Fedai, the information he'd recovered from Portman's floor safe and his subsequent murder at Kusadasi, a little about Yafa and her merry band of monsters, the time spent in the cistern, what we knew about Thurlstane and the desalination plant in Kumayt, and finally the overnight trip to Paris and the meeting with Rivers.

The doc sat back and shook her head in amazement. "At least this confirms for us that these murders were not committed for psychotic reasons."

"You're only saying that because you haven't met the killers."

The doc freshened up the hors d'oeuvres with cheese and bread.

"Just to change the subject a little," I said, "you still not wearing a *türban*?"

"No, I am not. I have thought about this. I have been dishonest with God, and my family. It will be difficult, but I will not wear it again.... Now, if you will allow *me* to change the subject, did you and your Special Agent Masters make love when you were trapped?"

"No," I replied, almost choking on an olive.

"But you wanted to, yes?"

I thought about lying, but decided against it. I nodded.

"Yes, I could feel this between you," she said, toying with her food.

"So I guess there won't be any more Turkish baths in my immediate future?" I asked.

Aysun locked those spectacular eyes of hers onto mine and smiled. "When I saw you at the door, your last visit—our last lovemaking—it was all I could think about."

"Sorry, doc."

"No, do not be sorry. I never expected you would be the one presenting my father with five camels and a goat." Aysun stood and went over to a large bouquet of pink lilies. "I received a call and these flowers from the man I met at your hotel. . . ." She picked up the card near the vase. "Colonel Richard Wadding. You know he asked me on a date?"

I snorted.

"I don't think he likes you," she said.

"Really? There's no doubt in my mind about him."

"I said no to the date. He told me you and Special Agent Masters were once lovers."

"Yeah, we were. But at the moment, we're just working this case together. I think the colonel's sore that Special Agent Masters finally saw him for what he really is."

"And what is he?"

"Someone you shouldn't get involved with."

Aysun studied the card for a moment, then dropped it in the trash. "Perhaps it is easier to remain celibate."

"Doc, I have a favor to ask."

"What is it?"

"I need a Geiger counter. Do you know where I could get one?"

"Would that not be something you could get through your embassy?"

I didn't give her my theory about the mole, deciding to keep that one to myself. It was a complication she didn't need to hear. "Asking for an instrument to measure radioactivity post-9/11?" I said instead. "It'd send them into meltdown."

"Yes, I suppose. Hmm . . . a Geiger counter. I think it would be possible, but I will have to accompany you. First, I must make a call."

The doc took her cell phone off the bench, scrolled through the memory. She leaned back against the cupboards, flicked her hair away from her face, and brought the cell to her ear. I couldn't understand what she was saying, but the way she spoke Turkish was soft and gentle, like silk on silk blowing in the breeze. She ended the call. "Yes, I can get this for you, but it will take an hour."

"OK. I'll just—"

"And now *I* have a favor to ask of *you*."

"Sure."

"Have you ever seen a Turkish woman dance?"

The show started with a kiss, a long, sensuous kiss, the kind of kiss that could earn a censor's rating. A kiss that steamed your shirt to your back. "One hour," she whispered in my ear, taking my hand and lifting it to cup her breast. Resistance was not exactly futile, it was nonexistent.

So while we waited for the doc's contact to call back about the Geiger counter, she danced for me. She danced without music, unplugged, the silence punctuated only by our breathing and the sound of her feet on the Turkish rug—the swell of her beckoning pubic bone moving back and forth like a hypnotist's watch.

The dance concluded with Aysun nude and lying on the rug, sweat glowing on her skin, her chest rising and falling with expended effort, her damp hair sticking to her neck and shoulders. "We have forty minutes left," she whispered. "How do you wish to spend them?"

Emir was talking to a well-dressed man in his fifties, who was sitting beside him in the passenger seat. I opened the rear door for Aysun and went around to the other side. Emir and his friend were already concluding the introductions in Turkish when I climbed in.

"So, where we going?" I asked.

"The Grand Bazaar,"Aysun said. "Emir knows the place." A brief exchange between them in Turkish followed, establishing the minor details.

Emir pulled away from the curb with a smile, his eyes darting to the rearview mirror as usual, unsure what to make of the woman sitting beside me. His allegiance lay with Anna Masters, but part of him also wanted to be nice to the extraordinary piece of ass occupying the backseat.

I read his mind. He was thinking that in the unlikely event he might get to have a crack at this woman, it would pay not to be churlish.

"This is my uncle I tell you about—Kemel," Emir bragged. "He has rug shop."

Kemel turned around, beamed a fistful of gold teeth at us, and said, *"Merhaba,"* which by now I'd figured out meant "hello."

"Of course he has," I said, and gave him a *"Merhaba"* in return. I waited for the sales pitch, but it never came. Emir must have briefed him. If so, the guy was learning.

Situated on the side of the hill facing the Golden Horn, the centuries-old Grand Bazaar packed four thousand shops into a couple of miles of covered, crisscrossing lanes. The place hummed mostly with tourists looking for sourvenirs that would sum up the essence of their visit to Turkey.

My mementos were memories, and all of them were bad—except for the ones involving the doc. My memories were of seeing Dutch Bremmel sitting with his head beside him, of watching Ten Pin getting gnawed by a jet fighter, and of pulling the skin off a rat. But, like I said, there were also a few good memories. I now had the memory of seeing Aysun dance, of watching her hips and pelvis move in a way I'd never seen a woman's hips and pelvis move before. And by the age of thirty-four, I figured I'd seen just about every way possible for a woman to move. In this, the doc proved me wrong. She apparently took belly dancing classes—it was her hobby, she told me afterward.

THIRTY-SIX

Emir stopped next to the Grand Bazaar's main entrance. I asked him to wait, and the doc and I joined the crowds moving back and forth like a restless sea beneath the arch. We passed by the gold and jewelry sellers, past the spice merchants and clothing shops, ducked behind the knife quarter, and ended up outside a shop specializing in technical equipment.

The shop was empty, as was every other retailer in this corner of the Grand Bazaar, it being a long way from the bargain T-shirt quarter. Aysun walked up to the old man in a threadbare cardigan who stood behind the counter. He put his cigarette down on the glass, the burning end hanging over the edge. The doc and the old guy then embraced and kissed each other's cheeks a couple of times, back and forth like Europeans do, and exchanged a few words. "My brother's wife's uncle's neighbor would like to know if you would stay for tea," Aysun asked me.

"Love to, but . . ." I jiggled my wrist. "Time."

Even though he couldn't speak English, the old guy got the drift. He reached behind his counter and lifted up a case with a handle. He opened it and gestured for me to come closer. Inside the carrying case was a yellow box the size of a brick with a large dial on it, a carry handle, a range switch, and a simple on/off switch—a Geiger counter. The old guy chugged on his cigarette, put it down, then showed me how to use the instrument, which, I gathered, was basically to turn the switch to "on" and walk the box toward the suspected hot source until the needle jumped into the your-hair's-about-to-fall-out zone. He pointed it in a couple of directions and the speaker gave off two crackle-like *pops*.

He said a few words in a voice that was thin and emphysemic. I shrugged apologetically, not understanding. He raised a finger, then pointed the box at his wristwatch to demonstrate. The needle went nuts, accompanied by a continuous stream of popping sounds. He adjusted the scale knob, the noise disappeared, and the needle settled down again. I got it—the scale was adjustable from radiation that was "background" to "Chernobyl."

I said thanks and told the old guy, through the doc, that I'd return the instrument when I was finished with it. He replied with body language that said, "No hurry."

Ten minutes later Aysun and I were walking back across the road toward where Emir had illegally parked, causing a minor traffic jam. A couple of uniforms in a patrol vehicle had pulled up behind his Renault and were attempting to get him and his uncle to move along. They were all waving arms at one another like Will Robinson's Robot. The issue was resolved when the doc and I materialized from the crowd, whereupon Emir acquiesced to the police demands and moved to hold a door open for the doc. The uncle waved at the officers, who had the surly look of traffic cops the world over. They got in their car and drove off to the next inevitable snarl, somewhere down the road.

"I'm going to go it alone from here," I said. Aysun was about to protest but I headed her off. "I have to do a little breaking and entering. It'd be best if you weren't with me. Emir will take you back to your place. If you like, I'll stop by later and let you know how I made out."

"Yes, OK. Please . . ." Aysun smiled, took my good hand, and squeezed it before climbing into the backseat.

Emir witnessed this apparently intimate and traitorous exchange between the two of us and shot me a poisonous glance—which, of course, I ignored. I whistled at a cab that happened along on the other side of the road, heading in the right direction.

Bebek was maybe fifteen minutes across town, enough time to think about why Portman, Bremmel, Ten Pin, and the *Onur* crew had been killed. Enough time also to wonder whether Masters would want to make good on her threat and go to work on me with her nail file. But that would only happen if I took the coward's way out, confessed my guilt, and told her what had happened. Assuming, that is, I had guilt.

The cab dropped me outside the Portman residence. The cop guards and their portable armor shields had long gone, replaced by a *For Lease* sign nailed to the front wall. I walked up the steps, case in hand, and tried the door, just in case the previous visitors had been careless. Locked.

I took my notebook from my jacket pocket, removed the thin, filed-down hacksaw blade tucked into the spine for just these occasions, and went to work on the lock. The door clicked open. I went in, closed the door behind me, and the scents of a house freshly cleaned but unlived-in washed over me.

Upstairs, I put the case on the floor in Portman's study and extracted the Geiger counter. I turned it on; the device was quiet. I pulled back the chair and the carpet, opened the floor safe; the box stayed silent when I waved it around inside—a couple of *pop*s, background stuff.

The wall safe was next. The painting in front of it hadn't been changed—the hunting party was still doing its best to bring down that elephant. I swung it wide on its hinge. The box sounded off a handful of *pop*s. I opened the safe door, put the Geiger counter inside, and the thing went crazy. I adjusted the scale and a screech came out of the speaker like the noise a badly tuned radio makes in a violent thunderstorm. The needle hovered over the 12,400-becquerel mark. The safe was hot.

There was another competing noise in the room. My cell. The screen told me it was Masters.

I switched off the Geiger counter. "Hey," I said, answering it. "Guess what?"

"Jesus, Vin..." There was relief in her voice. "So you're at Portman's?"

"Yeah, why? What's up?"

"Something terrible has happened...."

THIRTY-SEVEN

The early evening was still and quiet. Somewhere close by, people were crying. The Istanbul police had set up floodlights, getting right down to business, taking statements, earning their pay. Istanbul police forensic teams were already on the scene. Anti-terror guys picked and poked their way through the scene.

Just about everyone I knew in Istanbul was there. Iyaz and Karli were taking a statement from a witness, the same old lady I'd pegged earlier as the grandmother of the kids playing in the gutter. I didn't see the kids. The old woman was sponging her eyes with a hankie. A knot formed in my gut.

Goddard and Mallet stood around, shaking their heads, discussing something with Harvey Stringer. Masters had her arms around Nasor, Doc Merkit's nephew and sometime receptionist. Rodney Cain stood by himself in shock, staring into nothingness.

Ambulances and cop cars were everywhere, their flashing blue, red, and orange lights bouncing and shearing off hundreds of shattered windowpanes that now lay across the sidewalks, the road, over the parked vehicles—over everything—lending a jagged kaleidoscope effect to the scene. There was the gagging, sweet smell of burnt human flesh in the air, the smell you never forget once you've experienced it.

The epicenter of the explosion was a car-sized crater in the asphalt, twenty yards down from Doc Merkit's place. Opposite, Emir's Renault, now a twisted, scorched half-ton of metal, had come to rest upside down on the sidewalk against a tree trunk. A paramedic had climbed into the upper branches and was in the process of recovering blackened body parts caught up in them. The bomb must have detonated with pinpoint accuracy, which to me indicated an observer somewhere with a cell phone. Something glinting in the gutter, reflecting a bank of floodlights, caught my attention. I bent down and picked it up: the silver head and torso of a miniature human skeleton.

"Vin, I'm so sorry." It was Anna. I felt the warmth of her arms around me, but it couldn't chase that smell out of the back of my throat.

We stood there not moving for some time. Over Masters's shoulder, I watched the scene playing out around us with a detached emptiness. *We have forty minutes left. How do you wish to spend them?*

"I just spoke with Detective Iyaz," Masters said, leaning against the side of an ambulance. "The old lady saw Emir drive past. There were two other people in the car with him at the time of the explosion. One of them has yet to be positively identified."

"Emir had an uncle who lived nearby," I told her. "His name was Kemel. He owned a rug shop. He came along for the ride." I sipped the sweet, thick black Turkish coffee Masters had bought from a vendor a couple of blocks over. It didn't help.

"I'll pass that on," said Masters. "They're talking about this being the work of the KKK."

"I didn't know the Klan operated this far north."

"Vin, hereabouts 'KKK' stands for the Kurdistan Democratic Confederation. A local terrorist group. It's also called the PKK. They blow people up in Turkey every other day."

"This KKK claimed responsibility?"

Masters shook her head.

"You and I both know who did this. Forensics are going to find traces of the same explosives made in the U.S., shipped to Israel, and supposedly fired off at Hezbollah."

One of the many ambulances backed away from the scene and drove off quiet, in no hurry.

"I pressed Karli and Iyaz about Yafa and her entourage," Masters said. "I think they want to believe she's a figment of our imagination."

"Some figment," I replied. "She'd have had Doc Merkit's home staked out. They would have known Emir was our driver. The two people in the car with him were mistaken for you and me." I remembered circling the block with Emir, looking for what, I wasn't sure, but clearly my gut had picked something up.... "Where's Harvey Stringer?" I asked abruptly.

"Took off half an hour ago."

I swore.

"You think he's the inside man?"

"Maybe," I said. "His hall monitors, Goddard and Mallet, have been running around on his behalf, keeping an eye on us. He has full access to the day-to-day on this case. And he knows more than he's prepared to share about Yafa. Stringer would have known about Portman's trips to southern Iraq but has chosen not to come clean about them. Someone ran Portman's emails through a filter—Stringer has access."

"We should go to Burnbaum."

"When we've got something solid."

I caught a glimpse of the granny I'd seen earlier. She was helping a much younger woman herd the three young boys into a doorway.

"So what did you dig up at Portman's place?" Masters asked.

"Ays—Doc Merkit found me a Geiger counter. That's why she was in the car with Emir and his uncle." I knew I was wandering from the point. I felt Masters's hand on my shoulder.

"Don't blame yourself, Vin. This was just... bad luck."

"Yeah, bad luck." I watched Karli and Iyaz talking with a couple of guys wearing paper shoes—forensics. "Portman's wall safe was hot," I added.

"Radioactive?"

"Seems like it wasn't the perfect crime after all. I figure Yafa went too heavy on the explosives and accidentally burst the radioactive water sample. That would explain why the safe was cleaned out so thoroughly—had nothing to do with wiping away prints. If forensics found fluid in the safe, they'd have tested it. And that was the last thing Yafa and her people wanted."

"So when Yafa found out about the existence of the secret floor safe, they must have come to the same conclusion you did about the existence of a duplicate water sample and report. Which would explain why they were after Fedai. It also confirms your theory that an inside source was feeding them information."

Being right didn't give me a lot of satisfaction, not today.

"Vin, I can tell you a little about uranyl fluoride now, if you're interested. But it can wait till tomorrow."

What I wanted, needed, was to keep busy. "I'm OK. Fill me in."

"You get uranyl fluoride when you dissolve uranium hexafluoride in water. You also get hydrogen fluoride. Both are highly toxic, and I mean *highly*. Breathe too much hydrogen fluoride and it'll kill you."

"And what's uranium hexa-whatever?"

"Uranium hexafluoride is part of the cycle that ends in either fuel for nuclear reactors or thermonuclear bombs."

"Well, I guess if Karli and Iyaz's forensics people had found that in the residue left in Portman's wall safe, it would've shifted the murder investigation to different ground. We need to get out of here."

"And go where?"

"To different ground."

THIRTY-EIGHT

I zipped the flight jacket up tight under my neck as the MH-60 Pave Hawk climbed into the haze. "What's that?" I said into the mike, gesturing at the huge, obviously ancient ruin sliding by below.

"That's Ur," replied the flight engineer.

"Err... as in you don't know?"

"No, *Ur,* as in the ancient ziggurat of Ur, temple to the moon goddess, Nanna. That there's the world's oldest ziggurat, Special Agent. Over four and a half thousand years old—older than the Great Pyramids of Egypt. Back when it was built, it was sited near the mouth of the Tigris and Euphrates rivers, on the Persian Gulf. If the experts are right and all those ice shelves melt, maybe that's where it will end up again—on the mouth of the Persian Gulf. Ironic, right? If you're interested, I do a little tour guiding there in my spare time."

"Really," I said.

Masters made a sound that implied we might just take him up on it. I doubted it. Our schedule was tight. And even if it was loose, I doubted it.

"It's within Tallil's secure perimeter," the flight engineer continued. "Can't miss it—the only thing you can see rising above the plain. Perhaps when you people are done, you can look me up at the squadron."

Any moment the guy was going to hand us his business card. "What's with the haze?" I asked, heading him off. A band of gray tinged with orange sat on the horizon off to the northwest.

"That's a sandstorm we got coming in about two hours from now. If

Kumayt was any farther out, we wouldn't be going. Engines and sand don't mix, and these babies have been known to crash. But we'll get out and back before it hits."

My sphincter did the sphincter equivalent of nervously licking its dry lips. I'd only just gotten over a fear of flying, something I'd picked up on a tour of duty in Afghanistan—having two helo crashes back-to-back in one morning will do that. The Pave Hawk banked hard left, the rotors thudding as they chopped into the dry air, my arms and head heavy with the g's. "How'll we get back?" I asked.

"Wait out the storm and then we'll come get you. Pretty much all you can do."

"How long will it last?"

"The weather boys say it won't be a bad one. Day and a half, max."

I sat back against the bulkhead, the webbing on the body armor rubbing up against that problem rib, and watched Iraq slip past the Pave Hawk's open side. Down on the ground, temps were slightly below freezing, the sand frosted white here and there by the last of the moisture that the cold had wrung from the air. It'd been snowing here just two weeks ago. In six months, it'd be hot enough to melt lead. What a place.

The chopper settled into the flare, nose high and tail low, all 24,000 pounds of it shuddering from wind buffeting and the various rotating masses working hard to counterbalance each other.

Masters's voice bellowed in my headphones. "That must be the welcoming party."

I scoped the LZ out the door on her side and saw a platoon-size detachment of Brits—specifically, the Queen's Dragoon Guards—a Mastiff troop carrier and several Land Rovers equipped with mounted and manned machine guns, parked upwind. Platoon members had set a defensive cordon around the detachment. I guessed that the guy leaning against the windsock with a hand shielding his eyes was Lieutenant Hamish Christie. I'd talked to the lieutenant already, back when we arrived at Tallil. He'd drawn the short straw and been assigned as our liaison. Apparently, the Brit military police, our usual babysitters, were all down in Basra cracking heads. A riot had erupted there because some local politician had gotten himself whacked. The whole province of

Maysan was on alert, which, Christie informed me, had been the general state of play here ever since the Ottoman Empire failed to come to grips with this place. The lieutenant turned his shoulder into the clouds of dust spun up by the MH-60's rotors.

The flight engineer collected our headsets, food trays, and blankets once the chopper had settled onto its wheels. The pilot leaned over behind the bulkhead, gave us the hurry-up signal, followed by a salute. I figured the aircrew wanted to be nicely hunkered down back at Tallil with a Dr Pepper by the time the sandstorm hit. Masters and I obliged, grabbing our stuff, hopping out, and running clear of the rotors. The Pave Hawk was airborne before we'd reached the windsock. The flight engineer threw us a wave out the side.

"Welcome to Fantasy Island," Christie exclaimed, over the receding noise of the helo's turbines, with an accent I'd pegged as Scottish.

We checked the names on each other's shirts, then shook hands.

"Just to get the protocol right, what do I call you?" he asked. "Sir and ma'am? *Provoh* marshals? I'm at a bit of a loss. . . ."

"I get called plenty of things, so whatever you like," I replied, having already broken the ice with Christie over the phone. "But Vin and Anna will do, unless you want to go formal, in which case I'm Your Royal Highness and this is Special Agent Masters."

"I'll keep it casual, then, eh? So where do you want to start?" He headed toward a dusty, desert-camo-pattern Land Rover.

"What about the storm?" Masters asked.

"I understand we've got around forty-five minutes till it hits. But I wouldn't let a little skin-flaying dirt and gravel divert you from your purpose—keeps the snipers indoors. You're here to look at the new desal plant, right?"

Masters nodded.

"Then let's start there, shall we?"

"Say hello, lads," he said to his men as we piled into the Land Rover.

The lads mumbled a greeting.

"This is Special Agent Cooper and Special Agent Masters. They're cops, so I hope you've all got your parking fines paid up."

The driver did a U-turn.

"What do you know about this part of the world?" Christie asked us.

"That there are lots of ways to get killed," said Masters, beating me to it.

"You don't say. Well, Iran is around thirty miles over the horizon that way." He pointed directly ahead through the windshield. "So while this place might be within Iraq's national borders, its allegiances lie with the ayatollah. Muqtada al Sadr and his Mahdi Army are top of Ali Baba's tree around here. Those Shiite asshats run this rat hole and push everyone around—with the exception of Her Majesty's British Army, of course. Lately, another group called the Supreme Council for Islamic Revolution in Iraq has been trying to muscle in on the action, but so far they haven't become serious contenders, though it has raised the body count amongst the locals somewhat. The politician who just got a handful of hot lead inserted in his person is a case in point.

"The Mahdi Army recruits from the poor and the pissed-off, so it has a pool the size of a small ocean to draw from in this place. If you have a different political point of view, whether religious or secular, you'll end up with a bullet-riddled car, and usually while you're in it."

"What about the plant?" Masters asked.

"Kawthar al Deen, which means 'Sweet water is the way,' or 'Sweet water of life'—take your pick. We've been up here for the last month, tasked to protect the final construction phase. A crafty Egyptian gent by the name of Moses Abdul Tawal fronts the project. He flies in occasionally to kick a few arses for the fun of it. Has his own full-time private security force on-site, made up of mercenaries. And these lads are at least as crazy as any lunatic on the other side of the fence. Fortunately for Tawal, his lunatics are fiercely loyal to his checkbook."

"We going to pass through town?" Masters asked, establishing the geography.

"Through Kumayt? No, that's behind us on the other side of the Tigris. The plant is twenty-three miles northeast of it. We just follow the pipeline."

"Twenty-three miles. That would put it within spitting distance of Iran."

"It would," said Christie, "if you could spit ten miles."

The scrub of the airport gave way to low marshland, something I hadn't seen a lot of in Iraq. "What's the water like here?" I asked.

"Fucking awful, mate. Best you stick to the bitter on tap back at barracks. Failing that, take your own supply. That's why there's a desalination plant here. The groundwater had a high salt content and traces of DU were found in the surface water. There's supposed to be a burial ground of contaminated Gulf War I scrap out here somewhere."

"We heard. Does anyone know where that burial ground might be?" Masters asked.

"No, though I'm sure someone in one of your government departments would have the coordinates tucked away somewhere."

"You wouldn't happen to know why the water was tested in the first place?"

"When you're in Kumayt next, call in to the hospital and visit the children's ward."

"What'll we find there?"

"Birth defects, many times the national average."

The marshland came to an abrupt end, becoming the Iraq I was more familiar with—a flat and empty moonscape of powder fine enough to blush a woman's cheeks. The convoy zigzagged through a half-dozen dry riverbeds called wadis, eventually hooking up with a broad, smooth strip of two-lane asphalt tracking a fat pipeline that disappeared into the haze. I didn't see another living thing the entire journey, not even a goat. We followed the road for twenty minutes, the elevation climbing steadily, plenty of signage along the way keeping us informed of the miles remaining to the plant.

"You ever meet a Colonel Emmet Portman?" I asked Christie.

"Colonel Portman? Aye, he didn't invite me over for tea or anything, but I met him a couple of times. Seemed like a good man. Friend of yours?"

"He was murdered," answered Masters.

"Oh, sorry to hear that. Is that why you're here? On the trail, as it were?"

"As it were," I confirmed.

"And here I was thinking perhaps it was the weather that brought you here. For what it's worth—and don't take this the wrong way—rumor had it Portman and Tawal hated each other's guts."

"Do you know why?" Masters asked.

"No—the rumor didn't come packed with a lot of detail. Take the turnoff, boyo," Christie instructed the driver. There was no turnoff that I could make out, just a bunch of divergent tire tracks in the mushroom-colored dust. "I'll take you to where you can get an overview of the project. Might as well do that before we drive you up to the front door. You seen a desalination plant before?"

Masters and I shook our heads. *No.*

"You're in for a surprise then. Our base is up this way, too."

Several corners later, the trail swept past the aforementioned base, barricaded with barbed wire, sandbagged machine-gun posts, and sentries. We motored by in a swirling cloud of choking grit that drifted toward the Brit guards, one of whom gave us a merry wave.

Not five minutes' drive past Club Dragoon, the convoy pulled to a stop on a low hill. Spread out below was a vast facility.

"Sweet Jesus," murmured Masters as we left the vehicle.

Countless shiny new stainless-steel pipes were laid out on the desert below like the sand had been sucked away to reveal the skeleton beneath. Here and there, clusters of vertical stacks rose into the air. There were huge water storage tanks, covered cooling ponds, an enormous power station to provide the facility with electricity, a ten-thousand-foot newly surfaced runway, hangars, garages, and several clusters of buildings that looked like office blocks. Surrounding the facility was a trench deep enough to swallow tanks. Inside it, there was a double perimeter of gleaming razor wire that reminded me of an exercise yard in a prison. Concrete bunkers that I guessed contained machine-gun emplacements dotted the perimeter every three hundred yards or so. "You'd think they were expecting trouble," I remarked.

The roar of jets at high altitude echoed around us. I squinted at the sky a long way ahead of the sound and spotted two tiny flecks of silver racing north, parallel to the Iranian border.

Christie rested the butt of his SA80 assault rifle on his hip. "Aye, like I said, Iran is barely ten miles across the plain. On a clear day you can see Khuzistan, the Iranian province Saddam annexed during the Iraq-Iran war. I've heard they're pretty jumpy over there. And while I think about it, best not to venture off the road. The surrounding area has been mined."

Masters peered through a pair of binoculars. "Who owns the white Eurocopter? That's a lot of money parked down there on the helipad."

"If it's white, it's Tawal's," Christie replied. "You're in luck. He must be in."

"He is," she said, passing me the glasses. "Take a look."

I refocused until a tall man in a long white robe sharpened in the lenses. Tawal—we'd seen pictures of him on the Net. He was beating two other men to the ground with a clipboard. The guys taking the lumps were cowering, trying to protect their heads with their arms.

"And don't you ever ask me for a raise again. . . ." Masters said, taking a camera with a long lens out of her bag and snapping off a bunch of shots.

I kept watching. The guys put up no resistance whatsoever. When Tawal had finished dishing out the punishment, he spat on the two men sprawled on the ground.

"I've seen Tawal do worse," Christie told us, peering through his own pair of glasses. "The place is a couple of months behind schedule. He's on edge."

While Masters took photos, I moved the binoculars over the facility. There were plenty of armed stooges wandering around, looking bored. One of them also had a pair of binoculars. And the guy was looking straight back at us. "Let's go introduce ourselves," I said.

A gray veil was suddenly drawn across the sun. Within seconds, the light intensity went from mid-morning to twilight. The sandstorm moved across the sky and the ground. I saw the guy with the binoculars become enveloped in a swirling eddy of sand that forced him to bury his face in the crook of his arm, and then he disappeared. I felt a shift in the air around us, sucked out just like seawater retreats ahead of a tsunami. A heartbeat later, we were consumed by a howling, blinding wind that stung exposed skin and filled my mouth and nose with a choking dry clot of dust and grit.

I put on the eye goggles and tied some camouflage netting around my face. Masters and Christie and his men did the same. Christie gave the "move out" hand signal; the shriek of the wind and the intense sandblasting made further talk a waste of breath.

THIRTY-NINE

Moses Abdul Tawal was in his mid-fifties. He was also somewhere around six three and 230 pounds; athletic, but with a stomach that looked like a pillow had been stuffed up his shirt. His hair was solid black with no gray—dyed, I decided. His skin was brown and smooth as tanned leather. Behind gold Porsche glasses, his eyes were small and surrounded by dark circles. Tawal either didn't sleep much or he was sporting a couple of first-class shiners. Maybe the workforce had fought back.

"You have blood on your sleeve, Mr. Tawal," I said once the formalities of introduction, namely our shields, were back in our pockets.

He saw the spatters, pulled back the sleeve, and investigated the skin on the underside of his forearm. "Oh, I must have injured myself somehow," he said in perfect, though Middle Eastern–accented, English.

Yeah, we saw.

Not finding a source for the blood, Tawal shrugged and moved on. "Can I get you two anything? You must be parched from being out in the storm. As you might expect, we do a very nice line in water here."

"Sure," I replied. "Water would be fine."

"Please." Masters nodded.

A young Iraqi guy in a white coat and black pants appeared from behind a black panel, a crystal decanter and two glasses on a heavy silver tray. He placed the load on the immense, and no doubt priceless, wood and ivory antique boardroom table. I accepted the glass as sand dislodged from the folds in my clothes and rained down onto the black granite floor around my feet. I shifted my boots, and the sand crunched. I gulped down the water, as did Masters.

Two walls of glass suggested this was a corner office. Beyond it, I supposed, lay the expanse of Kawthar al Deen—though, at the moment, the view was limited to a solid wall of boiling dust, the high overhead sun making its presence known by throwing an ethereal orange-red tinge throughout. There was a flash followed by a bolt of lightning. The building rumbled. Large drops of water, heavy with suspended powder, smeared the glass.

"So, how may I help you today?" Tawal asked, taking a seat at the head of the table and gesturing at us to sit.

"There have been a number of murders. You have probably heard what happened to the U.S. Air Attaché to Turkey, Colonel Emmet Portman," I said, kicking it off. "We believe you and the colonel met on a number of occasions and over a number of years."

"Why, yes, I did hear about the colonel. Very tragic. But I fail to see how his death might have anything to do with me."

"Colonel Portman spent plenty of time down here. There seems to have been a lot of effort expended to keep that quiet."

Tawal shook his head. "Not of my doing. I still don't see how I may be of any worthwhile assistance."

"We believe the two of you didn't get along."

"Who told you this?" Tawal frowned.

"I don't think it's any secret," I countered.

"There were certainly issues on which the colonel and I did not see eye to eye. But I would like to think that we had a common respect."

"What were some of the issues that came between you, Mr. Tawal?" Masters interposed.

"The colonel did not think it fair that this facility came to be built by an Iraqi-led consortium, given the amount of American blood sacrificed here in the name of democracy."

I believed in Tawal's answer about as much as he did. "You mean he didn't appreciate the way your consortium lied, cheated, and bribed its way into the catbird seat."

"Ah, I see you've been talking to the people at the Thurlstane Group. This is not America, Mr. . . ."

"Special Agent Cooper."

"Thurlstane was not prepared to conform to the realities of business practices here in Iraq, Special Agent Cooper. We were. That is why, as I believe you saw today, we have built a magnificent piece of infrastructure for the people of Iraq, for the future of this great country."

"A runway, lots of empty buildings, a nice thirty-mile stretch of highway—it all seems like a lot of trouble to go to for a patch of desert," I said.

"How very nearsighted of you, Special Agent. Water is even more important to the future fortunes of the Middle East than oil. Over the coming decades, you will see towns like Kumayt become cities, purely because of the presence of this facility. Along with the domestic consumption of potable water, we will also be able to supply industry and agriculture with their needs. I wouldn't be surprised if Kawthar al Deen itself becomes an important town and business center surrounded by lush farmland. Populations will grow on our doorstep."

"I hope they don't step on your mines."

Tawal stared at me without blinking. Then he glanced around the room—probably looking for his trusty clipboard with which to teach me some respect.

"Where are you from, Mr. Tawal? You're not Iraqi."

"I am Egyptian, from Cairo. Are you going to ask to see my passport?"

"No, and there's no need to tense up on us, Mr. Tawal," I replied.

"You have an aggressive interrogation style, Special Agent."

"This is Special Agent Cooper being nice, Mr. Tawal," Masters informed him. "He must like you."

The guy forced out a smile but he didn't seem in the least bit happy.

"We have some photos we'd like you to have a look at, if you wouldn't mind, sir," Masters continued. She pulled a folder from a satchel. "Do you know this man?" she asked, placing a print on the table in front of Tawal.

"No." He shook his head. "Who is he?"

"His name is Dutch Bremmel. Or I should say, *was*. He's dead." Masters produced a second photograph. "And this man?"

"No."

"His name was Denzel Nogart, though mostly he was known as Ten Pin. Also dead."

A blank expression suffused Tawal's face. It said he had no idea why he was being shown these photos.

"How about this woman?" Masters put a police artist's sketch of Yafa on the table.

"Is this woman also dead?"

"We wish," I said.

"Why are you showing me pictures of people I have never seen before?" he demanded.

We couldn't decide whether Tawal was a very dangerous man or a man in very great danger. Until we knew for certain what we were dealing with, Masters and I had decided not to stampede the guy. It was time to shift the tone into the conciliation range.

"We believe Colonel Portman died because of some connection with this facility," I told him. "And frankly, sir, we're concerned for your safety. Special Agent Masters could show you photographs of at least another twenty men and women, including a couple of close associates of ours, who've also been murdered. During the course of this investigation, there have been attempts on our lives."

"I did not know. And, of course, I am shocked and very sorry to hear this," Tawal said. "Naturally I will do everything possible to assist your inquiries. Come, let me show you what we have created here. We can talk along the way."

He stood. We stood. A poke around the joint was exactly what we wanted. Masters shuffled the photos back into the folder.

"Guts before glory," I said as she followed him out.

"Unfortunately, the storm will preclude the full tour," Tawal told us. "The facility is spread over a number of hectares. It is too far to walk so we often move about on golf carts. But not today, I'm afraid."

We passed though fifty yards of corridor to a second set of elevators and rode one to the basement. "Do you know how desalination works?" he asked.

"You take out the salt," I said.

"Well, yes, of course. The desert may seem dry, but beneath it are natural reservoirs containing many thousands of megaliters of water, deposited over millennia. Unfortunately, due to the high content of salts, this water is undrinkable. The salt content is not as high as seawater, but still it is not suitable for human consumption." The doors slid open on a wide underground corridor that disappeared in darkness in both directions.

"Saving on electricity?" I asked.

"We are not fully operational as yet," he said with a shrug.

Five men wearing jeans, body armor, and machine pistols strolled out of the darkness and walked past us. Tawal ignored them. We found it hard to. They moved with the confidence of combat vets. I wondered what their backgrounds were.

Moving to a heavy security door, Tawal punched a code into a panel and the door swung open on hydraulic arms. Behind it was a control room. Displayed on one wall of the room were flow diagrams illustrating the plant's main processes—power generation and desalination.

Two large control panels dominated the floor. A couple of additional rows of computer terminals, all with joysticks, backed them up. Four male technicians hovered over the control panels. One had a welt on the side of his face; he didn't appear to be entirely happy in his work and frowned at the control panel, avoiding eye contact with the boss. I recognized him. He was one of the men we'd seen Tawal discussing industrial relations with just before the storm rolled in.

"Kawthar al Deen is almost totally automated," Tawal told us. "The systems are monitored and there is a maintenance crew, but we can produce enough water for a city of three hundred thousand people with a workforce of just twenty."

"Then why do you need all the office space?" Masters asked. "Looks like you've got enough of it here for at least several hundred people."

"Yes. We have planned for Kawthar al Deen to be a business center. We have incorporated all the facilities of a modern Western-style workplace: a swimming pool, gyms, a nursery. Perhaps we will also incorporate a retail shopping mall one day."

He spoke brusquely to the guy with the facial remodeling. The man went to work on his keyboard and a section of the diagram up on the wall filled with green.

"There are two kinds of desalination processes—electrodialysis and reverse osmosis," Tawal continued. "Here we utilize reverse osmosis. The process begins when we draw off brackish water from the subterranean aquifers. The larger solids are removed, the pH is altered, then we pressurize this feedwater to 375 pounds per square inch."

Various sections of the diagram lit up to illustrate Tawal's pitch.

"The feedwater is then forced through water-permeable membranes, and we end up with brine on one side and virtually salt-free water on the other, all without the need for heating, environmentally questionable chemical processes, or phase changes. The only by-product is brine—salt-saturated water—and the impurities and minerals that have been removed, all of which is disposed of through the proven method of deep-well injection. The product water that remains is ready for distribution free of solids, pollutants, and bacteria. Cleaner and fresher than rainwater."

"So this process also removes uranyl fluoride," I said.

A pause followed that was pregnant enough to give birth to quintuplets. The guys on the control panels froze. "Excuse me?" Tawal asked.

"Uranyl fluoride. Apparently it's in the water around here, right?"

"No, I do not think so," Tawal replied. "Let us continue the tour." He moved to the door and held it open, frowning. I wondered whether it was something I'd said. "Would you care to see the gas-fired electrical power station we have built here? If desalination has one drawback, it's that it requires a lot of energy to pressurize the feedwater."

"What's down there?" I nodded toward the end of the blacked-out corridor.

"Nothing interesting. Storage, mostly."

The elevator doors opened. Tawal gestured that we should go first.

"Lamb before slaughter," I said to Masters, who smiled.

"I'm sorry?" Tawal asked, eyebrows raised.

"So you don't know anything about the uranyl fluoride?" I replied.

"No, but I can think only that you must be referring to the vehicles your American government buried that contaminated the surface water upstream of Kumayt. You may not know about this. It was because of such contamination that the Iraqi government decided to build Kawthar al Deen. In fact, I can give you a copy of the environmental report that revealed the problem. Depleted uranium is a terrible weapon," Tawal said, spreading icing on the guilt complex he wanted to serve us. "Your government gave Agent Orange to Vietnam, and they have given Iraq depleted uranium. This will be a problem for a thousand Iraqi generations to come."

"A copy of that environmental report would be handy," Masters cut in.

"I will see to it."

"Wasn't shredding it part of the bidding process?" I inquired.

Tawal paused. "Only the unsuccessful bidders were asked to destroy materials. The file is confidential, but I'm sure you agents have the appropriate clearances."

"I don't suppose you might know where this radioactive graveyard is located?" I asked.

"I'm sorry, Special Agent. Your government doesn't share its secrets with me."

Seemed to me a lot of people knew about the stash of buried hot wreckage, only no one would—or could—produce the smoking gun.

The elevator came to a stop and the doors opened. A man with an M4 carbine, body armor, and a pistol in a hip holster stood in the doorway. I recognized him, too—the guy with the binoculars who'd seen us looking down on the facility. His eyes were hidden behind the wraparound sunglasses, so I wasn't sure if the recognition was mutual. He gave the boss a nod and was about to step past us into the elevator when Tawal said, "Oh, Jarred. Would you mind doing me a favor and showing our visitors our special defenses?"

The man nodded. "Yes, of course."

"Jarred is our deputy head of security."

Jarred's accent was interesting—I couldn't place it. He was tall and blond, with sagging cheeks that suggested his eyes probably drooped at the corners. The guy looked depressed.

"I will get a copy of the report and see you again when you are finished—in, say, around twenty minutes," Tawal informed us.

"Take thirty minutes, if you like," I said.

Tawal switched on a smile that held about as much warmth as a photo of a long-life bulb and left us.

"So where's the head of security?" I asked our latest guide.

"On leave."

"Uh-huh."

"Would you like to see our crows?" Jarred asked cryptically.

"Your what?" Masters was going for clarification.

"Yes, I will show you our crows. You will see what I mean." Jarred turned and walked in the opposite direction from the one Tawal had gone in.

We followed along behind. After a few steps, Masters gestured at his sidearm. "An unusual pistol you've got there, Jarred," she said. "What is it?"

"A Barak."

"Never seen one before. Where's it from?"

"Kmart."

Masters and I shared a glance. Another Barak SP-21: nine-millimeter, fifteen-round magazine, and as Israeli as a Jaffa orange. Maybe Israel was Jarred's adopted country, which might explain the ambiguous accent.

"Which Sayeret unit you serve in?" I asked, playing a hunch. The Sayeret was the Special Forces arm of the Israeli Defense Forces.

Jarred turned his droopy eyes on me. He heard the question, but wasn't going to answer. Maybe he'd already used up his daily quota of idle conversation. He took us up a couple of floors via another elevator, along one more corridor and into a loading dock, passing at least thirty surveillance cameras and half a dozen armed men, who nodded respectfully at our guide.

A dozen golf carts were parked in the bay, the shutter door banging and rattling with the weather pounding against it on the other side. A fine dust hung in the air and tickled the back of my throat.

"I hope you don't mind a little sand." Jarred hopped down a small flight of stairs and made his way to the cart closest to the shutter.

FORTY

The sand in Iraq is not the kind of sand that kids build castles with at the beach. It's about fifty times finer and, when pushed around by a wind that's eighty-plus miles an hour, about a thousand times meaner. The small, abrasive particles penetrate everything. They get inside your nose, your ears, and your hair, inside your eye goggles and your gloves, under your fingernails, into your clothes, your pockets, your webbing, your shoes, your socks, your underwear. Even your cracks—*especially* your cracks. It penetrates everywhere, and I do mean everywhere. Machinery has it worse. The dust combines with lubricants to form a paste that destroys bearing surfaces, which explains why our golf cart stopped dead fifty yards from the bunker and had to be pushed the remainder of the way, into the lee of a concrete wall.

"These damn crows had better be worth it," I shouted into the howling wind, Masters beside me, bent behind the cart.

"What?" she yelled back.

I shook my head. Translation: *Forget it.*

The bunker rose out of the orange-red hellscape, the concrete curved dome of its roof a black silhouette in the haze. Jarred punched a code into a keypad, jerked open the heavy steel access door, then closed it behind us. Masters and I pulled off our Kevlar helmets and goggles while Jarred coughed up a clod of brown paste and spat it on the floor.

"Sweet Jesus," said Masters, shaking the grit out of her hair and blinking it out of her eyes. The air about us swirled with vortexes of stinging powder.

A phone on the wall rang. Jarred answered it while I took in our surroundings. There was nothing special about the bunker—just your usual reinforced, armor-plated speed bump for mobile attacking forces, though this one did have a twist.

"That was Mr. Tawal," said Jarred, interrupting my scoping. "Your escort has been recalled."

"They're not coming back for us?" Masters asked.

"Not until the storm is over. It is getting worse. Mr. Tawal has made accommodation arrangements for you."

Nothing we could do about it. And maybe it wasn't such a bad thing. It might provide us with the opportunity to do a little more snooping, this time without a tour guide.

"So, do you like our crows?" Jarred asked.

I realized what Jarred had been referring to as soon as we'd walked in—the five .50-caliber M2 machine guns arrayed around the bunker wall. Each was set up as a Common Remotely Operated Weapon Station, or CROWS. I'd seen CROWS mounted on Humvees, but this was a variation on the theme. We went in for a closer look. I knew they could be programmed so as not to shoot off parts of their own vehicles, or in this instance, their own facility. A thick rubber boot between the wall and the barrel kept the dust out of the bunker, although I wouldn't want to be in the vicinity if a round went down those barrels before they were cleaned.

"This bunker, and eleven more like it, have been built around these CROWS," Jarred announced. "Some use your American Mk 19 forty-millimeter Automatic Grenade Machine Gun instead of the M2. The sensor array for the system is built into the hardened external concrete shell and includes a daylight video camera with a 120-power zoom, a thermal imager for night operations, and a laser range finder for pinpoint target acquisition. Each is furnished with a fully integrated fire control system. And if one array goes down, an array on a neighboring bunker can take over. In this way, they are all as one." Jarred stroked the barrel with a lover's touch. "Using a simple joystick, each weapon can be fired individually or linked together, and from a remote location."

"We've been there, seen that," I said, Masters nodding. The bank of screens, each with a joystick—the facility's control room was also the fire control center.

"The system can also be set to shoot automatically and will do this in all weather, day or night."

"You work on commission?" I asked.

He smiled. "I like this weapon."

"Never would've guessed," Masters said, arms folded.

"How many mines you got out there?" I asked.

"I am not authorized to answer this question."

"What kind of mines are they—anti-personnel, penetrator?"

"I am not authorized to answer this question."

"How many men you got enrolled in your private army here?"

"I am not—"

"We get the picture," I said.

"Let us go back," he said, giving the machine gun a parting fondle.

On the way here, the sand blast had been at our backs, but it was into our faces on the return journey. Arriving in the loading dock, we stopped to shake the sand and grit out of our clothes.

"Please let there be a damn shower in this place," Masters prayed aloud.

"I will take you to Mr. Tawal now," Jarred said.

A short walk later, Jarred left us back in the boardroom, waiting for Tawal. I had no skin left in my crotch area or under my arms, where my shirt combined with sweat and dust to rub the skin raw.

"So, what do you think of Kawthar al Deen?" asked Tawal as he came through the door. His good humor had returned along with his smile.

"Like Evian crossed with the Maginot Line," I said.

"Yes, we are well defended, if it comes to that."

"And a handy place to launch an attack from, if you were so inclined," Masters observed.

Tawal's smile left in such a hurry I almost felt the draft. "I have the report here," he said, "the environmental impact study that preceded the building of this facility. It is your copy to keep."

"Thanks," replied Masters, accepting the five or so pounds of printed report, tucking it under her arm.

"I believe Jarred has told you about your escort?" Tawal asked.

I nodded. "They were told to come inside out of the wind. Jarred informed us you're going to put us up here."

"If that is suitable?"

"If it comes with a shower, it's suitable," said Masters.

"I am sure that can be arranged. So, I am happy to answer any further questions you may have. . . ."

I wanted to ask Tawal, just to gauge his reaction, if he'd had Colonel Portman, Bremmel, Doc Merkit, Emir, and the others killed, only I had no follow-up answer if he responded by asking why he would want to do that. And as far as we could see, there was no motive wrapping this guy up with the murders. "Not for the moment," I said instead. "Though I suggest you don't leave town till we've concluded our inquiries."

"You have no authority here—over me."

"We know that, Mr. Tawal," Masters replied. "Like Special Agent Cooper said, it's just a suggestion."

"I have a conference in Cairo in two days' time."

"I'm sure we won't be keeping you that long," Masters promised cheerfully.

Tawal snapped out a phrase in Arabic. The Iraqi servant appeared and stood stiffly at attention, waiting for instructions. Tawal spoke to the guy like he was something that needed a saddle on its hump. He turned back to us. "Achmed will show you to your accommodations. I am around, should you desire to discuss anything further. Achmed doesn't speak English, by the way, so there's no point asking him anything. If you leave your uniforms and any gear you want cleaned outside your rooms, he will see to it." He got to his feet, eager to leave. "Now, if there is nothing more, I have a desalination plant to get operational. . . ." He was out the door in four strides.

"Shall we leave our sidearms and body armor outside for a little sprucing up?" I asked.

Masters answered with half a smile.

The dust and sand blew across the windowpanes in heavy red waves, the glass flexing under the pressure. We could have been on Mars. Achmed cleared his throat to catch my attention, then gestured for us to follow, holding the door handle. The three of us retraced part of Tawal's earlier tour, passing several armed personnel, who checked us out far more thoroughly than when we'd been accompanied by Jarred, their boss.

Rounding a corner, I collided with a guy in a white coat. I recognized him from the welt on his face. I noticed he also had a split across the bridge of his nose. He was one of Tawal's whipping boys, the one I'd seen earlier in the control room. I looked at him, he looked at me, and then he dropped something—a small scrap of paper. And then he hurried off, leaving the scrap behind.

Achmed came back around the corner to check on the delay, but by then I was bent down, tying my shoelace, the scrap beneath my rubber combat sole. While fumbling knot number three, I checked the area for cameras. There were plenty, but all of them were pointed in other directions; we were in a blind spot. It occurred to me that the guy who left the note knew exactly what he was doing. Achmed glanced at Masters, giving me enough time to palm the scrap.

After another five minutes spent walking around endless corridors, Achmed left us in adjoining rooms, Masters in one and me in another. I wondered whose reputation Tawal and Achmed were concerned about. Theirs? Masters's? Mine?

I looked around—a bed, no television, no minibar, no view. Not even of drainpipes on an adjacent building, on account of there being no windows at all. We had to be at least three floors underground. Off the main room was a small bathroom with a head, washbasin, and shower. Folded neatly on the bed was a towel and a galabia—a jaunty orange number with a blue-and-gold geometric pattern around the collar and down the front.

I tried the front door, the door I came in through. Locked. I heard Masters rattle the door between our rooms. Locked. "Are we under house arrest here?" Masters asked on the other side, stating the obvious.

I picked the lock with the little tool from in the spine of my notebook and opened the connecting door. "Look what I found baked in a loaf of bread," I said, showing her the hacksaw blade.

"You find a tunnel in there, too?" she asked as I went to her front door.

The lock was too heavy and complex for the blade, so I went to the door connecting her room with the next and put my ear against it. Nothing. I picked the lock and did the same on the next two doors until I found a room with a main door unlocked.

One of the rooms was three times the size of the area Masters and I had been allocated. I counted ten bunk beds. I wondered how many rooms like the ones we'd just been through were duplicated here. I checked the hallway: clear, but well lit and covered by surveillance cameras. It was also long and ended in a right angle. I'd seen enough armed personnel walking about to know that this part of the facility was patrolled, especially now that we were occupying it. I closed the door.

"Hey, before I forget, you must have tied your boot a half-dozen times back there," Masters said. "What was that all about?"

"Did you say you wanted to take a shower?" I asked, heading back to our rooms.

Masters took the hint instantly. "Yeah."

I led the way to her bathroom and turned the cold tap to full on. Water blasted from the faucet. We checked the mirror, lights, and ventilation grates for pinhole cameras. None.

Reasonably satisfied that the room was secure, I took the scrap of paper out of my pocket. Maybe it was nothing special—the guy's grocery list. For all I knew, we'd seen Tawal beating up on him for dropping litter and here he was doing it again.

"The technician, the one we saw Tawal working over. You didn't see, but he bumped into me on purpose. He dropped this." I unfolded the scrap. "Might be nothing, or . . ."

"Or what?" she asked as I handed her the note.

"Possibly a hell of a lot of something," I said.

"Lat-long coordinates."

"You want to fire up your laptop? Think you'll get a signal in this storm?"

"Ought to," she replied. "Got ultrawide band, and thanks to the U.S. Army, there are plenty of repeaters." Masters went out and came back with her Toshiba. "Let's do this quick and easy," she said as it booted. A minute later, Google Earth was up and running. "Give me a read on those coordinates and I'll punch them in."

"Thirty-two degrees fourteen minutes, two point nine-zero seconds north—forty-six degrees fifty-two minutes, sixteen point eight-six seconds east."

Masters finished tapping the keys and the familiar blue earth rotated to focus on Iraq before the view zeroed in for a close-up.

"Where are we?" I asked.

"You are here—Kawthar al Deen," she said, placing a yellow electronic pin in the map, almost on the border with Iran. "And whatever's sitting on these coords is 14.99 miles west/southwest of us."

"Can you get in close on the location?"

She played with Google Earth's buttons. "Nope, it's pretty fuzzy. I guess the DoD isn't keen on giving al Qaeda ground resolution it can use."

"Has to be something there. The guy risked his life getting us that scrap of paper," I said.

Masters gave me The Look.

"OK, he risked getting another good clipboarding. Fact is, we don't really know what this Moses Abdul Tawal is capable of."

"Perhaps whatever we find there will give us a clue," Masters observed.

"Can you get on to Christie through his regiment?"

"I'd say yeah, probably."

"Without giving him the specific locations, ask him whether there are any restricted areas—Coalition or Iraqi—on this side of the border, and within, say, twenty miles of this place."

"OK . . . so, we done?" Masters asked. "If we are, I might take that shower."

"Don't let me stop you," I said, leaning against the sink.

"Alone."

"Sure. And after you've emailed Christie, you might as well upload those photos you took earlier. Maybe the FBI or Homeland Security has something we can use."

Masters nodded.

I gave her a smile.

"Alone."

FORTY-ONE

Masters was toweling off her hair as she walked into my room. Like me, she was wearing a galabia, only hers was cream-colored. Despite it being cut for a guy, I couldn't help but notice it fitted in most of the right places. And the places looked good.

"That suits you, Vin," she said, motioning at the orange, blue, and gold thing I'd slipped into.

"Makes me look like an Inca ruin. Did you get through?"

"To Christie? I think so, but I haven't heard back." Masters sat on the chair beside a small writing shelf anchored to a wall. She seemed troubled.

"What's up?"

"I flicked through that report Tawal gave us. They tested the surface water at a number of sites, one of them being Kumayt, and found various isotopes consistent with depleted uranium contamination. I've been thinking about the DU supposedly buried around here."

"Do we need the cone of silence, chief?" I asked.

"I think maybe we do."

I walked into my bathroom and turned on the faucets. "They bury contaminated material where it's geologically stable," Masters said. "They also bury it where it's *dry*. Have you noticed the ground in this part of Iraq is totally the wrong kind? Remember what it was like near Kumayt? It was soft, wet, and porous. You drop something radioactively hot in a hole dug in marshland and sure as shit it's going to work its way back out."

"Is it possible someone just went ahead and buried stuff here anyway—made a mistake? The Army has been known to make one or two."

"Vin, Cain and I were snooping around in the Department of Energy before we left, remember? We were hoping to get a lead on the contamination burial sites. The people we spoke to have checked their research with the DoD and sent Cain an email, which he has just forwarded to me. DoE says there's *no* chemical waste or DU-contaminated wreckage buried anywhere around here—in their words, 'unsuitable containment characteristics.' In short, too marshy."

"So if there's no DU dump, why does this environmental impact study say different?" I asked.

"According to DoE, inquiries into the existence of a dump in the Maysan province had already been made by our mission in Ankara."

"Really? Does it say who made the inquiry?"

"Nope," said Masters. "But it was six months ago. Five'll get you ten it was Portman doing the digging."

"If there's no DU in the water, I'd like to know what messed with those children."

"I'm sure the colonel asked himself the same question. I'd say, with that independent water-quality assessment he commissioned, Portman found some answers along with that uranyl fluoride."

"Yeah." What the hell were we really dealing with here? "We done?" I asked.

Masters nodded. I turned off the taps and walked out into the main room as the Iraqi in the white coat, Achmed, came in through the front door carrying a tray with food on it. He glanced at me, then Masters, glowered, shook his head at our shameless display of immorality, and mumbled to himself while he put the tray on the shelf. He then checked the state of the adjoining door, no doubt wondering whether he'd contributed to this lascivious behavior by leaving the lock unlatched.

"Don't get the wrong idea, Mac," I said. "She's my mother."

He looked at me, puzzled, went out the door, and then came back in with another tray, which he deposited in Masters's room. On his way back out, I stopped him and said, "Clothes," pinching the galabia's collar to help him get it. "Clothes, uniform," I repeated.

"Ah!" he exclaimed and held up ten fingers, flashing them a second time. My interpretation: our ABUs were being returned in either twenty minutes, twenty hours, or twenty days.

Achmed left us to eat. I went to the tray and lifted up a couple of lids. Slices of lamb, lettuce, yogurt, tomatoes, and cucumber. Again. From Istanbul to Iraq, that's all anyone seemed to eat. Masters lifted a lid on her tray and screwed up her nose.

"I know what you're thinking," I said. "What wouldn't you give for a nice, juicy rat."

A *ping* sound came from the laptop in Masters's room. "Mail's in," she said, going to fetch it while I sat on the end of the bed and picked at the food. "From Christie," she announced. "Says he'll pick us up at seven-thirty tomorrow morning and has informed Tawal of that."

"What about the sandstorm?"

"It'll still be with us, but the wind's supposed to drop some before sunrise. And in answer to your question, he said there are no restricted areas around here—too close to Iran. Kawthar al Deen is out here on its own."

Masters sat down on the bed beside me with her tray. "Do you miss her?"

I didn't need to hear Doc Merkit's name to know who Masters was referring to. "Yes," I replied. No point denying it.

"Were you in love with her?"

Was I in love with her? I liked her. I enjoyed being in her company. I liked her smell, her warmth. I liked the way she looked, her eyes, the way her hair fell around her shoulders. I liked the whole Turkish-girlfriend thing—it was exotic. I enjoyed making love to her; loved the touch of her breasts against my back; loved watching her move; loved watching her move on me. . . . "Did I love her? I don't know. 'Love' is a pretty complex word," I said. "Could you be more specific?"

"I know that before you left the consulate, before the explosion, you visited her. I know you went to see her, because you told me you were going to see her. Emir called me."

"Emir called you?"

"He said you were with her for at least an hour and that I shouldn't trust you."

I was starting to think that Emir was lucky he was already dead. "So you want to know whether you should go get your nail file?" I asked.

"No, actually I want to forgive you. I was the one who went and got engaged. *I* tried to manipulate *you*. Maybe I wanted to hurt you. And then, when it was all over with Richard, I just assumed you'd come running. Turn you off, turn you on, make the rules and expect you to follow them. That wasn't fair."

"I guess, if you put it like that—"

"The slate's clean, Vin. You don't owe me any excuses."

"Are you trying to talk me into coming up for coffee?" I asked.

"I don't know, maybe I am. . . . Is that something you might be interested in?"

I came awake suddenly, instantly, too fast. It took a few blinks to work out where the hell I was. It was dark and the surroundings were unfamiliar. And then it came back—an explosion, a silver skeleton, Iraq, Kawthar al Deen. Through the door between our rooms I could hear Masters's soft and steady breathing. Before going to bed, she'd made me an offer I couldn't refuse, except that I'd refused it. There was only one reason why that made sense: It was just too soon.

I thought about the doc. She'd still be alive if we hadn't become involved, and the realization gave me a pain in my chest.

I woke Masters with a cup of Turkish-style coffee left by Achmed, who'd also brought us a breakfast of cheese, tomato, and cucumber. I was thinking I'd happily kill for a bagel. Achmed showed me our clothes, which were folded on the floor outside our respective doors. They'd probably been sitting there all night, so maybe he'd meant twenty minutes.

Once we'd eaten, showered, and dressed, Tawal paid us a visit. "I trust your stay here hasn't inconvenienced you, Special Agents," he said as we collected our helmets, weapons, and gear.

"No, though I haven't been locked in my room since I was a kid," I informed him. "You got a good reason for that, or did you want to prevent us from going on an unguided tour?"

Tawal gave us his phony smile. "You and I both know that these rooms held you for less than two minutes, Special Agent. You would also be aware that, with so much security in this facility, no harm could possibly have come to you. And should you have chosen to explore this facility on your own and become lost, finding you would have been a simple matter indeed. Shall we proceed? I believe Lieutenant Christie is waiting." He turned and walked off.

Tawal had a nice way of saying, "We kept an eye on you every second." I wondered about the bathrooms. Had he seen us and picked up our conversations, despite the precautions?

"Do you think he's disappointed we didn't put on a little peep show for him last night?" I said under my breath.

"Maybe," replied Masters. "Are you?"

"Please, this way," Tawal said before I could answer, holding a security door open for us.

We were led on a brisk walk through the facility. I couldn't figure out whether it was a meandering tour or the most direct route to what was probably the main entrance, a black granite and mirror-lined reception area with an elaborate fountain. I timed the walk: seven and a half minutes at an average speed of around three miles an hour. Up three floors, past twelve armed goons, under twenty-seven surveillance cameras, along two hallways, and through four security doors. Subtracting thirty seconds for tapping codes into keypads and another minute spent listening to "The Girl from Ipanema" in the elevator left six minutes. A walk of around a third of a mile and I still had no sense of the extent of the facility belowground.

Jarred appeared to be loitering around the front reception area. I gave him a nod, which he ignored. He was wearing dust goggles, dressed for a walk outside and, for all I knew, he was looking at his reflection in one of the mirrors. Or he could just have had a bowl of assholes for breakfast and, as they say, you are what you eat.

The reception windows faced an open courtyard filled with concrete bollards that limited the speed and direction of any traffic. Specifically, any traffic that might have intended to blow itself up. The airborne sand had thinned a little, but the wind was still blowing waves of it across the sky. Out front there was a small garden blanketed in about a foot of sand that had built up against the glass of the external door. It was a great day to be somewhere else. Lieutenant Christie's vehicles were parked thirty yards away, black shapes against a morning sky shifting from red at the horizon to yellow overhead. The lead vehicle gave us a few dirty yellow blinks, flashing its lights. Time to move.

"I hope you have both enjoyed your impromptu stay with us," said

Tawal. "If you have any further questions, please do not hesitate to contact me."

"Thanks for your hospitality, Mr. Tawal. We'll be in touch," Masters replied, handling the good-byes while I matched the guy's fake smile with one of my own.

Jarred held the glass door open for Masters and me as we walked into what felt like an airlock. We dropped goggles over our eyes and pulled scarves up over our mouths, preparing for the short jog across the open ground to the lead Land Rover.

As I pulled open the door, the wind caught the built-up sand and lifted it into a swirling tornado that ripped at our clothes and stung the skin on the back of my neck. I put my head down and ran for Christie's Land Rover, Masters half a pace in front of me.

"Good morning," chimed Christie as we threw ourselves in the back.

We shook the grit out of our gear. A water bottle was passed back to us and the Rover began to move.

"Sorry we had to leave you there last night," he told us. "I thought perhaps it might be to your advantage anyway."

"It was fine," said Masters, taking a drink and then offering me the bottle. I passed.

"Tawal's an unusual guy," I said. "When he flies in, where does he fly in from?"

"He's Egyptian, so perhaps from somewhere there."

"So, we've got Egyptian management, Turkish technology and construction, and Iraqi labor, maintenance, and supervision," Masters summarized. "And probably the whole thing's compartmentalized—no one on the ground except Tawal knowing what the left and the right hand are up to."

"Who put up the money?" I asked.

Masters shrugged. "Maybe all three countries. Maybe someplace else entirely."

The Land Rover rounded the last of the concrete bollards and drove through the heavy front gates.

"Y'know, Vin," Masters continued, "Thurlstane must have been in the game just to provide a check quote, just to give the process the impression of fairness."

"Because Kawthar al Deen's a front," I said, picking up on her train of thought, "and an American company would've blown the whistle."

"What sort of front?" Christie asked.

"Before it's anything else, Kawthar al Deen is a forward military base," said Masters. "The whole desalination plant thing is just a cover."

I nodded. Masters was making a lot of sense.

She took a few more pulls on the water bottle, then wiped her mouth with the back of her wrist. "Only, who'd want to build a private, clandestine military base right on Iran's doorstep?"

"I don't know," I replied. "But I'd bet that finding out was how Emmet Portman ended up getting himself butchered."

FORTY-TWO

Ahead, whole sections of the road that linked Kawthar al Deen with Kumayt lay hidden beneath sand drifts, the only indication that a road existed at all being the roadside post markers placed at twenty-yard intervals disappearing into the red haze. I leaned forward, a scrap of paper in my hand. "You mind tapping these coordinates into your GPS?" I asked our host.

Christie examined the numbers: *32°14′2.90″N, 46°52′16.86″E.* "This got anything to do with your question about restricted areas in the vicinity?"

"It's related. One of Tawal's people slipped us the numbers. The guy was shitting himself."

Christie fed the numbers into the handheld device. "Aye, well, whatever it is, it's out in the middle of nowhere—a drive of around an hour and a half from our current position. As far as I know, it's all rock, dust, and wadis out there. Any idea what you'd be hoping to find?"

"Answers. Only don't ask us what the questions are. Like I said, the way the guy slipped me those numbers, I got the feeling they were important. Can we head there now?"

"Sorry, can't. There's a situation brewing. Remember that politician down in Basra who got himself whacked yesterday? There's been a lot of revenge sabotage at Al Amaran and Kumayt through the night, using this sandstorm as cover. The boss has tasked my lads to defend the hospital in Kumayt. We don't want people getting dragged out of their beds and decapitated on the telly."

"I hear you, Lieutenant," I said. "But we need to check out that location, and the sooner the better."

"I'll see what I can do," he replied.

We were too late for at least two people at Kumayt. Their heads were planted on steel concrete-reinforcing rods on the outskirts of town, presumably as a warning to someone. The blood in their hair and beards had congealed with the dust, and only the wisps flapped in the wind.

Christie pulled the patrol over to the side of the road. His men were deployed around the vehicles while photos of the scene were taken for the police. They also bagged the heads. Masters and I walked the area. The rest of the bodies were nowhere to be seen.

The force of the wind had tapered off some, and while there was not so much airborne sand, the haze was still impenetrable. An open truck appeared suddenly out of the murk before Christie's men could react, loaded with armed men all wearing scarves over their mouths and noses. Everyone relaxed a little. Blue uniforms: local Iraqi police. The truck swept past and was almost instantly swallowed by the dust soup.

We drove into a square near the town's center. A couple of buildings were on fire, one of them the police compound. There were men everywhere—mostly civilians—shouting instructions at each other, ferrying buckets of water and sand to dump on the flames, directing traffic, helping each other.

Our unit continued on to its original objective. The streets were mostly empty away from the police station. We passed a permanent vehicle checkpoint supposedly manned by Iraqi police, an old bullet-riddled vehicle occupying one of the blast-protected inspection pads. The place was deserted.

The hospital was big by small-town standards—four stories, with a couple of stubby wings hanging off either side of the main block. Concrete blocks and heavy steel gates manned by Iraqi Army units protected the entrances to the grounds.

The Iraqis waved our vehicles through into a parking lot protected by more concrete walls and razor wire. The Iraqi flag, I noticed, was hanging limp on its pole.

Christie turned around in his seat. "We've got to have a chat with the Iraqis and then probably send out a patrol or two," he said. "What're you going to do?"

"Go talk to the hospital staff," Masters replied. "Got to be a few people who knew Portman, right?"

The lieutenant nodded. "Have a word with Dr. Bartholomew. He's an Aussie. He's the one who raised the alarm about those birth defects. And you might like to give him the heads. He'll put them on ice till the Iraqis get around to finding out who they belonged to."

"How long we here for?" I asked.

"The duration, I'm afraid, however long that is," said Christie. "It's up to my boss—he doesn't tend to consult with me. I haven't forgotten about your problem."

We left Christie to get his unit organized and went to collect the heads from a warrant officer in the Mastiff. A couple of Iraqi soldiers were looking in the bag, shouting at each other. One of them had tears running down his cheeks, cutting valleys through the dust caking his skin.

"What's up?" Masters asked.

"One of the heads belonged to this man's sister's husband," explained the WO in an English accent as thick as a bowl of rolled oats. "It appears he was a copper, manning that empty checking station we passed."

"Can you explain to the man that we're taking his brother-in-law's remains into the hospital?"

"Do my best," said the WO.

The Brit spoke to the two locals in a mixture of Arabic, mime, and English. He seemed to get the point across. The Iraqis drifted away with slumped shoulders.

I swung the bag over my shoulder and turned toward the front entrance. Inside the hospital, it was standing room only. The sandstorm had been the cause of plenty of accidents—broken limbs, burns, motor vehicle accidents. Folks were either asleep, groaning, or arguing, a couple of men in particular giving an Iraqi nurse a hard time, yelling at her.

Masters found someone who could point us in the right direction. She led the way through an access door and down a hallway, which eventually opened out into a large ward. The place stank of disinfectant, blood, and urine. Here and there a few people moaned.

I walked up to one of the nurses, an Iraqi woman wearing a full black burqa, and gave her a peek in the bag. "Dr. Bartholomew?" I asked.

It took a few long seconds for the contents of the bag to register with her, and then her eyes widened behind the black slits. She grabbed my sleeve and excitedly pulled me into an annex, where a tall guy in jeans and a T-shirt with a stethoscope around his neck was bent over a sink, washing his hands. The woman waved her arms around, talked animatedly, pointing at me and the bag I was holding. The man talked to her in Arabic briefly before she swept out of the room, muttering to herself.

"Got something there for me, mate?" asked the doctor in a broad Australian accent, walking toward us. The guy had unkempt longish blond hair that was graying slightly at the roots. His olive skin had a blanched look, and his brown eyes were rimmed with red pinstripes. I guessed he'd been up a while.

"They're probably more for your fridge," I replied. "We found them on the outskirts of town, welcoming visitors."

"It has been one of those welcoming kinda nights," he said, looking into the bag. A stink rose from it. He shook his head. "I know these guys. They're police. The one there on the left—I took his tonsils out only last week."

"So he hasn't had much of an opportunity to miss them," I suggested, always looking for that silver lining. "This is Special Agent Masters and I'm Special Agent Cooper, Doc. We're with the OSI. Mind if we ask you a few questions?"

"What about? These two?"

"No, about Colonel Emmet Portman."

"Sure, what about him?"

"He was murdered."

Bartholomew blinked a couple of times while this news registered. The guy was clearly exhausted.

A nurse walked in, a European woman—dark, Spanish-looking. Bartholomew spoke to her in a language that sounded Italian. She looked in the bag, shook her head, and carried it away.

"I've just finished a triple shift and things are getting quieter. Let's go to my office."

Along the way, he was continually pulled into corridor consultations with other doctors and nursing staff. Dr. Bartholomew was obviously an important cog in this machine.

His office was windowless and airless and small enough to wear. There was room for a tiny desk, which was covered in piles of reference books that leaned against his computer screen and swamped the keyboard. A chair for visitors and the one behind his desk took up most of the floor space. A whiteboard with various meaningless names and lines drawn in red and green marker pen swallowed up most of one wall, while on the other hung the framed photo of a green wave, curling perfectly, shot by someone in the water aiming back down into the hollow barrel. A brown, muscled guy was inside the tube, casually dragging his hand along the glassy concave face of the wave.

"You?" I gave the photo a nod.

"A long time ago. And in another life," Bartholomew said as he cleared a pile of magazines off the spare chair and motioned for Masters to sit. "So what happened to Emmet?" he asked.

"The killers cut him up into itty-bitty pieces," said Masters.

The doc shook his head. "Well, you know, there's no justice in the world, is there? Emmet Portman was one of the good guys. He spent a lot of time here, mostly with the kids in the cancer ward." He leaned back in his chair, his hands resting on his stomach. "Now, what is it exactly I can help you with?"

"Lieutenant Christie said you were the man to talk to, that you and Emmet Portman were tight," I replied. "There are quite a few odd factors connected with the attaché's death, and we're looking into them."

"Such as?"

"Radioactivity in the water supply here. Vast sums of money disappearing and a water treatment plant out in the middle of nowhere. One of Portman's squadron buddies mentioned that the colonel had a connection with a hospital around here. We're assuming it's this hospital, and our investigation has led us to you."

"Mr. Christie will vouch for you?"

"I don't know," I said. "Why don't you call him and find out?"

"I will." Bartholomew pulled out his cell and walked out of the room.

Masters and I glanced at each other and shrugged. I picked up a model of an eyeball from the doc's desk and looked it over.

A minute later, Bartholomew walked back in and locked the door behind him. "I know I'm taking a hell of a risk here, but with Emmet dead, that just leaves me."

"I take it Christie gave us the nod?" Masters asked.

The doc gave half a grin and said, "He told me you gave Tawal a major dose of the shits, which makes you my kind of people."

The Australian went to his filing cabinet and unlocked the bottom drawer. Then he pulled it out entirely and tilted it over onto its side. Taped to the underside of the drawer was a folder. Bartholomew pulled away the tape, releasing the folder. He opened it, took out a handful of photographs, and spread them across his desk. Each one showed a baby or child with horrible deformities.

"Jesus," said Masters quietly. "This stuff breaks your heart."

"After Gulf War I," Bartholomew began, "the staff at Basra Hospital became highly concerned at the number of leukemias among children in the area, as well as the alarming number of congenital malformations in newborn children. From 1990 to 2001, data showed an incidence increase of 426 percent for general malignancies, 366 percent for leukemias, and over 600 percent for birth defects. At Kumayt, we're almost double those figures. Or we were. There had to be a reason for all the abnormalities suddenly turning up. We thought it might have been something to do with a depleted uranium dump supposedly somewhere upstream of us, a hangover from the first Gulf War—perhaps the stuff had finally worked its way into the water supply. That was over three years ago. Around the same time I met Colonel Portman. He'd flown down here from Turkey, looking into something to do with a reconstruction project."

"Kawthar al Deen?" Masters asked.

"Yeah, but I didn't know anything about it back then. Anyway, the colonel had cut his hand, nothing too serious. He stopped by to get the wound cleaned up. While he was here, he toured the hospital—saw the children's ward. It got him pretty worked up. Said he felt a personal responsibility toward the kids. He sent gifts and toys. About a month later, he phoned. He told me in confidence that the authorities in Baghdad were aware of the problems with the water supply here. An environmental study of the area had been undertaken and high levels of depleted uranium had indeed been found in the water. Locally, promises were made to clean up the dump and build a desalination plant to treat the groundwater and make it drinkable. Bids went out for the project."

"That was when Portman met Tawal," I said.

"Yeah—talk about oil and water. . . . Anyway, I gather there were some issues around the way the bids were conducted, complaints from other companies involved. To say that Emmet didn't like Tawal would be an understatement, and from what I've heard, the feeling was mutual. Emmet told me he didn't believe there was a DU dump in the vicinity of Kumayt—couldn't find records within the Department of Defense of the existence of such a dump. His conclusion was that the whole desalination thing was crooked. So, around six months ago, he had the water tested independently."

Bartholomew handed me a photocopied report pulled from the packet taped under the file drawer. It was dated three months ago. I recognized the black-and-white logo in the top left of the page. *Sage Laboratories, Ca.* I passed the report to Masters.

"There's a lot of competing noise about depleted uranium," the doctor continued as Masters scanned the report. "Some experts reckon that breathing the dust will fuck up the immune system and alter your genetic code. Others say it's harmless."

"Only there's no argument about uranyl fluoride," observed Masters, examining one of the pages. "Radioactive *and* toxic like you wouldn't believe."

"The toxicity is the real problem," said Bartholomew. "The levels of hydrogen fluoride they found are just as bad. That stuff is seriously gnarly."

"Any ideas how these chemicals got into the water?"

Bartholomew shook his head. "As you can probably understand, I've become a bit of an expert on all this stuff. Depleted uranium is a dense metal. It oxidizes and small pieces get weathered off it. It's radioactive, but it doesn't turn into uranyl fluoride, and certainly not hydrogen fluoride."

"That doesn't exactly answer my question," said Masters.

"Do I know how it got in the water?"

"Yes."

"No, I have no idea how, but I'll give you one guess *who*."

I didn't need to guess, and I didn't believe Masters would have to either. I said, "So Tawal somehow got his hands on uranium hexafluoride and contaminated the water with it, just so there'd be a good excuse to build a desal plant here."

"So, you know.... Yes, that was Emmet's conclusion."

And Bartholomew didn't need to remind me that it was the one Emmet Portman had reached before being gruesomely murdered by persons keen to throw us off the scent.

"You obviously know about the link between HEX, depleted uranium, and uranyl fluoride?" Bartholomew asked, breaking into my thoughts.

"We know it's their common ancestor," I said.

"HEX is a major part of the nuclear fuel cycle. You can't just go to the corner store and buy it," observed Bartholomew.

"Yep," I agreed. The realization had already occurred to Masters and me. If HEX was used—and as far as we knew, there was no other way to produce uranyl fluoride—where the hell had it come from?

"What's your water like now?" Masters asked.

"Salty, but not lethal. I had it tested again a month ago. Not a trace of either DU, uranyl fluoride, or hydrogen fluoride."

"Where did you get the sample you tested?" I asked.

"Straight from the tap."

"Do you know where Portman got the sample he tested?"

Bartholomew balked. He was about to say something, then changed his mind.

"Problem?"

"You know, it never occurred to me to ask. The truth is, I don't know for sure where he got it from. I just assumed he took a sample of the local drinking water."

"Can we keep this?" Masters tapped the report on the palm of her hand.

"Sure. I have copies."

"Doc," I said, "if I were you I'd burn them. Keep your knowledge to yourself. Folks who know about that sample tend to end up whacked."

There was a knock on the door followed by a female voice speaking in Arabic. After a brief exchange, the Australian turned to us and said, "Your transport has landed."

FORTY-THREE

That crack about there being copies—I don't think he trusted us."

"Can't say I blame him," I said, tightening the lap restraint.

The air quality had improved. Outside it was now like LA on a bad day. The sudden absence of wind had allowed much of the choking dust to settle. And it had settled over everything, a gray blanket of ultrafine powder that boiled into mini mushroom clouds around every footfall.

"You can thank Mr. Christie," said the English flight sergeant over the front seat of the Land Rover we were traveling in. "The chief pilot, Flight Lieutenant Robear, owed him a box of Scotch, a debt your Dragoon mate was prepared to forgive if we gave you a ride. So now you'll take over the chit, I suspect."

"Interesting way to run a war," Masters observed. "You're headed north anyway. It's not like you're doing us a favor."

"Oh, really? Well, then, I'd keep that way of thinking to yourself, ma'am, if you want the ride. Robear has a cow-eye waiting for him at Balad, and hanging around playing taxi driver to you is keeping him from her."

"A cow-eye?" she asked.

"A woman with dark eyes, ma'am. And just so that you're abreast of all the terms and conditions, this is a one-way ticket, OK?" the flight sergeant continued. "As I said, we're heading up to Balad Air Base, so you'll have to catch a train back."

"A train?"

"Of the camel variety," replied the Brit, smiling at his devilish cleverness.

"What about Christie?" Masters asked.

"If you're still out there this afternoon, he'll come get you."

"Dickwad," said Masters under her breath.

I smiled to myself.

We'd been expecting a Land Rover or two, but a Lynx was better. Once airborne, it'd do the leg in six minutes. Putting up with Flight Sergeant Jerkoff here was a small price to pay. The flight sergeant, the chopper's loadmaster, was accompanied by a couple of British riflemen, one of whom was behind the wheel. The corporal swerved the Land Rover through the streets of Kumayt, dodging humans, dogs, chickens, donkeys, and other vehicles. The place had come alive with the passing of the storm.

"So what do you think you'll find out there in the desert besides train shit?" the flight sergeant asked, clearly enjoying the sound of his own voice.

"You asking questions about our mission, Sergeant?" I replied. Or, in other words, "Mind your own damn business, Mac."

It took fifteen minutes to reach the patch of dirt being used by the Lynx as a helipad, and another fifteen for flight checks before we lifted into the blue-gray mid-morning haze on a cushion of dust. Flight Lieutenant Robear leveled off at 2000 feet. Far off to the north, the rear end of the storm was flinging spikes of dust high into the air. Down on the ground, it was the usual moonscape.

After what seemed like minutes, because it was, Robear called back to us from the cockpit. *"OK, we're coming up on your coordinates now, Special Agents. You like us to do a little scouting around at a hundred feet—help you get the lie of the land?"*

"Thanks, Flight Lieutenant, appreciate it," said Masters.

We peered out of the Lynx's open side as the helo banked hard over.

"There's plenty of razor wire down there," Robear noted.

Masters and I picked it up a couple of seconds later—a twelve-foot-high double razor-wire fence, just like the one circling Kawthar al Deen. The helo overflew the coords a couple of times from different directions, but there didn't seem to be anything on the ground—only dirt and wadis surrounded by a square half-mile of razor wire that didn't even appear to have an entrance gate at any point. Odd.

Robear's voice came over the headset. *"I'll put you down inside, close to the fence. That OK?"*

I gave him a thumbs-up, then fitted my eye goggles and scarf in place.

The Lynx went into a flare, bringing the nose up and filling the cabin with swirling grit that stung like birdshot as we touched down. Masters and I climbed out, stayed low, and ran at a crouch beyond the arc of the main rotor. We kept our backs to the aircraft as it lifted off, holding the scarves tight against our mouths. The noise of the helo quickly receded and the loud silence of the desert rushed in to fill the void.

"Well," Masters said, stretching her scarf and then slapping the dust and dirt out of it, "here we are."

"Yeah."

"Why the fence?"

"Maybe they're keeping some vicious wadis here," I suggested. I sucked some water from the bladder in my backpack and it turned to mud in my mouth. I spat it out and sucked some more. "Let's walk the fence. There has to be a gate somewhere."

Half an hour later, we found it. The road in, which was really little more than a track, had been covered by sand, keeping it hidden from the air. Lengths of cable and chain and a couple of seriously heavy locks secured the gate, which was caked with dust and looked from a distance like any other length of the fence.

"Wave," I told Masters, gesturing at the small, covert surveillance cameras covering the gate.

"What?"

"You might as well. There's no way we can avoid them."

"There's nothing here. Why would anyone bother keeping this area under surveillance? I still don't get it," said Masters. "Let's go stand on those coordinates."

I pulled the GPS from a thigh pocket. "Three hundred yards that-away," I told her, pointing toward what would have been the center of this mystery compound, and started walking.

Above the last of the suspended dust, the sky was blue with a few wisps of high cirrus cloud bringing up the storm's rear. The air felt cool and dry but the sun had a bite. I sucked some more water, which was now warm. We walked up to the edge of a drop-off. Spreading out below it was a deep, wide wadi. I took a few steps down into it and stopped when I caught the movement: A large shiny black snake, coiled in the sun, had felt our vibrations through the ground and was making a lazy retreat. It vanished into a rock fissure obscured by weathered rubble as we continued down into the wadi.

I stopped for another drink and a bearings check on the GPS. The device told me I was standing on the X marking the spot.

"Still nothing," Masters observed.

I offered her a drink from my camelback tube, which she declined.

"So, what now?" she continued, hands on her hips, walking a small circle, eyes scanning the sloping walls of the wadi.

"Split up," I said. "I'll head left. Looks like this valley might come to a dead end up there. You go right. Meet back here in, say, half an hour, unless you find something, in which case let me know. We're going to walk every inch of this place." I wound up the volume on my brick and adjusted the squelch. Masters did likewise.

I repositioned my body armor and the weight of my backpack to give my rib some relief and headed off. I could see that the walls of the wadi actually became quite steep farther along, more canyonlike. Perhaps whatever there was to be found was where the shadows lengthened. I turned and saw Masters disappear behind a boulder.

Her voice suddenly burst from the radio handset clipped to my shoulder. *"Vin, come quick. You gotta see this."*

I jogged back, kicking up sand and dust, and as I came around the boulder, the one Masters had disappeared behind, I was in time to see something that tied my brain in a knot. It was Masters. She'd hoisted a rock that would have weighed maybe ten tons over the top of her head. As I watched, she tossed it aside.

"Huh?"

For an encore, Masters tugged at a face of the wadi itself and it came away like netting. Jesus, it *was* netting.

I ran closer as she ducked under the camouflage and vanished. A cave was hidden behind the net. I stopped at the entrance and pulled out my sidearm. Fluorescent tube lights set in the ceiling blinked on as I stepped inside. Masters closed a small steel cupboard on the wall that contained a number of switches, circuit breakers, and fuses. "Scratch the surface . . ." she said.

I glanced around, then holstered the Beretta. It was obvious no one was home, but I could see where they'd been. An empty water bottle and several crushed drink cans lay scattered around on the concrete floor, as well as chocolate and cracker wrappers. Two large Caterpillar bulldozers, a massive John Deere backhoe, and a much smaller version sat side by side in what appeared to be a large garage. Various items were collected here and there, hanging on hooks or leaning against walls: jackhammers, fifty-five-gallon drums, shovels, heavy steel spikes, overalls, hard hats, shower stalls. The air stank of diesel fuel and rock. A heavy layer of dust blanketed everything.

"What do you make of this?" Masters walked between the bulldozers, scooping sand off a track guard.

"Stuff to dig with," I said.

A red steel door built into the rock wall at the rear of the cave caught my attention. It was secured with a heavy padlock and chain. I took a sledgehammer to the links and got nowhere, so I smashed its hinges, then pried it open with one of the heavy spikes. It was a small room, well ventilated with ducts in the ceiling. Stacked on the floor were a number of drums of varying size—some plastic, some steel. I opened one of the plastic drums, reached in, and grabbed a handful of pellets that reminded me of chicken feed and smelled like chicken shit. Ammonium nitrate prills. I guessed the steel drums contained fuel oil, which a quick inspection confirmed. ANFO—ammonium nitrate and fuel oil—beloved of terrorists the world over, was also the most common explosive used in mining. A locked case caught my eye. I made short work of the lock. Blasting caps.

"Look what I found," Masters called through the broken doorway. "Nuclear biological chemical suits," she said, holding one up. "What do you suppose they need these for?"

I gave her a pair of raised eyebrows. NBCs. Interesting.

"Y'know, it doesn't look to me like this place has seen a lot of use lately," Masters continued.

I left the bang room and wandered over to the machinery. She was right, though the layer of dust on the backhoes didn't appear to be as thick as the one blanketing everything else. Maybe they were more multipurpose items than the dozers.

I found a screwdriver and climbed up into the driver's seat of the smaller one. Using the screwdriver, I dug out the ignition lock and joined the hot wires. I went through the starting routine illustrated by a decal on the dashboard, and the motor fired without hesitation. The fuel gauge indicated that the tank was half full or half empty, depending on your disposition. I killed the ignition and climbed down.

"Somewhere around here," I said, "there's gonna be a big hole in the ground. Let's go find it."

The midday sunshine was now brutal overhead, a hint of the summer to come. The GPS informed us that we were now 120 yards from the coords provided by Tawal's battered employee. We followed the course of the wadi as it meandered through the surrounding sand and rock.

We both saw it at the same time. The trick with the entrance to the garage had been repeated on the ground. Camouflage netting covered with fine gauze and light rubber rocks, mimicking the surroundings, covered the wadi bed for a distance of half a football field. I lifted a corner. A steel framework supported the camouflage roof. Simple, but effective. We'd flown over this very spot a few times in the Lynx and seen nothing other than a continuation of the usual monotone landscape.

Somewhere there was probably a switch that made the netting retract like the awning over a veranda. Masters found the edge of the netting on the other side of the wadi and rolled it back, revealing a pit that disappeared into darkness.

"A pair of headlights would really help here," I said.

Masters caught my drift. "What is it with guys and power tools?" she replied.

I jogged back up the wadi, retracing our steps to the garage. A couple of minutes later I was driving to the pit in the larger backhoe, which was also easily hot-wired. I took it around to the far side of the netting to a point opposite Masters, hopped down, and hooked the camouflage onto the trench-digger's tines. After climbing back up, I gave it some gas and pulled the netting away from the supporting framework.

Sunlight revealed that the pit was maybe a hundred feet deep, an access road cut into the near-vertical wall descending into it corkscrew-like. This was a pretty serious feat of excavation. But I figured that the people who'd dug this hole—Tawal's people—probably had a lot of experience in engineering those deep wells for brine storage.

I drove around and picked up Masters, who took a seat on the steel guard over the rear wheel.

"It's nice in here," she remarked.

"Climate-controlled air," I said.

"Got an MP3 player?"

We descended into the hole, the headlights cutting into the gloom. After several complete turns, the road flattened out and became the base of the pit, which was smooth earth and cool rock. We climbed down off the machine. I wasn't sure what I expected to find, but finding absolutely nothing didn't exactly top the list.

The cool airflow coming through the vents held the tang of mud and something else I couldn't identify.

"What's that smell?" Masters asked.

"Not me," I said.

The walls of the pit were solid rock. "There's a lot of dirt down here. I'm going to dig a hole."

"Like I said, men and their power tools..." Masters climbed down from the cabin and walked across to the access road, which she followed for half a turn up the side of the pit until a view was provided of the backhoe action below.

Meanwhile, I reversed the machine into the center of the pit, lowered the stabilizers until the rear wheels lifted clear of the earth, then engaged the digger's hydraulics. It took a few moments of uncontrolled operation before I had it squared away. The narrow bucket buried its tines into the earth and scooped up a load of reddish gray soil, which I tipped off to one side. I glanced up and saw Masters with her hands on her hips, head tilted, and a frown on her face—the combination every man in the universe recognizes as impatience. I backed off on the revs as Masters motioned at me to open the cabin door.

"Vin, you'll strike China any time now," she called out. "It's a dead end."

I thought, No one bothers hiding stuff that doesn't need to be hidden. And we were given these coordinates for a reason. I gave her the shorthand version: "Give it another ten."

Masters shrugged. I shifted the digging site a little and went back to work. Five loads later, something came up with the dirt. Masters stood, then walked down the road for a better look. I hung out of the cabin doorway.

"What is it?" she asked.

"Looks like a piece of steel." It was six inches long, slightly concave.

One side appeared to have a rusted iron liner. It exuded that unusual chemical smell. "There's corrosion of some type on it."

"Dig up some more," Masters suggested.

"Now, there's an idea," I said, giving her suggestion the smile it deserved.

I hopped back behind the controls, deposited the load off to one side, and went back for another. The bucket sank into the trench, the tines bit, and the machine began to balk and tug at something with a lot less give than dirt. The arm shook and jolted, then whatever was causing the resistance suddenly broke free. I pulled it up. Another chunk of steel similar to the last piece, only much larger. And from what I could see, this stuff had numbers stenciled on it. I set the throttle to idle and climbed down for a closer inspection. I wiped the dirt away from the stenciling while Masters trotted down the road again and picked her way across the tailings.

The flat snarl of a big chopper suddenly filled the sky overhead. I looked up and wondered why Robear and his Lynx had returned.

"What have we got?" she asked.

More corroded concave steel with an unidentified smell. And then a thought hit me. I jumped up onto the backhoe and pulled down my backpack. I dug around until I found what I was looking for and wrenched it out—a yellow box the size of a brick.

"Oh, shit." It suddenly hit Masters, too. "That smell—it's uranyl fluoride and hydrogen fluoride, isn't it? That's a HEX storage cylinder down here."

I flicked the on switch and the little yellow box borrowed from the old guy back in the Grand Bazaar went nuts. I tossed Masters my pack and said, "The camera. We need a record of that serial number."

I walked the floor of the pit like it was a crime scene, looking for the hot spots.

Masters's camera flashed half a dozen times.

The hottest spot in the entire area turned out to be the soles of my boots. "We need a sample of this mud," I told her.

"Use your camelback," Masters suggested.

It was nearly out of water anyway. I unscrewed the lid and used it to ladle a few pounds of wet dirt into the bladder. "How radioactive is this stuff?" I asked.

"It's not the radioactivity we have to worry about. It's the toxicity. We're OK, but we'll need to shower."

"Together?"

BANG!

Masters and I ducked. A chunk of the sky had fallen and hit the backhoe's steel roof. It slid off, bumped into the backhoe's arm, and slumped into the fresh hole I'd just dug.

"Jesus! What—" Masters exclaimed, shocked.

"Shit!" I added.

"Who . . . ? That's, that's the guy!"

Masters was right. It was the guy—the one who'd palmed us the coords for this place. He looked a lot better the last time I saw him, when both sides of his head were where they should be. In the interim, he'd apparently taken a soft-nosed round through his left earhole, not to mention a half-twist with pike off a 160-foot diving board onto a plate of rigid quarter-inch steel.

The helicopter hovered overhead and slowly maneuvered to one side of the hole. This time, I got a good look at it. It wasn't a Lynx. It banked hard over and suddenly the world was full of .50-caliber slugs sparking and ricocheting off the rock walls. Hot brass casings rained down around us and steamed on the moist dirt.

The burst of fire stopped as the chopper repositioned itself for another crack at us.

"That's Tawal's," Masters yelled as she went for cover behind the backhoe's meaty, water-filled tire. "It's the helo we saw parked on the ramp, the Eurocopter."

The sun flashing off its sparkling, virgin-white fuselage eliminated any doubt. Examining its profile, I noticed what appeared to be a large bulk attached to the machine gun's barrel.

"Oh, shit—there's a CROWS system up there," I said, pulling out my sidearm and checking the magazine.

"That's bad," Masters said.

"Could be worse."

"How?"

"Looks like whoever's operating the gun can't get the angle on the barrel depressed far enough. That Browning can't get a clean shot at us."

"Jesus, Vin. What's the difference between dying from a hit with a ricochet or a clean shot?"

"Hell of a time for riddles, lady," I replied as we ran for cover beside the John Deere.

The pit filled with the roar of high-velocity lead smacking off the walls. The cabin above us exploded in a swift succession of bangs, showering us with granules of safety glass. A couple of ricochets tumbled too close for comfort past my head, warbling on their merry, deadly way. The brass casings followed, tinkling musically as they bounced off the backhoe's roof. A regular symphony. What to do? We could just wait this out, hope for Christie to turn up. But, for all we knew, the helo was merely the advance guard. Now that the thought occurred to me, I was sure Tawal would have a few Humvees on hand, manned by Jarred and his flunkies, itching to do something other than shuffle around air-conditioned corridors smiling at cameras.

Overhead, the helicopter moved in a lazy circle, hovering around the rim of the pit. It had to be difficult for the pilot and gunner to coordinate with each other and get the craft positioned just right for the kill. And we were presenting a static target. If we were mobile, keeping a bead on us might prove beyond pilot and gunner—at least until the barrel didn't have to be depressed almost vertically downward. Once we were clear of the pit, and within the CROWS's operational limits, its advanced sensors and tracking would take over. I considered the options: stay put or go. On the move, we were ducks. But at least we weren't sitting ducks.

I leapt back up into the driver's seat and goosed the throttle. "C'mon. Time to go," I shouted. I retracted the backhoe's support posts and secured the rear bucket as Masters climbed up and crouched in the space between the driver's seat and the wheel guard.

"By the way," she said, "I agree."

"What?"

"You're right. We're better off making a run for it. I'm just pleased you weren't going to argue about it."

"Sure..."

"What about him?" Masters asked, gesturing at the remains of the guy whose name we didn't even know, who'd risked his life to blow the lid off Tawal's multibillion-dollar scam, and lost.

"We'll worry about him if we don't end up joining him," I said, raising the machine's bucket high overhead.

Fifty-caliber rounds zinged and fizzed around us, holing the guards and sparking off the engine's crankcases. Water sprayed from the punctured rear tires. Masters made herself as small as possible and buried her head under an arm. A round that missed my face by inches made a noise like a door buzzer. I tried not to think about what would happen if either of us was hit by a tumbling, misshapen .50-caliber round moving at nearly the speed of sound.

I retracted the stabilizers, slammed the machine into second gear, gunned the throttle, and dropped the clutch. The backhoe did a massive wheelie, the front axle pawing at the air, and accelerated toward the stone wall of the pit.

"Shiiiit!" Masters yelled.

With the engine revs nudging the red line, the beast was a handful to control. The rear bucket bounced off the dirt with a jarring crash and brought the front wheels back down into contact with the ground. Just in time. I wrenched the steering wheel, the front tires bit into the dirt, and the machine turned, following the road as it took us clockwise up toward the light. And the prowling specter of Tawal's gun platform.

I stamped on the gas again and the rear wheels lost traction with the massive torque pumped into them by the turbocharged diesel. I fed in the opposite lock and wrestled back some control. I checked the sky. As I'd hoped, the pilot was having trouble positioning the chopper. The Browning was on the wrong side to get off a burst, angled away from us. The helo pivoted in the air to bring the M2 around, but by then we'd moved to the far side of the pit and out of the gun's sights. In fact, the Browning had not been fired since we started moving.

"It's working," Masters shouted.

I relaxed a little. Bad move. The rear wheels suddenly gained some extra unexpected traction, catching me by surprise. We were headed for the pit's vertical rock wall. I swerved. The rear wheel came around like a pendulum and smashed into the rock, which bounced us toward the edge of the road and a drop-off that was now more than seventy feet. I swerved again in the opposite direction and somehow managed to avoid the edge of the road and a drop to certain death.

"You want me to drive?" Masters yelled.

I ignored her, fed in more throttle, and the backhoe stormed up the hill, gathering speed. "When we reach the lip of the pit, speed's going to be our best friend," I said, thinking aloud. From the corner of my eye, I saw Masters's knuckles whiten further as she renewed her grip on the machine.

The exit from the pit was fifty yards ahead. The road steepened and straightened a little. I red-lined the engine and shifted up a gear. The backhoe surged forward, water spraying from the tires as if they were giant showerheads. I lowered the bucket to give the machine a little better balance. The helicopter swooped low overhead as we roared out of the pit, launched into midair by the ramp. Ahead and below, a white Humvee with a roof-mounted CROWS had been positioned to block our escape. Through its windshield I caught a glimpse of Jarred's eyes, wide and startled, a moment before we landed on the vehicle, crushing it.

The backhoe bounced off it and the thing bucked and skidded left and right as I fought the steering wheel. Jarred's Humvee suddenly exploded behind us, the heat and the blast wave rolling over us. No time to look back.

"Where's the chopper?" I shouted.

"Coming up on our six o'clock. Don't drive in a straight line."

"Thanks for the advice."

"Vin, there's another Humvee . . . two of them—up there."

They were tracking the edge of the wadi, heading in the opposite direction from us. At this point, the wadi's sides were too steep and rocky for them to attempt a descent without the risk of a rollover. The Humvees would have to go farther down toward the pit and turn in there.

"Are we going back to the cave?" Masters screamed over the roar of our engine and the thump of the Eurocopter's blades.

"Unless you've got a better plan . . ."

More .50-caliber slugs began clanging into the backhoe's trenching arm, which protected our backs. The gun platform was in a sideslip, coming up directly behind us, now with a clear line of sight.

"I'll hit the brakes and it'll fly right by," I said. I stomped on the pedal and the whole machine shuddered. The wheels locked and slipped as the tires fought for traction. At the last instant, I turned into the cave, the backhoe teetering on two wheels for a frightening instant before righting itself with a thump. It rolled forward slowly and came to a stop between the Caterpillars and the smaller backhoe. The rear tires oozed water and the motor steamed. Hydraulic fluid dripped steadily onto the floor. It was like a half-dead animal.

FORTY-FOUR

I'll hit the brakes and it'll fly right by?" Masters yelled—pissed—climbing down.

"Worked in the movie."

"That was a *movie,* Vin! Jesus, you could've killed us."

"We're still breathing, aren't we?" I hopped across to the other bulldozer, jumped onto the ground beyond it, and picked up a couple of empty plastic water bottles. "Hey," I called out, "if you see another one of these, I need it."

"Why?"

"Because a couple of Berettas up against three Brownings, and who knows what else, won't cut it. The odds require a little evening-up."

We didn't have much time, not enough to explain. Tawal's chopper was close; from the hard grind of its turbines and the dirt-filled windblast from the main rotor blades filling the cave, it was hovering just outside, no doubt covering the entrance, trying to keep us bottled up inside. In a minute, two at the most, the Humvees would arrive, the cave would be stormed, and no corny lines from *Top Gun* would save us.

I handed Masters my M9, exchanging it for an old Evian bottle. "Might be worth taking a few shots at the bird, just to show them we're not completely toothless."

Masters nodded. "Where are you going?"

"To make a few surprises. You got spare mags?" I asked.

"Two," she called out at my back, as I ran for the room with the red door busted off the wall. I cut up one of the bottles with my knife, made a funnel, and used it to fill the other bottle with ammonium nitrate prills. The ideal ratio of prills to fuel oil was around fifteen to one. I tipped in about the right amount of fuel oil. Outside, I heard Masters firing off the handguns.

"Vin!" I heard her call out. "Need help here!"

The box containing the fuses was open. Damn: Most were of the ISFE variety—igniter safety electric fuses. I lifted out the tray. Beneath it was a roll of Primacord plus a few nonelectric delay detonators.

"Smokin'," I said aloud, and went to work quickly. *Carefully.*

The big backhoe went out first, heading west, still spraying water, bucket raised high in defiance. The vehicle had hit twenty miles an hour by the time it reached the sloping sides of the wadi and turned, veering back and heading toward the pit. The weight I'd attached to the bottom of its steering wheel was doing its job, keeping the vehicle behaving in a generally controlled fashion so it appeared that the dummy made up of drums and wearing my ABU was in control.

One of the Humvees sped off to run it down, the roof-mounted CROWS Browning hurling several hundred rounds at it. The helo took the bait, too, and hovered off to one side to join the Humvee in pumping as much copper-sheathed lead as possible into the dummy propped up behind the wheel. I kept my eyes glued to my watch and prayed that those nonelectric delay detonators were as accurate as the explosives folks I knew said they were.

My heart raced. "In three . . . two . . . one . . ."

Masters stood on the gas pedal, and the tires on the small John Deere squealed and spun momentarily on the concrete floor. We shot out of the cave and into the sunlight, heading to the right. Masters hit the brakes almost immediately, broadsiding into the second Humvee before it could get out of our way. We skidded around and the trenching bucket smashed into its windshield.

"Go, go, go!" I yelled.

As we separated from the Humvee, I pitched one of the water bottles through the hole in its windshield, throwing it hard. Five seconds, four, three . . .

A hand appeared through the hole, clutching the bottle, about to throw it. And then, *BOOOM!* Bits of Humvee and human clanked and thudded into the Deere. The tremendous blast wave blew us sideways.

We were both groggy from the concussion. I tapped Masters on the shoulder and shouted, "Let's go!" My ears rang from the explosion. I turned to see how the big John Deere was doing. How long was it going to take before a hot .50-caliber round hit the Primacord and detonated the ANFO dummy?

Answering my question, the backhoe suddenly and completely blew apart on the edge of the pit. A massive fireball engulfed it as it rolled in and was swallowed by the hole in the wadi floor. More explosions followed, sending black smoke rings into the sky. The Humvee following it was slowing, turning away. Its roofline had a deep gouge through it. A large piece of backhoe shrapnel had ripped into the CROWS, tearing through the roof and probably disabling or killing the driver. The Humvee straightened again and kept going until it, too, disappeared from sight, tipping over the edge of the pit.

The white helo carved a wide circle around the smoking carnage.

Time to move. I jumped from the cabin and scrambled up the side of the wadi, the undersize chemical suit grabbing at my crotch. After a few moments of disorientation, I found what I was looking for. I shoved the bottle in the fissure, leaving most of it exposed. For its sake, I hoped that the shiny black snake living here was off visiting a buddy somewhere.

I scrambled back down the wadi and ran for the backhoe. The Eurocopter had climbed well out of harm's way. Maybe the pilot, or whoever was in command—Tawal, perhaps—was having second thoughts about trying to corner us. Or more likely it had gained some altitude to get a better tactical overview of the situation.

I squeezed Masters's shoulder and nodded toward the rear of the wadi. She crunched through the gears and reversed us into the shadows. The chopper descended, moving from side to side, looking for the safest approach. Those steep walls of the wadi were providing us with protection on three sides.

There was only one approach. The helo hovered sideways, cautiously edging toward us and no doubt using the CROWS sensors to check for surprises. And then it stopped and suddenly backed away. The pilot must have seen me scramble up to the snake hole and figured some kind of trick was in store.

The Eurocopter came toward us again, this time from the opposite side. I felt sweat breaking out in places it had never broken out in before. That flying gun was lining us up, and this time the pilot was making no mistakes. Except for maybe one.

Just behind him, the whole side of the wadi suddenly burst toward the sky in a massive geyser of rock, dust, and flame. Masters and I dived beneath the John Deere for what little cover it afforded. I glanced up in time to see the helo's tail rotor destroy itself among a shower of rock. The aircraft started to spin, slowly at first, then picking up speed. I watched it climb before turning on its side and descending in an uncontrolled death spiral. It hit the ground with a *whump,* the main rotor blades whirling and shattering against the wadi floor, causing the wreckage to spin, twist, and writhe. And then its fuel tanks exploded, flinging shards of metal across a two-hundred-yard range.

We stayed under the backhoe until well after the secondary explosions stopped. Eventually we crawled out, stood, and brushed the dirt out of our clothes. My throat was dry. Grit crunched between my teeth. I checked that the bladder was still tucked under the backhoe's seat, then picked my way up the side of the wadi, taking it slow, no longer in a hurry. The bottle was easy to find. It caught the sunlight and flashed like a navigation strobe, as I'd hoped it would. I bent down, plucked it from the fissure, and gulped down the warm water inside.

Four columns of black smoke rose into the sky, accounting for three Humvees and one Eurocopter. The shock waves from the main explosion had caused the hole in the ground to collapse, burying the HEX storage cylinder beneath thousands of tons of rubble. Hanging over everything was a mushroom cloud of dirt and dust from the destroyed cave. The larger particles blown skyward now sprinkled down in a sand shower. ANFO sure had a kick to it.

"So, Special Agent Cooper. You've been busy."

I looked over my shoulder. It was Lieutenant Christie. With the ringing still in my ears, I hadn't heard his unit approach. Six vehicles were lined up behind him, his men already moving out to reconnoiter the area.

"So, Lieutenant Christie. You're late. Got a shower in one of those trucks?"

The steel gate protecting Kawthar al Deen from truck and car bombs swung open to admit the convoy, a wise decision given that a Warrior, the British equivalent of our Bradley Fighting Vehicle, headed it. Not quite a main battle tank, but not to be argued with nonetheless. Lynx gunships hovered overhead. Christie's CO, a lieutenant colonel, headed the op. There was no resistance to our show of force, which made everyone feel a little overdressed for the occasion.

Tawal had apparently left the country that morning, as soon as the storm lifted. His security force had been reduced to five personnel. The Brits disarmed and detained them. No authority had been granted to us to search and occupy the facility, and the Iraqi parliament was indignant on Tawal's behalf. There was nothing to do but withdraw. Masters and I withdrew all the way to Istanbul.

FORTY-FIVE

The FBI confirmed it—from the same batch of explosives used on Portman's safe. Ours, or the Israelis', depending on how you want to look at it," said Captain Cain.

Masters came in and took her seat.

"You missed the funerals, by the way." The captain had trouble deciding where to look, so he walked to the window and watched the Bosphorus traffic. "But then, so did I," he continued. "Dr. Merkit's family didn't want infidels present. I bought her flowers from the three of us. Karli and Iyaz delivered them. I sent flowers to Emir's family, too."

"Thanks, Rodney," I said. "I know how you felt about her."

"Actually, I doubt that, Special Agent. But what can you do?" He wasn't expecting an answer. "I know it wasn't intentional on your part—how things turned out between you and her . . . just happened."

Cain had his back to me. Beyond him, through the window, a Russian oil tanker drifted down the waterway.

"Do you want to hand your involvement in this case to someone else?" I asked him.

"No," he replied, turning to face me. "I want the satisfaction of helping you nail the fuckers who killed her. The FBI just came through with IDs on those photos you sent from Iraq." Cain opened his briefcase and removed a folder. Inside were the photos, which he spread out across my desk.

I picked up the one on top. "Moses Abdul Tawal."

"And that's his real name, not an alias," Cain continued. "Stop me if I'm telling you stuff you already know. Tawal's a heavy hitter in Egyptian business circles. Well known to Egypt's politicians. Helped build the Aswan High Dam. Could be why he was brought in on your desal project, water and heavy construction being common to both. You need something big done, call in Tawal. He owns at least two dozen companies, is a major shareholder in double that number, and not all of them aboveboard. Rumor has it he also deals in illegal arms—the hard-to-get high-tech stuff—but no one has managed to hang anything on him. Interestingly, Interpol has had their eye on Tawal for a while in a low-level kind of way. One odd thing: He's Jewish. You can count the Jewish population in Egypt on the fingers of one hand, by the way. They're a statistical anomaly. Apparently, he takes his religion seriously, but it doesn't seem to have hurt him in business. Tawal doesn't have a police record, although he has been implicated in a large number of assaults, none of which has ever gone to court. He probably punches them in the mouth, then pays them to keep it shut. It's safe to say the guy has a temper."

I nodded. We'd seen one of his tantrums.

"Tawal has a number of addresses, in Paris, New York, and Cairo. Also has a houseboat on Lake Nasser—he likes to feed the wildlife."

Masters picked up another familiar face from the pile. "And this guy?"

"Jarred Ben-Gari. Formerly of the Israeli Defense Forces, rank of captain. Good record. Fought in the September War against Hezbollah. Then one day he just resigned his commission and walked away. No reason. Turned up at your desal plant."

I recalled the look on the guy's face the moment he died. "I don't think we'll be running into him again," I said. In fact, for all I knew, maybe Tawal himself was also getting debriefed on eternity. "Was Ben-Gari with the Sayeret?" I asked.

"Good guess," Cain replied. "He was. Something went wrong and he was transferred. Ended up in artillery."

Masters and I exchanged a glance. Both of us had caught the connection, even if Cain hadn't. The explosives used on the safe and in the car bomb had come from Israeli artillery shells supposedly fired in the September War. Jarred, military HEX, Tawal, Portman . . .

"What about the rest of these people?" Masters asked, picking up a photo of a guy wearing sunglasses who was strolling along arm in arm with an AK-47. He was either whistling or puckering up.

"Just your usual ragtag bunch of former shooters," replied Cain, "graduates from various combat units who quit to make some real money doing the same job they were doing for their governments. Nothing special about any of them. No apparent common factors."

I leaned back in my chair and stared at the ceiling, trying to put the pieces together. The exercise made my head hurt.

"Anything else you need a hand with?" Cain asked.

"No, not really. Not just at the moment, anyway," said Masters. "Thanks for all this, Captain. And Vin and I are both deeply sorry about Dr. Merkit."

Cain nodded and said, "Yeah." He was about to say something else, but then decided he should leave before whatever it was just came out of its own accord and shot him in the foot.

Masters looked at me and I looked back at her. We were both thinking the same thought: *Could Rodney Cain be our mole?*

"You stole his girlfriend," Masters told me. "That's a motive right there."

I wasn't ready to point the finger at Cain quite yet. And my relationship with Doc Merkit came along *after* someone had passed the information about a second safe to Yafa. "I need some air," I said.

"No, you don't. We need to talk. About the case. There are holes."

"You want to talk about the case . . . here?" I opened my hands wide and looked around the room. For all we knew, you could shake more bugs out of this room than a picnic rug. Whoever the mole was, he had plenty of resources, along with high-level access. There were at least ten people on the short list.

The phone on my desk rang. I picked up. "Special Agent Cooper."

"Hello, Special Agent. It's Sage Laboratories calling." The voice on the line was young, female, and black. "Says here on the instructions that we're to fax our report, rather than email it."

"That's correct."

"You provided us with a couple of security questions for proof of identity."

"Yep, I remember."

"Usually these are your mother's maiden name, that sort of thing. . . ."

"Uh-huh."

"OK...um...Who did the Redskins trade for on April Fools' Day, 1964?"

"Sonny Jurgensen."

"What year did George Allen take the Redskins to the Super Bowl?"

"1973."

"OK, Special Agent Cooper. Your report is being faxed as we speak. And...have an NFL day."

"I'll try to," I said, hanging up.

"What was that all about?" Masters asked.

"To the fax machine, trusty sidekick," I said.

It was cool but sunny down by the water; warm, as long as I didn't move about and gave the sunlight enough time to accumulate on my exposed skin. A few small fishing boats bobbed at their moorings close to the retaining wall. I finished reading the report from Sage Laboratories as Masters dodged the traffic and skipped through a break, a steaming apple tea in each hand.

"Here," she said, holding one out to me.

"Thanks."

"I could get addicted to this stuff."

"Jarred...it's possible," I said. "Thousands of shells were fired into southern Lebanon. The captain of an artillery barrage could've made a few of them disappear."

"If we could prove that," Masters added, "it would connect Tawal to Portman's wall safe, and to Portman's murder. From there it'd be a hop, skip, and a jump to all the other murders. What did Sage come up with?"

"I haven't read the whole thing, but pretty much what we expected." I handed her the report on the soil sample we'd taken from the pit and sipped my tea while she skimmed through it.

"*Concentrations of uranyl fluoride...hydrafluoric acid...adducts of uranyl fluoride...consistent with the exposure of uranium hexafluoride to water...* Jesus, you know what this means?"

"That Tawal is a good reason to use the electric chair more often."

"The bastard really did poison the water supply to give the desal plant a reason to exist. Then he produced a fabricated water report to make it look like DU contamination." Masters shook her head. "Fuuuuck... All those poor kids, their parents..."

I held my hand out to take back the report, but she stopped me.

"Hang on. There's a note here about the HEX." She turned the page and continued reading as I watched a tanker the size of the Chrysler Building squeeze through the narrow strait, and thought about what I'd like to do to Tawal if I caught up with him. "Oh, man... listen to this," she said. "Most of the hot isotope of uranium, U-235, had been removed. The percentage of uranium-235 was 0.3."

"Can you give that to me in English?"

"Depleted uranium is the feedstock for nuclear fuel that ends up either in reactors or bombs. The stuff gets put through a process called gaseous diffusion. What comes out one side is depleted—HEX with very little of the U-235 left in it, remember? That stuff goes into storage. Out the other side comes enriched HEX, which goes on to be made into the fuel. Sage says that because the sample we provided contained a specifically small amount of U-235—0.3 percent—our uranium compounds came from *depleted* uranium hexafluoride from a specific source. Vin, they're saying the storage cylinder we dug up was one of *ours*!"

"Ours?"

"The good old U.S.A.'s—ours. Somehow Tawal managed to get his hands on one of our depleted uranium storage tanks—or more than one, who knows?—shipped it to Iraq, and buried it in the ground.... Jesus, Vin, we have to take this to somebody."

"Like who? We don't know who we can trust, remember? We've got the cylinder's serial number, and we keep that card close to our chest till we're ready to play it."

Masters's cell started bleating. She juggled the report and the tea and took the phone out of her jacket. From the look on her face when she checked the screen, I could tell she didn't know the caller. "Special Agent Masters... Yes, of course I remember you, Colonel."

Masters lowered the phone and mouthed, *Woodward*.

I nodded—the Reapers' commanding officer.

"No, I'm in Istanbul," she said. "Yes, a beautiful city... Yes, Special Agent Cooper is here with me.... Uh-huh... Uh-huh... sure..."

I drank the last of the tea and walked the twenty paces to a trash can. When I returned, Masters was still on the phone.

"Yeah . . . So you were aware that Colonel Portman had lost his appi-8 status? . . . Uh-huh . . . Fair enough . . . Yes, sir . . . You were? Really? . . . Uh-huh . . . What did he have against them? . . . Uh-huh . . . What? . . . OK . . . Well, thanks very much for the heads-up, Colonel. Special Agent Cooper and I appreciate your cooperation. Good-bye, sir." Masters gave me a half smile. "Y'know, I cannot understand that man. What the hell is a SWAG?"

"What was the colonel having a 'scientific wild-ass guess' about?"

"He knew that Portman had been grounded."

"Why didn't he mention it to us?"

"Probably didn't trust us—us being ground pounders and all. Though his excuse was that he was unsure about what he could and couldn't say. Anyway, his superiors have cleared him to talk. The SWAG related to him believing that Portman had a problem working with the Israelis."

"Portman was anti-Semitic?"

"No, nothing like that. The Reapers were going head-to-head with the Cheil Ha'avir, taking on those F-16 Sufas we saw down at Incirlik. The Israelis were practicing bombing runs—lofts."

"Lofts? Shit . . ." A loft was a bombing profile designed to throw ordnance a long way, where the delivery platform flew a parabola and let the load go near the top of the arc. "Practicing the delivery of nuclear ordnance?"

"That's what the colonel said. And while the Israelis were doing that, it was the Reapers' job to come at them, mimicking the sort of tactics an opposing force might use."

"Was he specific about what kind of opposing force?" I asked.

"Block said his squadron was flying intercept profiles that might be used by F-14s."

F-14s. There were only two places in the world where F-14s still flew. In reruns of *Top Gun*. And in Iran.

FORTY-SIX

OK," I began as we headed back to the peach fortress on the hill, "this is what we know. . . . After making like an Iranian fighter-interceptor against the Israelis, Portman gives up his flying status to concentrate on the shit going down at Kumayt. Then Yafa and her eunuchs come along and kill him in such a way that the police believe he's the victim of a serial killer, a theory reinforced by subsequent murders. Portman's gruesome death turns out to be merely the cover for the murderers' real goal—securing the only report they believe to be in existence on the HEX-contaminated water at Kumayt.

"The explosives used to blow Portman's safe, as well as the car bomb that later kills Doc Merkit and Emir, turn out to have come from Israel, from artillery shells supposedly fired off in the September War. And this brings us to Jarred, who happens to be a former IDF artillery captain working for Tawal, the guy who's poisoning the water at Kumayt with U.S. nuclear material. Why? Because he needs an excuse to build a vast desalination plant on the Iranian border that will be used as a secret military base. Have I missed anything?"

"The U.S. connection—the HEX. We're up to our necks in this somehow," Masters said as we went through the front security check.

I agreed. Plus, there was the mole; the tampering with Portman's email; the general obfuscation, the leaking of confidential information.

The women in their head scarves and body stockings smiled at us from behind the bombproof glass like we were old friends. Masters smiled back for the both of us. After passing through the X-ray machine, we walked in silence to the elevator. We'd just missed it. Masters pressed the button and leaned against the wall.

"I've been thinking about who we can check that HEX tank's serial number with," she said.

"Any ideas?"

"Well, the Department of Energy runs all nuclear storage facilities. When I was asking around about the Iraq DU dumps, I developed a pretty good rapport with a woman in the DoE's middle management. She was high enough to have reasonable access, low enough to pass under the radar, and jaded enough to want to help."

"OK, see what she can do with it."

"I've also been thinking about something Dr. Bartholomew told us. That Portman said he felt personally responsible for the children affected by the contamination at Kumayt. Why would he say that—that he felt *personally* responsible?"

"You think we've missed something?"

"Maybe nothing important... Portman stumbles across the hospital at Kumayt and he gets involved. He gets drawn into the bidding process and doesn't like what he sees going on. Maybe he plays a few hunches and comes up with some frightening information that leads to even more frightening conclusions. And when he learned what his squadron was up to, he wanted no part in it. Portman had the full picture. I wonder what he was going to do with what he knew."

The elevator arrived.

"If Portman blew the whistle on the shit going down in Kumayt, what would that do to the governments in Israel and the U.S.?" I wondered. "It's our HEX and Israel is our ally. Once the scandal hits the media, both administrations are going to be in for a rough ride. What would Jerusalem and Washington do to protect themselves?"

They'd do plenty. And what instrument would they use for that protection? The Israelis would call in Mossad. Washington would use the CIA. Masters and I looked at each other, arriving at the same place at the same time: *Stringer*.

The elevator stopped and the doors opened. The coast was clear. We hurried to our office. I opened the door and—

"Ah, just the people I was hoping to bump into." Harvey Stringer was seated behind my desk. "In fact, I've been trying to do that with you in particular, Cooper, for some time. But you're elusive, aren't you?"

"Am I?" I said.

"You are." Stringer tapped his fingers together and stared at us like he was considering his next move.

Goddard and Mallet were loitering around Masters's desk. I noticed they'd switched to wearing suits now that their cover was blown, the cheap variety that give out electric shocks on warm, dry days. I had the impression we'd caught them all in the act of a little invasion of privacy.

"In my office in an hour and a half. Both of you," Stringer ordered. The desk seemed a lot smaller with the big man behind it. He stood up and performed that big person's trick of appearing weightless as he swung out from behind it and reached the door in two giant steps. Without turning, he bellowed, "Be on time."

Mallet and Goddard followed their boss at a respectful distance.

"Flotsam before jetsam," I called out as they reached the door, which caused them to pause.

"Cooper, admitting you're an asshole is the first step in the program," said Goddard with a smile.

"Doesn't seem to have worked for you or your throwback buddy. Did you happen to find what you were hunting around for back there? A few good ideas, maybe?"

Mallet shook his head. "Aside from your partner's spectacular ass and her exhibitionist tendencies, you two got nothing."

"Catch you in your next X-rated performance, honey," Goddard said to Masters as he stalked out, looking smug, Mallet in tow behind him looking smugger.

Masters headed back to her desk, steamed up. "Do men always compete with each other to see who can be the biggest shithead?"

Yeah, often. Redirecting her energies, I wrote on a pad and passed it to her: *Agree we might have missed something important on Portman. Need to go back through the case notes.*

She nodded.

I went to the filing cabinet, unlocked it, pulled the files, and dropped them on her desk. We reread the translations of Iyaz and Karli's notes, neighbors' eyewitness accounts, the crime-scene report, the initial forensic report on Portman's remains, the lists of evidence collected, my notes on the Thurlstane Group and the interview with Bob Rivers, Portman's phone and bank records, his will and insurance papers, the phone interview with Portman's wife, his flight records, and a hell of a lot more besides. Nothing popped, for me or Masters. After nearly an hour she rose and got a glass of water from the cooler.

I had a problem. "There's nothing new," I told Masters.

"What do you mean?"

"Aside from the Flight Records stuff, nothing new has been added to the case file." I reached for the phone. "Rodney, Vin."

"What's up?" Rodney Cain asked.

"There are a few preliminary reports in Portman's file. None of them have been updated."

"Such as?"

I picked up the one at the top of the pile. "Such as the full, unabridged report from Istanbul homicide forensics."

"Well, yeah, as a matter of fact, got that one right here. Arrived the day before yesterday. Took longer because they had it translated. I didn't know you were sweating it."

"Nothing else come in?"

"A few of the neighbors have been re-interviewed.... To be honest, I think Istanbul homicide have moved on. They're expecting us to make the miracle breakthrough."

I felt a twinge of guilt. Cain had just inadvertently reminded me that I'd kept him well behind the play. But then I remembered the hint of suspicion and the guilt untwinged itself. "Can you fax what you've got?" I asked him.

"Sure."

I hung up and checked my watch. Half an hour till Stringer Time.

Cain sent the final forensic report through on the machine a minute later. It had fattened considerably, but I wasn't expecting to see anything particularly new or surprising, just a lot more detail on what we already had. I started flipping pages. Yep—the missing bones, the number of pieces he was cut into, the damage done to the back of his larynx by the chloroform... There was half a rain forest of recorded tedium. Say a guy gets an axe buried up to its handle in his forehead, you'd think the forensic autopsy would stop somewhere above the neck, right? But no, when these guys are good, they're thorough. They take tissue samples, hundreds of them, from all over the body. If the thickness of the report was any indication, Istanbul forensics was thorough.

"Hey," said Masters. I glanced up. She pointed at the face of her wristwatch. In twenty-two minutes Stringer would start drumming his fat fingers on his desk, wondering where we were.

I speed-read the summaries. At some point, some surgeon had botched the posterior cruciate ligament in the knee joint of Portman's left leg. No more skiing for him. There were no signs of arthritis in his fingers or toes. There was a low-grade case of hemorrhoids and a little diverticulitis. Tut-tut, not enough fiber in the diet. Portman's renal function was poor. His lung function was excellent—well above average for a guy around fifty, and his liver function was normal. His—

Wait a minute. Poor renal function—why was that? Why weren't Portman's kidneys working? I flicked back and read the pathologist's more extensive overview. The word "necrotized" got my full attention. "Shit," I said out loud.

"What?" Masters inquired.

"You got Portman's files there—his medical records?"

Masters passed it across.

"Turns out Portman was down to one kidney. The other one was almost completely dead." I searched for the paragraph I knew should be in his last flight physical, but it wasn't there. Somehow he'd fooled the system. "Jesus . . . I think I can tell you why Portman felt personally responsible for the situation down in Kumayt. Because, in Desert Storm, he flew Warthogs and buried a few tons of depleted uranium in Iraqi ass."

"You have to call his wife," said Masters.

"Ex-wife," I corrected her.

"She has a right to know," Masters replied, as she reread the information rushed through from Andrews.

It had taken some fast talking, but the Flight Surgeon's office had come through. The guy on the desk there pulling an all-nighter must have been bored. He'd faxed us the relevant page in Portman's flight log within nineteen minutes of our request.

"You're better at this stuff than I am," I said.

"You've already spoken with her," Masters said, holding the handset out to me. "I've dialed the number. Take it..."

I took the phone. It was ringing, and then someone picked up.

"Hello?" said a familiar voice.

"Mrs. Portman?"

"Yes...? Who is it?"

"Mrs. Portman, I'm sorry about the hour," I said, glaring at Masters. "This is Special Agent Cooper."

"What time *is* it?"

"It's seven A.M., ma'am." If I were her, I'd have hung up on me.

"Your voice is familiar. I've spoken to you before, haven't I?"

"Yes, ma'am. Special Agent Vin Cooper. I'm with the OSI, investigating Colonel Portman's death. You might not remember—you told me about your husband coming home and telling you he didn't want children, that he wanted a divorce."

"I remember. You were rude to my sister...."

"I was jus—"

"Why are you calling? Do you know who killed him?"

"Yes."

"Is that why you're calling? To inform me?"

"We don't have the proof as yet, ma'am."

"So you're not going to tell me who?"

"I can tell you positively that Colonel Portman was not the victim of a serial killer, ma'am. We believe he was killed by an organization that wanted it to look like a serial killing. He'd found something. The organization wanted to stop him revealing it, and stopped in a way that would have any investigation chasing its tail. I can't tell you too much more about it—not just now."

There was silence while she took all this in.

"Mrs. Portman, your husband saw combat in Desert Storm. Did he tell you much about it?"

"A little—not much. Why?"

"He was one of the pilots who stopped the retreating Iraqi Army on the highway to Basra. It was widely reported in the media at the time—it was called the Highway of Death."

"Yes, I saw the pictures. Horrible. I didn't know Emmet was involved."

"Did you know he was on the verge of complete renal failure?"

"What?"

"He was down to less than one kidney."

"No . . . no, I didn't."

"Mrs. Portman. Your husband was also sterile."

"Sterile? I don't believe it."

"Believe it, ma'am. You should also know that your husband loved you very much," I said.

There was silence on the line.

"Mrs. Portman?"

"You don't know what you're talking about. And I don't see that this is really any of your business."

She was right, it wasn't. But Masters and I had come to know a few things about the late Emmet Portman. Maybe passing on some of that knowledge might help her down the line. "Ma'am, my investigating partner and I believe your husband divorced you so that you could meet someone else. He wanted you to have children. He wanted children with you."

"I'm hanging up now. . . . This is . . . I don't believe you."

"Mrs. Portman . . ."

She didn't hang up.

"Colonel Portman was flying A-10s," I told her. "Tank-busters. The ammunition they use is called depleted uranium, or DU. Have you heard of it?"

"Yes, I've heard of it."

"When this ammunition burns, it turns into a uranium oxide aerosol. When inhaled, there's a view among a number of medical experts that it can cause problems."

"What kind of problems?"

Masters handed me a page downloaded from the Internet about some of the disorders being blamed on DU. A paragraph was highlighted. *"Kidney damage, cancers of the lungs and bones, respiratory disease, skin disorders, neurocognitive disorders, chromosomal damage, and birth defects."*

"Oh, my god . . ."

"During the attack on the highway, the A-10s were pretty low, and they shot off a lot of DU," I continued. "Your husband could have breathed in a lot of uranium oxide."

Silence.

"Ma'am," I said, "the stuff he was breathing probably killed his kidneys, and sterility is another symptom. As I said, we believe your husband left you so that you could have healthy children with someone else."

"Dear God," she said. It was barely audible.

"Mrs. Portman, if you want, I can provide you with the numbers of a support group. . . . There's a class action being put together. . . ." I went on to tell her a little about Kumayt, and Portman's work in the hospital there, helping and caring for those children.

She told me that since her divorce from Emmet, there had been no one else. From what I knew, there'd been no one else for Emmet Portman either.

I left her in tears.

FORTY-SEVEN

Harvey Stringer glowered as we walked into his office. "You're late. Ten minutes late by my watch."

"Our apologies, sir," Masters jumped in. "But we just got a call from Colonel Portman's ex-wife. She wanted to know if there'd been any developments. She and Emmet were still close, despite their divorce, and his murder hit her pretty hard."

Stringer tapped an enormous finger on the desk in front of him, considering his response. After a moment, he grunted and said, "We have no room for romantics in our world, Special Agent Masters. Don't waste my time again." He aimed a small remote at a spot on the wall, the lights suddenly dimmed, and an LCD screen descended from a slot in the ceiling. "Now, Special Agents Telopea and Blitz tell me that you've had contact with these people already," Stringer continued, shifting his focus to a selection of familiar faces tiled across the screen.

Telopea and Blitz, alias Mallet and Goddard, were seated opposite. They remained deadpan, feigning good behavior.

I nodded. Yeah, Masters and I had had contact with these creeps. "We understand the woman's name is Yafa," I replied. "We don't know the name of the guy with her, though usually he's chewing on a silver toothpick. The guy in the smock is an Egyptian industrialist and gun smuggler by the name of Moses Abdul Tawal."

"The woman's full name is Yafa Fienmann," Stringer said, taking over. "The man with her we've identified as Ari Shira. They travel under Czech passports but they are in fact Israeli and ex-Mossad, though I'm sure neither nation would want to claim these two as their own. Both characters are serious fuckups. Shira went nuts one day and killed a bunch of Palestinian women and children. Just pulled them out of a marketplace and shot them in the street. Then he bought an ice cream and caught the bus home. He spent four years in a mental institution until they pronounced him cured. Fienmann was expelled from Mossad after a shoot-out that went wrong and she shot her partner by accident. There was another story doing the rounds that she killed her partner in order to sleep with his wife."

Beneath the table, Masters tapped my foot with hers.

Stringer continued. "Moses Abdul Tawal is Jewish, rich, without conscience, and open to the highest bidder. We believe that these three deviants are involved in activities against the interests of the United States, as well as in the illegal trafficking of extremely dangerous, high-value, high-security materials."

"Such as uranium hexafluoride," Masters offered.

Stringer fixed us both with an intense stare. If I'd been standing, I'd probably have taken a step back. But then the big man exhaled, the paper on his desk fluttered, and the immediate danger seemed to pass. "We don't know where the HEX originated from or how Tawal got his hands on it, despite a surveillance operation that has gone on over the last twelve months," he said. Stringer was feeding us a little worthless detail to make us feel included, but I wasn't buying it. The CIA would have known where the HEX had come from, even if they couldn't yet pinpoint the specific facility. But their intel would harden up substantially once they tunneled through the tons of fallen rock and dirt and recovered those storage cylinders. In the meantime, we still had our problem. I made a unilateral decision.

"There's an inside man," I announced. I felt Masters's stare.

Stringer's nostrils flared. "An inside man, eh? An inside man . . . How do you know it's not me?"

Was it me or did the room suddenly become very cold and still?

"As a matter of fact, Mr. Stringer, we have you down as a potential suspect," I said. "Colonel Portman was the point man in your surveillance operation. And yet you deliberately impeded the investigation into his death."

"The truth, Special Agent, is that Portman's murder took us by surprise. He went a lot farther on his own and didn't keep us in the loop. He'd become something of a loose cannon. As for impeding your investigation, if you remember I gave it a hand along with the Bosphorus shipping log when your investigation had hit the wall."

Stringer had me there. Unless, of course, he knew where the *Onur* was headed, in which case he'd given us the information knowing full well it would take us no farther than the bottom of the port. Had he done that just to throw off any suspicion?

"So tell me why you think there's an inside man, Cooper."

"Information to which only this mission and the Istanbul Police Department had access was provided to Yafa." I told him how our theory about the two safes at Portman's house had also become known to the killers, and the fact that Portman's email files had been selectively edited to remove any mention of Kawthar al Deen, Kumayt, Thurlstane, or anything that would have helped us cut to the chase and perhaps prevent further deaths. Dr. Merkit's, for example. I balled my fists.

The CIA boss smiled, his lips as big as a couple of porterhouse steaks. "Cooper, Portman's activities on behalf of the CIA were top secret. We don't leave information about Company activities—past or present—where it can be accessed by anyone who comes along. And we don't just acknowledge that such-and-such or so-and-so is on our payroll when asked—not even by senate committees. As for the details about the existence of the second safe . . . they could have been passed along by anyone on a very long list, anyone with low-level access who's looking for a little extra pocket money."

Stringer sat back in his chair; its joints begged loudly for mercy. "No, in our view Tawal *is* the top man, and he's on Jerusalem's payroll. Our next play is to remove Tawal from the board. By doing that, perhaps we can delay the game. An Israeli nuclear strike on Iran's nuclear facilities is imminent—Arak, where heavy water is made, is less than a couple of hundred miles across the border from Kawthar al Deen and well within the range of the IDF Special Forces they intend stationing there. We can't let it happen. People think the world changed on 9/11. But 9/11 will seem like a footnote in the history books compared to the day after an Israeli nuclear attack on Iran."

"Why are you telling us all this, sir?" Masters asked.

"Because you're on the team now, Special Agent Masters—you and Special Agent Cooper. You're going to help us capture Moses Abdul Tawal. I've been admiring the way you handle yourselves. You've done extremely well since you've been here. So, until further notice, you and Special Agent Cooper are working for me. Here are your orders from the Pentagon assigning you both to me for the duration of this operation," he said, tossing a fax on the desk.

I was lost for words. For once.

"Can you handle a weapon with that thing?" Stringer pointed at the cast on my forearm.

"Yes, sir," I said.

"Good. We leave for Cairo," he said, checking his watch, "in one hour. And this time, make me wait at your peril."

Cairo traffic reminded me of a landslide: Everything was headed in the same general direction, only that's where the cooperation seemed to end. Aged Fiats, Renaults, and Peugeots swarmed all over our Suburban and the one in front as we headed from the airport to the U.S. Embassy.

A sudden electric shock against the top of my hand felt like a pinch. Cairo was warm and dry—ideal conditions. I turned and said, "So let me get this straight, Mallet, or whatever your name is today. You actually bought that suit? With your own money?"

"The name's Special Agent Telopea. And we're about to go on a mission, Cooper. We'll have high-powered weapons and it's going to be dark. Get my drift? Thought you should be apprised."

"Just keep your suit away from matches and inflammable liquids, Mallet. In the meantime, move over."

Mallet put a couple of inches between us. We flashed past a ten-foot-tall concrete pharaoh standing in the middle of the road, its hands clenched. If I had to stand like that in Cairo traffic, hands wouldn't be all I'd be clenching. I sat back and let my mind wander.

Anna and I didn't have much time to talk back at the Consulate-General before we'd had to leave. Neither of us wholly believed Stringer. He'd fed us a mix of fact and fiction, making it difficult to sift one from the other. Israel was planning some kind of strike, and Kawthar al Deen figured in it somehow. No argument from us—we'd worked out that much on our own.

But we didn't accept that Tawal was the number-one man. How could he be? The plan was to get our hands on him; then, with the specter of a long stay in someplace unpleasant with bars on the windows and doors, there was a good chance he'd roll on everyone around and above him. Mostly, there was the issue of the HEX. Fact: Somehow, someone had acquired it from a U.S. storage facility. Fact: Masters and I had the serial number of the tank we'd unearthed, and that would tell us which facility. When we felt we could trust Stringer, the CIA would have it, too. What bugged Masters and me most was not that Stringer had fed us half-truths, it was that he'd fed us any truth at all.

The Suburbans crossed a sluggish river a fifth the width of the Mississippi. A sign on the bridge informed us that it was the Nile. We turned right almost immediately on the other side of the bridge into a world of silence, the madness of Cairo held back behind concrete-block chicanes manned by military types armed with old MP5s and AK-47s behind portable armor shields. The driver flashed his ID at the checkpoint, and the security guys eyeballed the passengers while another detail checked under the Suburbans' skirts with mirrors on poles. Finding nothing of interest, they waved us on.

Across the road from the U.S. Embassy, I noticed a large international hotel going broke with no one brave enough to sit in the bar. Backing onto the same street was the Egyptian Academy of Music, reveling in the quietest location in all of Cairo. The Suburbans carried us through the embassy's anti-blast gate, and parked.

It was not my idea of a good briefing. Several people I didn't know asked questions that suggested they hadn't been listening in the first place. Or maybe they just believed that a good briefing was a long briefing. I was expecting something different, this being my first full CIA-only gig—like maybe folks doing forward rolls into their seats, something dynamic.

Stringer did his best to make the operation ahead seem like just another day at the office. There were observation points, photos, targeting strategies, logistics considerations, Sudanese- and Egyptian-language issues, air-traffic control sectors, the boundaries of Sudanese and Egyptian Army and Air Force installations in the operations area, ATC and ground frequencies, as well as the usual SIGINT, ELINT, maps, and satellite intel. Need-to-know was paramount. By that I mean there was nothing provided to the folks at the briefing about Tawal, the target—who he was, and why the U.S. government wanted him in a nice secure place beneath the sleepless gaze of surveillance cameras. Just that he was wanted and that "Failure is not an option, people." The only CIA outsiders besides Masters and me were two women from State, neither of whom said a word. In the wrap-up, Stringer asked if they were OK with everything. I took it from the zombielike way both moved their heads up and down that they were. CIA can do whatever it damn well likes.

The overall picture of the mission was this: Tawal had taken up residence on his barge on Lake Nasser/Nubia, just south of the Egyptian-Sudanese border. Satellite intel showed fifteen to twenty armed personnel accompanied him. The strike team, which included Masters and me, would transit to a town in northern Sudan called Wadi Halfa. From there, Masters and I, together with Mallet, Goddard, and three sharpshooters, would deploy aboard a Sudanese fishing boat. There would be two other boats besides ours, also commanded by CIA teams. That was a lot of firepower. Tawal was a high-priority target: Stringer obviously didn't want to take chances.

All vessels would make their way north to points less than a mile from the barge, where Tawal could be kept under observation. An hour before first light, the squad from one of the three boats would disembark and position itself to become a blocking force/cordon on the landward side of the barge. There was to be no chance of escape. Half an hour before first light, three Pave Hawks would depart Abu Simbel Airport, Egypt, orbit five miles downwind of the operation zone, and wait for the radio call that the target had been secured. First light minus twenty minutes, and the strike teams would close with the barge. When within range, the sharpshooters would disable Tawal's security force. Coordinating via radio, Masters, Mallet, Goddard, and I would then board the barge and snatch Tawal. We'd all egress in the Pave Hawks, which would arrive three minutes after being summoned. Easy.

It didn't quite happen that way. We made it to Wadi Halfa without a hitch, but the boats weren't available. One day lost there. Then the boats arrived but one broke down in transit. A prayer held its ancient motor together and none of the gods were listening when we tried to spark it back to life. Another day gone. A third day disappeared when two of the translators and four members of one of the strike teams came down with gastroenteritis.

There was concern that our presence might be conveyed to Tawal by the locals, so we spent these additional nights bivouacked out of town where there was sand, scorpions, snakes, and not much else. Day four: ELINT and sat intel confirmed that Tawal was still on his barge, so we were cleared in hot.

FORTY-EIGHT

The moonless night was cold in the wind chill. High cloud erased the starlight, making the night thick and black. Occasional coughs from Nile crocodiles and the slap of fish clearing the water punctuated the low burble from our exhaust as we hugged the shore. An hour and a half till first light.

Two members of the fire team gave me a nod as they passed, heading below to get their equipment. Mallet followed. By now, the cordon would be in place. There was nothing to do but wait.

I yawned. Masters and I had checked our weapons a couple of times already—Tokarevs with three spare mags apiece, and AK-47 carbines also with fifteen spare mags, all of Chinese origin for ease of later misidentification by local authorities. Aimpoint Comp sights compatible with our night-vision devices completed our weapons ensemble. I couldn't get comfortable in the CIA-issue body armor. It was tight, especially across that rib. I lowered the NVD, turned on the sight, and aimed the weapon at the shoreline. Movement. There—a massive croc hauling itself up over the rocks and then settling onto its broad belly. The Aimpoint sight was first-class. I turned everything off, sat on the gunwale, and listened to the night.

With the lights off and without the night vision, all I could see of Masters was the glow of the narrow green strip on her black Kevlar helmet. The boat captain cut the motor a hundred yards out from our designated position and we slid across the water in silence, the drag slowly washing off our speed. We inched around a spit of land and the anchor went down without a splash. I turned on the electrics and trained the sight on the barge. Tawal was an early riser. He was waving something about, leaning out over the water. A huge shape suddenly reared up out of the blackness and then fell back.

"Must be breakfast time," said Masters, taking in the same show. "He likes to feed the wildlife, remember?"

I remembered Cain telling us.

"You'd think he'd put some clothes on, though, wouldn't you? Crocs might take the wrong item."

I looked harder. Tawal was wearing some kind of loose dressing gown, completely open at the front. He was erect. A woman appeared from a doorway, also in some kind of dressing gown. She let it fall off her and beneath it she was naked. Lucky Tawal. From what I could see, the woman had a hell of a body. She kissed Tawal on the shoulder and then went back inside, swinging her ass at him. "Honey, come back to bed," I said. "You might catch something out here."

"Or something might catch you," Masters added.

Tawal must have heard us. He followed the girl back inside.

"Do we know anything about her?" I asked.

"Not that I've seen," said Masters. "But Tawal's worth a few hundred mill. Gotta have a little black book."

"Crazy if he doesn't," I agreed. Everything went quiet on board the barge, though I counted seven heavily armed security guys. Four of them were smoking, begging to be shot. "With everything that has happened, I haven't asked you... you still getting out?"

The boat rocked a little, unexpectedly, enough that I had to change my footing.

"KMAG YO-YO," Masters replied.

"Did you get that from Block?" I asked.

"Kiss My Ass, Guys, You're On Your Own? A military chat room, actually."

"Any idea what you're going to do?"

"I still haven't made up my mind—not completely. Being a special agent was something I always wanted to do. Starting a new life was not something I ever seriously considered before Richard, but now that's over..." She shrugged.

"Then what *could* you do if you left?"

"Well, I've spoken to my sister and we've talked about me joining her in the West Indies, to work on my all-over tan while I learn how to scuba dive. Then perhaps I'd get my instructor's ticket and teach other people for a while. Vin, if I leave...I've been thinking...Come with me."

I thought about it for a moment. Could I? "Maybe I will."

"Maybe you should. But you won't. You like locking people up too much to quit."

Perhaps, perhaps not. Scuba diving with Anna anywhere sounded more attractive than another stretch busting heads in the OSI or CIA, or whoever it was we were working for. Maybe it was time I left, too, got out while the party was still going strong. And left with the hottest babe on the dance floor on my arm.

"And then when I get bored, I'll go back to school."

I snapped out of it. "School?"

"Law school."

"No way. *Law*?"

"Yes, way. I believe in the system. I've experienced law enforcement from this side. Maybe I could do some good at the other end of the process. Who knows, one day I could even come up against Richard and kick his damn—What's that? Can you hear that? Are they Pave Hawks?"

The thump of helicopter rotors reached my ears at the same instant. It couldn't be the MH-60s. They hadn't been summoned. Something had gone wrong. I moved to the other side of the boat.

The familiar *thump-thump* was getting louder, closer. I could hear them, but still couldn't see them. I flipped down the NVD, and aimed the scope toward the sound. Mallet appeared from behind the wheelhouse, obviously also wondering who, what, where, why, and a bunch of other goddamn questions besides. Goddard was right behind him.

And then I noticed Mallet had a pistol in his hand. It was a Chinese Type 67. We weren't issued silenced weapons. He raised it. The two-handed grip. Anna had her back to him. *What the hell are you doing?* He held the weapon's muzzle an inch from the base of her skull. *A silenced pistol...*

Mallet hadn't seen me. I didn't think about it. I fired point-blank into the side of his face. His jawbone separated from his head, taking his

NVD with it. The rest of him slid over the side of the boat. Gone. Just like that.

"Jesus Christ!" Masters shouted, spinning around.

Goddard came out shooting. *Phut, phut, phut*... another Type 67. *They didn't issue us silenced weapons.* The pistol jumped in his hands. A round slammed into the ceramic plate protecting Masters's front, then another—panic shots—the force of the hits sending her sprawling backward onto the deck. A third round zinged off a winch beside Masters's head as she rolled onto her side.

I dropped to a knee, fired into Goddard's legs as he stepped forward and past me—a three-round burst. The slugs sawed his boot off at the ankle. Overbalanced, he took another step onto the shattered bone stump and stumbled. A burst of fire, this one from Masters, caught him in the throat as he fell and cored it. He slumped to the deck with a soft *thud*. Anna was on her back again, breathing hard, frozen, smoke curling from her AK's flash suppressor.

The chopper roared low across the water a hundred yards to our right. It wasn't one of ours. It looked civilian, a Bell 412. I could see armed personnel sitting in the open doorway, legs dangling over the side.

"You OK?" I yelled at Masters.

"I'm OK, I'm OK," she replied. She got back on her feet, reaching for the railing. "Shit, that hurt."

"Welcome to my world. What the fuck's going down here?"

"You tell me."

The helo flared in a hover over the barge as a gun battle erupted on the shoreline behind it.

"The cordon's being attacked from the rear," I said.

Ropes dropped from the aircraft along with the rain of machine-gun fire. Tracers told me that Tawal's security force was returning the fire, though it was sporadic. Most of his twenty-man security detail must have been taken out from a distance by sharpshooters on the bird.

"Our boat driver's dead, and the radio's smashed," Masters called out behind me from the wheelhouse. I had a feeling that belowdecks would look like a slaughterhouse, which explained the odd shift in the boat's balance I'd felt earlier. Mallet and Goddard would have taken out whoever was down there first before coming up to whack us. Masters was incredibly lucky that my weapon was raised and in the firing position and that Mallet had just blundered into my sights. My thumb must have snicked the safety off without asking my brain's permission—I didn't remember doing it.

Our engine burst into life. Masters had decided we were going to charge right on in there. The throttle surged and the screw bit, launching us forward and ripping the anchor from the silted bottom. I braced myself against the wheelhouse, the helo and the barge filling the Aimpoint's lens and getting larger. Machine-gun fire spat from the side of the helo and chewed up the prow of our boat, flailing me with wood splinters. Masters spun the wheel and brought us on a course parallel to the barge and the shoreline. The other CIA boat was on the move, coming in. I wondered who was controlling it, whether they had a Mallet and Goddard on board.

Tawal appeared on the deck of his barge, hands on his head, pushed along by two gunmen. He was still wearing his robe. The attacking force had complete control of the vessel. The machine gun in the Bell gave us another burst and a cluster of geysers erupted just beyond our stern. Whoever was firing it didn't know how to lead a moving target, not that I was going to complain about it. What was going on here? The gunfire had thinned. An explosion flared green in the scope and the mast holding the barge's navigation lights, comms, and radar aloft toppled, allowing the helicopter to settle on the roof of what was the main cabin. The attacking force was getting ready to leave.

I refocused on Tawal. He was forced up on the side rail of the barge. The two gunmen behind him had ahold of the back of his robe. It seemed to me they were making him lean forward, way out over the edge of the barge like he was on a trapeze. I could hear a lot of shouting going on over the noise of our boat and the chopper, but couldn't see too much detail.

A black shape the size of a tree trunk reared up out of the water and Tawal was gone. My mouth fell open.

"You see that?" Masters called out. "They just fed the guy to the crocs!"

I started firing into the side of the helo. The machine gun in its side door returned the compliment, and .50-caliber slugs smashed into our hull below the waterline and raked us from the bow all the way to the stern. The assault force climbed aboard the aircraft and it lifted off. A well-oiled operation. Whoever these creeps were, they knew what they were doing. They also knew what the CIA was doing.

The helo altered direction and Masters brought the boat around to intercept it. I wasn't sure this was such a good idea, given their firepower, but it provided a better view into the side of the aircraft. I emptied the remains of the magazine at it, but to no apparent effect. A few of the men that I could see ripped off their NVGs and helmets—only, one of them wasn't a man. *Yafa.* The 412 banked around the spit of land, hovered there for thirty seconds, then climbed away.

Dawn wasn't pretty down by the lake. Large black birds circled high overhead as we picked through the disaster. The woman we'd seen getting impatient and naked with Tawal was of Middle Eastern origin, maybe twenty-three, and drop-dead gorgeous. Now she was just dead, a bullet through her left eye.

Masters had run our boat up on the shore. The .50-cal rounds had done a lot of damage and we were taking water. Down in the hold, as we'd feared, Mallet and Goddard had killed the three CIA sharpshooters. Masters and I were cuffed to the wheelhouse for an hour while the mess was sorted out and the senior agents on the scene came to grips with our story—that Mallet and Goddard were working both sides of the fence and that we'd shot them in self-defense after they'd slaughtered the agents belowdecks and came gunning for us. The silenced weapon in Goddard's rigor-mortised fingers, in addition to the 7.62 millimeter slugs prised from the wood behind the sharpshooters' heads, backed our version. But even after we were released, the suspicion still clung to us and soaked up the agents' anger and frustration. Goddard's remains were bagged with his boot, his foot still laced into it.

"I don't think Mallet and Goddard liked you very much, Vin," Masters remarked as an agent zipped up the bag.

"What makes you say that? I was nothing but helpful—charming, even."

"They didn't have to show their hand. There was no need to kill us. Putting a bullet in you must have been something they wanted badly."

"Gee, I can't think why," I said.

A gunshot rang out and a large croc retreated into the water. A couple of agents kept an eye on the lake's edge from the safety of the barge.

The last thing the CIA needed now was for an agent to end up an essential food group.

"After they whacked us, Goddard and Mallet were going to RV with the helo round the corner," I went on. "Must have been why it stopped there in the hover. I think it wasn't just me they wanted dead, and it wasn't just Goddard and Mallet who wanted to do the killing. You saw who was on that Bell."

"I saw." Masters screwed a black ball cap down on her head. "I hate Monday mornings. I'm going to go help out. You?" She climbed up on the gunwale and jumped down onto the mud before I could give her an answer.

None of Tawal's people had survived. All twenty were shot dead. Among our blocking force onshore, there was one dead and six wounded, one of them critically. They'd been surprised, outgunned, and outmaneuvered. After the shock of the initial assault, they'd at least had the good sense to keep their heads down.

Stringer arrived in a chartered helicopter an hour after sunrise to supervise the cleanup. We didn't talk. He was wrong about there being no one on the inside—he knew it, we knew it, and we knew he knew it. What we wanted to know was whether he was involved in it. How could Mallet and Goddard operate without him being involved in it? Nevertheless, here he was, assisting in the evacuation of the casualties, loading them into the Pave Hawks. The op was an unmitigated disaster. As far as Stringer's future in the CIA was concerned, a crystal ball wasn't needed to figure he wouldn't have one.

There was some confusion about what to do with Tawal's dead. We didn't have the resources to spirit them away, not in northern Sudan. So rather than leave them to the vultures, we set Tawal's barge ablaze along with our boats and cremated them.

As we lifted off on the last shuttle heading back to Abu Simbel, on the Egyptian side of the border, I saw a familiar long white coat. It was Tawal's dressing gown, lying up on the bank a couple of hundred yards from the barge, stained with silt. The dressing gown suddenly took off when we flew overhead, making for the water, the snout of a massive croc buried deep in its sleeve.

FORTY-NINE

Stringer was recalled to CIA HQ, Langley. We were recalled, too, though, as I pointed out to Masters, CIA wasn't the agency that had called us to Turkey in the first place so *re*calling us was technically incorrect. She told me to shut up.

The interviews at Langley were more like interrogations, mostly because they were conducted under hot lights in an empty room and ran twenty-five hours pretty much without a break. Masters and I were interviewed separately. Obviously, the interrogators were hoping to pounce on some divergence in our stories, which was unlikely given we had every intention of telling them the truth. Only just not the whole truth.

After these interviews, CIA knew what we knew: that Portman had been murdered by ex-Mossad agents employed by Moses Abdul Tawal; that he was killed because he'd discovered the secret of the buried HEX; that Kawthar al Deen was in fact a secret IDF base for Special Forces that would pave the way for an Israeli nuclear strike, which was imminent, on Iran's nuclear facilities.

CIA also knew that we believed there was an Israeli spy operating at a high level within the U.S. government. We told them that this same spy had helped obtain the HEX from a U.S. storage facility, and had been instrumental in the deaths of numerous U.S. and Turkish citizens.

The CIA told us they believed the HEX had come from Russia. The Company doesn't feed anyone information unless it has good reasons—

mostly related to disinformation. The good reasons in this instance were that it wanted Masters and me to go away and forget everything we'd seen, heard, and done. We were happy to oblige, but only because we wanted the Company off our backs. As far as we were concerned, the account had yet to be closed. We owed it to Aysun Merkit to see it through, as well as to Emir, Emmet Portman and Dutch Bremmel, Adem Fedai and Ten Pin, the dead and wounded CIA guys, and all the guys on the *Onur* who went to their graves in her.

Fortunately for us, Masters's contact at the Department of Energy was still being undervalued by her employer. So, to Masters's hotmail address, she forwarded a spreadsheet on the nation's inventory of depleted uranium hexafluoride. The inventory revealed that there were 686,500 metric tons of the stuff in 57,122 cylinders stored in three DoE facilities: Portsmouth, Ohio; Paducah, Kentucky; and Oak Ridge, Tennessee. A handy fact to have on hand for when dinner-party conversation slows, but what we really wanted—and what Masters's deep-throat connection provided—was the serial number of every one of those cylinders.

There was ice in the rain and it was slanting horizontally when we arrived at the security gate to the old K-25 site, Oak Ridge Reservation. I lowered the driver's window on the Ford rental, reached out, and slid our credentials under the glass, toward the security guy. He glanced at them and signaled by holding up a finger that he'd be just a moment. A few seconds later he jogged out of the bunker and approached the window.

"Mr. Jurgensen and . . . Ms. Swank. You're down from Washington, aren't you?"

"Yeah, how'd you know?"

"Never mind . . . but you're hoping to catch us with our pants down."

"I'm sorry?" I asked, frowning.

"Well, looks like you got a leak somewhere in head office. We all think that's kind of funny."

"Why's that?" I didn't need to have it spelled out, but it went with my disguise.

"You're hoping to arrive unannounced and check for leaks here, right? But all the while you've got one yourself back in Washington. Ha-ha."

"Oh, yes... ha-ha... I see," I said. "Funny. I don't suppose you'd care to tell me who that leak is?"

"Sorry, no can do. Gotta protect our sources," he replied, grinning. "So, anyway, I believe you're heading for the cylinder yard."

I pursed my lips and gave the steering wheel a thump. "Yes, goddamn it," I said.

"You been here before?"

"New to the job. Both of us."

"Well, head on straight. You'll come to a traffic circle—go left. Come to another traffic circle, turn right, and you'll find a security post two miles down the road. They'll be expecting you."

"Thanks, damn it," I said, splashing the frustration around like cheap cologne.

He handed our credentials and documents back with a smile. Despite his rain hood, mini waterfalls ran off the end of his blue nose and chin. "You folks have a real nice day."

The heavy boom gate lifted and we cruised beneath it, over a set of road spikes that clanged into their recess.

"Your friend at the Department of Energy—her talents are wasted," I told Masters. We had no chance of sneaking into this facility as OSI special agents without all kinds of authorities and paperwork we'd never get. But posing as DoE bureaucrats and then having our surprise visit "blown"? Genius. The letters Masters's friend had also supplied, as well as the security passes, could all potentially land her in a basket of snakes but, as the gate guardian rightly pointed out, you gotta protect your sources.

The windshield wipers were moving around like a conductor doing "Flight of the Bumblebee," but they still weren't managing to cope with the volume of water and sleet.

The first traffic circle suddenly appeared out of the murk. I turned left.

"There's a hell of a lot of real estate here," Masters observed, thinking aloud.

"Uh-huh." There was. The Oak Ridge Reservation was built on a colossal scale. It was the backbone of the Manhattan Project, which gave birth to the bomb in 1945.

We turned right at the next traffic circle. Signs told us where to go in case we weren't sure. The security gate for the cylinder yard eventually reared out of the rain.

"Just a suggestion," Masters said with a smile.

"What?"

"Try not to pour it on quite so thick this time. Acting's not your strong suit."

"Thanks for the pep talk," I replied before hitting the window button.

A woman in a gray hooded raincoat with broad yellow reflective strips came out in the rain to meet us.

"Morning," I said through the crack in the top of the window, holding up the paperwork.

"That's OK," she replied in a husky voice, waving it aside. "Milton called—been expecting you. Turn right after the barrier arm and keep to your right till you get to the main building. Kevin will meet you there."

"So much for the element of surprise," I said, giving her a shrug.

"Don't feel bad, Mr. Jurgensen. We don't get a lot of visitors to the cylinder yard. Nothing ever happens, so we're glad of the attention. We got nothing to hide here anyway. As we say, it's all out in the open."

"I guess you're right. Thanks." I edged the Ford over another set of spikes.

Masters gave the woman a wave and I watched her turn and go back inside her bunker.

Through the driving rain and the razor wire, I could see row after row of neatly stacked cylinders containing uranium hexafluoride. Like the lady said, it was all out in the open. The rows went on seemingly forever, disappearing into the driving rain. How easy would it be to misplace just one? Throw enough money around and anything was possible. And HEX was hardly plutonium—it couldn't be put to a lot of use, not even by terrorists. The containers were just sitting here exposed to the weather, getting old and leaky.

The main admin building was a piece of 1940s kitsch—small secretive windows and a tiled exterior. Inside there were probably still pictures of FDR and Ike on yellowed walls. A guy in the regulation raincoat was waiting in a driveway beneath a portico, waving us in. Kevin, I presumed. We parked and got out.

"Hello. I'm Sonny Jurgensen and this is Ms. Swank," I said as I shook Kevin's big wet paw.

"Kevin Greig. Glad to meet you. You want to come in and have a cup of coffee before you get started, wait for a break in the weather?"

I looked at Ms. Swank and she gave her head a slow and solemn shake. "I don't think so. We have a schedule to keep, Mr. Greig," she said.

"Then where do you folks want to begin?"

"There might be something wrong with our records, but it seems there are a number of cylinders that haven't been visually inspected for five years."

"Really?" Kevin asked doubtfully. "I don't see how that's possible."

"Neither do we, Mr. Greig, but we have a responsibility to the American people to ensure the records are up-to-date."

"You folks really are new to this, aren't you?"

"Excuse me, sir?" Masters asked.

The guy shrugged. "So this is not a snap inspection of the facility?" He sounded disappointed.

"No," Masters replied.

"Oh," he said, dejected. "We all thought it was. Don't get many visitors to the yard. OK... Well, follow me."

Kevin led us inside. "You folks going to poke around the cylinders, get your hands dirty, or you just want to have a general look around?"

"It's not a great day for gymnastics," said Masters. "But we have a job to do."

"Sure," he agreed. "Well, I'll break out a couple of NBC suits for you." He took a step back and sized us up. "The suits'll keep the rain out, too. At least, you'd hope they would...."

Kevin was expecting a chuckle. I gave it to him.

Ten minutes later, Masters and I were suited up and waiting beneath the portico for Kevin, as instructed. There was no break in the weather. A white DoE-branded pickup with a revolving yellow beacon appeared from around the side of the building and parked beside our rental. Kevin got out, leaving the motor running.

"You folks ready to roll?"

"Ready," said Masters.

"You got serial numbers for the cylinders you want to look at?"

"Right here." She waggled her notebook.

"I can take you down the line, if you like," Kevin suggested.

"Thank you, Kevin," I said. "We sure appreciate your willingness to assist, but we have to muddle through this sometime. Today might as well be the day."

"OK, I getcha. Well, the cylinder yard is laid out quite logical. The rows running this way are designated by letters; the ones at right angles by numbers. Mind if I have a look at your serial numbers?"

"Not at all," Masters replied. She opened her notebook to a laser-printed strip of paper containing half a dozen serial numbers, all but one chosen at random. The cylinder we were here to inspect was buried among them.

"Say you want to find cylinder BB-32-N101-A16," he said, pointing at the one on the top of the list. "Drive down BB till you get to cross street number 32. The letter N tells you your cylinder will be on the north side of block 101. The letter A tells you it's on the bottom of the stack—C on top, B in the middle. Those last numbers in the series tell you it's number 16 in the row."

Masters and I must have appeared confused.

"You sure you don't want me to take you?" he asked. "You don't want to get lost out there. A lot of it is signposted, but some of those signs have rusted away."

"No, it's OK, thank you," said Masters.

"Well, I'll see you folks when you're done. Got any problems, use the radio."

Masters went to the driver's door.

"Feeling confident, Ms. Swank?" I asked.

"I'm just the driver," she said. "You're the navigator."

We nosed about, locating some of the cylinders. Finding them wasn't so hard, but the sheer size of the yard was staggering, and the rain wasn't helping. The cylinders themselves were big. Each weighed around fourteen tons and measured twelve feet long and four wide—not the kind of item that could be loaded on the back of a pickup and just carted away.

After dicking around for half an hour, we found what we were looking for. On top of the stack should have been cylinder number JJ-74-E57-C25, and indeed there was a cylinder up there occupying the space, only it was a fake. Had to be. The real one was buried in the ground upstream of Kumayt, its poison leached into the earth. I took the ladder out of the truck, climbed to the top of the stack, and read the serial numbers off to Masters.

"They're the right numbers," she said. "What's in it, do you think?"

"Anything but what's supposed to be in it. Let's go talk to Kevin, see if we can get an introduction to his boss."

We drove back to the main office, past thousands of HEX cylinders. I wondered how many of them were the genuine article; how many had been stolen and for what reasons. Masters slotted the pickup beside our rental. Kevin wasn't around, so we found our own way back inside, showering in the suits first before removing them, as per the rules printed on a plate screwed to the wall beside the change-room entrance.

While I climbed back into my clothes, it occurred to me that with the serial number on the cylinder, we had something Portman never managed to get his hands on: proof. Portman had the lab report on the sample, but while the minute amount of uranium-235 it contained strongly implied U.S. involvement, what we now had was incontrovertible. The cylinder we'd uncovered was definitely one of ours, stolen from this facility. The one in its place was a phony.

I made one last check that I had everything: wallet, keys, cell, and my uncle's Vietnam War-era Colt .45, which I probably should have left back in D.C. The thing was killing me, sticking into my rib. I took it out and stuck it in my boot.

Time to go.

I pushed through the swing door. Masters and I could now hand everything over to the FBI and—

"Put you fucking hands over you fucking head."

The shout caught me completely by surprise. The guy already had Masters pressed against the wall with his shoulder, her hair balled up in one fist, a Barak pistol in the other, the black muzzle pushed hard into her ear. *Adem Fedai was found dead inside the car. He had been beaten and shot through the ear.* He rolled the silver toothpick from one side of his mouth to the other. I sniffed the air. There was something familiar in it.

He growled, "Do it, *ya chatitchat hara*."

I had no idea what he was saying but I did it anyway—stuck my hands up over my head. "You probably don't know this, but there are only two kinds of people who wear sunglasses inside," I told him. "And you're not a rock star, are you?"

"Cooper..." Masters warned.

"Shut you face," he said.

"Who? Me, or her?"

"Both. I will kill her if you do not do exactly as I say." He wrenched Masters's hair so that her head was pulled back, then slammed it against the wall. Masters's knees buckled for an instant, then recovered. She didn't make a sound.

"Hey!" I yelled. "I've done it, OK—see?" I wriggled my fingers above my head. "What next? What do you want?"

"Up the stairs. Go!"

I took a step toward the stairs, and he swung Masters around to face me, using her as a shield, keeping her between us. He was a well-drilled, sunglasses-wearing asshole.

"Your name is Ari Shira," I said as I moved past them and started to climb. "They tell me you like ice cream. I'm kinda fond of chocolate-chocolate chip myself."

"Shut you face."

"You're Israeli, ex-Mossad. So is your partner, Yafa Fienmann. They kicked you out and so now you're doing your best to give the Czech Republic a bad name. OK, an even worse name."

"Keep walking," he said.

"CIA knows all about you—" I rounded the landing and saw Kevin slumped on the floor, blood trails leaking from his mouth and nose and the air reeking of *that* smell. I recognized it now: chloroform. Kevin was either out cold or stone dead—it was impossible to tell. I couldn't see any gunshot wounds, so maybe he was lucky. Maybe he'd wake up later with a killer headache and a real sore throat, though I didn't like the odds on his luck being good. Yafa and this Ari character didn't seem all that interested in temporarily knocking out the people who got in their way.

The doorway at the top of the stairs was open. Yafa Fienmann suddenly stepped into it, a Barak held casually by her thigh. "Ah, so it *is* you. Have you brought your gorgeous partner?" She craned her neck to look past me. "Yes, she is here." The fruitloop clapped her hands—or rather her hand and gun—together with excitement. "Ari, do not hurt her. Not yet."

"Go!" Ari yelled to get me moving. I walked toward Yafa. "You and your beautiful friend. How do you manage it to stay alive?" she asked. "Someday we will sit down and you will tell me." The way Yafa was talking, she could've been asking how Masters and I managed to match our drapes with the carpet.

Shira said something to Yafa in an unfamiliar language. Hebrew, I guessed. She turned me around, shoved me against the wall, and frisked me with one hand while the other kept the pistol pressed into the base of my spine. She grabbed the fabric of my jacket, feeling for lumps of metal over the tops of my arms and then their undersides, my armpits, my ribs, belt line, small of my back, down the outside of my legs, the inside legs. The last port of call was my crotch, which she lingered over, with more interest than she needed to, looking for lumps of a different kind, cupping my testicles and then giving Little Coop a friendly squeeze.

I tried to turn around, thinking she'd missed the Colt.

"Stay, big man," she said, her hand pushed between my shoulders, cold metal on the back of my neck. She went down the inside of my leg a second time, and found the pistol tucked into the top of my boot. She pulled it out.

"Hmm... heavy. This is an old one. A man's gun." She rubbed my crotch again. Little Coop wasn't interested. Yafa flicked the weapon at me, indicating that I should move back and give her some room.

"I haven't searched the woman," Shira said.

"Thank you, Ari. You have left the job to me. You are *so* considerate."

He muscled Masters up the last couple of stairs and then let her go, pushing her toward the wall. Masters wheeled and glared at him.

Yafa held my Colt in Masters's face and said, "Turn around and face the wall, please. You will enjoy this."

"Get on with it, bitch," Masters spat.

Yafa put her through the same routine she'd just given me, only this search was conducted with her hand groping around inside Masters's shirt and pants. Yafa sniffed her fingers, waved them under her nose, and said, "I love your natural perfume."

Masters said nothing.

Yafa shrugged. "Inside. Now," she said, gesturing at the doorway.

I covered the distance in a couple of steps. It was a corner office—the boss's office. The reek of chloroform inside was almost overpowering. It had a sofa. It had a matching chair. In the matching chair sat a very large man. On the floor beside the chair and the very large man was another man in a suit, curled into a ball, blood leaking onto the carpet from a gut wound. He looked exactly like the smiling guy in the family photo on the desk. I figured he was the boss at the facility, and now he was a loose end being tied. If I ever got out of here and pulled the guy's financials, I suspected there'd be a very large sum of money deposited somewhere for at least one storage cylinder of HEX.

"Cooper," said Stringer. "Nice of you to pay us a visit. Where's your partner?"

Masters came through the doorway.

"Good," he said. "We're all together."

"You," said Masters.

"Yeah, me," Stringer replied, trying to get comfortable in a chair a couple of sizes too small for him. "Don't tell me you're surprised."

"Not surprised, Stringer," I said. "We just don't believe you're Mr. Big—and I use the term figuratively, of course."

Stringer gave me a crooked smile. "Were they armed?" he asked, addressing Yafa and Ari.

"Yes," said Yafa, handing him the Colt.

"Lemme guess.... Cooper, this is yours, isn't it?"

"Uh-huh." I noticed Stringer was wearing black leather gloves. There was enough hide in those gloves to upholster a car seat.

The CIA chief examined the Colt. "Nice weapon. Didn't figure you for a traditionalist, Cooper." He popped the magazine, saw it was full, and snapped it back in. He cocked the trigger. "Just in case you get any ideas," he said. I saw his thumb interrogate the safety as he slipped the weapon inside his coat. "Where were we? Yes, me not being Mr. Big. I had motive, access...."

"You were in Ankara the night Colonel Portman was killed," Masters said. "We checked."

"I had Special Agents Telopea and Blitz to help me out."

"I don't think much of the CIA, Stringer, but those two weren't special agents any more than their names were Mallet and Goddard. They were ex-Mossad or Marine Recon or SAS... dredged up from the ranks of the guys who lost it, or who never really had it to start with. Maybe Telopea and Blitz could put together a recipe for disaster, but not much else. One member of the team that killed Portman let himself into the house. He was known to the Air Attaché. This person had a key that had been stolen from the leasing agent along with a floor plan. After he'd entered the house and made sure Portman was alone, he subdued him with chloroform. Then Yafa and Ari arrived and went to work." While I talked, something clicked: *Damn!* I remembered the glass shard my boot had picked up in Portman's courtyard. "To make it seem like they broke in and did the job without assistance, and perhaps so we wouldn't find out about the leasing agency break-in and the stolen key, a windowpane beside the courtyard door was punched out *from the inside.*"

Stringer's hands were clasped across his gigantic belly. I watched them rise and fall with his breathing.

"You want more, Stringer?"

"Depends on whether you want to go to your grave with it—might as well get it off your chest."

"You were interviewed at Langley, same as us. We told them Moses Abdul Tawal's people killed Portman. While we didn't mention them by name, we believed that to be Psychokitten and Ice-Cream Boy here. Only, these two also led the raid that killed Tawal, the guy we thought was their boss, so something major wasn't adding up. While we didn't give Langley specifics, we told *you* who we saw riding in the helo, but you chose not to pass anything on to Langley. And they never questioned us about it. Why not? Only one reason we could think of. Because if CIA and OSI believed the people who killed Portman were dead—killed along with Tawal on his barge—then the case would be complete. That's what you told them, wasn't it? And they bought it. So now the real Mr. Big can continue with business as usual. In fact, why don't you ask him to come on in and join us?"

Stringer didn't have to. A side door opened and Ambassador Burnbaum walked in, drying his hands on a paper towel. He shook his head and said, "Spilled some of that chloroform on my hands. Damn near passed out cleaning it off. You know, Cooper, you and Masters have made this a lot more difficult than it had to be."

"You're under arrest for espionage and murder, Burnbaum. You, too, Stringer," said Masters.

Burnbaum picked up a paperweight, a six-inch-long graphite-colored spike—a DU tank penetrator. The depleted uranium it was fashioned from had no doubt been extracted from the uranium hexafluoride stored in this very facility. Burnbaum examined it while he talked. "Yes, yes, of course I am. This is about Iran. In a very short period of time, Iran will be nuclear-armed. We can't allow that to happen."

" 'We' being Israel," I said.

"I don't see anyone else having the nerve to do what needs to be done."

"Why is an American spying for Israel?" Masters asked.

"I'm Jewish, Special Agent, as is Harvey here. American on the outside, Israeli on the inside. Perhaps what you're really asking is why one ally would spy on another?"

Masters glared at him.

"The U.S. will stick by Israel only while there are common interests. And that's the issue here, really: The U.S. has no stomach for an attack on Iran, especially after the mess in Iraq. No, neutralizing Iran—it might have been a common interest once, but now it's off the table. For the nation of Israel, though, it's a matter of pure necessity, of survival, of life or death. We're looking down the barrel of genocide all over again. If we don't stop the Iranians, they'll do their best to kill us all as soon as they have the capability—they've said so time and again—which could be any time now."

"So this whole operation—the murders, the desal plant, the poisoning of the water—the whole filthy mess has been sanctioned by Israel?" asked Masters, incredulous.

"You should know better than to ask, Special Agent. And if the answer were no, would you believe it?"

Masters was furious. "What damn well makes the value of *your* life greater than anyone else's? What about the children at Kumayt?"

"You're talking about the effects of the HEX? You know as well as I do that in this game, you have to use the tools available to you, and some of them are blunt. However, we have to look at the positive side. We're focused on the lives we'll save. And, yes, they'll be Israeli lives. We needed a facility like Kawthar al Deen. Reliable intelligence is a real problem. We can get a lot of it from the air and from shared intelligence links with Washington, but if we're going to go in with ordnance—especially of the nuclear sort, to surgically remove their assets—we need quality boots on the ground. And that means a base from which Special Forces can be launched at a moment's notice."

"Why the orchestrated killing?" I asked. "Why Portman, Bremmel, then Ten Pin?"

"Well, yes, why indeed. Tawal was a businessman. We promised him a bonus of twenty million dollars if he could keep the base at Kumayt a secret, at least until the strike. Incidentally, you and Masters should consider yourselves fortunate. Too many people knew you were paying Kawthar al Deen a visit. That meant Tawal couldn't kill you while you were there, not without risking his bonus."

I thought about the advice I'd given Dr. Bartholomew. I sure hoped the guy had taken it.

Burnbaum continued. "Portman was a problem. He figured it all out. He'd even uncovered the secret of the planted HEX cylinder. He talked to me about it, told me he was going to go public, and I passed that news on to Tawal. If Portman released what he knew, Tawal would have lost a fortune, which signed the attaché's death warrant. Tawal was looking for an excuse anyway. I don't think he liked Portman a whole lot. And, ironically, if Tawal hadn't become emotionally involved and hadn't *insisted* on Portman's elimination first, before those other two, Yafa's plan to link their deaths with the F-16 upgrade might have been a little more convincing."

"We had to deal with Portman fast," said Stringer, chipping in, "before he talked."

Burnbaum shrugged. "Well, there you are. The enterprise was flawed from the beginning. Might there have been a better way to achieve the desired result? Quite possibly, but you pay people to do a job, in this particular instance to maintain security and buy time. And I'm happy that at least we've succeeded in that, and time has been bought."

"Time for what?" Masters asked.

"Turn on CNN tomorrow and you'll see some very nice smoking holes in Iranian soil. Oh, I forgot, you're not going to be around tomorrow." Burnbaum smiled. "Stringer—kill these two." He indicated which two, as if he needed to, waggling the DU penetrator at Masters and me.

When I looked back at Stringer, the CIA station chief already had a gun in his hand. It was my gun, the Colt .45, and it was pointed at my sternum. From this distance he couldn't miss. Even a bad shot would be fatal. Stringer's eyes were calm and cold. I flinched, expecting the soft-nosed anti-personnel slugs I loaded it with to tear a hole as big as a—

BANG! Something crashed behind me. I turned. It was Burnbaum, flung back from his seat and into the wall behind him. I watched him slide to the floor. There wasn't much of the guy's head left above his nose. The DU penetrator rolled slowly across the desk and fell with a heavy thud onto the carpet in front of me.

"Yeah, like I said, nice weapon." Stringer bounced the Colt in his hand. "I like a piece with some weight in it. These nasty Glocks with all their polycarbonate just don't do shit for me."

Yafa and Shira seemed pretty relaxed about what had just happened to Burnbaum, the guy I believed had been pulling their strings. Which meant they were either quick to jump onto another horse when theirs fell over, or Stringer was their mount all along. Yafa stepped across to Burnbaum and bent over him, checking the damage. Then she pulled his piece from a shoulder holster—one of those nasty Glocks—which she handed to Stringer.

"You were Burnbaum's handler," I said. "You ran him."

"And he never knew," replied Stringer. "Can you believe that? And Burnbaum was a Cold War graduate. Well, I guess you can believe it—you didn't get it either."

Stringer placed the Colt on the arm of his chair, and shifted Burnbaum's Glock. "Thanks for killing a dangerous spy for us, Cooper. Washington will give you a medal. Posthumously, of course."

I shook my head, almost in admiration. Stringer had it all thought out. The guy they bought the HEX from was dead on the floor; the spy who organized it was dead beside him, apparently killed with my gun by me, the special agent on his tail. And no doubt Masters would be killed by Burnbaum's weapon—all nice and neat. Stringer could then go back to what he was doing, being Jerusalem's man on the inside. No doubt he'd work it so he was first on the scene, having cracked the plot wide open. He'd earn Mossad's Man-of-the-Month plaque for sure.

I heard a series of thumps coming from the other side of the main door. And then suddenly it burst wide open and shoved Yafa Feinmann hard in the back. The force of the impact pushed her forward. She stumbled and fell into the corner of the desk before hitting the floor. There was a bloody divot in her forehead at the hairline. She groaned, semiconscious, licked her Ferrari-red lips.

Kevin stood unsteadily in the doorway, blood running from his mouth and nose. He coughed up a glob of red ooze into his hand, looked at it, then collapsed.

There was a moment of complete and utter silence, tension having squeezed every ounce of sound and movement from it. Stringer, Shira, Masters, me. We all looked at each other, calculating the angles, weighing the odds. Four pairs of eyes flitting left and right.

I broke first. I dived for the floor. The room exploded with gunfire.

Deafening. BANG! BANG! Masters twisted and sank an elbow into Shira's gut. I saw her get a hand on his pistol. BANG!

The Glock in Stringer's hand was pointed at the both of them. BANG! He squeezed the trigger again. BANG! And then again, only now at me. BANG! I was on the move, finishing the roll.

He missed.

As I came up, I snatched the DU penetrator from the carpet. Shira saw me. His gun jumped twice as Masters wrestled him for it. BANG! BANG! A round missed its intended target—me—and buried itself instead in Yafa's back, between her shoulder blades, shattering her spine.

The penetrator was in my hand—warm and heavy. I had the angle and the momentum.

BANG! Stringer, thinking I was shot, had shifted aim again. Now he was targeting the swirling duo of Masters and Shira, fighting for his Barak.

I carried the swing through its arc, using its energy, rising up off the floor. Stringer's massive head tipped back with surprise when he saw me coming. His mouth opened. I caught him under the chin. The heavy DU penetrator pierced the soft muscle beneath his jaw. I pushed forward, putting my weight behind it. The DU continued up through the roof of his mouth, through his soft palate. I gave it a final thrust and the pointed tip crunched out through the back of his skull, plastered in hair, blood, and gray matter.

I snatched the Colt from the armrest. I had a clear shot at Shira as he wrestled with Masters. He saw me turn. Our weapons jumped at the same instant. He spun away from Masters as the jacketed round from the Colt smashed through his arm, into his abdomen, and out his back, taking his liver with it.

Masters stood, swaying. She lifted her head and I saw the dark stain spreading from her chest, soaking her jacket. I took a step toward her as she faltered. I caught her as she fell, her face suddenly ashen and bloodless. I unzipped her jacket, tore through her shirt and T. The ragged hole in her pale skin was big and black and red, a sliver of wet pink bone poking through. Beneath a ragged crimson flap of skin, I could see her lungs pumping. I reached behind and checked her back. Blood was seeping away through the entry wound, warming my hand, soaking the carpet beneath her.

"Anna! Can you hear me!? Hang the fuck on. Anna! Jesus . . . !" My head swung around. What was I looking for? The room was full of dead people, unconscious people. No one to help. Nothing to do. Jesus fucking Christ. Masters whispered something but I couldn't hear her. I bent down, put my ear close to her lips. Her breathing was shallow, red froth bubbling from the hole in her chest.

"Vin, I've . . . made . . . up my mind," she whispered, her breath shallow, fading, the wound sucking. "I . . . I quit."

ABOUT THE AUTHOR

DAVID ROLLINS is the internationally bestselling author of *A Knife Edge* and *The Death Trust.* An avid pilot and a journalist, Rollins has done meticulous research, giving his military scenes an awesome precision and his backroom politics a chilling truthfulness. He lives in Australia, where he is at work on his next thriller, *Zero Option.*